MY LONG-PLAYING RECORDS

and Other Stories

My Long-Playing Records

and Other Stories

Richard Jespers

Library of Congress Control Number: 2014913030
ISBN-10: 1500372323
ISBN-13: 978-1500372323
Printed by CreateSpace Independent Publishing Platform,
North Charleston, South Carolina
www.richardjespers.com

The stories in this collection, in a slightly different form, first appeared in other publications: "A Certain Kind of Mischief," *Beloit Fiction Journal*; "Ghost Riders," *Gihon River Review*; "The Best Mud," *Cooweescoowee*; "Handy to Some," *Westview*; "Blight," *riverSedge*; "A Gambler's Debt," *The Mochila Review*; "Tales of the Millerettes," *Eclectica*; "Men at Sea," *Green Hills Literary Lantern*; "My Long-Playing Records," *Boulevard*; "Basketball Is Not a Drug," first appeared in *Blackbird* and was also anthologized in *Best of the Web 2008*; "Engineer," *The Ledge*; "Snarked," *FRiGG Magazine*; "Killing Lorenzo," *Harrington Gay Men's Literary Quarterly*; and "The Age I Am Now," *Colere*. "Bathed in Pink" was a Tennessee Writers Alliance Contest winner.

To Ken

Acknowledgements

Beginning in 2007 I was fortunate enough to become part of a caring group of writing peers, who hold MFAs or PhDs in creative writing or related fields—all of them practiced and published writers. Barbara Brannon, Melissa Brewer, Dennis Fehr, Michelle Kraft, Juanice Meyers, Jewel Mogan, and Marilyn Westfall—members of this esteemed group—read and commented on a number of stories in my collection. Because their criticism was often so spot-on, I came to trust it in order to make meaningful revisions. Ms. Brannon, a talented editor, deserves a big thank you for giving the manuscript a crisp copy edit, as well as an insightful overview. I thank Walt McDonald, who served as my creative thesis director in graduate school. A special heartfelt thanks I extend to Daryl Jones, who at significant moments in my career has supplied me with help and encouragement when I needed them most. Others who provided strategic instruction and support in the last decade are Edmund White, Elizabeth Stuckey-French, Mark Jude Poirier, Pam Houston, Diane Thiel, Jeffrey Davis, and Ron Carlson. I am grateful to all for the part they played in my development.

Since 1976 visual artist Ken Dixon and I have shared home and hearth in Lubbock, Texas, and during that considerable period he has never ceased to encourage me in my work—sacrificing time together, vacation trips, and much more for the sake of it. I love him for providing me with the first of many blank journals and for always standing by me during my extended apprenticeship. To my departed parents, Norma and Louis, I owe my love of books and reading, and to my brother, Vic, and my niece Rachelle, thanks, as well, for their quiet but sure support.

Finally, I wish to thank the staff of CreateSpace for all their help in producing this book. Without it I'm afraid it might have been a much different product.

After silence, that which comes nearest to expressing the inexpressible is music.

—Aldous Huxley

CONTENTS

Preface	xiii
A Certain Kind of Mischief	1
Ghost Riders	22
The Best Mud	42
Handy to Some	59
Blight	65
A Gambler's Debt	71
Tales of the Millerettes	83
Men at Sea	136
My Long-Playing Records	155
Basketball Is Not a Drug	175
Engineer	208
Snarked	225
Killing Lorenzo	238
The Age I Am Now	256
Bathed in Pink	270

PREFACE

The conventional wisdom concerning short story collections is that once a writer has placed a healthy number of stories in journals—fifteen or twenty—the stories should be published as a collection. Well, as conventions go, this one now stands on its head. Companies are usually willing to publish a writer's collection only *after* he or she has premiered a novel, preferably a best-selling one—and often editors would prefer that the stories be *linked*, making a collection seem more like a novel. Of these fifteen stories, fourteen *have* appeared in small literary journals, and they *are* linked, linked to my biography.

Because I lived my first twenty-two years in Kansas, the region informs my fiction in many ways—a grandmother with mental problems, viewing at age fourteen *West Side Story* in Wichita's old Miller Theater, life along a torpid Arkansas River—and so I reserve a place for those stories. Yet because I've lived, since 1970, in the state of Texas, I stake out a place for those narratives, as well—the bustle of Dallas in the seventies, the rigors of living in a semiarid West Texas for more than forty years, coming to terms with a religious faith I long ago abandoned. And because I've occasionally traveled outside the country, I include a number of stories inspired by those trips—a young boy's journey with his uncle across the Atlantic, a translator who witnesses the assassination of a Dutch filmmaker, an old woman who takes a brief glance back at her trip to Madrid. The most important link may be that of a musical motif signaled by the title story, "My Long-Playing Records." A number of narratives reflect the fact that I earned a degree in music and played keyboards publicly for more than two decades, that I've collected almost a thousand LPs, CDs, and digital files covering a wide range of music that still informs my life. Music is found everywhere throughout the days of my characters. It's live. It's recorded. It's in movies. On stage. At church. Between their ears, as they listen to their devices. In most of these stories, music determines more than setting. It produces character-driven narratives that play out to their own hard-earned beat.

As I prepared this manuscript, I considered separating the stories with straight protagonists from the stories with gay ones. Wouldn't the "straight" stories appeal only to the straight person and the "gay" ones to the gay reader? I decided against such a move. My experience has shown that my "gay" stories may not be gay enough for editors of gay journals and yet too gay for mainstream publications. Must I ramp up the gay aspects to please the former and eradicate them to please the latter? Heaven forbid that readers or journal editors wander into a life that might be a bit different than their own and yet astonishingly similar. My characters hail from perhaps a broader spectrum of humanity than if I'd separated these stories and published two different collections. The time for that has passed.

By publishing this collection myself, I have found the perfect venue. Yes, I've been able to produce exactly the book I wish, without sacrificing my artistic interests. I hope the reader, too, will bow to the habit I've developed while reading a collection, which is to enjoy perusing one or two stories before turning in for the night. There is a sense of completion you experience before dousing the light—giving you something to ponder as you submit to your dreams.

Richard Jespers
October 2014

A Certain Kind of Mischief

I guess our alliance begins when Brad, an eighth-grader, waves me to the back of the bus. I don't hurry—Ragland's the scariest dude in school—but my hesitation seems to agitate him, causing me to walk slower and slower until I arrive at his feet.

"What do you think I'm going to do, Buckaroo, stab ya?" His green eyes boil as he glares up at me.

Slouching in the middle of the back row, he allows his legs to sprawl up the aisle. I stand near his scuffed ropers—almost falling on him—as the bus lurches away from Heritage Oak Middle School, and he fakes like he's catching me. If you're going to get kneed in the balls, now is the time for it to happen because Doug the driver is preoccupied and everyone's acting like maniacs. If I got stabbed, they'd all point and laugh—like I was the kid always getting whacked on *South Park*. *Hey, look, they've killed Lenny.*

Brad scoots over. "Ho, Lenny Lubowski, I hear tell you're a real whiz kid, got like straight As. Is that true?"

I've seen Brad's dick in the showers after gym. It's long and usually very red. I don't think he uses deodorant because he smells oniony at times. His dark hair looks like it came off a Ken doll, and two or three zits spoil a face that would be pretty good looking if it didn't have a permanent scowl. His body seems to be covered with scabs and bruises. I'm almost as tall as him, but he must have ten to fifteen pounds on me.

"Hey, eff you, Buckaroo, bet I'm just as brainy."

"Why don't you just say 'fuck' like everybody else?"

"Maybe my mama don't like it, a-hole," he says, draping his arm around me and giving me a quick ping to my earlobe. It doesn't hurt. "How's ever*thang*, anyways?" He pulls me tight against him and whispers, "Some day when you ain't looking, I'm going to kill you with my bar hands."

"What?" I say, turning my head.

"You heard me," he says, grinning. His mouth is filled with teeth that are perfectly white except for an upper incisor that has a gray, dead look to it. Of all the kids on the bus—the student council president, a couple of cheerleaders, the science fair winner, ordinaries like me—no one hears his threat of murder.

I shrug as if it doesn't matter. And in a way it doesn't. I was happy until I was six, before Mom up and deserted me and my dad. With no one to do our laundry and cook our meals and keep our house clean, Dad still walks around with his head up his ass. Since my mom left, he and I stopped reading to each other at night. And now that I'm in the sixth grade, the one way we connect is through IMs. I have our complete text history from when I got my first phone, and sometimes when I look at it, I can't believe I have the same dad as back then.

got to skool
hav good day
bus had flat tire. stuck @ 98th/milwaukee
txt me when you get home
ok, luv u dad

My dad, who's a dentist, never responds to my affections, no matter how thick I lay it on. I think I remind him too much of my beautiful but reckless mother: the curved bridge of her nose, her ocean blue eyes and silky blond hair. She took our dog Woofie and went off to an art colony in New Mexico to live like a Bohemian. I googled it when I overheard Dad on the phone referring to her as *some damn Bohemian*. It described her to a tee, but Dad didn't divorce her, and she never asked him for a thing—not even me. I have a few items to remind me of her: a faded photo of her smoking a cigarette and holding me in her lap, the mood ring her father gave her, some Atlantic jingle she collected along with some other shells at Myrtle Beach when she and my dad were on their honeymoon. And I have to admit, I do miss her and Woofie, the way he'd snuggle up with me at night. After my mom left, my dad started wearing Eternity. Whenever I get a whiff of its woody smell, it gives me a feeling that the world's coming to an end.

My phone makes its Sherwood Forest fanfare, and I take it off the clip hooked to my belt. *wil be late go ahed and eet if no hot pockets call piz hut*

O-k, I punch in. Then I tap "Send" before Brad can grab the iPhone Dad got me for my birthday. It's my second one in three years. I couldn't live without it: it has all my music, a calendar, a Kindle, and all kinds of cool gaming apps.

"Nice little dee-vice you have here, Lenny. What's your effing pass code?"

I tell him and Brad taps it in. "Cool wallpaper, I like monarchs." He begins scrolling through my messages, but he won't find anything. I only text Dad.

"You lead a pathetic little life, don't you, Buckaroo?"

"I guess so."

"Don't worry," he says, gesturing to everyone on the bus. "You ain't alone."

We're halfway through the scheduled loop, and the bus empties as we stop at Megan's corner, then the block where Sean, Pegeen, and Tiffany get off. Some of the remaining kids nap. Some jabber on about Justin Bieber and rappers and such, putting their earbuds up to each other's ears. A few kids even try to finish their homework in all this hubbub. I glare at Brad's scarred hands fingering my phone like it's his.

"My pa up and left us two years ago, went off to work the oil fields around Odessa," Brad says, flipping through my photos—mostly of trees and flowers, a video I shot of this ant speeding along with a breadcrumb on its back. I followed it for two blocks, which must be like fifty miles for an ant. "Pa used to be a rodeo clown, but a buddy of his got him this job as a roughneck. What he really is, is what they call a worm, which means he's everybody's bitch, doing all the shick no one elst wants to do. Told me that hisself. His hands and arms is black and he walks like a cripple, he was butted so many times back in his rodeo days. Man's only forty-four." Brad takes a breath, tapping each picture twice to look at some things, like the pistils and stamens of a lily, up close. "And my mom don't have a clue about how to make money. Right now she's temping and spams at night. She don't bring in as much as you're supposed to—probably 'cause she's an effing drunk, glugs it down like a old sailor. My dad makes the house payment and pays the electric, so we got a roof over our heads, but that's about it. He got a new wife and twin boys and sends a few hundred dollars whenever he feels like it. You can guess how far that goes."

"Life's a fucking shithole," I say, and Brad laughs, laughs for something like thirty seconds, which is pretty long for one that sounds so fake.

"That's one mouthful of filth," Brad says, putting his lizard-skin hands over my ear. "Maybe I won't kill you after all," he says. The bus jerks to a stop, and Brad gets up to leave. He bends over as the door up front *pssts* open and whispers, "You can see my dick any time you want, you don't have to wait till we're in the shower."

I shrug and act like I don't know what he's talking about.

"Come on," he says, tossing me my phone. "You know you want to."

He propels himself like some kind of hip-hop hipster up the aisle—bouncing on one scuffed-up boot then the next, slapping every other seat—and kicks at some sandals in the aisle. *Owww* goes Jeffie, one of what Coach Darby calls the Whiners, and Brad waves as he ambles backward down the street. I can't take my eyes off him.

One afternoon before Doug the driver has a chance to ask me for a permission note, I scoot off the bus with Brad, and we race down his street. Every house in the subdivision has a different design or bric-a-brac around the windows—something that makes you think your place is unique, but when you look at all the roofs you see it's not. Brad takes a jangly wad of keys out of his pocket and unlocks the front door. I see the layout is much like ours five blocks over except it's minus one bedroom, a bath, and what my dad calls the solarium. Brad punches in a code on a keypad by the door to quiet their alarm.

"It's not hooked up," Brad says. "My mom cain't pay the bill, but she says we have to make it look like we're doing okay. Oh, yeah."

I text my dad that I'm home now, and then we drink some water from the tap in the kitchen. "Blecch, I hate the local H_2O," Brad says, shaking his head like he's drunk poison. He washes our glasses, dries them with a towel, holding them up to the light, and puts them back in the cabinet. Taking my arm, he leads me down the hall to his bedroom. It's tidy, with an old iMac sitting on a small desk. Several shirts are hung in an open closet that includes maybe one sport coat and some jeans and slacks hung by the hems from old-timey pants hangers. There isn't a dust bunny in sight.

"It isn't what I expected," I say.

"What, you thought I'd have a bunch of Richie Rich kind of stuff?"

"Huh?"

Brad takes off all his clothes, and again I'm fascinated at how thin yet powerful his body looks—sort of a human arrow. Various cuts and scrapes pepper his skin from the forehead all the way to his ankles: an X probably made with a knife, several that seem like fruits split open raw, and a bruise big as an eggplant on his left flank. "I'll bet you're wondering how I got this," he says, wincing. "Fell on the swing at the park, trying to do a loop-the-loop. This—this here I got when I crashed my skateboard." He points to a brown scab crusted over like an egg roll on his left shin. "These, these I done myself." Brad indicates a dozen more cuts as if doing a TV commercial for Band-Aids. He takes a nail file from the top drawer of his highly polished bureau and pretends he's cutting his wrist. "It's fu-un," he says, tossing the file back in the drawer. He tiptoes across the floor like a woman in high heels, and it makes his dick flop from side to side. I giggle, something I often do when I'm caught by surprise. "My ma makes me change my underwear twiced a day, she's a real freak about it." From the same drawer he removes a pair of white briefs. Before sliding them on, he twitches his eyebrows and says, "You want to jack me off?"

I shake my head and watch as he puts on some cargo shorts and a faded yellow T-shirt with a smiley face on the front and frowny face on the back. I hear a door open, and a woman's voice says, *Bradley . . . Bradley Thomas?*

"In here, Ma. I brought this here buckaroo home with me." He winks.

"Who?" his mother says as she sticks her head in the door. She's a hard-looking woman, skinny like Brad, but her face is wrinkled and her cheeks are sunken. Still, her arms look as if they could hit the moon with a bowling ball. Her red hair has about an inch of gray at the roots, and she stinks from smoking. "What's your name?" her husky voice says, leaning against the door frame with her arms crossed.

"Lenny," I say, stepping forward to shake her hand. She ignores the gesture but smiles, exposing yellow teeth and a few molars black with fillings. You can just tell she used to be pretty.

"You need to get them thangs up off the floor, Bradley Thomas," she says, snapping her fingers. "Pronto, young man."

"Yes, Mother," he says, and for a second I think he's being sarcastic, but when I see the obedient look on his face—as if he's four—I realize he's scared to death. He picks up his school clothes, folds and slips them into his drawer.

"No, Bradley Thomas, you wore them thangs all day long, they go in the laundry, *remember?*" She makes her voice go all syrupy as she grasps her son by the neck and gazes into his eyes. He squints and smirks.

"Oh, yeah," he says, withdrawing from her embrace so he can trot his clothes down the hall. Brad's mother leaves me alone, and a door slams. Then I hear her muffled voice, and when Brad returns, he says, "You'd better skedaddle."

"Did I do something wrong?"

"Mama don't like me having friends around too much. They make her nervous." He crosses his eyes and mimes like he's drinking from a bottle. Then he puts an arm around my shoulder and walks me to the door. I see that the living room is furnished with a love seat and a console TV that, my guess, doesn't work because there's no cable box feeding it the digital signal. For the first time, I pity Brad. I don't care for the feeling, so on my walk home I try to think of a way of not seeing him again—you know—like sitting behind Doug the bus driver with the little kids or hiding under a seat. But as I unlock our front door, I realize that whatever this is, I've jumped in with both feet.

Because I'm two years ahead of my grade level in math, I'm able to help Brad with his homework. He seems to have trouble understanding sets, so I tell him it's like putting the same colored marbles in separate bags. He smiles and says, "Well, ain't you clever." When he starts getting As, Old Man Drake keeps him after school to quiz him, makes him do a couple of equations. After that, I make sure Brad misses two or three of the hardest problems on the page. When we finish our assignments each day, Brad and I entertain ourselves by using his mom's land line to make prank calls. We block her number first; if someone uses anonymous caller rejection, we choose a different listing. Brad's voice is deep, and he cooks up a totally believable way of talking as if he's thirty and working as a deejay for KONE. Most people are too hip to fall for such juvenile crap, but one afternoon Brad manages to hook a woman he hand-picks from the phone book.

"I know it's a lady," he whispers, "because she's got just the one initial by her last name." *Oh, howdy, Ma'am, how you doing this fine afternoon?*

In a few minutes he convinces the woman to buy a hoodie that covers the whole body. "Nice for lounging around when you're watching TV, Ma'am. The best way you can take advantage of our exclusive offer is to pay by credit card. I'm standing by to record your number." He winks at me lying on his bed, which is covered with a beige comforter smelling like Bounce. I suspect his race-car sheets are stained with blood, but I can't be sure. He points to me, and I take down the card's sixteen numbers plus the three-digit security code and expiration date as he dictates them. He spends several more minutes keeping the woman on the line while I use the computer he and his mom share to order several items from Hammacher Schlemmer. When I nod that the website has accepted the credit card, Brad ends his call, remaining polite as ever. He erases the Internet history and puts the turquoise iMac to sleep.

"Bitch only *thinks* I use it for my homework."

All of a sudden, he drops to the floor, rolls over, and slides under his bed. "Git down here," he says, and I pull in next to him. It's quiet, like being in a cave.

I watch as he gingerly undoes the thin gauzy material concealing his box springs and pulls out a miniature copy of *The Adventures of Tom Sawyer*. "Found it on my teacher's desk in fifth grade," he whispers. "I've read it like twenty times." He replaces it by wedging it between a spring and the mattress. Untying some strings, he produces a jar filled with grasshopper legs.

"Gross, dude," I whisper, and he giggles, tying the jar back in place. He produces a small jewelry box.

"Here, open it." I do and inside there's a gold ring with a red stone. "It's my Meemaw's high school ring."

"She give it to you?"

"Last summer when I was over to her place in Guthrie, I kiped it out of her drawer. She's blind as a bat."

"Your mother would kill you if she knew."

"No shick, Shylock."

We slide out, and I rest my head on his stomach. We tell each other about our families, why, for different reasons, we both feel like orphans. You'd think that knowing his dad left Brad like my mom left me would make me feel better, but it doesn't. When Brad tries to kiss me, I slug him, and he laughs, but I don't think it's that funny.

Five days later we find a couple of cardboard packages on the porch minutes before Brad's mom gets home from temping at an office in Briercroft Center. For forty-eight hours we tuck away our riches—including a digital TV with a five-inch screen—until his mom calls to say she'll be working late.

"She's really on her way to Crossroads to play *pool*," he says. "She won't be home till midnight."

Holding the TV between us, we surf, stopping to watch Dr. Oz. "Look how he paws over them women like some effing perv. Makes me sick to my stomach."

In the same shipment, we receive a little robot that picks up your toys and puts them where you want and a CD player in the shape of a Darth Vader helmet. The robot does okay with a baseball and even Brad's Eric Cartman doll, but when Brad tries to make it pick up his boot, it says, *Too heavy for me.*

"Effing lame," Brad mutters.

While we race the robot around Brad's wood floor, we play a couple of his mom's CDs he keeps hidden in his box springs. We both like "Windy" by the Association, but he goes ape wild over Led Zeppelin. The CD player, which is made of black plastic, rattles like an old car when he turns the dial.

"Dude, my brain feels like it's on fire when I ramp this shick up. Every bad thought in my head melts away, and I'm on cloud ten," Brad yells over the music. I'm happy just being next to him in this little underworld he's created.

All of the merchandise—except for the TV, which Brad insists I accept for helping him with his math—we hide behind a small door in his closet that accesses the bathtub plumbing. On the next afternoon, we use the same woman's credit card number to order a stun gun. Don't ask me why. I guess it's because we run across a picture while googling topics for school. Its arrival—again, before his mom gets home—is something that both excites me and fills me with dread, and I can hardly tell the difference.

The one we order is made to look like a cell phone—but at six inches long and an inch thick with silver plastic and black buttons, it looks more like a handset model. The booklet says if you hold the gun against a dude for three seconds or more, you can disable him long enough to tie him up or get away and go for the cops. It says the stun gun can *turn a grown man into a quivering pile of Jell-O, and cases of death are very rare.* We agree to use it on each other *once*—for no longer than a second. Brad holds it next to my chest and grins—then he gazes down at me with something like great sorrow. After he zaps me in the chest, my body snaps in two and my muscles tingle like when I hit my funny bone. But it also seems like a gorilla is sitting on me. I can't move, and I don't want to as I stare up at the ceiling with thoughts of my mom and dad and my grandparents in Abernathy ambling through my head. When I've recovered, at least half an hour has passed. I shove Brad away and tell him it's his turn.

He shakes his head. "And if you try to take it away from me, Buckaroo, I'll zap you again." He grins and I shrug. I should be interested in getting even with him, but I feel too weak to fight, and besides, a little spot on my chest hurts if I breathe too deep.

To lessen the possibility of getting caught with it, we pass our cellphone stun gun back and forth on the bus each afternoon—which doesn't look as weird as you might think. No one ever asks to see it. At night, under the covers, if I can't sleep, I watch Jimmy Fallon or Carson Daly on the little TV, and when one of them says something funny, it makes me wish my friend could be in on the joke.

Since Brad is two years older, gym is the only class we have together. He's always in trouble for not suiting up or not having a permission slip to play intramural games, or talking back. You name it, and he's done it.

Son, I made you section leader to help you develop some confidence, a sense of responsibility, Coach Darby says one day. *And all you've done is betray me.*

Brad has trouble making free throws, unlike the other section leaders, who are Coach's *stars*. None of us ordinaries are very good at the free shots. We'd rather try our hand at three-pointers, which Coach has told us to forget about. The only jump shots he wants to see us attempt are in the elbow or block zones because he says that's where you have a better chance of scoring a few points. He keeps telling us we have to learn to play the game in the correct stages, or else we'll never master it. One day when he says that for the billionth time, I roll my eyes at Brad, who's standing in front facing our squad. He laughs and is demoted from section leader to the back row.

"Some time when you least expect it, Buckaroo, I'm going to kill you with this thang," he tells me later on the bus. "A hundred and eighty thousand volts."

Jeffie, who's also in sixth grade, turns around and sticks his face over the back of the seat. "Hey, Brad," he says. "How'd you get that scar on your forehead?"

"Why don't you go eff yourself, you little horny toad," Brad says.

"Because I'd rather jack off like I seen you do in the shower."

"Go on, you little perv, go irritate somebody elst for a while." Brad pops Jeffie on the forehead, and the kid staggers up the aisle like he's been stabbed. Doug the driver yells at him over the PA. *Take your seat, Master Fuller, or I might have to rough you up.*

"I'm sorry for getting you cut as section leader," I say in Brad's ear.

"Fudge, I don't give a shick. The only perk I ever got was leaving third period to beat the rush to gym. Now I'll have time to pick on you and old Jeffie-poo."

"You're not that mean," I say. "Not really."

At first I think the bus has hit a bump; then I realize Brad has rammed his elbow into my ribs. It hurts worse than the stun gun. "Ow, damn. Fucker."

"See how mean I can be, you little prick."

"I'm . . . sorry, Brad," I say, tears rolling down my face.

"Eff the waterworks. The more my mother does that the more I'd like to kill her. I mean, I want to effing stab her when she starts that business."

It's my turn to keep the cell-phone stun gun overnight, but I take it out of my back pack and hand it to Brad.

"Keep it, Buckaroo," he says. "And quit blubbering. The best way you can square this with me is to take little Jeffie-poo down a peg or two. You heard him: 'How'd you get this scar, how'd you get that scar?' I wish the eff he'd mind his own effing business."

"I could kick the dude when I get off the bus," I offer.

"Naw, you need to have on some sturdy roper boots like mine . . . but I guess you could give him a little shock with our trusty dee-vice."

"Don't be stupid," I say. Quicker than I can imagine, Brad makes a fist and gouges me hard in my crotch. I'm seeing something like stars, and my insides are on fire. I don't make a sound but close my eyes and bend all the way over. I've hurt my testicles by falling on the bar of my bike, but this . . . the spot hidden deep inside me . . . seems to be shooting flames throughout my whole body. I rock back and forth, feeling like I do after I throw up.

"If you don't electrocute our little Jeffie Fuller, I'll make it so you cain't never get a girl pregnant," he says.

With my head still down, I nod. "But what if it kills him?" I croak.

"*Don't be stupid,*" he says in a high voice, laughing.

We're now at his stop, and I don't want to part ways—not like this, not with him having the upper hand.

"I'll call you later, Buckaroo."

"Okay," I say, staring after Brad as he hip-hops up the aisle and then runs like a gazelle toward his house. Soon he stops dead in his tracks. His mom is standing in their driveway holding a drink. As the bus pulls away, she gives him a couple of good ones across the kisser. At first I feel sorry for Brad, but when he lies about the incident a few hours later on the phone, I want to electrocute him and not just for a minute. *Dude, if I could stun-gun you, would the hate go away?* I wonder. *If I could stun-gun my mother, would I stop hating her guts?* I imagine sharing these muddled thoughts with my dad—if he would ever quit racing from chore to chore—but then *that* is as likely as me sharing my problems with President Obama. I sometimes imagine me sitting on his lap in the Oval Office and him telling me what a great kid I am. As busy as he is, I'll bet he still finds time for his two girls, and it makes me wonder what's wrong with my dad.

Brad and I work on The Plan for several weeks before trying it out on Jeffie. We decide to put the stun gun on half-power for one thing. The instruction book says that way you can simply daze your victim. I doubt it, so I say we should conduct a test.

"Like what?" Brad says.

"I don't know, find a dog. If it dies, what do we care? If it lives, it'll sleep it off and its owner will never know the difference."

"Buckaroo, it's no wonder they call you the whiz kid."

Brad's sitting on my bed cuddling an old teddy bear I forgot to hide. When he starts kissing it like it's a girl, I laugh, and he bats it across the room, where it lands sitting up against the wall. It's the one that soaked up all my tears when I realized my mom was never coming back. I call my dad at his office and ask him if I can invite Brad to come over for a burger, and he says yeah, he'll pick some up on the way home from work.

"Can't you cook them outside like you used to?"

Dad tells me the grill needs a new propane tank. "Brad isn't there with you, is he?" I tell him no and ring off before he has a chance to remind me of the *rules*.

"Aren't you going to change your clothes?" Brad says.

"I pretty much wear the same thing all day."

"I cain't believe you got five of these things." He twirls my yellow wrist bands around his index finger. "You know old Lance shot up drugs, don't you?"

"He did not," I say, gathering the bands from the floor where Brad's tossed them.

"Where the eff did you get that?" he asks, pointing at the slim TV on my wall.

"Christmas," I say, and I show him how to use my PS4. Brad gets into one game where these two monsters chase each other all over a kingdom called the Camel Lot. When my man destroys his man with one blow of my spiked battle flail and the screen goes bloody, he loses interest.

"Stupid video games," he says, tossing me the joystick.

"Ha, dude, I beat you," I say, and he pounces on me.

I like matching my strength against his until he starts choking me, and I knee him in the stomach. He lets go but he's breathing heavy and he has a fierce look on his face.

"Dude, what's wrong with you?" I say. "You might beat me next time once you get the hang of it. You have to make your hand work faster."

"I'll show you how fast it can work," he says, grabbing my crotch.

"Hey, don't," I say gripping his wrist, but he's too strong for me, and he keeps squeezing my balls until I spit on him.

He screams and runs to my bathroom, where he splashes water on his face and then rubs sanitizer over it. He returns, saying, "Don't ever do that again, a-hole. Do you know how many germs there are in one blob of saliva?"

"Then keep your fucking hands off my junk," I say, holding my sides.

Brad stands at my window looking out over our backyard, where my dad built banks of earth for me to ride my dirt bike on. He also made me a tree house and a wooden swing set. "When I was section leader, the six of us used to jack off together."

"That's a load of crap," I say.

"Come on," he says, whirling to grab my hand. "You know you want to." He throws his body on me, as if he's trying to soak me up inside of him. "Do you have hair on your balls yet?" he says, licking my cheek like a big old St. Bernard.

"I—don't—think—so," I say with all the air squeezed out of my lungs.

"Then you're too young," he says, jumping up. "Come on, we've got to find a dog for our little experiment, and I think I know just the one."

On our way we buy a pack of Beggin' Strips at a 7-Eleven on 98th. We meander our way to Brad's block by splitting a Big Gulp and tossing the cup in a drainage ditch. Brad then takes me to a yard at the end of his street where there's a German shepherd named Gingko. He says the folks there sometimes walk Gingko up and down the block, and once when the dog took a dump on their lawn Brad's mother made him run down and throw the dog's turds in the owner's yard. The property sits next to an empty lot at the end of a cul-de-sac crowded with tumble-weeds and overgrown with yellow stalks of what Dad calls prairie grass. We stand looking into the yard surrounded by a chain-link fence, and I notice the sky is about as blue as it can get in El Centro, Texas. A gust of wind swirls some pink dirt in our faces, and I turn my head away. We note that Gingko is occupied up near the side gate, and Brad whistles to get its attention. The dog charges back to where we are and cocks its head. With its mouth open and tongue hanging out, it looks like it's smiling. I open the box and hold out a Beggin' Strip to tempt Gingko, who barks as if it knows what we're up to.

"Put some through the fence," Brad says.

I clip a few links with Dad's wire cutter. It isn't as easy as he makes it look, but when I finish, I've made a hole big enough to stick my arm through. Gingko barks louder, so I drop a strip of food, and the dog tongues it before gobbling it down. I drop another one, and again Gingko goes for it. This time I push the cell-phone stun gun against its flank and click the button, holding as long as I dare. I can almost see the charge pass from the fake antenna to the other prong. The dog yelps and falls to the ground. It gasps, its eyes circling wildly, its tongue hanging out the side of its mouth.

"I don't think it's breathing," I say.

"The mutt'll be fine," Brad says. The wind is blowing stalks of grass in wavy patterns like wheat, and I sit staring at it, feeling sick at my stomach.

"*What're you boys doing?*" comes a voice behind us. We turn to see an old dude in khaki pants and a plaid shirt. He's got on big blue tennis shoes.

"Nothing, sir," Brad says. He stands and holds the Beggin' Strips behind his back.

I slide the stun gun inside my underwear, where it feels warm against my dick, and stand in front of the hole in the fence.

"What's wrong with the dog?" the old man says. His eyes look opaque.

"Old thang seems to be all tuckered out," Brad says.

"Well, I heard him, that's why I come over to see. He usually only barks when there's some kind of trouble. You all right, Gingko, buddy? You don't look so good."

"Shore is beautiful," Brad says. "We wanted to see it up close. We didn't do nothing to it." I throw Brad a look, and the old dude wrinkles his nose.

"Maybe you boys ought to get on home and not come back this way. I head up the neighborhood watch, you know. Is that your tool in the grass there?"

"No, sir," I say. Gingko now raises his head, but he seems disoriented. His tail is trembling like a leaf. As we race toward Brad's house in the middle of the block, the stun gun shifts in my boxers and begins sliding down my pant leg. I trap it against my thigh and walk a little bent over until we're out of sight of the old man.

"Hand that thang over," Brad says when we get to his house.

"It's my turn to have it."

He sneers at me with a certain disgust. "You can keep it, but only if you've got a plan to give Jeffie the full-voltage treatment."

"I don't know," I say. "You saw what half-power did to that dog. One shot and bam, Jeffie could be dead."

"It's either you or him," Brad says.

"Why are you so mad, dude? I told you I was sorry about gym class." He shrugs. "You can't hold a grudge forever . . . and you forget . . . I still have the weapon." I think about jamming the thing, hard, into Brad's chest—to jar some sense into his head—but he'd just spend the rest of his life getting even with me. Allowing the stun gun to slide down to my ankle, I grab it, saying, "Here, you can have it, I trust you."

He snatches it away and sparks it inches from my chin.

"Go ahead," I say, closing my eyes. "I can take it."

"Hey, Buckaroo, don't you know when I'm kidding? I'll be standing right beside you when we pull our little stunt on Jeffie-poo," he says. "All for one, and one for all."

I arrange for Jeffie to come to my house one day after school. He looks like he's still in fourth grade, his straw-blond hair in a crew cut, but he has a hard edge to him, like he might kick the crap out of you if you fuck with him.

"I take it your folks have this worked out," Doug the bus driver says, holding us back before he *psssts* the door open.

"Got it covered," Brad says, holding up a fake note from his mom, and Jeffie echoes Brad by flashing *his* note. Brad laughs and puts his hand on Jeffie's shoulder, as we all exit the bus. He leans over and says, "Good thang Mama made me work so hard on my handwriting, it looks better than hers." When we get to my front lawn, we start playing catch with an old football that's underinflated. Brad now has possession of the cell-phone stun gun. The idea is for us to pin Jeffie to the ground. Then we'll both put our hands on the gun and click the button as we shove it against him—that way we'll both be taking responsibility. It's bogus, playing the kid so we can build his trust, but I seem to do it without giving it much thought. Jeffie is less athletic than I am, so I call him Fumblethumbs when he fails to make a catch. Then I drop a pass, and Brad points and laughs at me. I remind Brad how Coach Darby fired him as section leader, and he does this *enraged* act by chasing me around the yard like he's Frankenstein.

Not long after that, the garage opens, and I groan. My dad turns in the driveway and parks his F-150 in the left-hand stall. Dressed in gray slacks and a new pink tie, his white shirt wrinkled from a hard day of pulling teeth, he comes over and says, "What's going on, boys?" He's trying to sound casual, which, of course, makes it seem like he's about to come unglued. "Yeah, well, I decided the lawn isn't going to scalp itself." He disappears into the house, but a whiff of his Eternity remains. A lady he once dated informed him he wore too much of the stuff, and he told me he *dropped her like a hot patootie.* In a few minutes, he stands at the door in a T-shirt and jeans and calls me inside. God, even after a full day, the cologne seems to envelop him like a cloud. I almost cough.

"What's our rule?" he asks, sitting on an ottoman, tying some old Nikes.

I shrug.

"Our rule is . . . no friends over unless I'm at home. You know that, Lenny." He makes a face. "Since your buddies are already here, they can stay. But play out back, I don't want you around in case the mower throws a rock."

"Okay," I say. "You want us to rake grass or anything?"

"Nope, you'd just be in my way."

Dad fills a glass with water from the dispenser in the fridge door and gulps it down. I follow him to the garage, where he pushes the mower from the right-hand stall onto the drive and attaches the large catcher. He presses the starter button, and a puff of blue smoke shoots out the rear. He begins mowing up near the house, and we go to the back yard like he said. After scrimmaging against me and Jeffie—he's leading twelve-six—Brad puts his arm around me.

"We cain't do it today, I'm going on home."

"What're y'all talking about?" Jeffie says, holding the football under his arm.

"Never the eff you mind, Jeffie-poo," Brad says, faking a punch to his stomach.

About this time Dad comes through the gate struggling with the catcher, which is now full of dead grass. He empties it in the alley dumpster, and we hear a screech of tires out front. Soon a figure appears at the gate. It's Brad's mom—with her arms crossed—and she actually looks kind of nice dressed in a gray pantsuit and black high heels.

"Bradley Thomas Ragland, you get your skinny butt over here this instant."

He creeps toward her like a cowed dog, and even though he's a little taller than her, he carries himself very small. She starts in on the dude, first for not telling her where he was going to be, and he barks something I can't make out. *I've warned you about that foul mouth of yours.* Then she slaps him and lowers his chin to make him look down at her, but in a second or two he jerks his head away. His face reveals a mixture of humiliation and rage, and she drags him out front. Jeffie and I race to catch up. Her car, a dented VW Beetle, is blocking the driveway. From the front window Brad's mom withdraws the robot we hid behind the small door in his closet.

"I heard your little *friend* talking while I was trying to take a bath," she shouts and slaps him again. "Where the eff did you get it, and that gee-dee boom box looking like death itself?" Brad folds his arms. His mom kicks him with her pointy shoes, and when he yelps and falls to the ground, she screams at him. "Tell me, you little a-hole, where'd you get all them thangs?"

In a casual but deliberate move, as if he's saying *Pardon me, ma'am, while I answer this here cell phone,* Brad raises his arm and shoves the weapon into his mother's chest. Her eyes get big—her face looking like, *Son, you cain't be serious*—and then he clicks the switch. Her body jackknifes before falling to the ground like Gingko's did. And then like Gingko, she shivers and kicks. Still on his knees, Brad bows his head—at first I think he's sorry for what he's done—and buzzes the stun gun against her body until it almost stops moving. He stares at her with the same satisfaction you get from half squashing a cockroach—watching its legs spin in slow motion, its body oozing white stuff. My dad pops around the corner, and I've never in my life been so glad to see him. When he catches sight of Brad's mom sprawled out like that, he dashes over, checking the woman's pulse rate. Her leg continues to spasm, her head rolls against the ground with her eyes open, and she keeps moaning. Dad then pulls out his phone and calls 9-1-1.

"I'm not sure," he tells the dispatcher. "What happened?" Brad and I stare at each other and then at his mom again. "Guys—tell me what happened."

I shrug and Brad makes the weapon spark for my dad. "I torched the goddamn fucking cunt with full power," he says. "Twiced. Goddamn bitch's been asking for it."

"Christ," my dad says, "somebody's used a stun gun on her."

He doesn't ask me any more questions, not right away. When the cops and ambulance arrive, Brad's mom is sitting up against her car door. Her red hair looks like a clown wig, and her face is milk white. She protests, mumbling she has no insurance. As they carry her away on a stretcher, it's like the anger has been drained right out of her, as if she knows a certain justice has taken place. Later I hear some kid at school say she has a big purple sore on her chest. Whether it's true or not, I have no idea, but if she does it would serve her right.

Of course, things get as squirrelly as they can possibly get. Brad can't help but spill the beans about his mother's abuse, and that sets off a whole chain of events. First, Mrs. Ragland is charged with assault and child endangerment. After a doctor examines Brad, he announces on TV: *Evidence exists that the mother has battered her son for quite some time now.* Then we hear that Brad's father in Odessa says he won't take Brad because he has a brand new family and can't afford him. Then Brad becomes a ward of the state. When I ask Dad if he could be Brad's foster father, he looks down the long side of his nose at me.

"I know you feel bad for him, but that boy's father is legally responsible for taking care of his own son."

Dad starts coming home early. In fact, he's often here when I get off the bus. It changes my routine. I used to watch my TV or take a nap, but now he's always suggesting we do something. And though I like it, part of me wonders if it'll last.

The cell-phone stun gun is taken by the police as evidence, which, to tell you the truth, is fine with me. When Dad demands to know how we got hold of it, I explain about making prank calls and charging items to that lady's credit card.

At first he tries to hide his smile, and then he falls into his chair, hanging his head. Tears fall to his gray slacks like big raindrops. He puts his arm around my waist and pulls me to his side. I resist, then a wave of sorrow splashes over me, and I fall back so Dad can hold me in his lap. Under his faded cologne, I can smell the father I once knew, and I bury my head in his chest. The world goes black. I find myself convulsing, crying for my mom and dad, for myself, then for Gingko and Brad and his mother, for all the bad shit that happens to people everywhere, every day. Dad holds me tight until I quit hiccupping; it's like being in a cocoon. I finally raise my head and stand on my own two feet. We're both embarrassed but smile and blow our noses. Things get real again.

"You're going to have to apologize to that woman and make it right with the credit card company, you know," he says, grasping my hand. Somehow I feel his strength passing from his arm to mine.

"How?" I ask.

"Oh, I'll pay the bill, but you'll have to work it off mowing the lawn and doing other chores—I've been too easy on you since your mother went away. Somehow I thought you'd just raise yourself." I make a face, and he kisses me on the cheek. It makes me shiver, and my eyes sting with regret at what an asshole I've been lately. "Your first job is to find out that woman's address. You're going to apologize to her in person. And don't be surprised if the police want to haul you in for credit card fraud." Even if he does wink, I visualize them showing up at our door, putting me in handcuffs.

Brad winds up in the county youth detention center, waiting the whole ten days a judge gives his father to collect him. I ask Dad if we can go see him, at least. He says straight up it isn't a good idea, and I ask why.

"Oh, I don't know," he says, untying his stark blue tie, kicking off his shoes. "Putting you and Brad in the same room is like lighting a match when you're trying to find a gas leak." He plops down on his bed and starts tickling me as he pulls me close.

"I hope Brad's father and stepmother will at least give him a chance. He isn't really bad."

"I have a feeling that once his dad gets hold of him Brad will turn out just fine. Or *not.* Son, he's got to decide what kind of young man he wants to be."

At first I miss seeing Brad on the bus, but now that Jeffie and I have become friends, we sit where Brad and I used to. It's like he's still with us. Sort of.

I have Jeffie over one afternoon and tell him about how we'd planned to stun-gun him, and, except for him being the victim, he thinks it's a cool idea. We get so busy doing our homework and calling girls in our class that we lose track of time. Last week Dad finally bought a propane tank for the gas grill, and when he gets home, he invites Jeffie to stay for supper. Later, after we're through eating burgers and deli potato salad, the three of us play Monopoly. I grab the top hat. Then way too soon it's dark, so we quit and me and my dad take Jeffie home. On our way back, I ask Dad to drive by Brad's place, which he does slowly . . . creeping toward the darkest house on the block. And yet, as we stop in front, I find it hard to believe Brad's not still inside, plumped up in his bed reading that tiny little copy of *Tom Sawyer.*

GHOST RIDERS

Driving Farm-to-Market Road 1585, I came upon a '73 Cadillac, a studio apartment on wheels, coasting, apparently with no driver. The car, a faded metallic green, moved on underinflated tires across the hard caliche, and a man in a dirty shirttail and lower-than-the-hip jeans slithered out the passenger side and up onto the roof. He began dancing to music that bore a savage thump, his bass speakers pounding contrary to the steadiness of my heart. Gawking as I passed, I gave him a wave and moved on. In my mirror the dancer made an obscene gesture, incorporated into his choreography. Still in awe of what I had witnessed—what if he crashed into someone or the car's accelerator got stuck and the car ran away with him?—I came upon Brewster's overpass. The intersection had been carved out of tawny pastureland, where a few black-and-white cows stood drinking from a rusty trough. I pulled in under the overpass and got out. Climbing upward, I found Brewster's home, a big indentation where the bridge met the incline, a place where people were advised not to ride out the fury of tornadoes; the vacuum could whisk them away to Oklahoma. The day's sun had warmed the concrete, making it an inviting space to weather the brisk spring air.

Brewster customarily stopped by the church on Tuesdays—he was one of our food voucher clients—and when he had failed to come in, I was struck with the feeling I got when a parishioner died. I was witness to many funerals, guiding earthly souls to part ways with those transitioning, and I was struck with the void the dead created, their utter *goneness.* Nothing I did or said would have allowed people to know I felt that way.

Our food voucher committee also distributed small bags with toothbrushes and striped toothpaste, shaving cream and disposable razors, turquoise mouthwash, amber shampoo, even laundry detergent. And so I had snagged a bag for him, along with his new wardrobe—a rust sports jacket my relatives had given me, pastel tailored shirts, even some new underwear I hadn't opened because my wife selected boxers—harboring a desire to witness his reaction.

The recessed area was deep, like a cave, but it was an aberration, as if the contractor had run out of concrete. On the opposite, otherwise symmetrical, side of the overpass, there existed a smooth slab of cement. Into the darkness I called out, and above the whistle of the wind, I heard a shuffle, maybe a groan.

"Brewster?" A face appeared in the light, and I moved in closer.

"Pastor man," he said, grinning toothlessly. I believed he had once been handsome—I could visualize his yearbook portrait, a black-and-white photograph buried in a row of other handsome youths, gleeful lunches spent eating sandwiches in the high school courtyard—but his cheeks were sunken like an old man's. An odd light, perhaps a sunray reflected from my car, illuminated Brewster. His bald scalp, often hidden under a ratty ball cap, was mottled and splotched with sores. Not a tall man, he wore a powder blue sweatshirt streaked with dirt and oil. His herringbone jacket was folded, lying next to his pallet of soiled blankets and refrigerator crates.

"I wondered where you were today," I said.

"I had a dream, Dave, that you would come," he said, wiping wine from his mouth. The bottle clanked against the concrete like a bell. "And you did come . . . bearing great gifts." The cheap wine seemed pungent to me, especially because I hadn't had a drink since my college days. There, far from the realm of parent control, I'd been a functional alcoholic for most of four years, able to quit as I went off to seminary. No longer tempted to drink, I remembered something raw, almost meaty, about the taste I sometimes missed with great aching.

Brewster's *bearing great gifts* made him sound like the preachers I had heard at revivals when I was a child, when my father would travel dirt roads of the Panhandle searching out venues to pitch his big tent and preach the gospel. I hadn't cared for those events, where I sat glued to my chair; my father, his face burning red, would frighten people from their seats to the altar, urging them to accept God's undying love or else. Counting his money and stashing it in his vest pocket before we moved on to the next town, he was a demon I'd buried a few years ago in a country cemetery near Childress.

Brewster attended the ten-thirty service on Sundays and sat on the third row, where the Cunnicutts had sat for generations, I was told. From the pulpit I scanned their faces, sometimes noting a quiver in their upper lips that registered contempt. Each week during the passing of peace I would speak to Brewster, taking his scaly hand in mine and saying, "Peace be with you, brother." The Cunnicutts would scatter like cats, exchanging pleasantries with friends as if they were at the country club. It would tighten a place in my chest, and I would forgive the Cunnicutts, and I would forgive myself for having so easily passed judgment on them. I would petition God to forgive us all, wondering whether I had gotten through. That was something else I kept to myself.

A short time before, our members had voted to become a reconciling congregation—seeking to help the needy, giving their riches to the poor, *accepting* the unwanted: people of color, two men drawn to one another, two women, any stinking wretch who walked in off the street—and I had been pleased with the attempts of those members who didn't slither away to another church. I hoped we could reach out and touch those whom Christ would love if he were to walk among us again. Anyone.

"How prescient of your dream," I said, handing Brewster what I had brought. Casting aside the toiletries bag and food voucher, he took a peek at the garments and lay them at the foot of his pallet.

"I'll wear 'em as soon as these are full of holes. That's my rule." Brewster smiled; his eyes were dull, red where there should have been white. It was late afternoon, and a ray of sunlight angled itself across his body.

"Where were you today?" I said.

"Overslept," he said, holding up his watch, an old digital that may have needed a battery. "I hate it when we change time zones. Nobody tells me to spring forward, and I get all pershimmeled."

"Yes, the man who bakes bread for communion didn't show up until nine on Sunday, and the early service had to take soda crackers." Brewster lay back and closed his eyes. "Is there anything else I can get you?" I asked.

"No, no, pastor man, I'm a-okay." His body rose from the cardboard bed, and he crawled out from the dark, squatting with me on the embankment. I wondered if he could smell his own rotten odor, a mixture of urine, sweat, and wine that made most people turn their heads. I wondered if he was like others, having *selected* his life, or had life zeroed in on him? I felt like asking him how he had arrived at that point, living but not living inside the guts of an overpass, but we were interrupted.

The same green Cadillac came floating by, crunching the gravel.

"Ghost Riders," Brewster whispered, calling out to what was now two young men, jeans sagging below their white Hilfigers. They waved.

"Hey, Brewski, what's . . . goin' . . . down?" The question was asked in rhythm to the bass. Twirling their bodies, their long hair flew in all directions; their open shirts revealed thin, rangy torsos swathed in dark green tattoos.

"Those boys sure can rhyme, cain't they?"

"Who's driving?" I asked.

"Why, they're riding the whip, pastor man," Brewster said, sliding into the cave to lie on his side. He groaned.

"You mean there's no one in control?" I said, sticking my head inside.

He grinned. "Are any of us in control?"

In the reflection of late sunlight, his gums were gray and sad. Every time I saw Brewster I had a great desire to embrace him, as if doing so would restore him to his former glory. In part I felt that way about most of my parishioners and maybe the world at large. I wished to restore it to some kind of *normalcy*, though it would have been difficult to describe such a state. War or no? Clean air or smog? Paper or plastic? I suppose I saw ministry differently than most pastors. My father had heard one of my sermons, one in which I'd urged people to forgive our president his adultery, as well as the men in Congress who had persecuted him for it; after that my father never spoke. My mother sent Christmas cards from them both, but her signature only confirmed a certain complicity with my father.

"No one's gotten hurt?" I asked. *Nope,* Brewster said, squirming like a dog, aching for that perfect position. I paused, and the wind swirled some of the gathered dust around us. "What do you do when it turns cold?"

"Drover Café on Avenue A. They'll let you sit all night if you buy a cup of coffee. And if you look pitiful enough and they're not too busy, you can curl up in a booth until the manager shows up. Then he kicks you out. Sad, isn't it?" He grinned. By then the Cadillac had floated down the road, distorted in a glimmering mirage. For a second it made me think of the burning bush and other biblical miracles and what constituted miracles. For some reason I hated to leave, but I shook Brewster's rough hand and drove off toward the city of El Centro. With every car I saw, I searched to make sure it had a driver. It seemed important.

My wife, Carolyn, was a good person, and I had loved her since we met in seminary, where she was earning her master's in sacred music. Carolyn's mother had chided her for going to Sunday School; her father had been quite devout, making sure she accompanied him to services while he was still alive. Several times since childhood had Carolyn forsaken the church, but she always came back, giving her ambiguity a kind of equilibrium. Carolyn led our quilting groups; she directed our children's choir. But she never took communion, and, as my secretary pointed out, she refused to be listed on the membership rolls. Her struggles—not to mention her lithe body, blonde hair, and spirited ability to argue—had endeared her to me for fifteen years.

"Dave, look at this," she said, handing me a section from the El Centro *Journal.* Headlines were a hobby for Carolyn, in the way that

some women collected recipes or *New Yorker* cartoons; se
stories of lives more bizarre than hers seemed to position her
securely in society. My mind at that moment was full of details like altar
flowers, the PA system, the organist's prelude coming in under three
minutes, the Bible being opened to the right place, picking up the last
scrap of paper off the carpet. I sipped my coffee and glanced down
anyway. *Vet Crashes Car Teaching Dog to Drive.*

"The woman put her Dane behind the wheel, not five miles from
here. Isn't that the damnedest thing?" she said, giggling.

"Carolyn, please."

Miming a mock apology, she continued to flip pecan pancakes
from the griddle and pile them in a warm oven. I could hear the sau-
sages crackling in the skillet, along with the sound of Javen and Jerrod
in the bathroom, thumping against the porcelain tub.

"Are the boys almost done?" I asked.

When Carolyn shrugged, I rose and walked through the living
room with the faux fireplace and minimalist bookshelves to either
side; smoke from the sausage hung heavy in the morning light, but the
hall was dark. Opening the bathroom door, I spied water puddled on
the tile.

"Hey, Jerrod, what gives?" His scrawny body was crouched beneath
the pedestal sink, his arm slinging a sodden sponge toward the tub. I
was often startled at how beautiful he was with his chestnut hair. His
brother's was a shade lighter, closer to being blond like Carolyn's and
mine. I liked Jerrod more than Javen because he stood up to Carolyn
and me. Javen, on the other hand, sought our approval. To my way of
thinking, Jerrod would survive the world's demands. Javen would suc-
cumb to them.

"Javen started it."

"Nunh-unh."

"You're too old for this," I said.

"Mama lets us."

"Well, I want you to stop. Stop!" I said, when Javen, crouching in
the tub, launched his last salvo. It landed at my feet, splotching the
hems of my slacks. "Now—Javen Jones!" I said, reaching over to pop

him on the shoulder. *Ow*, he said. I tossed my sons frayed towels from the back of the cabinet. "Some seven-year-olds better get this floor mopped up. Your mother almost has breakfast ready."

The boys began tugging on a towel, and I heard it rip. "Dang it, you two!" I rushed over and grabbed their skinny arms and shook them like my father used to shake my brothers and me. Once, when we had gotten into a similar tussle, he had taken us into the basement of our desperate little house and forced us to duke it out until all three of us drew blood, leaving us in a sobbing heap of skin and bones. "Does the word karma mean anything to you?" They turned their heads—their ornery, empty-headed faces—toward me and stared. "Down on the floor. Mop up this mess. Your mom and dad shouldn't have to clean up after you. You hear me?" I had heard those words before, and they made me shudder.

"Yes, sir," they said in unison. Those, too, not to mention that same tone of resigned resentment.

At that moment Carolyn appeared in the door. "Those towels belonged to my Granny," she said, as if we had snatched away her baby.

"They're rags, Carolyn," I said.

"They are now." Her voice bore a knifelike edge that communicated she was right. I fought hard to keep from telling her I knew that she had bought those towels in college, but it wouldn't, in fact, have been very Christian to start an argument on the Sabbath. I was running late and headed for the door.

"Boys, do as your mother says."

"Aren't you eating with us?" Carolyn said, toweling the twins' hair. "Can't." I wanted to look at my sermon and check the thermostat in the sanctuary. That turned out, most Sundays, to be the most important thing I did. Otherwise, the congregation could become too comfortable, and that was the last thing I wanted. On my way out, I grabbed a pancake and choked it down as I crossed the alley.

On Mondays, Wednesdays, and Fridays I exercised in our front room—after my hospital visits but before Carolyn brought the boys home from school. In addition to the treadmill, the parsonage had been furnished with a small weight machine. We had stationed a TV across from the treadmill, and when I could find nothing I started surfing, stopping at Channel 2. For a few seconds, the beige screen featured an unsmiling man, then flicked to another. At first the accompanying text meant nothing; then I realized city officials had put together a slide show featuring every sex offender in the area. I stared, transfixed by the entire cycle of zip codes: each doltish man's address, his birth date, and whether he had molested a male or a female. When I saw Brewster's photo, I became so rattled—because his address was located in a prosperous zip code with all the eclectic Disneyland architecture, where El Centro's bluebloods lived and worshipped—that I had to wait through the entire cycle to make sure.

I felt as if someone had fisted me in my stomach, and I tried to reconcile the image with the Brewster I knew. From my graduate studies, I realized he couldn't help his urges; they had been ingrained in him from an early age, the cruel irony being that he had learned to perpetrate acts on others because they first had been perpetrated against him. I stared, concentrating so hard I didn't, at first, hear the side door opening, the boys rushing around me, spilling news of their day, flashing graded papers in my face. I could smell the fresh air from a cold snap they brought in with them, and it made me think of my childhood spent in the far northern part of the Texas Panhandle, where winter was more of a condition than a season, a malaise that lingered far too long into the calendar.

"What's that?" Javen asked, and I told the boys to go put their things up.

"What *are* you watching?" Carolyn said. The boys thumped across the house to their room, where they slept in bunks with bright Scottish plaids.

I told her. "How can people who claim to be good Christians splash these men's faces all over the cable?"

"They have it coming," Carolyn said, removing her scarf in a brusque manner, as if I had offended her.

"They can't help it," I said.

"We all have urges," she said. "We control them or pay the price."

"So you have urges to molest?" I said.

"Not what I meant and you know it." She stomped into the kitchen to put away her groceries. I jumped off the treadmill and joined her.

"It's an electronic pillory, a way of punishing those souls in public," I said, standing over her. "Yet it's so sterile, unemotional."

"Come on, Dave, who'd you see up there?"

"Brewster. You know, the street man who sits with the Cunnicutts?"

"Why am I not surprised?" she said, cutting into a cake mix box with a knife. She tied a red apron around her waist and began to open cabinets.

"Look, I believe his neighborhood ought to be informed, but isn't there a better way? Couldn't the city send out fliers? Discreet letters to residents?" Carolyn became very busy, acting as if I had disappeared. She hadn't always done that. Before the twins arrived, she would have given me her attention, inviting me to converse while she cooked. And she would have engaged me back then. *Are you sure? What does the Bible say?*

I returned to the treadmill. When Brewster's picture came up again, I learned that his victim had been a fourteen-year-old male. I thought of Brewster sitting on that pew, and my heart practically turned to look up at me. The Cunnicutts had three boys, all teens. Finishing my three-mile walk while watching *Ellen* (I loved that she seemed to *get* everyone, no matter who), I tossed up a prayer. Then I sat and meditated to remove that awful image from my head: Bernard Brewster, born 5/11/63. He wasn't even fifty.

Feeling the moisture gathered under my arms and at the small of my back, I stepped into the kitchen for some water; Carolyn was now working on supper. The spicy chili made me dizzy with hunger, yet the pungency of steamed broccoli made me turn my head. I'd never liked broccoli, not since my father had forced three large clumps of it down my throat, making his point that starving children in Communist China would have been grateful for a full stomach of it.

"I sure would like to get Brewster away from that bridge," I said. "Back into society."

"Stay out of it," Carolyn said. "You'll only make people mad. Besides, you're wrong. No one can help those people. They're doomed."

I was amused by the street names found out in that part of the city: Canterbury Trails, Leicester Square Lane, Piccadilly Circle—where a decade earlier there had existed little more than straight furrows of cotton sticking out of the red earth. Had it been an even exchange, greedy farmers selling land to contractors hungry for land they could convert to a golf course? The house that matched Brewster's address was of the same design that had become popular in the 1990s: a high-peaked roof with arched ceilings, creating spaces where a second story might have been constructed—not excessive cubic feet that had to be heated or cooled. Irritated by such waste, I headed up the driveway and kicked the straw welcome mat, which landed on my feet. Surprised at my anger, I straightened out the mat and rang the doorbell. A thin matronly woman answered. Her hair had that monochromatic look of a regular salon appointment, a Kanekalon red that bespoke a life of regular meals and TV shows.

"Yes?" she said, through the glass storm door.

I introduced myself, and when she confirmed that she was Bernard Brewster's sister, I said, "Do you have a minute?" Her face turned stiff, and, in spite of wearing thick makeup, she looked well over sixty.

"I'm Melba Cunnicutt, come in, won't you?" she said. She led me to a room crowded with dark furniture, including an upright piano, blue goose-motif curtains that had faded in the windows. Box-camera photos of her ancestors had been enlarged and framed and were hung on the wall in clusters of three or four.

"Brewster could use your help."

"He goes by Hank."

"Yes, my secretary told me."

"Is this about Channel 2?"

"I . . . I'm not sure."

"Why don't I get you something to drink?" Her smile was more of a grimace.

"No, thanks, I won't stay long. The other day Brewster didn't show up for his food voucher, and I went out to see why."

"Out where?"

"One of Brewster's buddies told me he lives under a bridge south of town."

"Jesus Christ," she said, her eyes widening. "I thought Hank had gone to live with our brother, Buzz." Tears pooled. "I was sure Buzz was looking out for Hank since he got out of prison."

"Do you know anything about . . . ."

"Only what Buzz tells me. Hank had finally found a job driving a school bus. He had a contract. Regular hours. Insurance. Before the state began checking backgrounds." She looked out the front window and frowned. "Would you look at that." Passing quite slowly was a Honda Element, a boxy-looking vehicle with no driver. A scruffy boy and a long-haired girl, both blond, were dancing on top as the car seemed to float down the street, meandering out of view. Again I felt as I had when the vibrating Cadillac had appeared near Brewster's overpass, as if the Honda had a life of its own.

"Quite a fad among the young," she said. "If it's about giving up control, why don't they join the Army? I mean, if they're going to die, they might at least have a purpose." She toyed with a chain around her neck, dropping the fine gold cross into her cleavage.

"I can't get used to calling him Hank."

"Oh, he was the cutest little boy, one of the handsomest in high school, a cheerleader at the university. I don't know what . . . happened to him." Her eyes narrowed. "After that first incident . . . it was when he was teaching fourth grade and he fondled . . . I can't bear to use that word anymore . . . a boy he kept after school. After all that time behind bars . . . I went to see him once, it was such a horrible place . . . we found him a psychologist. He went twice a week for months and months, and we thought he had turned the corner. But dear Reverend, I believe there is no cure. It's like being an alcoholic. Your single cure is not to drink. Only Hank can't seem to quit. When he approached that boy on the school bus—it was his last stop—the kid beat Hank's face to a bloody pulp."

"Brewster always sits next to the Cunnicutts, the third row back. And yet they never speak to him," I said.

Melba sighed. "Hank's a great uncle to the boys . . . grandsons by my eldest," she said, crossing her arms over her chest. "They've never actually associated with him."

We were positioned in the middle of the room next to a large, dark coffee table strewn with magazines, when I realized I had not been asked to sit down.

"Guess I need to be moving along."

"If you were to fetch Hank from under that bridge, I'd see to him. I hate for him to burden your congregation. There are people more deserving of your charity."

"Let me talk to him." We exchanged phone numbers. "Be seeing you," I said, walking to my car. The neighborhood was less than ten years old, and most of the shrubs and trees were small. It reminded me of a model I had made as a kid, where I used tips of evergreen branches to make trees, little strips of green felt for a lawn. My father had taken one look at my little dream house and said I would never be happy if that was all I wanted out of life. I wove my car through the streets, and, out in the left-turn lane of the main boulevard I came upon the burnt orange Element capsized. An ambulance wailed in the distance and faded. I lurched to a stop behind the Honda, which was empty.

"Weren't there two kids?" I asked a man who had stopped.

"Yeah," he said. "Took off that way toward Kingsgate. I saw them go inside Heavenly Scents." He was referring to an upscale mall built of red bricks and arching windows, an architecture very similar to the rest of the neighborhood.

The gentleman, short and balding, had called 911 from his cell. When the police arrived, I gave them a general description of the duo I'd seen from Melba Cunnicutt's window, and then I left. When I got home, Carolyn informed me that the boys had been disobedient. She was in a pout, and I forgot about Mrs. Cunnicutt and the Honda.

"Why so angry?" I said, scooting in next to her on the sofa.

"The twins," she fumed, pulling both hands through her hair, shaking it out like a lion's mane. A gesture she had cultivated in college, it was one I still found very appealing. In fact, it was her distress that always seemed to arouse me; I tried to pull her close, but she pushed me away. "I sent the boys to bed because they were arguing over the TV. I'd already told them they couldn't watch *Survivor*. People eating live creatures, for Christ's sake!"

"*That* got you all riled up?" I said, caressing her neck.

She pounded a newspaper that had been folded into thirds. On page A10 was printed the headline: *New Hope for Sex Offenders (and Society, Too)*. I read the piece, which outlined innovative treatments: drugs inhibiting sexual behavior while blunting certain other sensibilities; amended aversion therapies; sanitariums, where skilled therapists taught new behaviors.

"I know you must be right," she said. "People like Brewster deserve a chance, but I swear, if one of them ever so much as touched our boys, I'd . . . ."

"Not going to happen," I said, putting my arm around her.

"How do you know?"

"I don't."

Early in our marriage we had spent nights talking and making love, to rise with but a few hours of sleep but feeling as if we could have conquered the world. Over time such periods fell away from our life. Not only that, but when we did converse, it was about the boys. I loved them, for sure, but I wondered what had happened to that couple snuggled together as if they were one creature. *Us.*

I often tried to weave current information into my sermons, something that would shake people up. For example, Saturday morning I had received an e-mail, something about world populations. Because everything seemed framed for Earth Day, I began.

"Did you know the following?" I asked my congregation, dimming the lights. With PowerPoint I flashed statistics on a screen dropped in front of the large oak cross hanging from a thick chain—all controlled with a remote I kept in the pulpit. "Did you know that if you reduced the current world population to a village of a hundred people, with all human ratios remaining the same, the demographics would look something like this? There would be sixty Asians, fourteen Africans, twelve Europeans, eight Latin Americans. And how many North Americans? Five! Out of a hundred world citizens, only five would be like you or me."

I tapped the screen's looming statistics and stared at the faces in my congregation—the majority of which were composed of pinkish white flesh. Congregants dressed casually, though a few of the older men wore ties. No fancy hats. No minks. I wanted members of my flock to turn to one another and nod. I wanted someone to raise her hand and ask for clarification, but no one blinked. After barraging people with several more slides, I stopped and stared up at the rafters from which hung large globular light fixtures. I had wanted to make a point, but now it seemed like bullying—as if I were trying to scare people into caring about our larger world. I had paused like that before and had learned to trust such moments. Appropriate words of some kind would rush into my head. Other times I would move on, as if I had planned such a grand pause.

At that moment one of the side doors squeaked open. It was Brewster. I had noted the absence of his pungent scent during the passing of the peace. He still wore the same clothes he'd had on the day I visited him; they had acquired, if it was possible, another layer of filth. Moreover, I had missed his watchful eyes, his craggy voice during the hymns. But I felt a stab of fear. Many of the calls and e-mails I'd received for days had been about Brewster, how I should have advised him to leave town, why I should have banned him from our church. I could have focused my sermon on the homeless again, yet I'd chosen to stay with the announced topic. What were we doing to save God's little orb that, at times, dangled so precipitously in the universe? Brewster scuffled along and sat where he usually did, next to the dark-haired Cunnicutt boys and their parents. No one in the sanctuary moved, not even the smallest child.

"In this moment we have an opportunity to test our commitment as a reconciling congregation," I said. Because I used a wireless mic strapped from ear to mouth, I stepped down from the pulpit, past the altar, onto the wide communion platform with wine-colored knee cushions, down to the main floor, and began to wander the center aisle. I touched Melanie Carter's cashmere sweater, caressing the fragile head of baby Carla slung over Melanie's shoulder. The young mother wore a joyous expression on her face, yet her lips were white with fatigue. I spoke and my voice boomed, coming at me from all directions. "Is there anyone who does not know what I'm talking about?"

Feet shuffled, several hundred heads turned, and a large murmur ensued. I had never turned my sermon into a dialogue before, but I liked the prospect, as if I were treading through a newly discovered forest.

"I know what you're talking about," came a voice, and I realized it was Brewster. "Would you let me say something?" He sounded like Gabby Hayes from the old TV Westerns, a toothless, brainless fool, but I swallowed hard and nodded.

Stepping up to the communion platform, where I kept a hand mic for parishioners making announcements, I handed it to Brewster. I watched him position himself next to the altar, next to the basket that held the morning's collection, much of which was designated for people like Brewster.

"I've done all kinds of bad things in my life." With one hand behind his back, Brewster paced back and forth in front of the carved image of the last supper. Then he faced everyone again. "I didn't have to run red lights and drive drunk—thank God I never killed anyone—I chose to do that. I chose to fudge on my taxes, when I was still employed. I chose to shoplift food, when I had no job and was starving. You get a lot of time to think about these things when you spend six years in a correctional facility."

His lips trembled and he looked up at the ceiling, at the same rafters I had stared at earlier, as if a divine message might await us there. "Yeah, I came out all corrected. For what I did I was considered the lowest form of life in prison, by the lowest scum on earth—liars, cheaters, thieves, and murderers—and they punished me, all right, but I'll spare you the details." He raised his head again, as if beseeching someone to help him; his eyes rolled upward before looking out over the congregation. "But you know, we all started out as little babies, who knew nothing about evil. Then something happened—something that made us different. It wasn't my parents, I came from a good home." He paused, as if he couldn't go on. "It could have been what my uncle did . . . on cold, dark nights, sliming his way into my bed . . . except he's not alive any more. No, you can't put him on trial, you won't see his mug on Channel 2." He looked over at me again. "But I can't make too many excuses. God whispered in my ear not to do it. And I didn't listen, I made the wrong choice."

I watched people in the congregation, their eyes: Selma Melchior, who often called to question my interpretation of the scriptures; Belmont Crane, a retired doctor, who taught a Sunday School class of men his own age; Mack and Mike who had adopted a Korean baby girl and led El Centro's PFLAG chapter. I watched as many folded their arms. I watched as some seemed ready to spring from their seats. I watched myself move and stand closer to Brewster. Before I could speak, the silence was broken.

"Everyone knows about the boy on the bus," came a loud, clear voice from the back. "And you deserve to spend the rest of your miserable life in prison." A beat.

"Judge not, that you be not judged," Brewster said, and up went a groan from the crowd. I touched his elbow. "Judge not, that you be not judged." He proclaimed it louder, and people twisted their shoulders to look at one another—almost as if he were speaking a foreign language. "Judge not, that you be not judged." Brewster was now shouting, and I pulled him to my side. His body was hard and bony, like an old elm that stood fast against the dirt-filled winds of West Texas.

"How can you touch him, pastor?" the same voice in back yelled out. It belonged to Cory Smith, a bearded man of thirty-two who ran his own carpet-cleaning business. His wife and four blond children sat unblinking, as if they were accustomed to such outbursts. "He's a disgusting and dangerous pervert." The crowd's energy rose up, with not only snatches of talk but a whirl of arms in motion, animated faces. I could feel their power shoving me around, and I jumped back into the aisle among them.

"Stop!" I yelled. The PA carried my voice to the four corners of the sanctuary and echoed off the walls. I raised my fist until they were quiet. "This man has suffered untold humiliation." A beat.

"I can stand up for myself, pastor man," Brewster said.

The congregation hushed its noise, but I could feel their discontent rolling beneath the surface like thunder. I looked at my feet.

"Yeah, I did time for my sins. And I vowed when I got out that I would be a good man. And then . . . I met that beautiful boy . . . it was a great temptation."

"Shut up!" Cory yelled from the rear, "or I leave now. This is the church where I grew up, that's the one reason I've stayed on, because I don't believe in all this reconciling mumbo jumbo. It's a highfalutin word for permissiveness. Pervert, if you say one more word, me and my family's leavin', and I encourage everyone who thinks so too to come with me." Cory's wife was pulling on his arm, urging him to sit down, but he jerked away. Both attended my Bible study class, Cory wildly intolerant of the idea that the scriptures were symbolic, mythological, rooted in biblical culture.

"Cory, don't, please," I said. Again, my voice boomed, so I shut off the mic. "We have an opportunity to . . . what Hank did was not right, not legal, not nice, not moral . . . yet we have an opportunity to embrace the unlovable. Hank can't help his urges, any more than the rest of us can help ours, whether it's eating something we shouldn't, drinking, taking pills. Gossiping. Everyone of us is driven to sin. But sin is not equal to evil, not in my book. Sin is nothing more than a human urge. Some of those urges don't hurt anyone. Some do. And no one knows it better than Brewster . . . Hank."

"Yes, sir," he said. "By lusting after that boy in the wrong way, I hurt him. He may or may not ever get over it." He pushed both fists to his mouth and then released himself. "And if I could take it back, if I could go back in time, and not do it . . . I can't tell you for sure what would happen. I might do it again, I don't know."

The moment tossed us all against one another like hunks of flotsam on a desperate sea. I turned on my mic, with my hand on his shoulder, and began to pray. The room seemed to calm. I said Amen and looked up to see that Cory and his family had already left. The choir began their Irish blessing—*May the road rise up to meet you . . .* I drifted with its harmony . . . *and, until we meet again, may God hold you in the hollow of his hand*—which signaled the organist.

The organist's silver head bobbed, and his fingers flew as he played a joyful piece, a flashy toccata that not only showcased his talent but the talents of the composer. The composer, who on some day in the past had risen from bed and inked black notes on staff paper, having taken whirling motions from his head and transformed them into music that now swirled among us like a glorious storm. I stood at the altar and greeted everyone who would offer me a hand.

Then I noticed Brewster had returned to his spot in the third pew, staring up at the gilded pipes of the organ. His head bounced; his eyes gleamed; his gums sparkled. The eldest Cunnicutt boy—almost in slow motion—sidled over and offered Bernard Henry Brewster his hand. Brewster looked up, his face frozen, and grasped it. The Cunnicutt boy, Blair, put his other hand on the man's shoulder and said something, and Hank smiled. The other brothers meandered over and offered him their hands, too. Brewster seemed to regard the boys like anyone else might have. I saw no leer . . . no lingering handshake . . . I saw no evil, only a goodness that corroborated the life I tried to lead.

Carolyn and the boys stood with me until the place emptied. I realized I hadn't finished my sermon, the one about God's corroding world. The postlude ended, and Brewster rose and came to where we were standing, shuffling his feet, smiling.

"Hank, why don't you join us for dinner?" I said, placing my hand on his shoulder. "Carolyn always makes extra food."

He nodded and smiled, his graying gums gleaming like a crude sea creature's. When I turned I saw that Carolyn's face had turned white.

"I'll meet you at the house," she said, ushering the boys out.

I slung my robe over the pulpit, and Hank and I headed for the door. Outside, the air was hot and heavy, a rare kind of oppression that could hit on a humid day in April, as if you were stuck inside a terrarium. I opened the gate to our yard, and we then stepped inside the kitchen. There Hank lingered in the doorway to the dining room.

Carolyn wouldn't look at me as she stood at the stove tying on her apron. Instead, she attended to lids clattering atop pots left warming since the Sunday School hour. The boys cavorted with their toy cars on the dining room floor.

"Could I use your bathroom?" Brewster asked.

"Sure," I said, showing him to the one where twin boys had warred over a towel. Hearing the whoosh of the shower, I returned to the kitchen. There I began to carve up a roast resting on a large platter from our good china. In a few minutes, Brewster returned to the table. His clothes were still soiled, but you could smell soap, you could see his face scrubbed clean. I called Jerrod and Javen to the table. I sat at one end, Carolyn at the other, the boys on one long side, and Brewster by himself opposite them. I said grace.

"I'm sorry," Carolyn said as soon as I'd finished, "I've forgotten something. You start without me." As we began to pass bowls of vegetables and I forked up slabs of roast beef, I heard the back door clatter. When Carolyn did not return, I slipped outside. I could hear Brewster engaging my sons. *Do y'all play sports? Yeah, Jerrod plays soccer, and I play basketball.* I followed Carolyn's scent—a delicate rose water she splashed behind each ear—across the alley. I entered the church that was now quiet and followed corridors until I reached the office. Next to it stood the tiny prayer chapel with the door ajar, and I peeked in; it was her favorite place to sit and think. There Carolyn knelt with her head bowed, lollipop colors from the windows bathing her back with light. I fell to my knees, with my arm around her.

"He's not going to hurt our boys," I whispered, praying that Brewster would, for the next few minutes, behave like a decent human being.

"I believe that's true," Carolyn said, taking my hand. "But the thought of him insinuating himself into our lives—playing with the boys on the carpet, tossing them the football, winning us over with good behavior . . . ."

"I know," I said. "Scares me to death."

"Then why . . . " She didn't finish but pulled away, leaving me with only her scent. As I listened to her heels chatter down the hall toward whatever it was she would find across the alley, I realized I couldn't explain it to her—my earnest desire to do more than what was right, to do that which we, mere mortals, were called upon to do by our invisible, robeless Lord who reigned over the universe every day of our lives.

The next week I was engaged in heavy damage control, keeping appointments with people who supported me, people who wanted to understand, and people like Cory who were about to jump out of their skin. I also sat down with Brewster, Melba, and their brother Buzz, and we discussed ways to help Brewster without enabling him, once I explained the difference. There existed among them a familial warmth that would see him through. Or not. What you could do to help a person was so tenuous, so dependent on his own desire to help himself. No matter how hard I prayed or how eloquently I sermonized, I depended on the human element to do that which was right.

Staring out my study window, I became aware of traffic slowing on University Avenue, as if there had been an accident. I ran outside, scurrying toward the curb. Up and down the street, young people were slithering out their doors and dancing atop their cars. I had finally read an article in the paper, one Carolyn brought to my attention, how youths from coast to coast were trusting their lives to driverless vehicles. *Some of our kids are going to get killed,* a Cincinnati woman said, *if we don't put a stop to these damned ghost riders. And soon.*

I looked north toward a darkening sky and realized autos in four lanes had slowed to a crawl. I ran between two cars and up the median, trying to tempt dancers back to solid ground, but it was as if I had become invisible. The wind stirred dust and leaves, and I shouted to a thin young woman with jeans clinging to her hips. I asked her what she was doing up there, but she smiled and kept swaying with the beat. Beneath her feet the roof of her little car buckled—sounding like the crushing of a soda can—and noting the utter surprise in her face, I reached out to catch her.

THE BEST MUD

C oop Mason turned and waved at the cab driver, who squealed his tires. "I give you all the money I got," Coop hollered, watching the yellow car careen down the street like a speedboat. Leaning forward, his back arched, Coop reached for the doctor's thick door and groaned. The place was built like one of those Mexican haciendas, with a red roof but no bricks to be seen. A building wasn't worth anything unless it was made of brick. He grunted to push open the door, and once inside, leaned against the wall.

"Mercy," he said, gazing around. "This place come out of a magazine."

Coop scuffled over to the window, where a dark-haired woman in a blue dress sat with a headset over her ears. She flashed him a glance of alarm he got from most people. He didn't think there was anything wrong with his face. He'd had it his whole life. It never scared *him*: the broad forehead topped now with gray hair curling around his ears, the long chin, brown eyes the size of pecans, the roasted pink tan of his face and arms. Maybe it was because, at six-four, he towered over most people. *Hey, Frankenstein,* some kid had yelled at him years ago, before he flunked out of high school, *you could scare the wet offa paint.*

"Here's a pen," the woman said, sliding it under the glass. "Please fill these out."

Coop stared at her. "Ma'am, I don't have my glasses. If someone could fill in the blanks . . . I'll give the answers."

"Sir, we're not allowed to fill out patient forms."

"But I cain't see a darn thing without my glasses." Zipping his jacket open and closed, open and closed, he watched her as she turned and spoke into her headset.

After a few minutes, a woman with hair the color of corn silk stepped into the waiting room. She wore black scrubs dotted with pink poodles. A pink rubber poodle clung to her stethoscope, and when Coop reached out to touch it the nurse jumped.

"Hey, Nursey, shouldn't you be wearin' white?" Coop said, giving her a big grin.

"Mr. Mason," she whispered, "is there anyone who can come back here and help you fill out these forms? We'll reschedule your appointment."

Coop tilted his head. "What do you mean?"

"Is there a relative who could help you with these forms? We're not allowed."

"Ma'am, I cain't take no more days off from work. I skipped today, 'cause I'm about to jump off a house." He was bent forward as if leaning into a fierce wind.

"I'll be right back."

Out of her side pocket fell a capped syringe, and she caught it before it hit the floor. Coop jumped. He might allow the doctor to look at his back and give him pills, but he wasn't taking no shots, no sirree. Shots hurt, they made holes that never healed. The nurse returned with a clipboard.

"Come with me," she said.

"Hey, you aren't mad at me, are you?" He'd often been able to tell if his teachers were angry, and then he would do something nice for them. Like the time he gave Mrs. Waddell a blue vial of Evening in Paris, and she dabbed some behind her ears, telling him that for being so much trouble he sure was sweet. He'd danced all the way home, and a heavy snow that night made it the best Christmas of his life.

Coop followed the poodle nurse to a small room where there was a little desk and two chairs. She shut the door and they sat down.

Squirming, he said, "Mercy, I hope you can make me stop hurtin'."
Coop reached for the pink poodle climbing the stethoscope, and this
time the nurse made no objection.

"What seems to be the problem?" she asked, releasing the stethoscope to Coop, who continued to caress the plastic poodle as if it were
a baby mouse.

"A couple a weeks ago I was workin' on a new house. I bent over to
pick up a stack of bricks. And when I lifted 'em up, my bones made a
cracking sound. My back's been on fire ever since."

"Has your back ever hurt this bad before?"

"Nope," he said.

"Okay, what year were you born?" she asked without looking up.

"Nineteen forty-eight, right here in El Centro."

She wrote it down. "How old are you?"

"Forty-six."

"Don't you mean fifty-six?"

He shrugged. She asked for more information, including his Social
Security number. He flipped through the plastic windows of his wallet,
saying, "I don't know which one it is, I cain't read too good."

"Here it is," she said, and jotted down the number.

"Thank God you found it, I don't know what I'd do without the
good Lord's help, I really don't."

"Okay," she said. "Have you ever had diabetes or hypoglycemia?"

"What's that first one?"

"Where you have your blood tested and you take insulin shots."

"I don't do shots, Ma'am. No way, José."

The nurse flipped over to a new page. "On a scale of one to ten,
ten being the worst, how would you rate your pain right now?"

"Oh, about medium, I guess a five or six."

"Are you in pain at this time?

"Oh, yes, Ma'am."

"Do you take anything for it?

"Alka-Seltzer. I put it in my Pepsi."

"How does that work for you?"

"I use a big glass so it don't fizz over."

She looked up. "Okay, Mr. Mason, please sign here. Also, this form of consent."

"I don't know if you'll be able to read it, but I'll write my name." In a large loopy script, Cooper T. Mason took his time signing both forms.

"Mr. Mason, the doctor's been held up. He won't be able to see you until after three o'clock."

Coop returned to sit in the front room. Some child was eating from a popcorn bag. Coop gave her a little wave, which she returned. The smell of popcorn took his nose to the Lindsey Theater downtown, where he had taken Rosa Lorca when he was fourteen. The balcony had been filled with narrow seats. It was where his girl Rosa wanted to sit, so they climbed the dark stairway. As they were taking their seats in the front row, he cast his eyes up to the vaulted ceiling. It wasn't a real prayer, but Coop found that a look up gave him courage to look down. In his memory the golden scent of popcorn seemed to hover up in that ceiling.

When the movie was over, they descended the stairs to use the pay phone. A little later they stood shivering in the November chill, and Coop put his arm around the pretty girl whose family had moved in from Mexico. As his daddy pulled up in front of the Lindsey, Coop took Rosa Lorca's hand and opened the back door of the Olds. When they came to her street east of the canyon, he brushed her lips with his, and Rosa climbed her front steps alone. She waved back, as her slinky figure leaned against a porch post.

"Son," his father said, "you should've walked her to the door."

"I'm sorry, Daddy," Coop said.

"You love her?" his daddy asked, smiling at him in the mirror.

"Maybe," he said, thinking of his mother, who, not long before, had died of cancer and was laid to rest in the cemetery. He wondered if she got lonely in that box *for the rest of all time.* The words the minister had used when she was buried never failed to give Coop a shiver. Now the little girl with the popcorn offered him some, and he grinned, forgetting all about Rosa Lorca, the Lindsey Theater, and his mother's grave.

When the nurse announced that the doctor was stuck in surgery, the waiting room emptied fast. Coop went home with some packets of Ultram, but they didn't begin to touch his pain. Not since he was five and the lawn mower fell on his head—sometimes he could barely remember—had he felt this much pain.

All alone in the house, Cooper looks for his mother up past the constellation of a hundred stars his Daddy puts in the ceiling with Day-Glo thumbtacks—the same spot where his toy rocket hits trying to find his mama in the Great Wide Sky. Where the rocket makes a dink, sparkly powder falls from the sheet rock like snow over his head. He rises and puts on an LP and flops back on his twin bed. Staring up, he reaches for the wagon-wheel headboard behind him, grabbing onto its spokes if he has a bad dream. Like the one where his mama leaves the earth and never returns.

Coop usually rose about seven and helped his father into his wheelchair. Jess Mason had been unable to walk for some time, having been involved in a car accident. Coop would roll his father into the bathroom, help him clean up, and get out of his daddy's way so he could wheel himself to the kitchen to fix them breakfast. However, it was nearly eight, and the house was still dark. Coop, who'd managed to get a couple hours of sleep, woke with a start and stumbled to his daddy's bedroom. He'd walked down that hallway a million times since 1951, when they moved to El Centro from East Texas. Everything felt so closed up, as if it was going to storm.

"Daddy?"

Coop heard a muffled sound and rounded the side of the bed. There lay his father, sprawled like a sack of spilt potatoes. The wheelchair was turned over.

"Oh, God, Daddy."

"When you didn't come, I tried to seat myself . . . ." he said. "Call 911."

"I cain't see a thing without my glasses, Daddy."

"Cooper, bring me the phone, I'll dial the damn number myself. I've been on the floor for an hour now, I'm about to pass out."

"Yes, Daddy." Coop bent over the phone with the long cord, and flames of pain shot from the base of his spine down his left leg to his toes. A clap of thunder broke over the house, too, causing him to juggle the phone before it hit the floor.

"Coop, what's the matter with you, boy?"

The nurse must have been right about Coop's age. Yeah, if his father was eighty, then Coop had to be fifty-six. And still, Daddy called him *boy*. It didn't bother Coop. He would rather fish or watch movies than lay bricks, even if he'd never laid a crooked brick in his life. His boss, Lonny, said he mixed the best mud in Texas, a fine mixture of concrete, sand, and water that would never crumble.

But on the day he'd wrenched his back, Lonny said, "That's enough, boy, go home. You're no good to me now."

Coop rolled on his side and pulled his knees to his chest, the fire in his legs now reduced to a burn. He rolled onto his knees and grabbed the phone. The dial looked like swarming bugs after you flip a rock over. Since he was in first grade, printed words always looked like roly-polys. His doctor had prescribed glasses for him, but no one ever understood, not the doctor, not his parents. With his glasses on or off, letters and numbers still looked like little bugs. Lonny told him that the Scottish Rite Temple now had classes to teach people like him how to read, but Coop doubted it. That was why he'd put his glasses in a drawer with the wool sweaters, and for years, whenever his daddy asked him where they'd got to, he would shrug. Coop could hear rain pelting the windows. He crawled on his hands and knees to his father, who took the phone and punched in 911.

"God, yes, I'm talkin', ain't I?" he growled into the phone. "We're both down, you'll have to break the door open."

Still on all fours, Coop brought one foot up. "Ow, ow, ow," he said. Then he moved the other one and stood. He made his way to the front door. Another bomb of thunder made him jump, and in that split second, his needs became clear. He had to have two or three Alka-Seltzers; they'd work faster if he chewed them. He had to see the doctor. Most of all, he had to feel better so he could lay brick again and take care of his daddy. He shivered as he waited on the porch.

A few minutes later the ambulance men, who were soaked to the bone, would not allow him ride with them, and besides, Jess Mason said no.

"Boy . . . you call a cab and skedaddle to work . . . bet my hip's broke, ain't it, fellers?"

Coop watched the ambulance glide away, its red taillights reflected in puddles on the street. The flashers seemed to illuminate houses from the inside. All those years his daddy had cared for him, and now if Coop couldn't pay him back, he'd die. He went inside and felt the house breathe, as the AC cut on. Feeling chilled, he turned the thermostat up. Daddy's clocks never sounded off at the same time. The cuckoo from Japan would go first; then the one that chimed Big Ben every fifteen minutes would take over; and last, the oldest clock, with a big pendulum, would *pound pound pound.* The echo of its chime hung in the air like the smell of last night's roast, and it made the house sound empty. Stepping inside his room, Coop crawled into bed. He crumpled into a quivering ball, but in no time he began to snore.

After a while he rises and moves to his record player, a square box with flaky black leather, arm of gun-metal gray. He fingers the old needle and flicks off a wad of dust. He puts on an LP of Sing Along with Mitch Miller. *"Red Sails in the Sunset" is the first number. He plays it when he wants to cry or run away from home. Sometimes he becomes angry, but if he plays Red Sails he feels better. He's in a far-off sea, where the sun hits the sails and turns them red as the soil in their yard. He turns the knob, and the record drops. He never seems to forget the clatter, how it falls flat as a pancake and begins to spin. The arm no longer moves by itself; he has to swing it over. The song no longer makes him cry.*

When little Big Ben struck six, Coop sat up in a sweat and slapped his face. "I gotta get moving." As soon as he stood, he moaned, scuffling his feet to the front door. His daddy had put the cab number on speed dial, and he kept a wad of cash in a jar by the phone, but today there was but one bill left. Coop grabbed the phone and pushed the two buttons Jess had colored with red fingernail polish. He got the lady named Mabel, who dispatched a cab. All the way to the hospital the driver, an old man, kept trying to talk to him about one baseball team or another, but all Coop could do was grunt. When the driver stopped in front, Coop gave him the bill with Hamilton's face on it and said keep the change. The old man said thank you like he'd given him the earth, and it made Coop feel good, but now his wallet was empty. As soon as he swirled through the revolving door and neared the cafeteria, hunger hit him like a kick to the gut.

Hypnotized by the hundreds of aromas, Coop stepped up to the serving line, where a large girl in a hairnet waited to take his money. He nabbed two big pieces of cornbread and ran past her. Down the hall he noted the cartoon picture of a man on a door and entered. In one of the stalls, he sat on the commode with his legs wedged high against the door and stuffed cornbread into his mouth. It was dry, but he kept swallowing and chewing and swallowing and chewing until he devoured a wad of dough the size of a tennis ball. He did it again until the cornbread was gone. Now his stomach hurt. Under the tap he lapped water like a dog. Coop peed at a urinal and washed his hands. In the corridor he saw the security guard strolling toward him and wiped his mouth with the back of his hand. The guy didn't even look at him.

Coop wandered the halls, and a series of good people helped him locate the fourth floor. He looked into every room until he found his daddy. The bed was cranked so that the old man was sitting up, his head rolled to one side. Coop stood next to him.

"Boy, Coop, do we need to get you some deodorant!" His daddy opened his eyes and took Coop's hand. "What do you think of this?" he said, pointing to the IV drip that led into his wrist. "All I got to do, if I'm in pain, is squeeze this doohickey."

"Wish I could have that hooked up to me," Coop said, caressing the IV tubing.

His daddy sighed. "Lonny was here. He saw the ambulance in our drive."

Coop looked at the painting of a clown behind his father's head and laughed. What the clown wore wasn't near as good as his own costume.

"Being without a job ain't funny. Why didn't you tell me, boy?"

"I do gotta job. Bonnie called about making a delivery."

"You cain't make a livin' givin' away balloons, dressed like a clown." His daddy tried to stare him down, but Coop looked away, stuffing his hands into his back pockets.

"I stole some cornbread downstairs."

"In honor of your dear departed mother, you might want to keep that to yourself."

"Wish I could buy some damn cigareets," Coop said, looking up, as if his mother was floating near the ceiling, watching his every move. While his friends had been swatted for swearing, his mommy would only cast a sad, mournful look in his direction, and he'd apologize. Then she'd smile and tell him he was a good boy.

"Take one of my Camels," his daddy said, holding out the pack.

"No way, José. Them are too strong."

"Take some money out of my wallet and buy yur own, then."

"I need a job so I can buy my own cigareets. So I can go to the doctor, so I can take good care of you. God told me it was my turn to take care of you."

"God don't ask you to do more than you can."

"If my back didn't hurt so, I could lay brick all the way to China."

"Well, Coop, get up on that other bed and smoke a Camel. They's gotta be someone who can help you."

"Okay, Daddy. I'll be glad when we get you home."

He lets the record play. It makes a loud scratchy sound. His daddy comes in and asks him to quit. He's sick and tired of "Red Sails in the Sunset." If you don't stop, I'm a gonna have to take it away, he says. Cooper rushes to the record player, but his daddy scrapes the arm across the black vinyl. I reckon you won't play it no more, he says, leaving. But he's wrong. Cooper does play it, scratches and all, and with each rotation, it seems he gets closer to the boy in the faraway sea, where sails burn flame red.

Laying brick was Coop's real trade. He'd been doing it since he was eighteen, but he had more fun when he was a clown delivering balloons to kids and singing "Happy Birthday." They'd squeal as he came bounding into someone's house or patio. He made fifty bucks for each delivery, often at night or on the weekend when he wasn't laying brick. And he didn't always lay brick. At least once a year, when he didn't show up on time or at the right place, Lonny would stamp his foot and tell Coop to go home and not come back. During those layoffs, Coop would do as many balloon gigs as he could get. That's what Bonnie Billew, his clown boss, called them, gigs. She'd started Bonnie's Balloons, so she could put her kids through college. Bonnie did the gigs herself—dressed up in the same costume, filling balloons from heavy helium tanks in her dining room—but sometimes she had to be out of town. Then she trusted Coop to enter her house and fill the balloons by himself. She even let him use her big white van. When she'd given him the keys the first time, he looked puzzled.

"You can drive a van, can't you?"

"Sure can," Coop said.

Coop had made a D in driver's ed before he flunked out of school, but his daddy made him renew his license every four years anyway. Coop could drive as good as anyone else he knew; you put the thing in gear and stepped on the gas.

Coop loved wearing the costume, too. It was like dressing for Halloween. After he took a cab to Bonnie's house, he would begin by putting the clown suit on over his clothes. Bonnie had made the outfit with a big ruffle that he snapped around his neck after he'd put his makeup on. The costume fit him because Bonnie was almost as tall as Coop, and it was half red and half blue.

"Half Republican, half Democrat," he'd said, laughing, after seeing a TV map about all the red and blue states. He told Bonnie that Texas was a red state, but he and his daddy always voted blue, for the working people.

"You're damn right," Bonnie had said. "If only it counted."

To do his makeup, Coop put on a bib. He'd start with the white pancake, smearing it across his face like cream cheese. Then he'd take the black stuff and paint in eyelashes that reached way up into his forehead. After that, he'd outline an oversized mouth and paint it red, gluing the red bulb of foam rubber onto his nose and slapping on a fluffy rainbow wig.

"How's your father?" Bonnie now asked, having stopped by the house.

He shrugged. "Still in the horsepital."

"Are you sure you feel like doing this gig, what with your back out?" Bonnie asked, brushing the hair out of his eyes.

"Sure," he said. The skin around Bonnie's eyes crinkled, and her dark irises sparkled when she smiled.

"Okay, then. I need you to show up Monday morning for a big convocation at the Civic Center," she said. "You've got to deliver two dozen mixed colors to the superintendent of schools. The old man is turning seventy, for God's sake."

"Oh, wow," Coop said. "I been to the circus seven times over at the Civic Center."

Bonnie stood in the door with her arms crossed, her purse squeezed under her arm. "Two thousand teachers will be there. When you hear the band play 'Happy Birthday,' that's when you come bouncing down the aisle. You do that so well, but I bet I can outsing you." She winked.

"That's for sure," Coop said. "But I'll practice, I want to be good for this guy from the schools."

On Monday Coop took a cab to Bonnie's house and let himself in. After inflating all the balloons she'd laid out for him, he put his mouth over the nozzle and sucked down a little helium. One time Bonnie had taught him how, and all afternoon they'd sung "Happy Birthday" like chipmunks to mesmerized kids. But because the stuff wore off in a minute or two, you had to do it fast. He blew up a couple of extra balloons, and, tying them off with trash bag clips, attached them to his waist. On the way downtown he practiced "Happy Birthday" with his regular voice, but he sounded funnier as a chipmunk.

In the loading zone outside the Civic Center, Coop screeched the van's tires to a stop, got out, and put on the big floppy shoes. He opened the back end and grabbed the balloons. He almost didn't want to go inside, the air was so clear, the sky blue like a toy magnet he had at home. Making a flubbing sound, all those balloons made him feel light as a feather, as if he had no backache, and he goose-stepped up the long walk. Big double doors opened for him, and a draft swooped the balloons with the *babababoom* of a thousand geese rising from the canyon lake.

Inside the vast lobby of the Civic Center, Coop came upon another set of double doors. The stage down front was full of people in suits and fancy dresses. Most of them sat in folding chairs on the main floor, but some were perched up in the balcony, rattling their programs and chatting. A pretty lady up front was trying to get their attention.

Standing in the double doors, Coop turned and watched some delivery men. They brought in one brown box after another and stacked them across the lobby. He flomped in his big shoes over to get a better look. The balloons screeched and bubbled in his ears.

"What're you makin'?" Coop asked.

"Would you look at this clown," said one guy.

"Quit bein' a jerk and hand me that box," said the other guy.

"My back's broke, I couldn't lift no box," Coop said.

"Get outta here," the first guy said, giggling. "We're doin' important work."

"I was just curious," Coop said, patting one of the boxes.

Coop returned to the open door of the exhibition hall. The lady up front kept talking and talking and talking. He turned and watched the delivery men bring in more brown boxes. Pretty soon they'd have a wall, enough to build a fort or something.

"Sha-*zam*," he said.

He heard the band come to life, trumpets, the drums, the cymbals crashing. He untied a balloon from around his waist, sucked in some helium, and bounded down the aisle, waving and grinning at the audience. He took another hit, and a large woman giggled.

"Lord, would you look at that one," she said.

On stage Coop grabbed the mic. To the accompaniment of "America," Coop serenaded the superintendent of schools with "Happy Birthday," sounding like Alvin the Chipmunk. As he twirled to hand the balloons to the superintendent, stiff cold faces became blurred, and he felt like the fourth grader whose classmates had made fun of his pilgrim hat, saying it made him look like a witch. The important man smiled, shook Coop's hand, and thanked him. But Coop was spooked; he took off his clown shoes, ran down the aisle, and with applause fading in his ears, sprinted to the van.

Cooper's five, lying on the floor where his daddy is working on the Toro. He's always cannibalizing one mower to fix another. The mower is suspended in midair so he can reach underneath. He tells Cooper to get up; it isn't a safe place to play. The boy hears a crackle and tries to scramble, but the Toro lands on his head.

Life, at times, was like the tornado Coop had seen in *Twister*. There, whole cows flew by—and big boards, bathtubs, trees, a car flung like a piece of candy across the room. He figured he'd been standing in the middle of his own twister since he was in the first grade. He couldn't remember much before the lawn mower accident. Ever since then events whirled by so quickly he couldn't grab on, like when his pickup got busted up because he went mud thumping in his buddy's pasture and tore out the bottom. Life whirled him like a top. This job, that job. Finish laying brick at this house, start a new one on Monday. Lonny liked Coop's work, his mud. *The best mud I ever seen anyone make,* he'd said. But sometimes Coop became weary of stirring wheelbarrows of cement, sand, and water until it stood up like pudding.

Coop was sitting with his brother Mike and his daddy in the hospital cafeteria. The nurses had allowed Mike to wheel their daddy down to the first floor, so they could all eat together. To make his living, Coop's brother estimated losses on cars for a big insurance company. He drove out from Dallas every month or two to see them and do paperwork. In his sixty years, Mike had had two wives, no kids, and so many girl friends Coop stopped counting. He wasn't near as tall as Coop or their daddy, but he had a big voice.

Coop gazed up at people placing food on their trays, selecting the turkey and dressing. The three of them asked for the same, as if it was Christmas. His daddy took white meat and potatoes and two pieces of pumpkin pie. Seeing that, Coop grabbed two pieces, too, while Mike, slim as a rail, took no dessert at all. He paid for everyone, and they sat down at the end of a long table. Mike soon returned with three cups of coffee. Coop liked Mike's visits because he was good at stories.

Coop remembered the time Mike had told how he'd run into an old girlfriend at a bar. He'd said she was drunk like a lady in love.

"'Guess what, Mike?' he'd said, mimicking the poor girl, 'I'm living with a classical pianist!' 'What's a classical pianist?'" Mike had asked her.

On that Sunday Coop had raised his hand and waved like a kid in school. "I know, I know, he plays like Liberace."

Mike had looked down at the table and grinned. "Good one, little brother. You're very sharp today." Sometimes Mike talked about how stupid people were, especially his customers, who pulled all kinds of stunts to get Mike to fix things on their cars that had already been broken before an accident took place.

They all finished in fifteen minutes and sat sipping coffee. Coop listened and counted trays clattering down the conveyor belt to the dish room. His life had been full of these moments, with him counting the times the cuckoo cucked, counting drips that fell from the kitchen tap until he ran out of numbers. How many years Mama had been dead. How many girlfriends Mike had had. It hit him that Mike had come without his latest love.

"Are you and Janet still sleeping in the same bed?" Coop asked, repeating what he'd heard a lady say on a soap opera. Sometimes words were like that, popping out of his mouth like baby bunnies from an Easter hat. Mike lit another Marlboro and took a deep drag, his eyes flashing at him for a second.

"Don't you worry about Janet," he said, patting Coop's hand. "She went her way, and I went mine. I'm meeting my new lady in Vegas tomorrow."

"I kinda liked Janet," Coop said.

Mike shrugged. "You should give her a call."

Coop shrugged back and grinned. He hadn't had a girlfriend since Rosa, and Mike knew it. As they ditched their trays, Cooped waved to the toothless woman at the end of the conveyor belt, and Mike wheeled their daddy to his room, where he fell asleep. They both leaned over and kissed their father on the forehead, and Mike drove them back to the house. He flipped on the TV, and Coop went to his room.

Cooper doesn't black out right away when the Toro falls on his head. He lies there with his eyes circling themselves like flies, his father and mother standing overhead. Strange men in white come and pick him up. His mama screams as she leans over him, on the long ride to the hospital. He does not hear for weeks. They say things to him, but he can't make out the words. When he talks, they strain, wanting so badly to hear something they can understand. Later, a lot later, he does begin to hear, but then he talks too loud. He plays records too loud, the TV too loud. He yells like a man in desperate need.

Coop's back hurt about as bad as it ever had, but it didn't seem to matter when, a week later, Jess's doctor called and told Coop to hightail it down to the hospital by the lake. When he got there, his daddy's hand was cold, but the machine was still making its soothing beep every few seconds. As long as he held his father's hand, everything would be all right. Then, all at once, his father's head jerked, he sighed, his head almost falling off the bed, and the monitor made a big long scream. Within seconds a nurse entered and told him his Daddy's heart had quit.

"Do something!" Coop said.

"Your father signed a DNR, honey," the nurse said. "Go home and get some sleep. We'll take care of everything."

Coop didn't know what she was talking about, often a signal that he'd better leave things to others more qualified, but he continued. "Do something, do something, do something." But when the nurse touched his shoulder and left the room, he took a cab home to wait for Mike's call. There Coop lay down, but he couldn't sleep. The muscles in his back kept tightening like ropes, causing him to arch his back and moan. He felt as if he ought to cry, but he couldn't.

The next day Mr. Jacks, a lawyer, called to say his father left him some money, and he should come down to the office. Again, Coop took a cab to the address Mr. Jacks had given him.

"Where is it?" Coop asked him, expecting to see cash stacked on the big table in neat piles. "How'm I gonna buy cigareets if I cain't get my money?"

Mr. Jacks gave him a few tens and said the rest wouldn't amount to much, maybe enough to pay for the funeral and burial. They'd send a check to Mike, who was now his *guardian.*

"Mike still ain't called. How can he be my . . . guard?"

When Mr. Jacks didn't answer and didn't answer, Coop went home and called the pain doctor. While he waited for someone to speak to him, he listened to the music they played over the telephone. It sounded like dancing cartoon monkeys, and he bounced his feet across the floor like puppets until he heard the nurse's voice. Then he told her how bad he felt.

"I might jump off a building," he said.

She told him to come in right away, and he took a cab. When he got there, he had to wait, and so he kept pacing up and down the carpet in the outer room. After a long time, the poodle nurse called him back. Today her outfit was pale blue.

"Nursey, my pain's up to a nine now," he said, his leg bouncing against the table. His life was twirling faster and faster, crazier and crazier. His daddy in the hospital all those days, and now *kaput,* his hand turning cold in Coop's while the monitor's screaming off the wall. The men in the green scrubs taking his daddy's hand away from him and rolling the body down the hall like a bundle of dirty laundry. And Coop with no job. He couldn't even get a balloon gig.

The nurse now made him put on a polka dot gown that she tied in the back. She said she was going to give him a sedative, and he tilted his head.

"It's like a cocktail," she said. "You won't remember the next twenty minutes."

"Okay, Ma'am, how many pills do I take?"

"You won't even know what hit you," the nurse said, taking his arm, which he jerked away. "Come on, close your eyes." He felt something like a mosquito bite.

"Ow," he said.

"Now stop it, you'll be out in no time. You'll be able to take directions—like sit up straight and be still—but you won't remember what happened."

Coop began to count to see if later he could remember how far he counted before he conked out. He reached fifty, as the big tall doctor came in with a needle as long as his third finger.

"What's *that* for?" Coop asked.

"I thought the patient was sedated," said the doctor. His arm was hairy like a gorilla's, and Coop tried to touch it, but the doctor flinched and pulled away.

"What's your name?" the doctor asked Coop.

"Don't you know?" he said.

"*What is your name?*"

"Coop. Cooper T. Mason. I lay bricks, when I can get a job. I'm a real clown, too. Maybe you seen me at somebody's birthday party."

"Increase it," the doctor said.

"That long needle best be for somebody else," Coop said.

"As soon as I give you more cocktail, you won't remember a thing," the nurse said. "Now hold out your arm, Sweetie."

"No way, José!" Coop said, jumping off the bed and crashing through the door like a bird he'd once seen trapped in a grocery store window. Coop kept colliding with glass door after glass door until he found the curb. He felt dizzy but began to limp toward the hospital by the lake, a few blocks over. Maybe they hadn't really taken his daddy's body away; maybe he could see him one more time.

Mr. Jacks had said the funeral wouldn't be for another week, something about all the relatives flying in from Nacogdoches. His dotted gown flapped like a sail, and he felt the hair on his chest part in the wind as he stumbled down the street. If he ever got home again, he was never going to leave. Mr. Jacks said after the funeral expenses, he might have a couple hundred left. He told Coop he stood a good chance of getting help from the government, especially if they didn't locate Mike. Coop dropped to his knees on the hospital's lawn rife with patches of red dirt, and the earth began to spin faster than he'd ever felt it spin in his whole life, faster than a twister.

Handy to Some

In '43 the doctor . . . quite a different doctor than you . . . gave me an emergency shot in the hips. In less than an hour this shot turned me backward and inside out . . . I was like a drunk. As soon as I hit the car seat, I had to close my eyes. I couldn't tolerate watching the ground . . . it was the day Rudy died . . . yes, my youngest brother.

I wonder . . . how many stories is that building next door . . . it's so tall . . . . My teeth were set, and I could scarcely talk. This shot was supposed to relax my nerves. They were relaxed all right. My tongue was stiff. I yawned over and over until my mouth got tired. Saliva began to run from my lips, and at night I had to pad my pillow. Now there is a nerve or a muscle that is bothering at the sound of a noise or at the end of a long day. I lose control of my lips, and my tongue pulls to one side. That shot was either wrong, or it was too severe. I think it was a masculine hormone shot, don't you? Well, of course, it was fifteen years ago. I was exactly fifty then.

That building is so tall . . . .

Now you're really taxing my memory . . . let's see . . . I think I was a pretty girl. Mounds of dark braids wound around my head. My broad German nose was small and pert. "Dark eyes," my father would call me.

Not much *to* say about him. When Fritz was small, long before he left Germany, he had brain fever and was laid out to be buried, and, for some reason was discovered to be alive.

Oh, he was handy, sort of, with the cutting and smoking of meat, the rendering of lard, and the making of liverwurst, but . . . I can't help laughing . . . he couldn't milk a single cow in the county to save his soul. He did it the old way . . . the wrong way . . . .

Why he sat *behind* the cow, that's how! Once he nearly lost all of his teeth! But the joke was really on us, because we all learned to milk the wrong way. We learned a lot of things wrong . . . . Driving cattle to and from the pasture was our responsibility, Rudy's and mine. I didn't want to do it the first time.

"Tilde Roderick!" Fritz shouted. He called all of his six sons by their full names when he wanted, really wanted something. Guess I was no different to him. Taking my little hand in his ugly red one, he said . . . in his rough accent . . . "Tilde, I vahnt you to help Rudy bring in dem cattle." I jerked my hand away, shaking my head. I felt the flaky rawness of that hand swallow mine. "Now ged on out der' an' run dem cattle in," he said, throwing me to the ground. It seemed so natural then . . . I never took his hand again . . . yet it was too late. Already had it, didn't I? I remember, too, my hands seemed to get bigger.

Well, for one, Fritz always insisted on giving a big long German prayer at dinner. One time it was so funny, hearing all that gibberish come out of his mouth. I laughed. In the big middle of the prayer, without missing a *gott* or a *himmel*, he grabbed my hand and cracked it hard with a big silver spoon, the one used for dishing up potatoes. Like I said, my hand immediately seemed to puff up and get bigger.

What? Sure, it was hard work! If a calf got away, Rudy and I had to stake it out and bring it back. Sometimes, as the calves grew stronger, they'd drag us. We hung on. Didn't know any better. It was our responsibility, and Fritz had warned us.

Yes, well, a little heifer did get away from me one time, and Fritz chased it down with his horse, Bap. When he finally got it, he made me take it all the way home with my hands tied around its smelly little neck. You can imagine.

I can't help scratching, doctor, it itches. Hm, to think it happened a month ago already. My hand hung by . . . now what'd *that* doctor say . . . "by mere ganglia?" Made it sound so pretty . . . nicer'n these big black stitches . . . this festering flesh. My wrist is so stiff, doctor . . . the tendons didn't heal right, I know they didn't.

Oh, yes, *every* day. We had to drive the cattle south about a half mile and pump a wooden trough full of water. Later we moved three quarters of a mile south and over one mile west. We used a long black snake whip on their backs, which I know was cruel, but we were untrained kids, sometimes hungry, sick and tired . . . very tired after pumping water until the fingers on my hands became hard and unfit for a woman's dainty work, and muscles on my neck got large and ugly like those of an ox . . . oh, yes, it's true . . . look at 'em! Anyway, my large bony elbows would pump more. I'd grab the handle and jump up and down until my back played out and my ankle broke down. You know, I can't see modern kids, like my grandnephew, Nicky, doing this, but the queer thing is we never complained!

Yes . . . Nicky is the one who found me. A darling boy, just like his grandpa, my departed Rudy Senior. Rudy Junior, Nicky's father, was building the pretty new house for me in town, and Nicky came in right after . . . such a child! He ran to the door, for they were outside, Rudy and his wife, and all my nieces and nephews. It was . . . one of my quiet times . . . I'd only nod and grunt for weeks at a time . . . don't know why . . . no matter. I sat in my wheelchair, such a dolt I was for breaking my hip the month before that. I'd been helping to build the new house and tripped over a board!

. . . Got plumb away from the subject, didn't I? My . . . my hand was dripping, hanging by mere ganglia, and Nicky yelled out the door, "Aunt Tilde threw up her grape juice all over the place!" *Gott* . . . the blood was so dark . . . Nicky's dangfool statement makes some sense to me now. Anyhow, I could hear Rudy Junior shout from outside, quite faintly really, "Good, now maybe she'll talk to me."

I was always afraid . . . I remember once while we were still driving cattle, quite a scare came to us. We'd heard there was a mountain lion in the vicinity. It frightened me terribly. So sure enough, the devil had his fun with me. Rudy and I were as far as the broken-down bridge at Miss Lila's orchard when we saw something moving in the trees, and, of course, not being able to see plainly and afraid to move closer, we turned back home. The farther we got, the more scared we became. The lion was after us!

I'm coming to that. Later, Helmut, our oldest brother, went to the grove, and it's so amusing now that I think of it . . . Helmut found a lost bull in the grove. Naturally, if we hadn't known of the lion, we wouldn't have run away . . . .

How many stories did you say that building is? Twelve! My, my, my . . . yes, I remember bolstering myself. Had to keep the cattle going. I'd say, "Now I'm one foot from the top of the hill . . . " I usually began to mark the distance when I was getting tired. Had I had good health, a sound mind *and* body, I could've made part of it enjoyable . . . in fact, I did try. I kept a diary of sorts, writing down every little thing, good and bad, that happened. Somehow I had to keep the two separate in my mind, and scribbling helped. It even went so far as . . . well, when I was eighteen or nineteen, I wanted to write a real book. It was to be my secret way of telling the world how dreadful Fritz was towards me . . . and how beautiful things were, too, of course. There was so much beauty to write of, and no one noticed but me. Oh, Rudy saw it. He was especially sensitive, but even he didn't quite see things the way I did.

Well, for example, spun across the road on an early June morning were the finest of spider webs, big things, twinkling with dew spattering the wildflowers under our feet. Now Rudy walked right through it all, but not me! I crawled under the large webs, looking at the dewy jewels, wishing I could put one of them in a fine gold ring.

Lordy, no! I've since heard a few good jokes about people who thought they ought to write . . . but my feelings were no joke. I think the book was an attempt to wake up and see what was really wrong with my world, the most rotten deal one could ever get. The tragic thing was that I forgot about the book for years and didn't wake up until I was about fifty, the year Rudy Senior died and . . . I got that terrible shot in the hips. Only then did I see the truth.

The truth? I should have been born a man! I *can't* leave these stitches alone. I hate these hands . . . still want to get rid of 'em. They never pleased Fritz! Never did he take an interest in my crocheting, and I wasn't half bad. Really. But . . . now maybe . . . I see where I was wedged in . . . neither did he like my attempts at farming. Even after I learned from a neighbor how to milk a cow properly, he'd lift that snide nose of his to sky and spit! "*Dummkopf*," he'd say . . . I was no good . . . as a boy *or* a girl.

Please, steady my wheelchair, I can't stop shaking. No! Not my hands . . . the chair, the chair!

Mean? Yes . . . the old goat . . . sent every last stupid brother of mine to college, but *Herr Gott im Himmel*, I was the smartest! I was the only valedictorian in our family! And . . . what did I get? Sorry . . . my voice always does that when I'm excited . . . croaks like an old frog stuck in the mud . . . do you have a tissue?

Yes . . . yes . . . yes . . . I guess I should have been a man. Got the worst parts, my father's big Roderick hands, instead of Mother's dainty ones. His big German nose . . . I was beautiful, I know I was, but no one ever saw it except me . . . even I couldn't see it after a while. All I noticed were those big hands attached to my little body. They *had* been small when I was small, but . . . with every pump of water, every crack of that whip, with every squeezed udder . . . every fence post nailed, the joints became more prominent, the hands became wider . . . and they hung from my little frame exactly like the ones that hung from my father's.

Yes, funny, isn't it? It all came to me that morning, sitting in that wheelchair, during one of my quiet times. I'd kept it inside of me, though how, I don't know. I suppose it was the photos that jarred me. Rudy Junior had put a large box of snapshots next to me, hoping to cheer me up, get me to talking again. I hadn't looked at 'em in years! He brought the pictures in from the farm, into my unfinished house in town. The floors were dusty from sanding. Sawhorses were still propped up. I . . . I was between two lives and somehow I'd had enough of *that*, so I sat and chewed on it for a while.

Yes, as I said, it was the boy Nicky who found me. Came in and out a dozen times that morning, jabbering to his crazy Aunt Tilde as if nothing in the world was wrong with her. He . . . he was enchanted with the photos, especially the one of old Fritz standing on the deck of the ship . . . before he was thrown into steerage where he belonged. Stupid man with the fevered brain believed he'd paid for first class! There he stood in sepia, his large hand gripping the rail of that ship . . . my large hand gripping the arm of that wheelchair. Nicky skipped out the door, yelling for his daddy to take a look at funny old Fritz.

I don't know . . . I just reached down and took the buzz saw . . . I could only think of those big German hands my father'd given me— and that was all he ever gave me—and I had to rid of 'em. Of course, I only got so far as the one. Then Nicky came in and found the blood. I'll never know why he didn't notice my hand hanging . . . . Anyway, when he went to the front door and spoke of grape juice . . . funny, I sort of believed it myself. He came back to me, said he was sorry I'd thrown up, and kissed me on the cheek. I thanked him. I was in what they call shock, but I did thank him, I know I did.

BLIGHT

Jed was my neighbor when I was a boy of seven. If I was around, he would nod to me as he came home from tellering at the bank, loosening his tie before he hit the front door, where his wife, Millie, had a Pabst Blue Ribbon waiting for him. Millie was tiny with short black hair and a pug nose. She might have been his dog by the way he petted and caressed her, but she didn't seem to mind. He would kiss her, and inside they would go, where it was cool. Jed had installed a big Carrier in the front window of the living room, and I would squat under it to catch the condensation in my mouth. It had a sour, tinny taste and sometimes I spat it out. If I stood with my ear to the vents, I could hear Millie above the roar of the fan.

"You're always late," she once shrieked. "How can I plan a meal?"

If Jed answered her, I couldn't hear him.

The autumn before, Jed had bought a new '55 Bel Air hardtop, turquoise and white. It was a beautiful car.

"You can look inside, but don't touch," he'd told me, as I entered the driver's side.

The center post of the steering column had stood erect like a turquoise rocket cone aimed at your eye. Upholstered in turquoise and white and ribbed with a silver cord, the seats had emanated that aroma of newness a young man like Jed so cherished. Habitually, he would polish that car in his driveway, and I would join him, perched mere inches to my side of the property line. He didn't say much. And at times, because he and Millie had no children, I wished he were my daddy.

My own father was a kind of ghost who worked the second shift at Boeing, and he was either at work or in bed behind a closed door. On weekends he sat at our breakfast table in a T-shirt not much whiter than his skin and issued orders no one followed. Jed was in better shape than my father, whose doughboy figure had surrendered to the slow, tortured death of an assembly line. By contrast, muscles in Jed's calves rolled up and down legs with hair the color of chestnuts; his upper torso was solid, like the pictures of Charles Atlas. Oddly, I can't remember his face. I believe he was handsome, even if he did wear glasses that made his eyes look like blue marbles.

One Saturday in August, when the temperature ascended to over a hundred and the wind seared you in half with its velocity, Jed rolled down the windows on his Bel Air hardtop and invited me to the river to fish. He opened the long door split between white and turquoise and gave me a pat as I crawled in. I had seen him open it for Millie a thousand times, as she pulled in her skirts, and he flicked the door until it slammed. He did the same for me, but inside the car, the impact sounded different. At that moment it occurred to me that we should walk; it was a short block to the park and another block over the dunes and down to the river. And the cardinal rule of getting permission to leave the yard flew out of my head like a bad thought.

Jed, who'd shucked his T-shirt, backed into the street, his biceps dancing as he turned the wheel. The Chevy's Powerglide whined until the vehicle reached cruising speed.

"Smooth as a baby's butt," Jed murmured, smiling down at me with teeth like Chiclets, placing his arm on the back of the seat.

I could see only the turquoise dashboard, a bit of the hood, and the dying elms that whizzed above us. If I'd desired to view the street, I would've had to fold bare feet under my legs, soiling the white vinyl, so I sat still. As the hot air swarmed between us like a nest of hornets, I was hit with an urge to sit close to him like Millie did. I inched toward him, and the heat from his legs gave me goose bumps.

Jed turned right at Pawnee Avenue and, following the curve of the street, turned left at the entrance of the park. He stopped at a turnout closest to the river, and the big door gaped open. Large elms, half eaten with blight, blew ferociously. Long gone was the best part of summer, that pristine period before the elm beetles struck, before the heat hovered near a hundred for days on end, before the grass yellowed beneath your feet. A few of the leaves in the ash trees had begun to turn the color of bananas, telling me August was half gone. Then Labor Day would arrive and then school, and life as I knew it would end until next June. Such a thought nearly brought me to tears. Grabbing the turquoise steering wheel, I slid along where Jed's sweaty legs had rested, eyeing the rocket cone as if it might go off in my face. Jed slammed the door behind me. It was like a shout.

On the blazing concrete, I hopped back and forth from one foot to the other. When I could no longer endure the torture, I ran around the car and jumped in the grass, landing on two cockleburs that stuck to my foot like baby porcupines. With my eyes tearing up, I watched Jed open the trunk and pull out a ragged quilt with tree patterns of faded red and yellow polka dots. Clinching my eyes shut, I wondered how my feet could take it any longer. When all of a sudden he hoisted me up on his shoulders beaded with perspiration, lumbering like a jeweled elephant toward the river, I was astonished. I wiped my eyes as we reached a dappled spot under an old elm. There was hardly any shade, as beetles had threshed the leaves to shreds, and yet a smarmy breeze rolled off the Arkansas, torpid as an old turtle. As cicadas rose in chorus, Jed knelt and delivered the little prince from his back. He told me to lie down and he would remove the thorns from my feet.

"Where are your fishing poles?" I asked, sniffling.

"In the trunk," he said.

"But why didn't you get them out?" I said.

He shrugged, and I lay back on my elbows. With soft teller's hands, he held my right foot and tweezed out thorns with fingernails kept a bit longer than most men's. When all at once he lifted my foot and sucked my big toe, I giggled like a bad boy I'd heard in church once, before his mother smacked his leg. And when Jed sucked at all five toes like a turkey leg, I threw my head back and screamed with delight. Then he let go.

He landed on his side, this leviathan, and pulled me to him. I squeaked and inhaled, my chest going flat. Then I exhaled and snuggled close to him. I could feel his furry chest and dewy abdomen against my bare back. He smelled like my father, except that Jed didn't smoke twenty Camels a day. And my father had never invited me to be precisely this close. But I liked it. It felt like something good ought to feel.

"Do you want to be my little boy?" Jed whispered, digging his chin into my neck.

Before I could answer, he released me and lay back against the quilt. I jumped and straddled his abdomen that felt taut as a drum. My older brother James had pinned me like that hundreds of times, so I relished the dominant position.

"Ride 'em, cowboy," I said, bouncing against his flanks. Jed smiled and chucked me under the chin.

"After you become my little boy," he said, "I'll have to throw you in the river."

"I can't swim," I said, giggling.

He laughed and let me win at slap fighting, shielding his cheeks from my attack. Tiring of that, I leaned back on my hands, and slid into something hard beneath Jed's Bermudas. I gasped and his hands seized my wrists, in case I should try to escape, which instantly became my only thought. I reared my head and screamed. Frightened, the giant released my wrists. I jumped up, but he snared me by the heel.

"Oh, no you don't," he said.

Rising, he jerked me down and dragged me across the quilt, stinging my bare back. Then he dropped to his knees and curled my hands inside his, which hurt me, and I heard his foot rip the quilt open. His head hovered one breath away from mine, his tongue depositing fire on my brow. "Oh, baby," he breathed, tossing his glasses in the grass and breathing more fire into my mouth. He came up for air. My lips were soggy from his slobber, and I hawked up a wad of snot from the back of my throat and spat into the blue eye established on me. When the Cyclops screamed and cursed, the hands suddenly released me. I crawled away and ran with the celerity of a hot wind.

No never mind the dozen cockleburs that pierced my feet or the searing concrete as my feet sped up and down the dunes and across Pawnee, and never mind the black Cadillac that swerved out of my path and onto someone's lawn, plowing furrows that remained in the soil until I graduated high school, and never mind feet pounding against a hot pavement, which did nothing but drive those tiny knives further into my feet. Before I knew it I was home. It only occurred to me, as I whizzed past Jed's driveway, crossing onto our lawn, the noise Jed had made, how, when I spat, he had *oomphed* like a punctured tire, sounding the immediate deflation that occurs when you hit a nail. And how the giant had roared with laughter, as if it all were a stupid mistake! That laugh haunted me still, as I sat on the back porch and removed more thorns from my feet. My mother suddenly appeared, asking me where I'd been.

Early the next morning Jed took a bus to Omaha, where, Millie said, he'd found a new job.

"Can you believe it, overnight, just like that!" she said, "leaving me with all the dirty work."

This she told her sister Mindy as they giggled, drinking Pabst Blue Ribbon and packing the Bel Air, which was parked nose toward the street. Millie put on a stack of forty-fives and opened her living room windows. Each time the music ended, she turned the records over or started a new stack. All day I sat on my side of the property line and listened and watched them pack the car's rear seat to the ceiling. The last thing they crammed into the trunk was a sewing machine covered by the tree quilt.

"When did that happen?" Millie muttered, running her fingers along the gash Jed had created. "That was Grandma's favorite quilt." Before they pulled out at dusk, Millie called me over to the car. "Jed's going to miss you," she said, tousling my hair. "Last night he told me he'd like to have a son just like you some day. And," she said, turning to Mindy, "if everything goes right, by this time next year he'll get his wish."

Millie and Mindy laughed with glee as they got in the car. Millie then jammed the gearshift into drive and waved. The rear tires spun and she tore down Main Street, leaving a cloud of blue smoke. It was something Jed never would have done. He loved that car more than anything in the world. And suddenly I wished to tell him.

A Gambler's Debt

Mrs. Prine would board the jetliner first. Instead of sitting up front, she would take a window on the left side of the seventh row. There she would place her purse in the middle and a pillow or blanket on the far seat. Then Dr. Prine would join her after the hordes had passed and take the seat on the aisle. (*I refuse to stand in line, holding a number like a goddamn fishwife.*) After that, if the flight wasn't full, the space between them would remain empty, providing a place for their incidentals. And the Prines did it all without exchanging a word or even a look. One might have thought that they were traveling separately.

In 1990, when Neville Prine was forty-four, he had conducted a riotous affair with his head nurse, May Dorsette, who also happened to have been Mrs. Prine's best friend—they had been roommates in college, and they both were married to men who had matriculated at the same medical school. Mrs. Prine didn't have a sister, but if she had wanted to select one, May Dorsette would have been her first choice— at least back then—for May and she could have talked for hours, speaking of their husbands as if they were dunces, little prigs who were too stuck up for their own good. But when Mrs. Prine discovered the merry tryst between May and her husband, she had been struck with one thought. *How can I leverage things so that I never have to touch Dr. Prine again and at the same time see that he touches no one else . . . not even me . . . not even if he wants to?*

In the past Mrs. Prine had served as president of the city PTA. Their own children were out of college, so the organization gave her what she felt was a useful connection. She also volunteered as school nurse three days a week, leaving time for golf or tennis, time to have her hair and nails done, time to read if she wished. In all, her activities equaled almost a full work week.

At the school where she volunteered, Mrs. Prine often spoke with teachers, who would confide in her; she was good at drawing them out and coaxing them into feeling as if they were the most important one in the room. *Little Billy's home is filthy,* Miss Thorne had told her. *Not a stick of furniture in sight.* And so Nurse Prine had visited the lad's home in an official capacity, obtaining copies of his immunizations, but also to see if Miss Thorne had been exaggerating. *Would you be insulted if I sent over a sofa? It doesn't do what I thought it would for my living room,* she said to a boy's mother, who had grinned with one tooth hanging down, a crooked, yellowing spike creating a bereft smile. Each month Dr. Prine wrote out a separate check for Cecilia, one that he marked as Discretionary Funds on the memo line. Rather than spending them on herself, Mrs. Prine gave such funds to people with bad teeth.

After their last child graduated from Rice, Mrs. Prine had begun to occupy the guest room—leaving Dr. Prine the master bedroom and bath. She kept it and the guest bath looking so antiseptic that not even her children realized she no longer slept with their father. Or if they did, they didn't let on. Whenever they visited, Mrs. Prine slept in Dr. Prine's bedroom, occupying the recliner positioned in front of the TV, which sat next to the gas log Dr. Prine fired up on blustery winter nights. Sometimes she would rise, in a sweat, and turn off the fire in the log. By morning she would wake up shivering and head for the warmth of a shower.

Mrs. Prine hadn't occupied the same bed as Dr. Prine since the day in 1990, when, standing before the citywide PTA at the Holiday Inn atrium and seeing her husband and best friend flirting on the front row . . . she then *realized* . . . that they had been carrying on in front of her as if she weren't there, as if she were invisible. A crazy chill had run through her, shaking her like a hundred pounds of Jell-O, as she announced the winner of an annual scholarship program. The handsome lad had jumped onto the stage, and she'd handed him the check for a thousand dollars.

She'd kept glancing at Dr. Prine and May Dorsette caressing one another's hands as they joked and flirted during the young man's great moment, accepting a check that would cover but a fourth of his university tuition. She had wanted to give him thousands more, had wanted to lavish the handsome Latin man with adoration and praise. But he had shaken her hand and left the stage. When she finished speaking, she looked out past her husband and May, beyond their she-nanigans—while viewing them in her peripheral vision—to a future that included neither of them.

From that point forward, she stopped answering the phone if the call was from May, deleting messages suggesting lunch, even when May ventured over to their house in tears to patch things up. Mrs. Prine stopped appearing at her husband's practice in the medical district to help out on busy mornings, stopped phoning the office, except for an occasional call to his private line, which he didn't always answer. And when the cell phone came into existence, Mrs. Prine reached her husband that way, bypassing May Dorsette, never even nodding to her at the Christmas buffet Neville set up each year on the twenty-fourth. May seemed to shrink to the size of a big doll. She became drawn and gray, aging faster than Mrs. Prine. That day standing before the city PTA had been a pivotal one for Cecilia Prine, perhaps nothing as momentous as the Black Plague or AIDS or the Iraq War, yet her world would forever be altered. And because no one but she had witnessed the untoward nature of her husband's affair, witnessed its vapid hor-rors, no one but she and Dr. Prine would ever know of its shuddering effects on their lives.

Mrs. Prine checked her phone before the flight attendant told her to shut it off, to see if her children had tried to contact her; they seemed to respond to texting, a method marketed by the phone com-panies, she believed, to further separate youth from their parents. Nope. She turned it off and flipped it shut. Dr. Prine had been read-ing the El Centro paper since arriving at the airport. He continued to read, she supposed, the box scores of every game that had been played the night before. She never spoke to him while he was engaged like that, gliding from column to column. Instead, she perused her *Elle* or a novel or played Glamour Pinball on her little phone. Because she had disengaged the gaming noises, it looked as if she were texting.

They were headed for Las Vegas, a two-hour trip. At takeoff Dr. Prine reached over and took Mrs. Prine's hand. He had done so since their first flight, the one that had transported them to Paradise Island in the Bahamas for their honeymoon back when hijacking was the current terror. And Mrs. Prine continued to allow the intimacy because it was part of an unspoken superstition, one that assured their plane would never crash. Should they ever forget to hold hands upon takeoff, they would wind up in a burning heap at the end of the runway—little difference between their flesh and molten plastic and metal. Once they were in the air, Dr. Prine brought his wife's hand to his lips and kissed it. Mrs. Prine feigned a smile and tilted her head as if she were young again. Then she snatched her hand back and stared out the window.

Ever since 1990 Dr. Prine had played a great game of Win Her Back. As far as Mrs. Prine knew, he had not continued his affair with May, nor had he taken up with anyone else. No, he had begun all over, with a new period of courting Cecilia, and he had never ceased. *What are you doing for kicks?* she had asked him during one takeoff. *I don't know*, he had said. *What're you doing for kicks?* She had stared him down. Kicks were none of his business; he had no right to ask.

She could have one-upped him because she was attractive enough, and some of their doctor friends had flirted with her, but she had decided against it, taking a week-long retreat in California every spring instead to meet with her Inner Goddess (she never told anyone where she went, not even Neville). The one good thing she had learned from a tent mate was how to use a certain mechanical yet fleshlike device to overcome her own sexual drought. Of course, certain other juices were lacking, that, mixed with her own, would have made for a much more heightened experience. Yet she had come to rejoice in the cold, removed act of bringing herself joy—closing her eyes and imagining complex, romantic scenarios with various men all about thirty, Neville's age when they had conceived their eldest child.

When the Prines arrived in Las Vegas, a waiting car transported them to one of the older hotels. She didn't tell people at home which one and remained rather vague about it when asked (they were all snobs). *Oh, yes, that may be the one, I can't remember for sure. Our driver takes us there, we check in, and I forget everything. I couldn't tell you what it costs. Ask Neville.* She was also vague with regard to its appearance. Their reward for staying in such a place was that she could wear floral polyester pantsuits and Dr. Prine could sport faded Rugby shirts, so as not to stand out. Occasionally, like the time they went to the Spring Preserve, a large city park, they ran into persons whom Dr. Prine had treated or those whom Mrs. Prine had rubbed elbows with on her committees. The Prines would nod and say hello but that was all.

They knew the hotel staff by name. They visited so often that they paid little or nothing for their suite—points, it was all about accumulating points—his and her rooms, whose interiors had not changed over the years. The bedspreads, the draperies, and upholstery were worn, yet the place was clean and well cared for—like one's home.

The Prines made a practice of setting their own agendas during the day. Mrs. Prine shopped, shipping her plunder to their address so that she returned to town with only the luggage she had left with. She often pampered herself with a full-body massage. A bear of a man named Argon would speak with a German accent, his long silver hair would graze her skin, in which case she would ask him to watch it. But his hands were a gift, soft and yet firm, searching out her pain. He was able to get deep inside her muscles, her calves and her lower back, vulnerable through all her years of nursing—during which time she had rolled, lifted, and tugged at endless pounds of humanity—and the blessed massage would free her from a certain agony. When Argon finished his ninety minutes with Mrs. Prine, she would pay him in cash, a roll she kept in her terrycloth robe, twice his fee. She speculated that was why Argon would give her an appointment any time she appeared at the hotel; she imagined him rearranging his client schedule to accommodate her, and it gave her a certain thrill.

Sometimes, when she was tired of her girl at home, she would make an appointment with Sergei in the hotel salon. Before falling into his leather chair, she had already turned her life over to him. For more than any man ever, Sergei determined what things would be like when she left Vegas, whether men gave her the eye or ignored her or whether friends chuckled over a huge mistake. Red was not her color.

Dr. Prine spent his Vegas days on the golf course if it was nice—not too damned hot, in other words. If it was, he went to the movies. Yes, he could have done that in El Centro, but Vegas theaters were dark and cold. And he could see things he couldn't view at home. He took in foreign films with women like . . . the ones he hadn't married . . . torrid lovers, opening themselves like carnivorous flowers. At that theater he could sit alone and not be bothered—all of them could—and even into his fifties he could remain erect until he returned to the hotel and, sadly, take care of it in the shower or attempt, in vain, to interest Cecilia.

Long ago she had opened for him when they were about the business of bringing children into the world. Back then it had been chic to replace yourself and your mate and not to populate the earth with superfluous children. Cecilia had figured out how—he couldn't now remember what kinds of douches she had concocted—to encourage the conception of one child of each sex. He marveled at how glorious those times had been. Cecilia had opened up for him, not in a salacious manner but as if she were offering up the best, the most sacred, part of herself. And to his everlasting regret—which he had not succeeded in conveying to her—he had not appreciated her offering. Not only her body but her essence. That day in 1990, after the PTA meeting at the Civic Center, where he had sat with May Dorsette, playing footsy under the table laden with drapey white linen . . . that blustery windy day had pointed his life in a direction he could not change—like the Kennedy assassination, when Kevin Neville Prine was no longer a high school senior but a citizen of the New World Order, where one could shoot leaders with whom one had a fundamental disagreement.

Yes, after that day, their life was like a war ending with an unstable truce. His children—in college at the time—had to have noticed something was awry, and he had begged Cecilia to let up. *You want me to play-act our marriage for the sake of our children?* she had snapped. Dr. Prine had not answered. At that point he could have withdrawn, encouraging her to file for divorce. All the legal blame—mental cruelty, boo hoo hoo—would have shifted to a moral emphasis. But at least it would have been over; the endless days of monotonous civility would have come to an end.

Cecilia had never mentioned separation, and when Dr. Prine questioned her about it, she said, *I've divorced you in the most important sense, in case you hadn't noticed.* Yes, he could have filed, and he could have afforded a handsome settlement. May Dorsette would have left her husband to marry him. There were any number of women—attractive or otherwise—who would have married him, but he still loved Cecilia and whether she returned his love, whether she was ever open with him again, seemed irrelevant. He would always love her.

So on their sojourns to Las Vegas, the Prines would leave their daily pursuits behind and come together of an evening. Over the years they had attended kitschy shows: Joan Rivers and Wayne Newton. But they had also been entertained by a senior Sinatra, been graced with Streisand's presence before her voice became a feather of its former strength. And the Prines had, at times, camped out in the casino downstairs. It remained a remnant of the old Vegas they loved: raucous nights floating from table to table, slot to slot, bumping elbows with some of the wiliest, some of the greasiest people on earth. The Prines had never been to Luxor or any of the other hot spots of the new Vegas, establishments that seemed crude in spite of their grandiose airs. Each trip they would make a point to find a bench along the wide walkway and view the fountain shows at the Bellagio. All that water shooting up as part of a world where drought was a constant factor!

In their hotel, which exuded a dingy sort of elegance, Mrs. Prine played the slots. She told Dr. Prine that she did it to watch the people—that was her greatest pleasure, she said—but she loved collecting her wins, too, handing the slip of paper to a page, who would return with a plump check (she always tipped the kid well). She would in the old days buy a bucket of quarters and command one machine until it seemed to play itself out. Now she used a debit card loaded with her self-imposed limit.

In her peripheral vision, Mrs. Prine would watch others give up on a particular machine, one that might have been in play for the better part of an hour. She would slouch on over to the vacated apparatus. The handle would still be warm and oily, the chair soft, and she would take a moment to use a Wet One on all the handles and buttons. Sometimes her strategy worked. On occasion she had won big, more than her usual amount in the hundreds. Yes, once she had picked up close to $30,000.

Immediately, she had thought of her charities, what some of those groups could accomplish with a few grand. But she was torn. Her charities were where she had committed herself to frittering away Dr. Prine's discretionary funds. She had earned thirty Gs of her own! Why give them away? At almost the same moment (her mind was quick), she reasoned that she had all the *things* she needed: clothes, cars, amenities, jewelry, a grand home. Her grown children had gone to fine schools. They both made considerable incomes. When she tried to lavish funds on them, they protested. It was their turn to give back, they said, contributing to their own concerns.

Without Dr. Prine knowing of her bounteous win—he was a blackjack fan—and with no one to pass judgment on her, she had placed on her nightstand a single with ten one-thousand-dollar bills. Their maid, Milly Claasen, would think at first that she was getting short shrift, a stack of ones. Then her eyes would pop open, if she allowed herself to believe the bills were real. In the hotel lobby had sat a Lucite box for Jerry's Children. When no one was looking, which was difficult to manage, she'd poked the rest of her winnings down the slot. Among the flutter of ones and fives and all the coinage, the remaining bills didn't look nearly as large as she had hoped they would. But at the same time, she remained proud of what she had done. Actually, *proud* was not the right word. The choice made her happy, and that was something quite different.

Whenever he sat at the blackjack table, Dr. Prine kept track of which cards had been dealt. Clearly he wasn't supposed to do it. He could have been kicked out of the casino if he were caught, though the practice wasn't illegal. He always played with a certain strategy. For one, he never used the hotel casino; that was Cecilia's domain. Instead, he hopped aboard a long gold bus running up and down the strip, until he found a place he hadn't been to for six months or more. He dressed in a flowered shirt and long baggy shorts and flip-flops that had been his son's. He donned the same faded ball cap he wore to work in the yard back home. And he always took to the table a club soda and lime, which he nursed until he was through; it looked as if he were drinking a gin and tonic, and the ruse kept his mind clear.

While Dr. Prine did possess an excellent memory, he couldn't recall every card that had been played; instead, he had taught himself to average certain values and thus calculate whether the dealer was more likely to deal him high cards or low, and he would place bets accordingly. At the same time, he relied a great deal on intuition. You could never underestimate the value of a hunch. He felt he could have wiped out any casino, but instead, to keep playing, he won only enough to remain anonymous. In one casino he'd watched a man take his considerable winnings and bow out; in others winners became confrontational and wound up getting banned. Prine preferred a quieter path whereby he won a few and lost a few. And afterward he would hand his winnings over to Cecilia, who kept their personal accounts. If she won anything, she never told him. And he had never had the temerity to ask.

After dinner on their fourth night, a handsome young couple handed them a flier in the lobby of the hotel. The sight, as if the duo were doppelgängers of the younger Prines, gave Dr. Prine a shiver. The simple green pamphlet spoke of spiritual growth, of human potential, of eternal peace and satisfaction. In their lifelong skepticism about such matters—they attended the Episcopal church near their home, where their largest commitment was to place a check in the wicker basket each week—they looked at each other blankly.

"Sounds interesting," Neville said. "Don't you think?"

"Maybe," Cecilia said. "I'm not very tired tonight."

So instead of heading for their room, Neville called for a car, and a white Lincoln came for them in less than five minutes. A blond young man dressed in a white suit emerged and held the doors for them. Once he was in the driver's seat, he eased into traffic and confirmed that he indeed knew how to find the Religion of the Mind temple. He said he had a good friend who played drums in the combo up on stage. The young driver glided from lane to lane and turned smooth asphalt corners, and Cecilia closed her eyes. She was floating and drifting—she and her friend May shopping Saturdays like schoolgirls, sharing secrets about their children and husbands. Something inside her ached, as if she'd lost a loved one, and she almost grabbed an Advil. Then she felt the car slow. The driver stopped in front of a low-slung building that once had been a retail outlet, a Costco or a Sam's. The façade was tarted up with large red boulders and feathery palms, desert-loving ferns.

As they entered the building, Cecilia noticed women smoking at picnic tables outside. *You do it, you're the grown-up,* one of the children said. *No, you do it, you're the child,* retorted the adult. Cecilia and Neville stepped into the large foyer, where people loitered among rows of tables, and books and CDs were for sale. Then, spotting the doors to the auditorium, they accepted bulletins from the ushers and proceeded down the aisle. *And why are we doing this?* Cecilia whispered to Neville. A small ensemble composed of piano, bass guitar, drums, and synthesizers sat on the right side of the stage. A lectern stood in the middle. Lyrics to a song were projected high on the walls to either side of the stage. *We are one, we are one, we are one,* sang all the people. After the song the Prines held up their hands, as visitors, and they each were presented with a rose. Not a word was uttered about Jesus Christ or Buddha or any other figure. Instead, the liturgy seemed to be a mix of many religions, with poetry for good measure.

The practitioner stood at the lectern and spoke. He had a strange name, a strange accent, yet Cecilia was taken with the sing-songy up-and-down nature of his speech. He spoke of materialism, not as if it were a sin, but as if it were a choice, and how, by degree, one could select its pleasures—but to remember that none of it mattered one whit. And yet, to her relief, there was no word of an afterlife. At home, the minister, the liturgy, the anthems, the hymns, always spoke of materialism in judgmental terms, then turned around and valued it in terms of what was needed for the church and its important projects—almost (it was a subtle manipulation) as if one's entrance into the next world were dependent upon gifts you made in this one.

The practitioner ended his talk with a story. A man had carried in his heart a lifetime of resentment against his mother for an intimate indiscretion she had committed against his person when he was a youth—seducing him into her bed. He had long nursed his anger, for she had ruined his ability to make love to women. Later in life the man's mother died of a sudden heart attack, and still he refused to view her in a kinder light. *One day his grown son came to him. Dad, remember when you used to lay into me with a board, and yet you never touched my brother? I hated you for many years, but it has become a burden I can no longer carry. It's . . . all right, Dad,* the grown son said. *I forgive you.* The practitioner seemed to stare at Cecilia, and she tuned out the rest of the talk, searching for her bottle of Advil. She flipped off the lid and swallowed two tablets without benefit of water.

At the end of the service, the congregants held hands, and the fingers of the woman next to Cecilia felt rough and cold, Neville's warm and dry. As the combo played something quick and modern, Cecilia hurried to the rear of the hall, where she was forced to linger because Dr. Prine was desperate to locate a restroom. Without quite realizing what the sensation was, she felt a sting behind her eyes, also something like bile rising in her throat, and she leaned against the back wall, listening to people chat. She knew she must regard Neville differently, but could she say the words? What one item could she give him, instead, to let him know? And yet, because of her renewed recalcitrance, she felt returning to her chest a certain hardness—picturing it as a shining chunk of coal multiplying over the years into an even larger malignancy—one that threatened to kill her. She shielded her eyes with her hand as if a blinding light were blazing up through the floor, and she wept, sobbing with a voice that almost shrieked. When Neville returned, he touched her arm.

"Oh, Nevi—I'm so sorry—Christ, I'm so sorry. Forgive me, please."

He said he was sorry, too, and held her, as if they were about to dance, held her as if she were fragile, which, in spite of her bravado, she was. Their bodies swayed; the folds in their garments shook. A third party—it was the practitioner who had led the service—gathered them in his arms, loosely and yet with great care.

"Would you like to see me in my chambers for a few minutes?" he said. "I've helped a lot of couples, often with a word or two."

Cecilia looked at Neville, who gave an imperceptible shake of his head, and said, "I think we've solved it," and the practitioner left them standing along the back wall of an empty hall. They heard the shuffle of feet, the murmur of voices in the lobby.

"I've had enough fun for this trip," Neville said.

"Mm," Cecilia said, squeezing his hand, wiping her eyes.

And when they returned to the hotel, they made arrangements to leave on an earlier flight. The entire way to West Texas—located in two seats closest to the window—they held hands. No one could hear them above the noise of the plane, as they spoke to one another. Oh, how they hoped to cut their losses before their plane, against all odds, fell to a rust-colored earth and ended their renewed attempts to love one another.

Tales of the Millerettes

1922 — Velma Flirts with Trouble. More than anything else Velma Bernard loved about being an usher was the gardenia she wore in her lapel each Saturday night. A scrawny high school girl dressed as a French maid would come around to all of the Millerettes in the lounge and pin to their lapels one of the aromatic blooms shipped to Wichita from Alabama. Every weekend since the Miller had opened, Velma would take the trolley home and hang her gardenia by a thread. When she had dried a half dozen, she would arrange them in a milk glass bowl and place it on the vanity in her room. Though the white petals turned brown, a certain aspect of the gardenia's beauty would remain. Prior to opening, Mr. Miller had given the girls patterns for black satin pants and fitted jackets of black gabardine. Giggling, they had shopped together at Innes Mercantile to obtain the material, the same fussy white blouses, identical bow ties and Mary Janes. The cumulative effect was that the Millerettes looked cute as penguins, so cute that their picture had made the paper.

Guiding customers to their seats was an occupation that might have been beneath the dignity of a recent college graduate like Velma, if hadn't been for Mr. Miller's kind attentions: a tempting leer thrown over his shoulder, caressing her posterior on the sly. While thrilling to each flirtation, she had serious intentions that did not include Mr. Miller. And yet there was a strong pull toward both, as if she were being grabbed on either hand by enthusiastic friends, one you liked and one you did not.

At Fairmount College Velma Bernard had trained in business administration, to please her mother, but her real dream was to become a film star. Yes, Velma Bernard. Her name had a certain heft to it; she wouldn't need to phony one up like a Pole or Czech with a thirteen-letter name ending in "z." She was pretty, but her lips were thin, and so to disguise the fact, she reddened the skin above her lip line in two curves. They gave her mouth the shape of a little heart, like the mouth of Clara Bow, whom she had admired since high school. Velma possessed short, wavy hair of blond and projected a smile that could be seen from the back row. Her boyish body could sport a shimmering chemise like a mannequin in one of the windows along Douglas Avenue. Her appearance gave her a vague sense of power over women, who tended to befriend her, and men, who wanted to possess her (it was an old story). But most important, she had certain other talents. She could sing rather well, having soloed in the Fairmount choir. She could perform simple tap steps and was a quick study for more difficult routines. Returning home from an evening of lessons, she would flop down on her bed, her muscles quivering from overuse. And at the same time, it would take hours for her heart to slow, for her brain to go black so she could sleep. Sometimes she didn't. Sometimes her mind contrived beautiful scenarios whereby she would build her own home in Los Angeles. She would marry another film star. They would have lovely children. But all that those scenarios did, at times, was stir the beating of her heart.

On a mild May evening in 1922, the night after Velma collected her diploma, the Miller had opened with great fanfare. The temple to filmdom had been built by an attorney, Jacob Miller, from Chicago, and towered three stories above the street at 115 North Broadway. The cost of his venue had amounted to a sum of $750,000. "Such a high price tag," the Wichita *Eagle* quoted Miller, "is due to the extensive use of brass for railings, the staircase built of Tavernelle marble, and a ventilating system that refrigerates the air." Opening night Mr. Miller had gathered his Millerettes on the draperied mezzanine and pointed down to the crowd queued up outside; Velma heard the murmur of voices growing. She saw one boxy limousine after another drop off yet another privileged party (the mayor and such), who were ushered in early. Those less fortunate hoofed it to the end of the line, which snaked its way around two blocks (ten thousand customers had competed for only two thousand seats). As the place opened, she watched footmen open doors to carriages, Cadillacs, and Packards. Doormen greeted theatergoers, and *directors* showed customers to the aisle, where she and other Millerettes would escort them to their seats. The console of an eleven-rank Wurlitzer was sunken in the orchestra pit, the squalling pipes located three stories up behind two decorative grilles. A funny little man named Shelly Hand was playing "Ain't We Got Fun?" and it quickened Velma's step. Mr. Hand received a score for every film and was paid to make sure he ended when the movie did. When the showing was over, he would sometimes bow to great applause.

"You are their gateway to Heaven . . . at least for tonight," Jacob Miller had told them all. "Make sure not to disappoint." His baritone voice was sure and strong, his consonants clearly enunciated. He didn't run his words together like some of the galoots she had gone to school with.

Velma's father had died when she was a baby, and so her voice softened when she spoke of Mr. Miller. "He treats us as if we were his daughters," she said one night before heading off to work. Her mother rolled her eyes, and Velma's thoughts drifted to Mr. Miller and a whiff of his wool jacket, which always seemed redolent of his musky perspiration—so unlike the smell of college boys.

"Oh, Velma," her mother lamented. "I wish you weren't working at that awful place. It's so common, so ungodly."

"Do we have any cheddar?" Velma asked.

"Hm, I suppose I forgot to put it out. Check." Her mother sniffed a handkerchief she held perpetually in her hand, like a figure from an old painting.

Velma stood and opened the white enamel cabinet whose galvanized compartment held a block of ice the man had just delivered. On the top shelf, she spotted the big orange wedge. Velma removed it and cut herself a slice to put on her roast beef sandwich. She grabbed a jar of bread-and-butter pickles. "Anything else you want, Mother?" Velma asked, winking over her shoulder.

"Oh, no, dear." Her mother sat and toyed with some potato salad on her plate, forking out the purple chips of red onion. Because her father had died when she was so young, Velma had grown up helping her mother do most everything. Velma didn't mind, but she wondered how her mother would handle that large house once she left town. And she had determined that she *would* leave, that she would have her own house one day—on a hill far away, and across its ridge would be nestled the dazzling letters that spelled out HOLLYWOODLAND. She had clipped a photograph from a magazine and taped it to her dresser mirror. The letters, soon to be lit with four thousand light bulbs, represented a future of freedom, of recognition, of visible means.

"All you'll find in that outfit is trouble," Vivian Bernard said, her eyes flitting toward Velma's form-fitting jacket. "If I'd known how lewd you were going to look, I'd have refused to make it for you."

Velma fussed with the jacket, which fit her torso to perfection, exploiting her modest bosom, her boyish waist. "Oh, Mother, you have no idea! The customers go wild over us," Velma said.

"That's because you're a vixen."

Satisfied with her pronouncement, her mother cooled herself with a fan she had been given by her Sunday School class. Furnished with an ivory handle and stiff yellow paper tinctured with an image of Christ in faded ochers and browns, it was a prop Vivian Bernard swung with great gusto. She often told Velma that if she would only pray, there wasn't a problem God couldn't handle for her. At the same time, she was terribly fatalistic. "August will be murder if it's this hot already. I don't know if I'm up to it."

"It's cool at the Miller," Velma said, trying to cheer her mother. "It feels like an autumn day. You almost need a sweater."

"I never heard of such a thing. Only God can cool the air."

"You should come down," Velma said. "I have an extra pass!"

"'Conditioning' the air!" her mother said. "That's as sinful as bobbing your hair, wearing dresses above the knee."

"Oh, Jeez," Velma said, swallowing her last bite. "I'm going to be late."

And with that proclamation, she ran to the front hall, grabbed a wrap, and soon caught a trolley that clattered down the tracks embedded in the brick pavement. The windows were open, and the wind blew her hair; she liked the feel of it, the sense that she was moving through time and space at a faster rate than most folks. After the short ride down Douglas, past manicured lawns, she hopped off at Broadway, not far from the theater. As her heels clicked along the sidewalk, she studied the marquee.

Beyond the Rocks had been held over. Velma had seen it so many times that she was able to mouth Miss Swanson's parts, and she could have given a synopsis to anyone who asked. *Gloria Swanson is on her honeymoon with her husband (you see), who is older than she, when she becomes infatuated with a younger man, Rudolph Valentino (don't you know). It only gets better from there.* Six reels, an act per reel, the film unfolded like a stage play. Something about staring up at the huge screen gave her a thrill, as if she, too, were participating in the intrigue of infidelity. Some day others would gaze up at screens all across America and admire *her*, participate vicariously in *her* deadly sins. Yes, she could see herself flirting with that imaginary but very real audience.

Sometimes when Velma's attention waned, her gaze was drawn from the screen to the gossamer curtains appliquéd with silver stars or to the dozen chandeliers made of brass and crystal. To her the Miller was not just a theater. With all its glittering bric-a-brac, it was a palace. The fact that she worked all week long at the Miller seemed to make it her home: she had sat in nearly every row; she had climbed among the ropes and curtains backstage, helping with live productions; she had visited the projection room and the concession stand to see how popcorn and cotton candy were made. She usually stood throughout her shift, swinging a leather swagger stick Mr. Miller had checked out to each of the girls; in the dark she sometimes twirled it, toddling like Chaplin down the aisle, instead of fending off an aggressive customer, as Miller had suggested. On that evening, however, Velma sat in one of the red-cushioned chairs trimmed in ivory and gilt paint. The Miller Theater was far grander than any place in town. In the future she expected to appear on large screens like the one in front of her and captivate audiences from coast to coast. In California she would stand under a marquee outside an even grander theater, like Grauman's Egyptian, and experience the thrill of her own success. *Velma Bernard Held Over for Fifth Week!*

"I like the way you work," came a voice.

Velma looked over her shoulder. "Oh, Mr. Miller, I didn't see you standing there," she gushed, feeling as if she had done something stupid. She jumped up, holding the stick behind her back.

"Call me Jake, Doll. Come, I want to speak to you in my office."

Velma drew in a quick breath. It was the only place in the theater she had not visited. She turned and followed him, handing her stick to one of the other girls, who would pick up the slack in her area. From the mezzanine they began to climb stairs.

They rose past the little lounge where the Millerettes took respite—puffing on Chesterfields, sipping Coca-Colas—up the burgundy-carpeted stairs, to the very top, where Mr. Miller opened a dark oak door. Inside he switched on a green library lamp over his desk. He opened a small window in the wall, and Velma could hear the click of the projector in the next room. The projectionist, an old man she had met once, sat and stared at the screen through that square in the wall. He was smoking a cigarette.

"I've told you not to light up in there," Mr. Miller spoke gruffly into the square. "You're going to burn the place down." He slammed the little window and nudged a red leather bench with his leg. "Sit over here, Doll." If it hadn't been for a chipped tooth and an oblong mustache that engulfed his mouth, his smile would have been boyish. Yet the pores in his face were big, as if he had already lived a full life somewhere else, as if he were only biding his time in a jerkwater town like Wichita.

On the bench they both watched the movie, like the projectionist, through a window facing the screen. Mr. Miller put his arm around her, and Velma sighed. She liked the gingery smell of his talc and leaned into his shoulder. She had heard rumors about Mr. Miller, that he had been banned from practicing law in Illinois. That's why he had set up shop in the hinterlands, where dopes like her weren't supposed to know the difference (she did try to think the best of people). She snuggled further into his prickly wool shoulder. Pulling her toward him, he kissed her hard, snaking his fingers inside her blouse where they kneaded her breast, sliding his other hand down past her waistband. When he finally released her, her lips felt as if they had been sucked by a leech, and a wonderful ooze flowed from her like a fountain. She felt on the verge of doing something, and though her mother had warned against its hazards, she knew exactly what that something was. Mr. Miller stood her like a big doll against the door and undid the cord of her slacks, and they, along with her undergarments, rather floated to the floor without a sound. Velma gasped. When Mr. Miller's pants fell, she hopped up and wrapped her legs around him (it felt quite natural). With their complementary parts so close, Miller thrust his hips, and Velma emitted a little cry (she could feel the letting of blood). All she had been taught told her not to go on, not to let him finish, but the world was changing. Women smoked in public; they swore; they earned their own living. And this, too.

All through the evening, Velma felt little trickles, cold and riverlike, running down her legs, and she would run to the ushers' lounge. "Here, take this," said Gladys Gorges, a large girl with a knowing look. She handed Velma a fluffy handkerchief, whispering something into her ear. Velma blushed but entered the bathroom and closed the door. The thought that she would have to stanch the flow of Mr. Miller's attentions never occurred to her (she thought she knew the score), but the handkerchief seemed to do the trick. (When the evening was over Gladys told her to throw it away.)

After the final showing flickered to an end, Shelly the organist bowed, and the crowd applauded. Cleaning up her station, Velma realized she was the last Millerette to leave the lounge.

"Hey, Doll, this way."

And Mr. Miller guided her to the alley. From there he drove her home in a long black Packard, where she sat snuggled against his shoulder. He pulled over and stopped under a tree whose limbs drifted down over the car, the long fronds of a weeping mulberry gently lapping the surface, as if sheltering them inside its arms.

Miller said in very soft voice, "God you're so beautiful," and his fingers once again found themselves going straight up her skirt, locating their earlier destination; she moaned as he kissed her deep and pulled her close. "I think I love . . . ." He remained inside her for the longest time, as they listened to the wind rustle branches against the car. Finally, he sat up straight, as if something had just occurred to him. "If you get preggers, kiddo, you're on your own."

His pronouncement sounded so logical at first, but it was like yelling "King's X" during a game of tag. It protected you somehow, but from what, getting tagged? For some reason she was not frightened. If life without a father had taught her one thing, it was that fear was not a luxury one could indulge in. No sirree.

Velma accepted a cigarette Miller offered her and lit it. She coughed on the first inhalation. "It's the wrong time of the month," she said, looking up at him, letting the cigarette burn. "Miss Dunne taught us to calculate our *safe* days. The only sensible thing I learned in her health class at Fairmount."

The big-boned woman with bronze skin had told them in a tightly shut classroom how to arrive at such a deduction based on one's cycle, and she had said if they ever told, she would deny every word of it. As Velma smiled up at Miller, she tried to count days, but her head spun. She would have to check her diary. She blinked, attempting again to remember how many days it had been since her last time, but the information seemed just out of reach, like a dream you try to recall. Mr. Miller turned and leaned against her one final time. His was a dry, sour kiss, and of a sudden she couldn't wait to reach the safety of her own room. As her Mary Janes clicked up the front walk of her mother's home (a three-story Victorian painted a sad, pale sage trimmed in lavender), Velma felt as if she had never been there before in her life. It was a fleeting feeling, about as quick as a sigh of wind, but it was sure. Once inside she removed her shoes and tiptoed up the carpeted stairs that knew no quiet way. Squeaks in the floor usually woke her mother, who would call out and Velma would have to answer, but that night Velma could hear her mother's snoring as she passed her door. She padded down the hall to her room and placed her newest gardenia in the milk glass bowl, where it browned and curled up immediately.

After that evening, whenever Velma worked, she headed straight to her station. No matter what, she had determined she would not leave it, not even if Mr. Miller begged her to follow him upstairs again. At the same time, she dreamed of doing exactly that, yes, of course, refusing at first and then, after exacting a promise of marriage from him, fleeing with him on a train headed for Florida or California. Imagine her chagrin, when, on the Monday following their tryst, Mr. Miller and his *family* set off on a month-long trip to Chicago and New York. (If she had had any idea he was married, would she have carried on so? It was hard to say now. Should she have asked him of his status?) The theater's management was handed over to a young man who hadn't yet finished high school. The redheaded fool gave orders that no one followed; they all did their jobs without being told, and the life of the Miller went on without Jacob Miller.

When her *Aunt Flo* (such a vapid term) failed to arrive on time, just prior to Miller's return, Velma dismissed it; often she had been late in college. To get over the thrills Mr. Miller gave her, she had spent the entire month of his absence flirting with men on the trolley. She had been a trolley's trollop, that's what, and she had loved it, plopping down next to a dapper man in a pinstripe suit and derby. Some of the young men even followed her home, making breathing difficult, but she would ditch them at the door. *Why don't you invite your young admirer inside?* her mother would ask. Each time Velma would shriek as if laughing at the devil himself and hurry up the stairs before such a devil could seduce her into doing his more daring work, like bank robbery or embezzlement. Removing her uniform and a layer of underwear, she would study her form. Yes, she still looked the same; she *must* look the same.

After Jacob Miller returned to work, Velma often sat in the exact chair where he had first approached her, hoping upon hope that he would tap her shoulder again, but all she got for her efforts was a reprimand from the redheaded manager. To emphasize his point, the lad took his swagger stick and tapped her knee. One evening Velma felt his hand on her shoulder, and then grazing her breast.

"Don't touch me," she said, slapping it away.

"Shhh," he said, digging his fingers into her shoulder, looking up about the crowd, some of whom turned their heads to see what the fuss was about.

"I said, take your hands off me." The louder she spoke the deeper his fingers dug into her shoulder. "Stop."

"You're finished, Lassie," he whispered, leaning over. "Clean out your locker and be on your way."

"You fool. You know that's what everyone calls you, don't you? Wait till I tell Mr. Miller of your overtures."

"Who do you think sent me here?"

Velma stood and rushed past him to the rear door, up the staircase, past the mezzanine, to the top of the stairs. When no one answered the door, she turned the knob and entered Miller's office. Light from the film flickered across the darkened room. She heard a giggle, a definite slap, and a little whimper.

"Care to make it three?" came his voice.

Velma couldn't see Miller's face. If she had been able to, perhaps she could have communicated to him her desperation, the great desire that welled up inside her.

"Either join us or scram," shot Miller's voice through the dark. Yes, a certain something about his invitation was tempting, but the thought of sharing him with another woman made Velma's blood curdle.

She thudded noisily down the entire staircase, out the door, and to her trolley stop. *Fire me?* she thought, smacking her hand with the leather-covered stick. Had the redheaded fool not noticed she had worn a bulky cardigan all evening? *How could he fire me, when I planned all along to quit?* As she ran up her street and opened the front door, she realized she had left her swagger stick on the trolley, but it was too late. By now it had gone on without her, toward the far reaches of town. The conductor would by now have picked it up and kept it as his own.

Each day Velma viewed in the mirror the changes overtaking her body: the widening of her hips, how her abdomen protruded, how her breasts drooped like pears. The larger Velma became, the lighter she felt, the lovelier her aspect (so she believed). She ingested more and more meat and cheese and refused to leave the house. She wore Vivian's discarded Mother Hubbards, blousy frocks that engulfed her, even as a woman in her condition. Theirs was a tacit truce. Her mother would say nothing, because if she did, Velma would flee the house forever. In return Vivian would quietly knit tiny items of clothing, stitch little quilts. She repapered and repainted Velma's room in dark pinks, setting up Velma's old crib in there. The sun would strike its new white paint, and its cheerfulness would propel Velma through another day of gestation, where she did little more than stare out the window at birds nesting in the elm beyond her window. *How do they do it, blindly laying eggs and feeding one season after another till they die? No recognition. No one to help.* One morning when it was chilly and gray, her mother knocked and entered. She sat in the rocker and began a slow steady rhythm of movement, her chin always parallel to the floor. A portable Victrola was playing "Make Believe," and Vivian lifted the arm to stop it.

"Your dear father had so many plans for you, plans I've not been able to fulfill. Before he passed, he would hold you in his arms and tell you of trips we all would take around the world. He wanted you to marry, but he'd hoped you might station yourself above us. On one of his marryin' trips, as he called them, you would be introduced to a German baron or a wealthy London merchant and be set for life. Of course that was before the Huns went crazy, before your dear father took a deep sigh and fell over in his chair. Had it not been for that event, he'd have taken you round the world. He'd have married you off fine by now."

"That's a lovely story," Velma said. "It becomes lovelier every time you tell it." If it hadn't been for a hint of longing in her own voice, her statement might have sounded like a reproach. At any rate her mother left her alone after that.

The night Velma's baby was born, Vivian Bernard attended her. With contractions increasing, Velma spoke. "Oh, I do hope you know what you're doing, Mother."

"I witnessed more barnyard births than you can shake a stick at, not to mention the birthing of ten brothers and sisters. Every spring I watched and learned while hands pulled and tugged at flesh reluctant to enter the world. I used to feel as at home between two spread legs as I do in the kitchen. It's what women do," Vivian said. Wiping her brow, she appeared as tired as Velma. "All, it seems, we're good for." After thirty more minutes of contractions, Vivian stood poised, a frown upon her face. With little struggle, however, Velma's cavity opened. She didn't scream, as Vivian had predicted she would. Her mother grabbed the scrawny, squalling red lump and placed it inside a soft towel in her arms. She cut the cord; with what Velma could not see.

"Oh, Mother," Velma sighed, pulling baby Vera close to her in bed, "she's so beautiful." She was exhausted, and the center of her body, not just the obvious place, hurt terribly. She had been stretched beyond endurance, and it was as if she had evacuated something awful, something wild. As she spoke her mother cleaned blood and goo from the baby's skin, rubbing oil over the tiny body squirming in perpetual motion. Velma wanted to be left in peace with her baby nestled in her arms, so that they would both fall asleep. Perhaps, she mused, they would wake up in a dense quiet forest, where they where they would live for the rest of their lives, undisturbed.

"Why don't you get up so I can wash the sheets?" Vivian said.

"She's going to be hungry soon, can't I lie here and enjoy her for a while?"

"It'll be the last bit of enjoyment you have for a long time, girl." Vivian laughed and began to pull sheets from the corner. Exhausted and woozy, Velma rose, holding her baby. "If I get them in cold water now," her mother said, "they won't stain. You can rest with her over there in granny's rocker. A lot of babies were nursed in that chair."

In her weakened state, Velma hobbled over to the wooden rocker with its thick gingham cushions and nearly fell into the chair. She almost panicked when baby Vera refused to take hold of her nipple. It was as if the infant didn't know what to do with her mouth, worming her little lips in and out, twisting her head.

"Was it worth it, my daughter?" Vivian asked, huffing her way back in from the laundry room, smelling of lilac water she sprinkled over her linens.

"Mother, she won't nurse," Velma said.

Vivian gently but firmly took the babe's head and made sure it latched on to Velma's nipple, as if she were attaching a trailer to its hitch. Velma sucked air against her teeth upon the little mouth's contact with her breast; the sensation at first was nearly erotic but gave way to a contentment she had never felt before. Their communion caused her mind to flop from one silly thought to another. Her mother. Her father. Miller. Her career. The letter V: it was a naturally strong consonant that overtook her mind. It stood for victory, valor, even vengeance, and she would continue the family tradition: Vivian, Velma, and now baby Vera.

"Mr. Miller was so strong, so sure of himself. I couldn't have stopped him if I'd wanted to." It seemed a lifetime ago since she had allowed him his way.

"The act is a sacrament shared between a man and a woman in the sight of God."

"Yes, that would have been best," Velma said, toying with her daughter's fine hair, kissing her soft little head. "But I'm so happy now, it doesn't matter."

Vivian sighed and walked over to the chair, placing one hand on Velma's head and one on Vera's. "God help you." The hand felt cold and moist against Velma's scalp. She shivered, in fact.

"Mother, I've come to a decision. I shall raise Vera in California."

"Gal, you can't be serious." Her mother dropped her arms and bowed her head, her eyes flashing.

"I've made up my mind. I'm taking the train as soon as Vera's able to travel, as soon as I work off a little of this fat. I must make a career, and I must prepare her for a bitter world."

"Oh, I don't want a delinquent for a grandchild," Vivian said, placing a hand over her chest and grimacing as if she had gas. For the first time in Velma's life, her mother appeared old. For so long her mother had looked the same, slightly gray, slightly large, but active, always alive. But now she looked old, more of her life behind than ahead.

"I only meant that with my love, Vera can shoulder the strength to fight anything. Knowing she's loved will save my little Vera."

"Has it saved you?"

Velma raised her head and smiled at her mother. "Why, yes. Yes, it has."

Vivian Bernard, whose parents, the Himmlers, had hailed from the Austrian Alps, carried 150 pounds on her tiny frame and had done so for as long as Velma could remember. Her grandparents had both died young of vague heart problems. So she wasn't surprised when one morning she found her mother stiff and blue, lying in bed with her eyes wide open. During her night's sleep, which had been fitful, though baby Vera slept quite peaceably, Velma had felt nauseous, her head swimming. She had heard of such things, experiencing the same symptoms as a loved one at the very instant that person was slipping into the next world, but she had never expected it to happen to her. It was mildly unsettling that she had done nothing about it, but had she risen, the baby would have cried. And anyway, what action could she have possibly taken to save her mother?

Vivian's portly body was taken away by the mortuary and prepared for the funeral, which was set for Friday. Her mother's people were all gone; it would only be Velma, baby Vera, the pastor, and a few souls from Grace Methodist-Episcopal who would appear at the service to come to grips with Vivian's death. She was barely sixty-three.

Velma stood with the others in the warm June mist of 1923 and half listened to the words any pastor would have spoken at a burial—words gleaned from books with torn leather covers. She was already thinking ahead, to a place where fresh words were spoken with each reel. She couldn't help it. A new life was creeping into view, and in it she would be freer than she had ever been! She could barely contain her excitement, as the first clod of dirt was thrown in on her mother. Yes, she was sad, but her mother had made what she could of her life, and Velma was about to do the same, only with much more zest, much more direction.

Following the service at the cemetery on a steep hill dotted with stone markers dated no earlier than 1849, the funeral director dropped Velma and her daughter at the house. Velma put Vera to sleep, and, with a strange new energy, envisioned putting Vivian's things out on the large front porch: clothing, books, furniture she had never liked as a child. The house would look bare, but if she was moving to California, she would need to rid herself of it all. She would sell the large house, take the proceeds and begin a new life. In the midst of her quandary, the phone rang. Expecting yet another solicitous caller, she sighed and ran down the hall. "Yes, hello?"

It was Clive Prince, a fellow member of Grace Church, who was also a vice-president of their bank. A thin, prissy man married to a dark-haired woman much like himself, Clive and his wife had no issue of their own.

"You'll need an income," he said.

"Yes?" Velma said.

"We have a repossession, an odd case really. The building is located on Douglas, not far from your home. The gentleman's mortgage account is in arrears. If you can come up with the last three payments, and pay them up from now on, it can be yours. It's a sweet brick building with a large front window, perfect for a dress shop."

"Mr. Prince, I know nothing about making dresses," Velma said.

"Your mother left you a sum, I guess you know," he said, "untouched from the day your father bequeathed it to you. Mrs. Bernard always lived off her parents' money, which is almost kaput. What your papa left is a rather modest sum, but with it you could pay this merchant's debt, pick up the payments, and as soon as you start bringing in an income, you wouldn't need to rely on Vivian's sums anyway."

Velma held the phone tight to her chin. "Mother never said a thing about it." In a twinkling, she saw herself with Vera, taking that train to California. Yes, along with this windfall, she would sell the house and its goods, gather all her things, her daughter, and make a new life where no one knew them. She would tell people she was a widow, her husband having been killed in a train accident.

"Velma," he said, "let me speak frankly, if I may. In your position, you won't be able to teach school. You won't be able to do secretarial work. Most places won't hire you, once they discover you've had a child . . . ."

"We're headed for California. Hollywoodland to be exact."

She could hear him take a breath. "Do you know how many people out there actually make a living worth spitting at?" Velma let the time pass without an answer. "Precious few, that's how many," he said. "Here you can set up almost any kind of business you want."

"Yes," she said. "I do see what you mean. Give me a day to think about it, and I shall call you tomorrow."

"That's fine," he said, "but don't take too long. I've got a line stretching around the block. I'm holding off the others because I think you deserve this repossession more than anybody else." He paused. "They all seem to have a leg up on you."

"Yes, thank you, Mr. Prince, I surely do appreciate it."

After she had hung up, Velma dug into a cinnamon roll some callers had left, pulling it away from the other dozen, swallowing before she had actually chewed the first bite so that she could devour the next. With such sweetness rolling about her mouth, her feelings turned a complete 180 degrees. As she consumed whole pieces of a second roll, she mused. It was as if she had become, for a short while, someone new, but because she was now coming to her senses, she was reverting to her old self. Yes, she could always sell the business, or at least the building, if it didn't satisfy her, or if the enterprise failed. She could still go to California if she wished, but she had to be realistic. She was no longer a girl; she had another mouth to feed. She became giddy with the thought of her decision, wearing it like a warm stole around her shoulders. The shop would insure a roof over their heads, money coming in. Gosh, she was so relieved to be doing the right thing. Sure, evenings she could do community theater, to keep her hand in. There was a part of her that would never relinquish the thrill an audience gave her, but for now her own desires would have to wait. Her mother had provided little earthly guidance, allowing her to do as she pleased, while admonishing her of God's wrath if she took the wrong path. Yes, she would provide Vera with what had been missing in her own life. If she succeeded in her work, then how could little Vera do no less?

The next day, without calling, she and Vera rode a trolley to the bank, and she signed all the papers. Everything was typewritten neatly in triplicate—two for the bank and one for her—triple proof that she was now a merchant. With threatening skies all around, she contacted a sitter and spent the rest of the day making preparations to remodel her building. It would drip with lavender: the main showroom, the dressing cubicles, her desk, which, instead of being shoved into the back, would be set up center stage, near the front window, where she stood staring into the street. From there, she would conduct trade; after all, business was what she had majored in. Oh, she had never sold dresses before, but she could have sold clams if that was what she had decided to do. At that moment Velma witnessed a change in the light, a flicker. Then a jagged line of electricity split the sky in half, slicing the trunk of a huge elm across the street as if it were a simple log. The smoldering disaster was followed by a bomb of thunder. She stared at the subsequent streaks of lightning illuminating her shop like ten thousand bulbs—as if they were a minor disturbance—and returned to her work.

1944–48 — Vera Seeks Her Fortune, Too. Vera Bernard had concluded you couldn't just be a good actress; you had to offer something extra, a quality that the other beautiful girls didn't have, something her mother called *flair*. Her mother couldn't really define flair, but Vera continued to imagine what it might be: a fur wrap thrown over her shoulder, a pair of heels made from alligator, a silk purse. In addition to helping out at her mother's dress shop, Vera worked at the Miller in the concession stand evenings and weekends. At home she kept her earnings in a cigar box, with a rubber band wrapped around a wad of cash that continued to grow. Wartime had done away with half the ushers and all the directors, so there was stiff competition to be the pretty face that sat in the glass cage and took in nickels. As Vera tore the customers' tickets, she would smile and encourage them to buy popcorn or a bottle of Coca-Cola in the lobby. And since she had worked there concession sales had risen threefold. The job was dull, but when her shift was over she would head for the third balcony, stepping over the rope that closed it to the public, and watch every film that came through town. She had seen Ann Sothern's Maisie movies a dozen times each. She knew the patter of the sassy, ambitious blonde: the plots, makeup, costumes, how the scenes faded from one to the next. She had no grasp of the technical jargon, but she believed she could move freely in front of a camera, and when she got to the coast, it would be as if the fish out of water had finally found the Pacific Ocean. From reading the magazines, she knew that thousands of starlets came to Hollywood every year and failed, but she was one of the few who knew she was going to make it.

When Vera was little, her mother, with great patience and verve, had taught her how to sing and dance. Vera had demonstrated a great aptitude for entertaining and soon outgrew her mother's teaching abilities. She had participated in community theater, playing every little-girl part that came along (one time opposite her mother), but now each day she spent in Wichita made her feel as if she were breathing through voile. Her mother had gone on and on about her days at the Miller—almost fairy-tale in nature, as she raved about marble stairs, gossamer curtains, brass handrails—and it was a pleasant enough place, but Vera often wanted to break out of the ticket booth that made her feel as if she were in jail. She would be smothered, completely suffocated, if she didn't get out soon; a tiny fan humming like a bird overhead did little to freshen her mood.

Vera was taller than her mother, nearly as large as her father (she had been told). Though her mother remained vague about who he was, Vera often looked at her face in the mirror and tried to imagine what a father of hers *could* have looked like. Yes, she had some of her mother's traits: light hair, average breasts, good hips. But where her mother was petite, Vera was statuesque. Her feet often pounded as she hurried down the two flights of stairs at home. She had to duck to get through certain doorways. Though she had towered over a number of leading men, she was undeterred. She would be marvelous. Where her mother had been soft and afraid, Vera would be hard-nosed and courageous. On her final night at work, three Millerettes, who now wore black slacks and any old sweater (it made her mother's blood boil), had thrown her a party. After one sip, however, she had given her glass of "firewater punch" to the girl replacing her and left. At home Vera packed, while Velma ironed her clothes and recalled lines from roles she had done in community theater: *Pygmalion, Eager Heart*—roles that Vera thought vilely tame for herself.

At midnight Vera witnessed Velma's stoic good-bye on their broad front porch. Vera then hoofed it alone to Union Station, swinging her suitcase as if it were a bundle of schoolbooks. She arrived with a thin layer of perspiration on her forehead and bought a ticket. Sitting in a coach that was packed, she soon stared into the darkness speeding past her and thanked God she was leaving this utterly flat land behind. It was as if she had been born in the wrong place, and now she was correcting that cosmic error.

Vera had been extremely thrifty, stashing away her earnings like an animal living in the ground. And at age twenty-two (she had refused to go to college), with her mother smiling and crying both as she released her hand, Vera had left. Now she was chugging through the large ranches of western Kansas. Yes, she was headed for Los Angeles with one cloth suitcase to her name—several hundreds coiled inside an empty lipstick tube and a fifty-dollar bill her mother had slipped her at the last minute.

"Here, take this," her mother had blubbered. "If you don't need it to eat, buy something nice for yourself."

As the train clucked along, Vera kept thinking of the bill clutched inside her glove. After the conductor took her ticket, she made her way to the restroom and folded the fifty into fours, placing it in a compartment behind the mirror in her compact. She wouldn't spend it until she absolutely had to, until she was near death, if it came to that. After changing trains in Albuquerque, Vera met a rather rotund man returning to California. They were located in the club car, and he slouched in an upholstered chair that sat next to hers.

"Uncanny," she said, lighting a Lucky he proffered, his greasy eyes glimmering like a toad's. "Uncanny that I would meet a *director* right here, on the train to Los Angeles. What do you direct, traffic?" She flashed her eyes at him and laughed. He was uglier than a stump, but Vera had learned that if she only smiled and lured a man in with her eyes, she could get him to do almost anything she wanted him to (although a rich boy at school had once told her to piss off when she asked for a dime to buy lunch). After several rounds of drinks, the man invited her to his compartment, and on their way, they bounced off the narrow corridor walls through several cars, laughing at their trouble. She vaguely recognized him, having seen his picture in *Movie Talk*: he had been posed with several starlets, a guy she assumed was at least second from the top on some kind of celluloid totem pole. On a tiny bunk, the man nearly squashed her to death as he splayed himself across her, and she squealed.

"Wait," she said, squeezing her way out from under him. "My time of the month." She then coaxed him into placing himself inside her mouth and she took care of his rampant, coarse needs that way.

"Ah, dear, what can I do for you?" he sighed when he was finished. It was almost too easy. In the tiny private bath, Vera hawked into the corner sink the residue of his passion and washed up. Entering the compartment again, she remained saucily quiet until the man was ready to retire.

"Well," she said, toying with the buttons of his pajama fly, arousing him into another frenzy, "there is one teensy thing you could do for little Vera." And she whispered it in his ear.

"My child, if you can improvise like you did tonight, you can play any role you like," he said, with a quick wink. And Vera threw her head back and laughed. Twenty-four hours later, when they rode into Los Angeles Union, and the train chuffed to a stop, the director sent her in a taxi to the Dormitory for Young Actresses (*That's where all the starlets begin*, he told her). The DYA was a nickel's throw from his studio. She couldn't have written the script better herself.

For weeks she made the rounds with a number of other girls. They would pay a cabbie up front, and he would take them from studio to studio. It seemed there was more flirting involved than actual acting, but sometimes the line between the two became blurred. She learned to let her stance speak for itself, as she lifted her chin and smiled. She had already landed a few bit parts, which was better than being an extra, which was what most of the DYA girls wound up doing before heading back to places like Des Moines and Pittsburgh.

In her off hours Vera sold stockings at the oldest department store in Los Angeles. From the dorm she would take a smoky old bus downtown in the morning, and if she were lucky, she would hitch a ride back in the afternoon. Having worked in her mother's shop, she knew how to approach a customer. You didn't want to scare one away by talking too much or too loudly. You held the silk stockings over your arm, so that the women could feel the luxuriousness themselves. Or you were allowed to don a pair and raise your skirt an inch above your knee to show off the sheen they made in the low ocher lights. After wearing them for a week, you were given the pair to take home. By then there was usually a runner in one of them, but you didn't care. You were in a land that never turned cold. The sun shone more than it didn't. And there was often a delicious breeze that seemed to come out of nowhere. It seemed like a kind of heaven.

Vera sat perched on a stone wall, legs crossed, smoking a Lucky she had bummed from the best boy. Bub was a short, pudgy man of fifty years with kids her age, and he always managed to cast her a leer that gave her a shiver of revulsion. But still she hit him up for cigarettes, Coca-Colas, even cash (he didn't tell her to piss off). Vera exhaled, waiting for the director to make up his mind. The script suggested she enter the yard from the main walk to the residence on the hill; then the camera would follow her to the front door. But the director had gotten a wild hair up his ass that she should sneak onto the lawn from a side gate, tiptoeing with her shoes off. She didn't get it. The character was coming to babysit. Why would she want to sneak in from the side? She wouldn't find out until the film was in the can that the babysitter was only a vixen in disguise. A trollop, as her mother would have said. The script had not revealed what she would become in the mind of the director. Your last part often became your next—a certain director liking you as a French maid or a trollop—and so you had to be careful.

"Oh, Miss Vera, Miss Vera," came a voice. It was Bitzy, who minced her way up the sidewalk in mousy steps that made Vera laugh. "Mister Man's ready fo' yo' shot. Let me freshen yo' face, and take that cig'rette out yo' mouth."

Vera took one more drag, flattened the end, and saved it in a metal case for later; she jumped down from the wall. "Oh, Bitzy, I don't think I can do one more thing. I'm sick sick sick of that man, I really am. He's not near as good as you-know-who." She was referring to the pig she had met on the train, the clod she hadn't heard from in weeks.

"But Mr. Man's a fine director, too. You jus' need t'let him does his job an' you does yours. I knows 'cause I played a slave for him las' year. He knows what he knows."

"You're the best part of impossible, aren't you?" Vera said, as Bitzy reached up and dabbed Vera's face with a powder puff. There was a gentleness, a softness Vera felt when Bitzy touched her, and Vera patted her hand. Bitzy smiled, and with a pencil darkened Vera's eyebrows, which tended to thin out in the light. The little woman had to be fifty if she was a day, but she seemed ageless. Wearing a sparkle in the corner of each eye, she walked miles to and from the studio daily. Though Vera felt odd about expressing it, she had great admiration for Bitzy. At home she had been told varyingly different stories about Negroes (a subject on which her mother had been strangely silent). There were those whose kin had been abolitionists; they said you had to be fair. If they were on the school board, they hired them as teachers. Others less couth called them names and derided their so-called smell. Bitzy had shown Vera nothing but kindness and bore only a redolence of mandarin oranges and jasmine, a scent she left as a trace of her love and good will for others. Yes, Vera was in the right place, where people could be free, regardless of their rearing, their skin color.

Still, the City of Angels was a funny place. Vera had lived there six months and still didn't know her neighbors, yet people like Bitzy, Lillian in Wardrobe, Guy at the commissary, were all family now. They greeted one another heartily. They joked and laughed. They commiserated over their plight during breaks. Not enough wages, not enough tips, but Vera could only listen to so much. Her experience was rather unique. Winning bit parts (quite different from minor roles) had seemed almost too easy. Then three minors in a row. Her mother had feared she might be destitute in six months, and yet here she was now with a featured role—little Vera Bernard from Wichita, Kansas. This was her fourth film, and this time her name would be listed in the credits. If she wished, she would be able to live in a bigger place, but her mother's business sense bore too strong an influence. Like Velma she put all her earnings in the bank. She occasionally footed someone desperate a small loan, but other than that, she lived like a church mouse. In her cigar box she kept a little cash for emergencies. Before stashing a few ones in her lipstick tube, she kept the box itself hidden deep within a hole in her mattress.

Still waiting to take direction, Vera straightened the stockings that the studio had provided for her (she had quit working at the department store). If she had forgotten to take them off, Leaping Lillian would have chased her down the street and ripped them off in ten seconds flat. They belonged to Wardrobe, and they were to be checked in at the end of each day. Lillian was a stooped reptile of a woman with gray curls falling across her brow. With a cigarette dangling from her lip, smoke enshrouded her like a fog, creating a permanent frown. Lillian's proprietary nature irritated Vera so much that one evening, when the woman went to tinkle, Vera lifted a new pair, still in the wrapper with the beautiful red-head on the pasteboard, and slid them down into her slacks.

Back in her apartment, Vera removed the hosiery from the packaging and rolled the stockings into the toes of some ugly green pumps that had come from her mother's shop in Wichita. She was saving them for a particularly swell evening. In her plan she would make a date with some hotshot producer . . . or rather, he would make a date with her . . . and she would borrow a gown from Wardrobe and pull out her elegant hosiery. She would be wined and dined and before morning, if she were lucky, she might become the next Mrs. Pudgy Producer, or at least his fiancée. Soon after, her stardom would light the night sky like a comet.

Her roommates, Alexis and Marion, drew straight dark lines for one another up the backs of their legs to simulate seams, but when Alexis offered to share her skills on Vera's, she laughed.

"Whom do you think you're kidding?"

"Where do you get off with this 'whom' crap?" Alexis said. "You're just a kid from Kanz-ass." They all laughed.

"I may be from Kansas," she said, "but don't try to hustle me. My legs look great without faking a seam."

"Oh, you think so?" Marion said, falling to her knees and kissing Vera's feet. Then they all plopped in a heap on an oval rag rug, laughing like schoolgirls. They were as different as they could be. Alexis was barely five feet, a fierce redhead with freckles; Marion was not much taller, dark-headed and plump, already testing for more matronly roles. And Vera had bleached her hair platinum. Unlike her mother's lips, hers were voluptuous, and she kept them dabbed with oily red lipstick. She often sat and rolled the tip in and out, in and out of the *golden* tube, for the fun of it.

"I'm so sick of this war, I could jump off a bridge," Vera said, her head on Alexis's stomach. "I hate going without stockings."

"Quit your gripin'," said Alexis (née Allred Kognowski, from Brooklyn). "At least we're all workin'. Compared to our GIs overseas, we've got it made. And you should remember that." She smacked Vera's leg.

"See, kid," Marion said, popping her gum and pointing a thumb at Alexis, "that's how this one stays happy. With low expectations she'll always be surprised. She'll marry the guy down the block and have twelve kids."

"Not me," Vera said. "If I expect the very best, then that's what I'll always get. Look at me. I fully believed I'd come this far in six months. A year from now I'll be starring in my own film, and Joan Crawford had better look out." She turned on the radio tuned to KECA. The Mills Brothers were singing "Paper Doll," and it gave Vera a lift.

A silence fell over the three of them, as they stood and went about their business, Alexis taking over the shower, Marion sitting down to write home to Michigan, and Vera studying her lines. She knew them cold, but she felt that she could improve her delivery, her character's aspect. After the long trip out, trapped with that walrus in his compartment, Vera had seen that she had some currency with the men in charge. As long as she didn't spend too much in one place, she would be able to get almost anything she wanted. The rest would have to come from a dark little part of her—she pictured it behind her liver—that she had yet to unleash before the camera. She imagined the spot as a cavern, from which she could mine whatever she needed: anger, frustration, humor, even murderous hatred. When she used these things, they felt real, but when she put them away, she felt a certain falseness about herself. At times she dreamt of the hours she had spent viewing cinema at the Miller. If she had never seen all those films, she might not have been making movies, and, though she wasn't religious like her mother, she thanked God for her fortune. Just in case.

For all her optimism, her valor, 1947 found Vera in a four-year rut of accepting minor roles: French maids (twice), chorus parts (three, one with Crosby), the gangster's moll (a scene that lasted twenty seconds), the dishrag behind the diner counter (she told Clark Gable *I'm out of pie and what are ya gonna do about it*). She had played parts in several Boston Blackie films, which were not exactly high art, but the elemental detective stories were viewed in wide release. People all over the country had seen her face as she raced from set to set, handing Blackie a gun from her purse; she had even received a few fan letters (mostly from young girls who wanted to know how you got started in Hollywood, and she hadn't even answered them). Combined with a job as a Loews usher, Vera barely made the rent some months. Frugal as she was, she had gone through her savings, and there was always something nagging at her coin purse: dental work, underwear, a new set of head shots for her portfolio. Still, she pretended like the fifty in her compact did not exist. To spend it would have been admitting defeat.

Vera believed the Blackie films were only the beginning of her Big Time. The ratty bombshell role featured her name in the credits, but when she made the rounds, she felt the receptionists' cold stares attempting to drive her away. She thought of Alexis and Marion, who had moved home to live with their respective parents, the dozens of roommates who had come and gone. She had even typed out rules for the bathroom and kitchen and made new lessees sign an agreement before she allowed the landlord to rent to them. (She kept him in her thrall by summoning him to her apartment to check her plumbing. Ha, that's what he told the wife. He'd been a handsome man when young, she could tell, but all he had left was a hardy-and-hale technique that scarcely left her breathless.)

Vera had recently met an actor, Perry Mitchell. Such an encounter was not that unusual; she met actors all the time. Unlike the women she knew—self-sufficient and strong—actors seemed to crave attention like beautiful dogs. Thankfully Perry was different. He was actually good—excellent, in fact, a quality that spread to others in the cast. In a screen test, he had opened Vera up so much that, when she got a callback, he began to give her the rush. Though she didn't land the part, she was, at least, worthy of his company. She was no longer alone.

Perry took her to restaurants where waiters wore tuxedos, and they sat in ocher-lit booths with individual telephones. His hair was slick with a vanilla pomade, his eyebrows still black with pencil. Women, and not a few men, eyed him as they entered those establishments. Keeping the interest in her own apartment, she all but moved in with Perry, a very serviceable Bauhaus on La Cienega. The light streaming in four square windows was warm and cheerful. Perry kept her in stockings and lipstick and champagne and magazines, too.

"I've been offered a big part, I have to go to Yuma," he told her one night.

"Where's that?"

"The desert," he said. Perry wasn't much taller than she, but on the screen his figure always loomed large.

"Want some company?" she asked, intertwining her fingers with his.

He exhaled smoke from his cigarette. "If you can stand a month in all that heat," he said. "I've let a place for the duration."

On a dry hazy day, they followed a line of cars and trucks from the studio all the way to Arizona, with only a few stops to restore water to the radiators. When Vera wasn't roaming Yuma's dusty streets and peeping inside filmy shop windows, she was at home in a concrete bungalow, tidying up, making curtains from dishtowels, cooking meals that Perry often came home too late to eat. (She knew how shooting schedules went, or she would have been jealous of Malva Staves, his leading lady, another slick one right off the train.) Late into the night Vera did scenes with Perry. Compared to theater, film was a strange kind of performing. On stage, even in Wichita, you were kinetic, alive as lightning. On the set you were more like a stone, waiting to be thrown across a pond. You waited and waited and waited for the director. While you waited, you memorized your lines, the lines of your film lover, the lines of someone you might stand in for should she get killed. You played cards. You smoked your brains out. But since Vera was only visiting, she wasn't allowed on the set. And though she knew what Perry was going through, it didn't alleviate her boredom. She was meant to act, too. She believed it was why she had been born.

"I want to go back to Los Angeles," she finally told Perry one night.

He shook the hair out of his eyes, staring past her. "A bus leaves the depot every day at six," he said, lighting a Camel.

Vera glared at him, hoping he might disappear for a few seconds, so that she could think of a zingy comeback. But none was forthcoming.

Day after day she continued to help him rehearse, bring him lunch, submit to his feral desires (when his moment arrived, he went writhing wild if she gouged his back with her fingernails). Because Perry refused to use protection, she employed the ways of rhythm, something Alexis had taught her, for if he came at her, with his member at a sharp angle, she couldn't say no. It was, after all, a big reason she had made the trip.

"Perry," she told him one night, "I'm late, me and my little friend."

"Verie, the shoot's almost over. I'm headed for New York in a few days, and I've only booked a single."

She sat up in bed and gave him a good whack across the chest. When he didn't flinch, she began to laugh. Perry sat up, shook his

jowls like Moe, and turned his back to her. She climbed on and he carried her around the room, both of them laughing like hyenas before
sleeping in one another's arms through a short night. The next day,
when the picture was in the can, Vera hitched a ride to LA, and Perry
boarded the Super Chief to New York. He did not say good-bye, but
neither did she. She should have felt anger, but all she could muster was a deep sorrow that she kept hidden, stashed in the little cave
behind her liver until it was needed.

Though her figure was still relatively slim, it was as if the casting directors knew there was life inside her, knew from her vague expressions
that her mind was trying to make sense of it all. And so, finding herself
in such a tenuous position, Vera considered having it taken care of.
Girls were sent downtown all the time, to a disheveled midget they
called Doctor Dirty. His method was actually quite antiseptic. With his
buggy eyes roaming the ceiling, Doctor Dirty would stand above the
examining table on a stool. Wearing a thin rubber glove over his tiny
fist, which shoved its way inside a woman's womb, he would remove
her issue (usually quite early) as if snapping a grape from a vine. Vera
had once accompanied Marion, who rose from Dirty's table (squeezed
into some sort of a janitor's closet), acting as if she had only had a
molar pulled: she said she was slightly nauseated but headed back to
work.

Yet since conceiving, Vera had acquired a visceral desire to give
birth to her child. It surprised her, but she really wanted to experience
what it felt like to carry the baby to term. It might help her play a part
some day. More to the point, perhaps Perry would take her back if she
could call him and tell him she had had a boy. After the third month,
she wore blouses with the tail out and sat around with Lillian, watching
the matron check costumes in and out. But Lillian had become gruff
and aloof. "You keep your filthy hands off those nylons," she snapped
at Vera more than once, staring out through her toady cloud of smoke.
When Lillian finally disappeared for only a moment to speak with the
director, Vera slipped her hand into a jewelry box, grabbed a plain
gold band, and crept out of the building.

When she was down to her last dollar and nothing could hide the truth, Vera waited tables at a sad chrome diner at the far end of Sunset, to pay the rent, making sure that the ring gleamed in the eye of anyone who might wonder. "My husband's overseas," she declared more than once, though the war was over. "Merchant marines," she said, when one woman gave her the fisheye. After a few weeks, when she had enough cash, Vera waddled toward Union Station (she wasn't going to waste money on cab fare). Along the way, to rest, she would lean against a storefront and stare into windows, missing the merchandise entirely, seeing a noose around her neck instead. When she finally arrived at Union, she purchased her ticket. She went straight to the bathroom and pulled out her compact. Yes, it was still there. She would have a little nest egg; she wouldn't be forced to work right away. She smiled and ran a damp towel over face and reapplied rouge and powder. Her face was puffy, but she was beautiful, still.

On the train, through endless miles of the western landscape, miles and miles of nothing but stunted yellow grass and cactus and sage, Vera tried to think of a way she could have stayed. The rhythm of the train told her *no, no, there was nothing you could do, nothing you could do, nothing you could do.* She could no longer work, and she had no one to support her, and so she would return to Wichita. Going to Dr. Dirty would have been an easy choice but for one thing.

Over the phone one day, her mother had finally, in a rather brazen tone, revealed to her who "Mr. Miller" was, his advances, and how she had allowed her physical desires to *cloud her judgment.* Vera now snorted, looking out the window as they chugged up a stark, dry mountain in New Mexico. What was *judgment?* Reading past the present to see the future? Denying yourself pleasure to prevent pain? Dying so you could live? There was only one person who might understand her plight, one who could have easily flushed Vera down the toilet. She stared at the seat in front of her to keep from crying.

As the train chuffed into Wichita's Union Station amid dozens of parallel tracks, Vera pulled her collar around her neck, straightening the band on her finger; "gold" had begun to flake off one side, so she twirled it under. She almost felt sorry for Lillian, who would be held responsible for its disappearance. Vera was now so large that it hurt her to move about. She desired to stand up straight, but the child within seemed to be climbing up her spine and wrapping its tiny fingers around her throat. The cloth suitcase she carried loosely at her side contained precious little: her head shots, scripts she had toted around for auditions long since past, and some cosmetics she had lifted from the studio.

The March day was a foggy one, a gray haze that held the buildings, the trees, even the people, in its control. Funny how she hadn't missed that aroma, wheat dust and mold spores mixed with a cool desperation. During the years she had spent in California, everyone had seemed so optimistic, even amid war. She had come to associate the warm scent of oranges with dreams that the studio made come true. But she learned the hard way that in Hollywood there were no parts for desperate actors. If a director needed an expectant mother, Wardrobe put a fitted piece of rubber under the actress's dress. In utter defeat, Vera was returning, just a few blocks from her mother's home, and she strode the sidewalk along Douglas as if she had never left town, as if she were hoofing it home from a shift at the Miller. How simple life had been then, tripping along beneath elms and cottonwoods that, in places, met overhead in a canopy, with patches of irises and tulips growing between the walk and the curb. Showing up at noon for a long day of hawking tickets and popcorn, she had tested seat after seat to see which one offered her the best view. Maybe she could get her old job back; maybe she could move up to manager. When her mother opened the front door and saw her state, she fell to Vera's knees and cried with joy. "Oh, Vera, I knew you'd come home."

Velma bought Vera all the latest magazines, though the last thing she wanted to read about was the life she had left behind. Velma closed up her shop and came home each noon to make lunch for them both. She spent her evenings taking Vera out to various cafés and tea rooms. One night it was the Orpheum with its phony Spanish garden motif; the next the Miller with a fat girl in the ticket booth. They saw films that nearly crushed Vera with their familiarity. She had read for any number of them. She knew the words that were about to come out of an actress's mouth before she said them, and she knew she had enunciated them better during her reading. Such injustice made her angry, because she was not finished. Women in Hollywood had babies all the time. They slimmed down; they returned to work. No one ever knew. Not really, not unless the mags made an issue of it. For three months Velma treated Vera as an honored guest, and, of course, Vera didn't fully appreciate it. She knew she was using her mother, but what else was she to do?

A night in June, when Vera felt as if a large dog had crawled inside her to die, Velma rushed her to Wesley Hospital in her black Chevy coupe. As the doctor slid his cold stethoscope along her belly, she made some calculations. Grammy Viv, whose walnut-framed portrait hung in the upstairs hall, had been born in 1859. Her mother, Velma, in another oval frame a bit farther down the wall, had entered the world in 1900. Vera, in the next portrait, 1922. And now her babe, if it made it through alive, 1948. In more than one movie she had seen, months flew off the calendar to indicate the passage of time. That's how she felt, that the pages of her life were flying off at gale force. Before she knew it, her kid would be one, then five, ten, fifteen, twenty, and she would be an old woman. It made her sick to be part of that kind of parade. She was not meant for this *petit bourguignon*, as Perry had sneeringly referred to a life of regular hours and acceptable mores. Yeah, she was different, special.

At three in the morning, she began to contract violently. She screamed. Amid the hospital's broken hush, the doctor was called. In less than an hour, he appeared and examined the space between her splayed legs.

"The baby's breached," he told her. "We shall have to call upon our friend Caesar." His black hair was slicked down, and he frowned as he spoke.

"Christ, I'd rather die," Vera said, flailing her head.

"You don't mean that," Velma said, seizing her daughter's hand.

"Oh, don't I!"

But while the doctor nodded, glaring down at her through his thick glasses, he injected her with something that made the room tilt. Yes, the room was spinning like a film sequence indicating a character's dream. When she woke hours later to see a nurse holding a bundle of pink skin in her face, Vera knew what was real and stared outside into the gray afternoon. Perry, Perry, Perry. Velma finally held the baby in her arms.

"Daughter, you've got to take her, or she'll go hungry."

"I can't look," Vera said. "If I do, I'll never be able to stop."

"Yes," Velma said, looking outside where the light had faded. "It's true."

A woman in a stiff white uniform and winged cap took the girl from Velma's arms. "I'll just start her on her formula then," the nurse said.

Velma sat on her daughter's bed. "You could name her at least."

"Ma," Vera said, "I couldn't name a cat."

"You look so tired."

"Yeah, well, I've just been butchered like a goddamn hog."

"In my day the baby would've died. The mother, too."

Vera closed her eyes. "I only wish." She visualized her mother having died young, Vera smothering inside her mother's womb, dying inside, yet dying to fight her way out, to live the life she was destined to live, and it made her glad she had had the little thing. Like her, it would now have a chance. But in that second, a certain other vision made her feel quite exuberant, something neither Velma nor anyone else could see. The vision of leaving the baby behind, well, it rather lifted her spirits—like reading the call board that she won the part Bette Davis had tested for.

"Be back tomorrow, dear heart," Velma said. "I'm opening the shop early for my yearly sale. If I'm lucky I'll make half my yearly take."

"Yeah, you go on," Vera said, waving her hand, blowing her nose after her mother left. She sat on the edge of the bed and grimaced as she padded across the floor. Without all that extra weight, her balance was off. Instead of bracing her weight on the front of her feet, she felt it shift once again to her heels. But she was unaccustomed to it, and she felt for a moment as if she might fall backward. Then she envisioned her escape again, and she convinced herself that she felt fine. Closing the door to the clanks and smells of the hallway, she groaned as she learned to walk again, across the room to her bath where she lifted her gown before lowering herself to the toilet. She touched the bandage they had fastened over her wound. The nurses had also encircled her tightly with long pieces of gauze taped down with wide strips of adhesive. She peed and fell into a snooze, until the rim of the toilet began to press hard into her legs. She woke with a start and stood, stumbling into the room where her mother had left a new outfit, fresh from her shop.

Vera slipped on new lavender panties that were way too tight, as well as the rest of her ensemble: a snug lavender slip and bra, the dress of purple velvet that, when she zipped it up the side, kept her guts in place, the purple hat with a veil, dark purple heels and matching handbag. She supposed her mother had seen something similar to it on the cover of *Vogue* and copied it, but it was like trying to build your own Cadillac; people would know the difference. Snapping her fingers, she recalled another pair of silk hosiery she had lifted from Wardrobe and went to her bag. Kicking her shoes off, she gingerly pulled the beige stockings up her legs, smoothing them out, binding them down with a couple of garters. She transferred all her worldly goods into the purple bag and placed it on a metal chest of drawers. Above it hung a scratched tin mirror, but it was enough for Vera to stare at her transformation.

"Dear God."

Her brown roots were at least a half inch long, her platinum tresses dulled from days of abuse, but she did her best to comb the mess into place. She penciled her eyebrows and put on a layer of dark lipstick. Then she powdered her face and rouged her cheeks, slipping into her shoes. Last, she took the pillbox hat and nestled it on her head, arranging it over her hair. Now she looked like a citizen of the world. She would make damned sure that anyone who saw her in the hall believed she was just another visitor leaving for the night. She pulled the same gag she had seen in one of her films, building the bed up with pillows to make it look like she was turned on her side. With the dark veil pulled down and her shoulders thrown back, Vera squeaked open her door, prepared to play the role of her life. As it turned out, the hall was empty, and no one at the nurse's station gave her a glance as she escaped into the night.

On the street Vera walked in slow, measured steps down Douglas toward the station. Several cabs stopped, but she waved them away. She continued on past the street where Velma slept, scuffling toward her mother's business. There she stopped and stared. A purple ensemble like hers was featured on the stiff white mannequin in the window, and, for a moment she glanced at it, wishing she had died in childbirth rather than look like anyone else on the planet, particularly a stiff plaster figure featured in a second-rate shop. As she hurried on, she felt as if her intestines were going to spill onto the pavement, yet, with her arms crossed over her middle, she walked until the marble columns of Union Station came into view. Though it was far less imposing than the Union in Los Angeles, it was as if she had come upon the Pyramids after traveling miles and miles between the humps of a camel.

She tripped over a raised section of sidewalk, and, recovering with only a mild stab of pain, she crossed at a light. She stared at the large columns then, pulling at one of the heavy doors, stumbled into the station. Dabbing at the perspiration on her face, she thought of the fifty-dollar bill behind her compact mirror. It was enough to buy her fare. The question was, would it be a ticket to New York or the City of Angels? She waited behind two or three others, and by the time it was her turn, she had made up her mind. She opened her bag and pulled out her compact: round, gold-plated, but scratched like a radiator cap. From behind the mirror, she removed the fifty her mother had given her long ago. Many times she had unfolded it, tempted to spend the money on frocks, a dye job, a voyage to Hawaii, but she had withstood the torture of her own desires. After a short man with a red face sold her a ticket, Vera bought a couple of packs of Luckies and slumped on a bench. She had enough left to let a cheap room when she got off at Grand Central and packed the cash away. Using her purse as a pillow, Vera lay down and stared up into the rotunda, dimly lit at dawn with dull yellow lights. The words scripted there were as hard to read as her future, where she would pound the streets of Manhattan. Her life had become a series of scattered puzzle pieces, pieces she was desperately trying to put into place, to form a picture. And the missing piece, the one that would put it all together, seemed to be Perry.

Velma had insisted Vera not smoke until after the baby was born. But now she tapped out a Lucky Strike and lit it. In her dizziness she was transported, for a second, back to California, where she had bummed cigarettes from Bub and pilfered loot out from under Lillian's bulbous nose. With her head barely erect, she shuffled back to the ticket window, where the same man stared at her and then allowed her to exchange her ticket. She waddled to a stand and bought a hot dog, loading it with mustard, relish, and onions. She gobbled it down and sucked on the straw stuck in her Coca-Cola bottle. She burped and sighed and found a bench where she could nap until her train was called.

The next day she switched trains in Albuquerque. And after that, she curled up in her chair and slept the entire way, except for moments when, forgetting her wound, she would move the wrong way and suffer a short stab of pain. Though she dreamed on and off, confusing conversations that wafted about her with the words in her head, the dreams were happy: in one she was surrounded by babbling children, floating above a field of wheat in another, reading with a dark-headed man for a part. As the train pulled into her city of angels, Vera was mesmerized by the western sun, how it created an aura of light around a palm tree, and how, for a time, its radiance blinded her.

1970 — Violet Makes a Heroic Effort. "I got wind of the news," Violet said before the crowd. She had heard it coming out of her voice lesson on campus—her head full of French and German lyrics learned by rote—but still, the information had startled her. Her auburn hair, straight and halfway down her spine, blew about her face, and she threw her head back to shake them away. Poised on the bed of an old red pickup resting half on, half off the sidewalk, holding her speech in one hand, a bullhorn in the other, she spoke with a slight tremor in her voice. "As you know, officers at Fourth National have made plans to build a parking garage where the Miller has stood for almost fifty years."

The crowd booed, giving Violet confidence. She was most at home when on a stage, certainly not as herself—tall, gangly, shy, and awkward. Yes, today she was one of the Weathermen, a war protester, at the very least a spokesperson.

"When I saw the truth corroborated in the *Eagle*, I knew I had to join in to save this place." Her voice echoed across a small canyon of buildings, and her words might have been tinged with a bit of self-importance if it hadn't been for the hundreds gathered around. "I see before me fans of all ages—men and women who have worked at the Miller through the years. There are people from the historical society. The press. Thank you all for coming." As she spoke the protestors formed an orderly loop and passed back and forth under the marquee. Their movement created a whoosh that beat against the magnification of her voice. "My grandmother was a Millerette. She worked here on the opening night in 1922. She carried a leather stick and guided patrons to their seats. The way she described the whole deal, it was quite glamorous. Most of that glamour disappeared a long time ago, but it doesn't mean we have to tear down this wonderful building. Even if it's 1970, we can bring it back to life!"

Violet lowered her bullhorn and jumped down to stand in front of a big bulldozer. She was taller than her grandmother, heavier, and her feet hit the ground with a thud. The crowd came to her defense with another cheer, and she picked up a sign she had made and held it over her head. IF YOU LOVE MOVIES, YOU'LL SAVE THE MILLER. The words lacked the power she had wanted to convey, but she hadn't the cleverness to come up with something more dynamic—not on the fly, not as quickly as that disaster had descended upon them all. The bulldozer's engine was reduced to a rough idle, and its exhaust pipe released a vertical puff of black smoke.

The operator, a porky, bald man, jumped down. "You can't stay here," he said. His voice almost quivered; you could tell he wasn't accustomed to such interference. "If you don't move, I'll have to call the cops." He reached up into the cab and drew out a microphone connected to a curly black cord. "I have direct radio contact with my boss."

Violet threw her sign down and jumped once again onto the back of the pickup. Using the bullhorn, she said, "My whole family has worked at the Miller. I put myself through college working here. You can't tear it down now. Not without a fight."

The operator shook his head and spoke into his radio. You could hear a static-filled response, and the man backed up and drove the bulldozer south on Broadway. The small crowd cheered, and the sound soon faded as their feet shuffled on the pavement.

It seemed that most of Violet's dreams met with disappointment. Every show she was in, every *honor* she had received, seemed to have been tinged with some kind of flaw. The third-grade play, where she played a princess, fell apart the night of the performance when the prince vomited all over her. She'd played Lola in *Damn Yankees* at East High, and the local critic had said her voice cadenced itself like a frog with laryngitis. She had cultivated that throaty, sexy, voice and he hadn't appreciated it!

Realizing that they must organize further, protesters quickly agreed to meet Saturdays at the home of Gladys Gorges Harrell. "They called me Gorgeous Glad," she said now, announcing her address into the bullhorn.

At their next gathering, fifty some showed. A gruesome group of people sat on Gladys Harrell's white furniture and mingled among her many antiques, including Persian rugs upon which they trod like cattle. But you could feel a power in their presence, something that might move others out of their complacency concerning the Miller.

"You're so pretty, what with Velma's eyes, so dark, too," Gladys said to Violet, handing her a glass of punch.

Violet took a sip. "My mother sold tickets at the Miller, and I've been working there since I was sixteen."

"Yes, I heard you say," Gladys said, taking her arm. She pulled out an album of stark black-and-white photographs. There were shots of young women on the stairs, on the stage, behind the concession counter making popcorn. In one photograph, more than forty employees stood out front under the marquee. You could make out —*dolph Valentino.*

"Yes, that's Mama Vee," Violet said. Knowing that Gladys and her grandmother had worked together gave Violet a warm feeling, as if she'd just discovered a long lost relation.

"Always admired Velma's spunk," Gladys said. "I know what a burden life was for her. How is she, by the way?"

Violet looked at Gladys. Hers was not one of those faces dull with pity for a girl who had grown up without a father around the house. "Still working in her shop down on Douglas. Says she'll never retire."

Gladys smiled and said, "I'll bet some of that spunk got handed down. We need a young one like you. You want to help out with what they call the nitty-gritty?"

"What will it involve?"

"Oh, just most of your time till we get those so-and-sos at the bank to come to their senses." She grinned and Violet grinned back. "Such a beautiful complexion you have, too." Violet could feel herself blush. Mama Vee always made her play down her looks. *Vera and I both learned that a pretty face isn't enough.* It might have been a perfect face—straight nose, high cheekbones, smooth forehead—if it hadn't been for eyebrows that were just a tad too thick.

After their encounter Violet was busy night and day, fired by the kind of energy that only someone under twenty-five could muster. She typed letters to officials at City Hall. She occasionally cut classes at the university to demonstrate in front of the theater, sometimes having to fall out of line so she could enter and work her shift. On a spring evening, as she stood before a group of picketers, Violet recalled, for people she hardly knew, an earlier scene at the theater; maybe it would soften them, make them see how important the Miller was, even to the young.

"It happened only a few years ago," she began. "I was crazy about a boy named Miguel Montemayor, a nice boy who lived not far from Mama Vee and me."

Miguel, with black hair slicked down, had been the boy all the girls wanted to date. He'd had high cheekbones, skin like velvet, and black eyes that snapped at the suggestion of fun. Violet had known him since the sixth grade (he had dubbed her Nana's Girl), where they had surreptitiously passed answers under their desks until they were caught, but in three years he had burgeoned from a skinny worm into a figure of young manhood. He was president of the tennis club, sang in ninth-grade boys' glee club, and played football. The fact that he had lowered himself to recall Violet into his life drove her wild with competing feelings: one, that she was totally unworthy and two, that she was the hottest thing going at Alexander Junior High. For hours she would sit in front of the mirror of an antique vanity in the room that had belonged to her mother and comb the auburn hair she'd fashioned to look as much like Annette Funicello's as she could; more than one girl had asked her how she got it to look so shiny. (Mama Vee had bought her a bottle of White Rain conditioner, which she sprayed on during her daily bath but told no one of its powers.)

The October nights were turning cool, and Violet shivered in the open window of her bedroom as she dialed Miguel's number. The white sheers blew around her, caressing her skin like a lover's fingers.

"*Hola*," Miguel's mother said, calling him to the phone. Violet heard her say, *No hablan demasiado largo. Sí, sí, sí,* Miguel responded.

"You want to see *West Side Story* Friday night?" Violet said, shoving the curtain out of her way. She had checked the *Eagle*; the movie was playing three times daily, including 8:30. She added, nearly gasping for air, "It won ten Oscars, and it's probably going to close soon."

"*Who* is this?" Miguel said.

"Huh?" Violet said, and Miguel giggled the same way he had in the sixth grade.

"How're we going to get there, Nana's Girl? I still can't drive, can you?"

"I hadn't thought that far ahead."

"There might be a way," he said. "Robert Stanley and a bunch of kids are going. And at lunch yesterday, he said I could come along if I could find a date. He's throwing a party afterward."

"Wow, to think I almost didn't call."

"Yeah, his brother's got a big old hearse. It'll hold about ten of us."

"Sounds great, but . . . I'll have to meet you."

"Robert's going to stop at my house," Miguel said. "Be here at eight sharp."

The thought of misrepresenting the truth to Mama Vee made the hair on Violet's arms stand on end. She had never been successful at such an enterprise, but perhaps she would have to learn to be more convincing. She had been named Violet after her great grandmother, Vivian Violet Himmler Bernard—a sour-looking woman (in the upstairs hall, Violet passed the 1920s photo each time she went to the bathroom). Violet had been told a million times how the woman had been able to read Mama Vee's mind, no matter how hard she'd tried to trick her. Worst thing was that Mama Vee had inherited her ancestor's tendencies.

"Okay, see you tomorrow night," she said.

"*Ciao*, baby."

Violet hung up. *Ciao*. When she opened her door and returned the phone to its nook in the wall, Mama Vee stood perched on the stairway with her arms crossed.

"Something you'd like to share, little Missy?" she said, peering up at Violet over her half-moons studded with rhinestones. Because Mama Vee kept up with women's fashions and maintained her petite nature, she always seemed younger than she was.

"Well," Violet said, "I've never lied to you before. Guess I won't start now."

"A wise decision," she said, heading down the stairs. "I've just frosted a cake. You can spill your guts at the kitchen table."

After she had heard Violet's story, Mama Vee said, "I shall deliver you and Miguel, and that's that. You'll have plenty of time to date, once you're sixteen."

Violet felt her eyes pleading with Mama Vee, but whenever the woman insinuated herself into Violet's plans, she was helpless to change her mind. She was tough that way.

"You have to drop us off at Douglas, and we'll walk the rest of the way."

"Don't be ridiculous," Mama Vee said. "Might as well let you walk."

"Why can't I ever do what my friends do?" she asked. "They're not criminals, you know."

"All it takes is one mistake. Believe me, I know from personal experience."

Violet knew what she meant. "Yes, but do I have to pay for *her* mistakes?"

Mama Vee smacked Violet's head and smiled. "Most probably."

Outside the garage on Saturday night, Violet and Miguel stood and watched Mama Vee start her '55 Bel Air as it coughed up a cloud of smoke. A mechanic had told her she needed to keep it tuned up, but she claimed she didn't have the money. When it fell apart, she said, she would get a new car, which made even less sense to Violet. Velma put the car in reverse, and Violet and Miguel crawled in back and slid across the straw mat upholstery. Velma glanced over her shoulder. She had told Violet she had her mother's hair, the dark, narrow eyes of her crafty grandfather, and Velma's very own lips, which had flattened even more through the years. *What about my father, do I look like him?* she had asked as a small child. *I don't think we'll ever know,* Mama Vee had told her. *Vera never sent us a picture.* "Vera" was an endearment Violet's grandmother tossed around like "Preacher Adam" or "Aunt Tilde." Violet couldn't quite "see" any of those persons Mama Vee was talking about, but she had stared at pictures of Vera in the photo albums until the face was frozen in her mind forever.

"You know I worked opening night at the Miller, don't you?" Velma said.

"Yes, Mama Vee." Though Velma's stories of sacrifice were often tedious, Violet liked the ones she told about the Miller. Filled with a sad but lighthearted nostalgia, the stories intrigued Violet. Her grandmother had watched the construction, the raising of black and gold marble walls of the lobby, the brass handrails being installed, little escapades of workmen running up and down the double staircase, the narrow one that led to the third balcony. There were other narratives hidden in her grandmother's words, but she usually only went so far before her eyes widened and returned to the present.

Violet examined the back of her grandmother's head. The woman's hair was still blond, streaked evenly with strands of silver white and sprayed into a flip. She possessed a timeless quality, unlike Miguel's graying and wrinkled *abuela*, who sat and rocked with a tattered lace shawl pulled over her shoulders, a white mantilla heaped over her head. She felt, for a moment, that she was lucky, then Mama Vee began to drone over the facts again.

"Well, it was a grand building, what with those marble stairs . . . ."

"*Refreshingly Cool,*" Violet said, referring to the photograph Mama Vee had hung in the upstairs hallway. There her grandmother and the Millerettes posed under the bubbly marquee, all of them raising the cuffs of their shiny slacks to show a little ankle. The promotional slogan beamed over their heads in bright lights.

"You young people take air conditioning for granted, but in those days the Miller was the only cool place in town."

"The coolest," Violet said, and Miguel snickered.

"Hundreds of people lined up to spend a hot summer evening. Charlie Chaplin did his vaudeville act down there once. Will Rogers spoke to a packed house, and Eleanor Roosevelt talked about the New Deal. I didn't work there all that long," she added. "Had to find a real career, so's I could support a family."

She scanned the mirror, neither smiling nor frowning, as if she were searching for a wayward child. When she turned the corner at Broadway and stopped in front of the Miller, she put the car in park and whirled around to face them both.

"Call me when it's over, and so we're clear, you are never to get in a car with a teenage driver. Under no circumstances are you to consume alcohol, little Missy. And Miguel, I have your mother's number, too. Understand?" Mama Vee was, if nothing else, thorough.

"Ah, I live the life of a princess," Violet said.

"Don't get smart, or I'll turn this tub around and you and Miguel can do your smoochin' in my parlor."

Violet grimaced and opened the door, holding Miguel's hand as she stepped onto the curb. When Mama Vee lingered, Violet tapped on the window, and her grandmother slowly pulled away, leaving them standing in a mist of blue exhaust. The lobby was already packed, and, after paying for their tickets, they headed across the worn floral carpet to the main staircase. Anyone who was anyone at Alexander Junior High planned to meet in the third balcony. It would be a riot. As Violet held Miguel's hand and they climbed the broad double staircase to the mezzanine, Violet said, "I love it up there, it feels like you're leaning out over a cliff." Throughout her childhood, the only section she hadn't occupied was one of three box seats, but only because they had been blocked off. She wished she could have been sequestered in one of them with Miguel, together on a red velvet couch, curtains slightly drawn.

For weeks thoughts of being with Miguel were usurped only by the coming of *West Side Story*. In fact, pondering the musical helped to sidetrack Violet's desires a bit. She had bought the songbook from Jenkins, and on Mama Vee's upright accompanied herself on all of Maria's solos. And as soon as she had been able to get her hands on it, she had acquired the LP of the soundtrack, too. As she watched the film, Violet would know all the lyrics! The overture. The entr'acte. The closing strains. She couldn't wait. Miguel had teased her about her enthusiasm, but she had told him, "I'm going to be on that screen some day, you just watch. I'll be in musicals that haven't even been written yet." She felt he had looked at her differently after that, as if he might stick around to see if her prediction came true. When Violet had been awarded a solo in the ninth-grade program, Lila Cain had tapped Violet on the shoulder and called her a cunt licker. Violet had turned around and knocked out one of Lila's front teeth. Aghast, the teacher had seen to it that Violet was expelled and had taken the part away from her, but no one doubted Violet's strength after that, nor her seriousness. Especially not Lila Cain, who, even a month after Violet was readmitted to school cut her a wide berth as they passed one another in the hall outside the gym.

Miguel now guided her up the marble stairs, where the hollows of a million footsteps swallowed their shoes. What a fuss Mama Vee always made over the place, as if it were the Taj Mahal. All Violet could see were long dull scratches in the brass rails, dingy yellow light falling from fixtures with tiny white bulbs. As they climbed the winding narrow stairs, she sensed only a bit of remaining life in the wood that creaked under faded wool carpet. Moreover, the air seemed stale, like that of an old cave. The third balcony was almost full, and Miguel waved at his friends, who had saved them both a couple of spots on the front row. Every step they took creaked the bare wood. The sound gave her a chilling vertigo, made her feet tingle. What if the balcony caved in?

Miguel took Violet's hand, and she squeezed it. It gave her confidence, a quality she had been lacking as a child, when she realized she didn't have a father like her friends. Mama Vee had said her father was an actor, but that was all Violet knew. Every time she watched something on *Saturday Night at the Movies,* she wondered if the leading man was her father. Mama Vee had admonished her: "If you get pregnant, even by our precious Mr. Miguel, as much as I adore him, you'll either live with his family or you'll be on your own. I shall not raise another child. No matter how much I love you." Her eyes had sparkled with tears.

"Yes, Mama," she had said. And she knew Mama Vee spoke the truth. Violet owned a box of condoms . . . just in case. Yes, she had proudly marched into the pharmacist's and demanded to buy a box of Trojans. She didn't figure on getting pregnant. Not now, and furthermore, when she went to high school she planned to take birth control pills if she could procure them.

Violet sat with her arm around Miguel. Particularly amorous, she cuddled and put her head next to his and encountered a scent she had never smelled before, a sweet aroma that made her temperature rise. She stared up into the gilded dome as if there were an answer there.

Miguel spoke up. "Hey, earth to Violet, earth to Violet." She giggled. "Here comes Robert."

Robert Stanley was student council president, a kid with slicked-back hair that made him seem like an Elvis midget. "Sorry your granny wouldn't let you ride with us, but you can still come by the house after the movie. It'll be over by ten."

During her confession Violet had also asked Mama Vee if she could attend Robert's party. "With no chaperones? You're some kind of crazy, Missy, if you think you're going to carry on like that." In Violet's mind her grandmother was going too far, but Violet could never seem to muster the power to overcome her will.

"The movie's not over till late," Violet argued. "I called the box office."

"Look, Violet, the party has to end by midnight, before my parents get home," Robert said. "See you there, or see you bare." And Robert left them to muddle it over.

"We *have* to go," Miguel said, taking Violet's arm.

Violet shrugged. "You heard what Mama Vee said."

"If you don't go to that party with me, I'll find another girl."

"Miguel," Violet said sweetly, touching his arm in hopes that it would quash his threat. "Did you know that dome up there was originally lit up like a rainbow? Mama Vee says the curtains shimmered like diamonds. There even used to be these huge chandeliers." Most of the large fixtures had been replaced with cheap white globes, ones like you saw in school hallways.

"This place is a wreck," Miguel said, looking over the crowd below. "They should tear it down before it falls down."

"Maybe, but this is where I want my movie to be shown when I make it big," Violet said, squeezing his hand. He looked at her and rolled his eyes. "I'm going to be an usher as soon as I turn sixteen."

"I'm going to work at McDonald's," Miguel declared, "so I can eat free." Then he laughed.

For a second Violet felt the way she always did when someone (particularly a male) debased her. She was big enough, yes, she could have tossed his scrawny carcass over the side, but then she remembered what had happened to her when she knocked someone's tooth out. Retribution always seemed to backfire on her.

As the lights went down and Violet's anger diminished, the overture began, and she felt like jumping up and singing. Through large speakers along the wall and behind the curtain, the overture blared out the melodies she had committed to memory, and, as flecks in the screen flitted before her eyes, she sank into her chair and squeezed Miguel's hand. The lights came down all the way, and Miguel squeezed back. His fingers were thick but smooth, and Violet forgave him. She watched the screen fade from one abstract pastel panel to the next, as the orchestra modulated from song to song. On the last chord, the screen transformed itself into the New York skyline.

As a child Violet had decided she was going to succeed in show business, where both her mother and grandmother had petered out. She had calculated that the mother who had abandoned Violet was about the same age as Donna Reed, and she sometimes dreamed Vera would get her own show on CBS, yes, *The Vera Bernard Hour,* and that she would insist on having Violet portray her daughter. She was certainly capable of following in her footsteps. She had studied piano since she was four and tap since she was eight, and had recently begun voice; Mama Vee had insisted, almost as if it had been she receiving the benefit. At the upright Violet had rehearsed "Tonight" so many times it came to her as easily as a nursery rhyme. And her voice would fill the room as she hit the last note, overpowering the one dubbed over Natalie Wood's, which, she believed, was breathy and tight as a drum. Her eyes began to follow the action on the screen as if it were she up there.

"J-E-T-S" is chalked onto the asphalt in big white letters, and it is as if you are viewing the scene from a helicopter. The Jets start to fight the Sharks; only it is choreographed into a dance, like a jazz routine Violet learned at the studio. She imagines it is she with the twitching butt dancing across the screen, attracting attention of all the boys, but especially Miguel. No one will get into trouble, if they keep dancing.

"Why don't they fight like men," came a voice down the row. It was David Kane, quarterback, and the other guys laughed. His girlfriend went *Shhh.*

On screen Tony begins to sing "Something's Coming." Violet often attributed a personal kind of meaning to the lyrics of show tunes. Unlike Mama Vee's church hymns, theatrical songs could guide and predict Violet's life. Something *was* coming, even if she couldn't see it.

"That Tony sure is cute," Violet whispered. As the two gangs are conned by the police into attending a function together, they dance something like a pavane Violet learned in class.

Everyone in the balcony seemed to be sitting on springs, whispering, waiting for the action to pick up, but Violet ignored them. Her world was up on the screen.

Tony and Maria "dance" in their minds because neither family will allow them to see one another. And Violet now had to admit that the movie dragged. She wanted the characters to get on with it.

"Fags," she could hear Robert's voice say, as three Puerto Rican guys "dance" together, though they are really just mimicking their girlfriends. Some other guys snickered, and it was tempting to shush them. After the Officer Krupke song and dance, Maria sings "I Feel Pretty." A girl—a large girl with a big voice—had used that song in the Alexander Junior High talent show, and it had tainted the lyrics for Violet.

"Hey, we're getting out of here," came a voice over their backs. It was Robert. "My brother's circling the block."

"Come on, it'll be fun," Miguel whispered, squeezing Violet's hand. "Robert's going to have beer and everything."

"If you want a ride to the party, you got to come now," Robert said. "We don't have room for all these kids." Some of Violet's schoolmates stood and began to follow Robert out as if he were a magic piper.

"No," Violet said, taking Miguel's hand. "We have to wait for Mama Vee."

"Nana's Girl, if we don't leave now, I'm going to drop you like a hot tortilla," Miguel said.

Violet stood as if she were wobbling on someone else's legs, and, looking over her shoulder at the screen, longed with all her heart to remain behind. She wasn't crazy about riding home with her grandmother, but she did want to see the end of the movie; she had been waiting for weeks. She stood at the exit until Miguel finally grabbed her hand and their feet pummeled the stairs, past the mezzanine, to the lobby. Having left that other world abruptly, Violet pulled away.

"I have to use the restroom," she said, and she took off toward the basement. Maybe when she was through, the crowd would have gone, and she and Miguel could sneak back to the balcony—maybe he would still be standing by the life-sized cutout of Natalie Wood running with her arm extended. Or maybe Miguel would leave her behind. Scooting down the stairs, she looked over her shoulder as Miguel began to talk with some other boys. He was quite handsome, her *Tony*.

In the restroom, there were a million other girls, mostly from Alexander, milling around, some waiting for an empty stall, but mostly smoking and fixing their hair. They laughed and joked as Violet stepped into one at the end of the row and sat down to relieve herself. At first she thought it was only cigarette smoke, but when there was a loud whoosh and a series of raucous screams, the place cleared out fast. Violet felt a great heat and emerged from the stall.

"I know what I'm doing, I've been burning shit down since I was seven."

Robert Stanley, the shrimp, stood shielding his face from the heat. "If you don't get out of here, you're going to go up in smoke, just like this old firetrap." He laughed and dove for the door.

"You're an idiot!" she shrieked after him. Flames were now licking the ceiling, shooting out in all directions, and Violet choked. As if the intense heat were a figment of her imagination, she leaped through the inferno and flung herself through the door into the hall. She could smell singed cotton, the stench of burnt hair. At the bottom of the stairs, Robert stood alone, bent at the waist, laughing at her.

"Get out, Meez Bernard-o, while you still can."

"No, you get out," Violet said, "before I kill you." Flames licked the edges of the bathroom door, and Violet realized girls weren't as weak as people thought. As she reached for the fire alarm, the red box with a silver handle, Robert rushed up and grabbed her throat from behind, his squat body falling against her back.

"I started this fire," Robert said, "and there's nothing you can do about it."

Violet pictured the guy who was a full head shorter than she and reached around to grab his jacket, but she couldn't get hold of anything. She then kicked her foot backward, raking it upward, and heard Robert cry out. Violet whirled and kicked his groin again, and the kid fell against the stairs.

"You—bitch," Robert groaned.

On the wall behind a glassed-in door of red, there hung a long fire hose coiled into a neat circle. Thoughts had never come so clearly to Violet, and she pulled the fire alarm, breaking the glass on the door with her elbow. She realized she would have to unroll the thick, heavy hose entirely before the water would flow. She kept pulling, but she could get it only partly unfurled. She could hear the roar of the fire, feel its heat about to destroy the door. She could hear a series of thudding steps, and she turned around to see Miguel. He had the most earnest look on his face. Together, without a word, they managed to free the long canvas hose. When they were finished, they stood holding the big nozzle and cranked the huge faucet to the left. Nothing happened, but before Violet realized it, the hose had jerked itself out of their hands. Squealing, she and Miguel stomped on it as if it were a riotous snake. Water shot across the hall in a great thrust of power, and they kept working their hands up the hose until they could grab hold of the brass nozzle. Just then she heard the tiny wail of sirens outside, and the power of the spray blew open what was left of the door. Holding the hose under her arm, and with Miguel directly behind her, Violet shot water at the fire, which had climbed up the oaken walls. She systematically kept imposing the rush of water on the fire until it began to diminish. She couldn't believe how, in places, fire kept creeping back to life. She coughed as she sprayed the little tongues of flame.

When firemen tramped down the stairs with their own hoses, Violet was almost sad. She had nearly become a hero. Firemen turned two more hoses on the flames, and in a little while the basement was a cave of soot and dripping water, smelling of petroleum that lingered like a bad cologne. A fireman thanked them and took the hose; he told them they should go outside. When Violet and Miguel emerged, they saw that the entire crowd had been evacuated and made to stand clear of the Miller. Miguel rushed up to Violet. "I thought you'd gone loco," he said. "But when I saw what you were doing, I couldn't just leave you there to fight alone." She threw herself into his arms and waited for Mama Vee to pick them up.

Later, when Violet told her grandmother who had started the fire, she said, "Ridiculous boy. Nothing could destroy the Miller."

"So you see, my friends, the only damage the Miller incurred, as it turned out, was to the women's bathroom, some charring along the

walls and baseboards, a testament to its great strength and beauty.
Management never remodeled, never replaced the oak, but we can
do it now." With the aid of her bullhorn, Violet's voice rang across
Broadway between the Miller and the Orpheum. The small but dedi-
cated crowd had hung around, shoulders hunched over like people
gathered for the burial of someone beloved.

"At sixteen I started as an usher here at the Miller. By the time I went
to college, I'd worked my way up to manager and put myself through
school. I often worked till midnight, studied, and went to classes in the
morning, so I could nap a little in the afternoons. This last spring my
sorority sisters and I went to see *The Happy Ending*. It wasn't much more
than a soap opera, but on that huge screen, it seemed like a saga. Jean
Simmons, John Forsythe, they seemed like real people." She cleared
her throat. "All the new theaters in town have screens the size of bed
sheets. Is that how we want to see movies?" *No,* the crowd yelled. "We
have to save the Miller, we just have to. Our group has collected over
seven thousand dollars, but we need a great deal more. Wood has to be
replaced and varnished. Marble steps have to be repaired. The brass
handrails are scratched, hanging by a single screw in places. A few surviving chandeliers are shorting out, and the air conditioning is nearly
shot." She paused again, looking out over the crowd. "Underneath the
shabbiness exists an elegance, and we must do everything we can to
save it." Violet paused. "As you know, Fourth National Bank is making
plans to demolish the Miller and put in a parking garage. Yes, it will
hold hundreds of cars, but is that what we want to do with this bit of
history?" *No!* "Can't they build it one block over?" *Yes.* Violet closed to
great applause, and people passed around hats.

In all, the committee collected less than a thousand dollars, which
bought them a few more weeks of legal help. They held additional
demonstrations until only a few weary people showed up. Weeks
passed, quiet meetings took place at the bank, behind closed doors at
city hall, and then the fight with Fourth National was over. The Miller
would be demolished, and Violet went home to cry with Mama Vee.
They swapped stories until it was time to go to bed, where Violet didn't
sleep a wink all night.

Because of fruitless appeals, the demolition failed to occur until a couple of years later, just as Violet was finishing her graduate work in theater. For months Violet would make a daily trek by the scene of demolition. Each day she would photograph the Miller, recording its demise. It had taken a long time to build, she mused, and the way things were going, it would take a long time to destroy.

Violet would sit across the street, watching, as the big ball struck the building repeatedly, unable to fell thick walls with one blow; it would take several hits just to knock down one portion. She would later watch as Miller devotees were allowed to carry off pieces of carpet, blocks of marble. Light fixtures. It was as if *her* home was being torn down. It was true. Velma Bernard had scurried up the main staircase opening night. Violet's mother Vera had sat in the ticket cage *and* appeared onscreen as a loudmouthed blonde in a detective series. And she, Violet Bernard, had worked her way through school. It was wrong what those people were doing. Buildings got old and needed repair, but they didn't have to be destroyed. They could be revitalized. Unlike human beings, they could continue on forever.

Yet Violet, too, bought a chunk of marble, one about the size of a grave marker. She and a friend carried it to her car, and she stored it away. Years later, when Mama Vee died, in 1986, Violet placed it at the head of her plot, inscribed with the following words: *Velma Agnes Bernard, Millerette Forever.*

Velma Bernard left her granddaughter a bit of money, and with it Violet made her first jet flight to LA. Taking a shabby stucco bungalow near Grauman's, she spent months making daily trips to the library and city hall. But when she had searched the city archives for anything—voter registration, utility records, births and deaths—it was as if her mother, Vera Bernard, had walked into the Pacific and simply disappeared.

She spent evenings going to movies. She could see cinema in LA that she would never see in Wichita: foreign films, independent films, classics. She went to the Los Angeles Museum often enough to witness two show changes. She took trips down to various beaches, tanning her skin darker than she could get it in Kansas. One day, she wasn't sure why, for there was no logical reason for her to do so, Violet walked until she located a public cemetery downtown. There she strolled among yellowing palm fronds, dusty aisles. She read one granite marker after another, until she was dizzy. Then she spied the large granite mausoleum and pushed open a heavy door labeled *Paupers' Palace*. The inside was illuminated with skylights only, but Violet persevered, reading every row across, then down. When she saw the name, she drew her hand to her mouth, as if it couldn't be true. This couldn't be her mother's final stopping place: *Vera Bernard, d. 1950*. Violet would have been only two! She didn't believe in God, not like Mama Vee, but what was the force that had guided her unimpeded, to find her mother at last, nothing more than a pile of ash in a drawer?

The city her mother had so adored, her grandmother, too, became a depressing place to Violet. There were a thousand people gathered everywhere where she wanted to be, whether it was the grocery, the queue for a film's opening, even the gym. In spite of her own ambitions, she didn't feel comfortable there, not as she had always believed she would. Often a brown smog enshrouded the city like a dingy veil, and on one of those days Violet packed her bags and flew out of LAX. Connecting in Albuquerque, she boarded a plane that bounced through fluffy clouds at Mid-Continent Airport and landed in Wichita.

Violet later ventured by 115 N. Broadway in her grandmother's old Impala—the first time since the Miller had been razed—and viewed the parking ramp that had been erected. She did a double-take to make sure that the cylindrical concrete edifice wasn't a blunder of her imagination. In a fog she drove back to the house she had inherited from Mama Vee and began to throw open windows. She trudged up the stairs. In the hallway where the arrangement of photographs had never been changed, she stared at the one of her grandmother posed with the Millerettes—at young women's eyes shining with hope, the daring bit of ankle they displayed, the gaiety of lights on the marquee. And Violet wept like a girl who had lost her best friend. She then wiped her eyes and stared some more. In the eternal vision of the photograph, Velma's gabardine still looked pressed, her wavy hair glorious.

Her gardenia still shone from that opening night, the petals open and fully fragrant with possibility.

The author gratefully acknowledges the following sources.

"The Acme of Art and Science Combined." *Wichita Beacon*, Miller Theater section, 30 April 1922, p. 3.

Hays, Jean. "Memories . . . The Miller Still Lives; Ex-Employees, Others Still Angry at Demise of Landmark Theater." *Wichita Eagle-Beacon*, 22 June 1982, p. 6-7Z.

Tanner, Beccy. "Miller Theater Was a Showcase: People Dressed Up to Attend Movies." *Wichita Eagle*, 11 July 1991, city ed., p. 7N.

MEN AT SEA

As a boy I crossed the Atlantic with my uncle on the SS *Constitution*, where we shared an expensive but cramped cabin on the Sun Deck. Bound for Genoa, the ship would be our home for nearly a week. With my bed unfolding from the wall and my uncle's sofa flattening to a twin, there existed at night a scant aisle through which we could pass to the tiny deco bath. I had traveled with Uncle T. once before, but not on a luxurious ship like this one. I thought he must surely be one of the richest men in the world. Uncle's colognes and talcs crowded the small vanity inside the stateroom door, while my toy soldiers and coloring books littered the floor. Amid the combatants of this tiny war were strewn articles that belonged to both of us: a black pair of my uncle's swim trunks, an oxblood sandal of mine that lay capsized with little soldiers clambering up the heel. I certainly was not tidy, but Uncle T. made a show; he always made a show of being impeccable.

"Dane Paul Adriane," my uncle said the first morning out, "I'm going to break my fucking neck if you don't keep these little men tucked away in your bed."

"No room," I said, folding the bed into the wall and watching the little men fall out the side. "See!" I said. And my uncle put his hands to his cheeks in mock perplexity.

Over his head my uncle spritzed some Pino Sylvestre, a tonic used to augment a physical plant that included biceps hard as baguettes, a stomach so flat it was unnatural, and thighs as plump as elephant legs. At least they appeared that way to me, a thin and retiring child who turned ten that summer of 1958. I primped in each mirror I passed, admiring my sunglasses with gold glitter embedded in plastic, tossing my head with the auburn hair my uncle had paid to have shaped into a Fabian cut the minute we left the slip in New York. To please my uncle I kept it neat, combing the ducktails to perfection, but I thought I looked rather silly.

Following a late lunch, Uncle said he wished to take a nap. I then collected my favorite soldiers, a general and a private, and Theodore Rex Adriane shooed me out the door to the ship's library. As a voracious reader, I had perused every book about dinosaurs I could find in Dallas, and I had committed to memory all the salient facts of the major species. In the darkly paneled room I located some books with information that was new to me.

On the second day out, I thought I was being clever when I asked, "Uncle T. Rex, are you a meat-eater, too?"

"Oops, you caught me," he said, planting his hands on his hips. His gesture created a secret that thrilled me, even if I didn't yet know what it was. When he hugged me, I squealed and squirmed out of his grasp.

I'm positive T. Rex Adriane, who also wore his hair in a ducktail, was probably the first in America to have had blond highlights struck into his warm brown locks. They grew whiter each day we were at sea, and, against the skin that became darker, he appeared every bit as handsome as Cary Grant, who starred in the film *An Affair to Remember.* Because it had been shot on board the *Constitution,* the movie showed continuously in one of the ship's four theaters, and we viewed it several times that crossing. (Uncle T. Rex viewed it; I usually went to sleep against his shoulder, awakened by his sniffling. It wasn't until years later that I watched it on cable, finding it quaint and sophisticated but hardly worth a tear.) With a forest of hair on his chest, which he showcased beneath a voile shirt, Uncle T. Rex regaled the captain's party with many a charming tale. Everyone at table laughed as he spoke of his prep school days in North Dallas, his years as a Southern Methodist Kappa Alpha (a fraternity that initiated him by making him streak—before it was called that—along Central Expressway between Mockingbird and Yale), graduate school in New York. These tales were told with raised eyebrows and made no sense to me, partly because he used the adult shorthand that one employs around little pitchers, but partly because I had no understanding of how much he adored men and what he would do to procure the one he desired.

In the afternoons Uncle T. Rex would leave the ship's newspaper protruding from beneath the door, and as long as it was there, I was not to enter. It didn't matter. I had a grand time making acquaintances of my own. Schoolboys engaged me in shuffleboard or card games like Eights or Concentration; two elderly men indulged me in rounds of Chinese checkers. They attempted to *court* my uncle, but though he was polite, Uncle T. Rex never allowed himself to be seen with them if he could help it. *Agents of death,* he would mutter.

And there was a woman, a Mrs. Boatwright of Newport. Though I think her name was Winifred, she always introduced herself as Mrs. Boatwright. Her husband was deceased, yet she still wore a gold band next to a dainty solitaire. At dinner I watched her eat. I'd never seen a person who was so adept at using a knife. It was almost menacing to see her slice off a thin piece of prime rib and hold it near her tongue, which shot out like a lizard's to grasp its many gifts. She walked with an ivory cane, though I detected no limp. And sometimes she stood behind me during a game of Chinese checkers, where she rested her hands on my shoulders. I was intoxicated by her perfume, which seemed to emit the scent of a new rose.

"That may not be the move you wish to make," she would say, as I picked up a tiny white marble. How she knew which direction I was going, I never figured out, but I would change my play and win the game against one of the elderlies. "That's my boy," she'd say. "See you at dinner, love."

Then she would move out on deck to share tea with her three sisters, all spinsters (she had no problem saying when they were absent). I think Mrs. Boatwright might have adopted me if she could. She and her sisters made this trip to Italy every year, and while the sisters ignored me like death, Mrs. Boatwright fussed over my shoes, my clothes, my hair as if I were a little doll. I liked it. My own mother seldom demonstrated affection in that manner. On the second night out, Mrs. Boatwright was placed in an open spot at our table next to Captain Strombley, far from her sisters, whom you could see complaining bitterly across the room. If, on occasion, she wasn't seated adjacent to the captain, she would sit next to me and give me pointers on how to wield a knife as skillfully as she. Her hair was totally white, but something in her eyes made her seem far younger. A look of savagery perhaps.

In spite of this attention, I was often left to my own devices, feeling as if I were one of those ghosts that existed on television, like *Topper*, who wandered in and out of polite company without being detected. Because I was dressed in the finery my uncle had purchased for me—an ecru linen jacket with matching shorts and long white socks, and my oxblood sandals—no one suspected my mother was the widow of T. Rex's brother. She waitressed six nights a week to raise my sister and me in a tiny clapboard dwelling west of Dallas Love Field, a house Uncle T. had bought for us when my father died. Mother was a sad person, as if she'd been born that way and none of us would ever be able to cheer her up. Although I missed her, I didn't miss her melancholy.

In my wanderings I happened upon one of the ship's many bars. It was a dark, cozy sort of cave, and I could hear someone playing the piano quite proficiently, but it was not classical music like I studied at home. It had the edge of jazz, combined with curlicues of arpeggios that the church pianist used during the hymns. I stepped inside, where my eyes became accustomed to the darkness, and sat down. A rotund man who sat like a blob of Jell-O on the piano bench was playing "Beyond the Sea," one of my favorite songs, tinkling his way up and down the entire keyboard quite entertainingly. When he stopped, he spotted me and struggled over. He really was quite large.

"You shouldn't be in here," he huffed, sitting across from me, wheezing hard and wiping his brow with a well-worn handkerchief. "But since you are, can I get you something to drink, like a Coca-Cola or root beer?"

"No, thank you," I said. "Would you mind if I played that piano?"

My teacher had only a spinet in her tiny apartment, and at home I practiced on a paper keyboard. My mother wanted to buy me a real instrument, but she couldn't afford it. And even though Uncle T. had offered to secure one for me, my mother adamantly refused. *You've done enough for us, Rex, thank you,* she would say.

"Not at all," the man said, guiding me over to the long, white concert grand. I sat on the bench, and, barely able to contain my excitement, played some Chopin. It was the simplest of pieces, one of two preludes I'd learned, Opus 28, I believe. My fingers remembered where they should go, even though it was a different instrument, and I played the minor chords as if I'd been born knowing them. The piano emitted deep, rich tones, like a big cat purring, and, since I hadn't played for weeks, I felt as if something dormant had been unleashed. I held the last chord with the pedal and finally released my fingers.

"Very nice," the big man said, popping a cracker with some cheese into his mouth. "How long have you played?" Little crumbs spewed out of his mouth.

"A couple of years," I said, running my hands over the keys that had been warmed by the mingled oils of our hands.

"My goodness, Chopin after only two years, but I'm not surprised. Look at those hands. You have such long fingers for a boy your age."

"That's what my teacher says."

"I just spotted my boss. I'd better escort you out," he said. "Come back sometime. I'll teach you a song."

"Okay," I said, and skipped out the door. Playing always left me happy.

On the afternoon of the third day, as I had every afternoon, I put on my trunks and found the pool. The sky was clear and the sun warmed my skin, but it wasn't really hot like a summer day in Dallas, as the air at sea remained crisp. I clung to the side of the pool as Olympic hopefuls swam lap after lap, until one muscle-bound god began holding me afloat like a toy, instructing me in the finer points of the backstroke. His arms felt strong, held beneath me like a hammock. For a few moments, I gazed into this young man's blue eyes and wished he were my daddy, so strong and capable, so warm and available. To entrust my life to these hands seemed like the most natural thing in the world, until he released me to the bottom of the pool. I was not frightened down there; I knew how to get back to the top, but for a few seconds I stroked the floor of the pool as if I were one of those mermaid dancers in Florida, as if it were my home. Then as I spluttered to the surface, the swimmer grinned and told me to keep practicing. I shoved water in his face and swam for the ladder, ignoring his laugh. At that moment my uncle opened a gate and came onto the pool deck. I scrambled out of the water and to his side, shivering with a thick towel draped over my shoulders. He handed me my sunglasses, and, putting them on, I grimaced at the young man, who watched us with a certain curiosity. From a highly varnished chaise, Uncle T. Rex returned the gaze of the one who had let me sink and purred his drink order to a steward.

"That man tried to drown me," I said, pointing.

"Are you sure?" Uncle asked, not perturbed in the least.

"Well, he did let go of me, and I sank to the bottom."

"Sorry about that," the young man said, splashing over to the side of the pool and resting his chin on his crossed arms, drops of water dangling from his eyelashes. When my uncle failed to strike up a conversation, the young man swam away, but I sensed a certain agitation on the part of my uncle, as if I'd deprived him of something.

"Once I walked around in Margaret's plastic shoes, the ones with the silver straps she got for Christmas, and I broke the heel off. No matter how hard I tried, I couldn't get the little nails in the heel to match up with the little holes in the sole."

"*Whatever* made you think of that?" Uncle T. Rex said, sipping his gin and tonic, continuing to eye the man in the pool, as if he were a cat patiently waiting to pounce. I could almost see his tail bang the side of his chaise.

"No reason." I stroked the hair on my uncle's arm, and he patted my hand.

My father, who once shook my hand because I had made ten free throws in a row, was now a faint memory. *Put her there, little buddy,* he'd said. The next day I could make only two shots of fifty, and he lost interest. A year later he was massacred in a spectacular accident on the Dallas Central Expressway, and, at that point, *I* lost interest.

When strangers saw us, they often thought that Uncle T. was my father, but to me, he occupied a class by himself. He'd always seemed to possess a great deal of money, something my father, uneducated and unambitious, could not have claimed. When I would visit Uncle, staying in the guest room of his penthouse atop one of the earliest high-rises in Dallas, he seemed to be a man of leisure, for he always took time off from his design firm to be with me. Uncle's houseboy would arrive at nine and stay until four, and, unlike many servants who were treated by the rich as if they were robots (my uncle told me), Juan was accorded a dignified respect. In turn Juan *slaved* to keep the place luminous, as if it were a scene from *Imitation of Life* (another trashy love film my uncle adored). If Juan reached a point where he didn't know what to do, he would ask Uncle T., who would always find one more chore. Under ordinary circumstances, my uncle worked long hours. He made a great deal of money, yes, but unlike his clients, who had inherited vast buckets of it, he knew from which client he had earned every penny, and he courted them all like royalty. Each crystal vase, each exotic rug represented great sacrifices of time and effort— sometimes hours on the phone convincing a client to accept a certain color scheme. And yet years later I believe the man could have lived on far less and been just as happy—as long as he was in the company of the right man.

The fourth day out, black clouds engulfed the sky, and the ocean, if you could bear to look, became this series of rolling mountains. It seemed to me, as I stood at a large window on the promenade deck, that the ship climbed each one and then plummeted downward and rose, over and over again. In spite of her sheer bulk, the *Constitution* rocked from front to back, rolled from side to side. Uncle T. Rex spent the day prone on his studio bed or in close communion with our tiny toilet. Seasick pills were ineffectual, and meals in the bowels of the ship out of the question.

"How do you feel, Dane?" he mumbled into his pillow.

"Fine." I lay on the carpet, coloring within the lines of a picture of the *Constitution.* I had decided the ship should be lavender, and I was almost bored with it.

"You lucky thing," Uncle T. said. "I wish I had your fortitude, your constitution."

"What's that?"

"I mean that you're the strong one," he said, moaning as the *Constitution* shuddered. I could hear its steel beams screech deep within. "You should go out, since I'm sick as sin, and do what you wish. Live a little."

"Like what?" I said, feeling my tongue lodged at the corner of my mouth as I colored the ocean a dark blue and went back over it with black.

"I don't know, but I'm sure if you approached one of the stewards, he'd be more than happy to help you."

"Am I bothering you?" I asked, finishing my ocean.

"Ah, little Dane, you're so funny sometimes." In a few minutes he was snoring, and I grabbed a navy windbreaker and locked the door behind me.

Trying to swim or play shuffleboard seemed futile, so I climbed and descended the corridors that made me feel like I was in a funhouse. As the ship tilted, I would run headlong downhill, and, as it pointed the opposite direction, I climbed upward. I knew I could read in almost any position, uphill or down, because I did it at home all the time, so I headed for the library.

Upon entering that cozy room, I realized I had become weary of dinosaurs. Once you had memorized the various species and all their vital statistics, the information either became repetitious or too difficult. Some of the books jiggled side to side, but thick glassed cases were snapped tight to keep the volumes from tumbling to the floor. I scanned the nonfiction section and found several titles on the *Titanic.* I carried them to a smooth leather chair that engulfed me.

This interest in a major disaster came to me naturally, since my father had perished in one where his car was split in two by a large truck. Mother didn't realize it, but I had perused every clipping on his death, staring over and over again at the UPI photo of my father's bare leg dangling from the wreckage. But also an article in *Reader's Digest* about the *Hindenburg* had fascinated me for months, that fiery skeleton falling to earth like a crumbling cucumber. And when the *Andrea Doria* had gone down a couple of years before, I devoured everything I could find. It gave me a perverse thrill to think that a famous actress like Ruth Roman had been aboard that ship. The idea of extraordinary people (if the rich were extraordinary) fighting against extraordinary odds, and some of them surviving, captivated me. Or, as in the case of the *Titanic*, hundreds of steerage poor perishing at sea made me wonder what I would do if faced with impending death.

I turned the pages of a large book with cutaway diagrams and photographs. I tried to read the text but didn't understand a lot of the technical language, so I studied the pictures. How large the shell of that ship looked next to the hundreds of tiny men who assembled her with nuts and bolts! The splash it must have made when put to sea! I released a great sigh as my chair seemed to slide a bit with the ship's lurch.

"My grandmother was aboard that ship," came a voice over my shoulder.

I looked up. It was Randall. He and his sister dined at our table, too. Mrs. Boatwright and he sometimes exchanged terse comments, which always seemed to be about manners or movies or how good or bad the weather was. He quickly sat on the ottoman, nudging his legs between mine. I couldn't take my eye off the large pimple in the center of his forehead, a dried clot of blood that brought to mind an Indian princess with a red jewel embedded in her skin.

"Hello, Master Adriane," he said. My legs fitted like teeth of geared wheels between Randall's knees, which he didn't seem to mind. I watched him worry that pimple with his finger, staining the tip of his fingernail with blood before sticking it in his mouth. "Enjoying this book, are you?"

"Oh, yes," I said. Rather formally Randall extended his hand, still damp with saliva. He didn't squeeze mine, which I found nice, and we shook hands.

"Grandma*mah* is one of the few hundred who survived."

"Does she talk about it?"

"I'm afraid not."

"Do you ask her?"

"Oh, my, yes." He shifted to the overstuffed arm of my chair, and though I had heard Randall speak at table, it suddenly hit me that he was British. It made me shiver to think how different he was from me, and yet we were chatting like old acquaintances. "But she is not forthcoming about what happened."

"Maybe it was too harrowing," I said, trying out a word I'd gleaned from my disaster literature.

"Aren't you traveling with your uncle?" he asked me.

"Yep."

"He and I had tea one afternoon."

I paged through the scratched photos taken in 1912 until Randall placed a hand over mine. I stared up at him.

"Look at that suite. It's so large, unlike the cubicles on this tub."

I laughed. "Uncle Rex keeps griping about how my *little men* take up too much room."

"I should say . . . he had to kick the tiny buggers out of his path on the way to the loo. You were out, I believe . . . the other afternoon . . . when he and I had tea."

"He's sick today," I said, making waves with my hands and pooching my cheeks as if I were about to vomit. I loved mugging; it always made my sister laugh.

"Aren't you the least bit ill?" he asked. I shook my head. "Nor I. I've been making this voyage for at least ten years now. It's complicated. Mumsy lives in New York, father in Italy. Anyway . . . takes more than this to make me *toss me scones*." He laughed and placed his arm around my shoulder. Randall's aroma of sandalwood and tobacco made me long for my father or someone like my father, someone who would laugh with me, help me with my homework, teach me all the things a boy should know.

"I left an expensive scarf in your stateroom," Randall said, caressing my neck, "and I must retrieve it or Irma will have a fit. Have you a key?"

"No, Uncle T. always takes it, so I won't interrupt him, *but wait.*" I removed the key from my pocket, as if it were a magic bunny, and Randall won it from my hand. My neck still prickled where he had fondled me, and I was puzzled. Yes, a burgundy scarf did hang from the mirror over the vanity, but it belonged to my uncle. On behalf of my mother, I had given it to him myself. And I knew for a fact what my mother had paid, and it was far from expensive. Perhaps he meant a different scarf.

"Let's stop by," he suggested.

"Nope," I said, lunging for my key. "We might wake him."

"He won't even know we're there." Randall tousled my hair and made a game of holding the key out of my reach as I grabbed for it. Giggling each time he jerked it away, I also felt a certain desperation to get it back.

To keep from falling, the two us grasped the rails attached to the corridor walls and rode the lift to the Sun Deck, where we staggered some more. Wobbling along the floor and giggling whenever one of us hit the wall too hard, we came upon my uncle's stateroom.

"Let me knock first," I said. "And then *I'll* unlock it."

"Certainly," Randall said, standing behind me, his hand planted on my shoulder.

I tapped lightly, then harder. No one answered, so Randall reached around me and slipped the key into the lock.

"Wait!" I said, noting the ship's paper, but Randall had already pushed open the door.

The steward had straightened the room, raising my bed into the wall, but my eye fell to the studio, where four bronzed legs became a sculpture. To his credit, Uncle T. kept his composure, pulling the sheet over the two of them. "*You forgot our little signal,*" he sang out. His companion had drawn a pillow over his head with a hand that was tattooed with a faint red rose, and I studied it. Why, I wondered, would anyone want a rose tinctured upon his skin, especially if it would later wither to the shape of a cabbage, like the rose tattoo on the arm of my grandfather, the one who lived out west?

As we fell into the room, Randall began to laugh into the higher registers of his voice. With a crazed expression, he waltzed over and snatched the wine-colored scarf from the vanity mirror.

"I always appropriate one souvenir," he said to my uncle. "Do you mind, love?" He wrapped the scarf tightly around one hand.

"Hell, no, just take it and get out. Dane, I'll see *you* later."

So this is what Uncle did behind closed doors, took naps with men we hardly knew? I was somewhat peeved that Uncle T. was giving away *our* scarf, the one my mother had slung hash to pay for, but since it seemed to mean more to Randall than my uncle, I let it go. I could feel the lilt of the ship pass from my left to my right foot, and it reminded me of balancing myself on a seesaw.

"I need money," I said.

"Take what you need and *go*." Uncle T. pulled the sheet higher, so that it covered both his head and his companion's.

"One moment, please," Randall said, pushing past me, standing over the two supine men. "Am I not due more than this?" he said, sniffing the scarf.

Uncle T. groaned, and I could hear his voice filter through the pillow. *Go now and we'll talk about it later.* Unsure of what was happening, I tripped over and slipped a bill from the back of my uncle's wallet. Cologne bottles tinkled against the raised edge of the vanity, as our mother ship rolled once again.

"Wait, little one," Randall said, "allow me to accompany you." He left Uncle's door ajar and caught up with me, both of us bouncing from one side of the corridor to the other. It was not as hilarious as before. I turned and saw that Uncle was standing at the door with the sheet wrapped around him.

"If you touch him, I'll kill you," my uncle shouted.

Randall waved without looking back, and I laughed, wondering why Uncle was so upset. Randall may have been devious, but at least he hadn't tried to drown me. He wasn't hiding his head under a pillow like the mystery man in bed with my uncle.

Objects in the duty-free shop diverted my thoughts, and Randall shuffled his feet among the narrow aisles as he huddled me close. I gasped when I discovered I'd nabbed a fifty, unaware that such a large bill existed. "Is this real?" I asked, and Randall raised his eyebrows, letting me go. My eyes scanned the shelves of amber liquor and Scottish sweaters, but when I sighted a model of the *Constitution* suspended in a bottle, I cried out and took it to the register. I purchased for my sister Margaret a large stuffed lion, one with a long mane that she could comb and braid for hours. For my mother I found a gold locket with a space for a photograph (I later placed there a tiny one of me made by the ship's photographer). And for Uncle T. Rex, I bought a leather-bound calendar, the kind that scheduled each hour of the day. When I had finished shopping, Randall helped by carrying the lion back to my uncle's room, dropping it next to the door, where it reigned as a floppy sentry.

"It's stopped!" Randall said, leaning against the corridor wall.

"What?" I said.

"Don't you feel it? The storm has passed."

Yes, my legs had quit fighting the imbalance of things. For a moment Randall stood quietly. We stared at one another, and then he placed the key in my hand and walked away.

"I would have liked you to visit my room, little boy, but it's too late now to play." He laughed devilishly, flinging the burgundy scarf over his shoulder.

I remember such a mixture of emotions: relief that the ship had stopped rocking; anger over the cavalier treatment of that scarf; puzzlement at Randall's mysterious departure; anxiety about invading my uncle's privacy; oh, and a pervasive fear of abandonment, that my uncle would find the bronzed legs on the studio bed more appealing than being with me. At the base of Uncle's door, I noticed the ship's paper had disappeared, but I dared not enter uninvited. I knocked, and Uncle T. opened up. Desiring to make amends, I thrust the calendar in his face, dragging the lion behind me, kicking it to the spot on the floor where my bed usually stood open.

"Very nice," Uncle T. said, caressing the leather cover as if it were alive. "And so very clever."

"What?" He closed the door.

I stared at the studio that, for once, was neatly made and standing in its upright position as a sofa. The air seemed cleansed of colognes and talcs and a heavy scent I had never quite been able to put my finger on. He caressed my face.

"You're smarter than you let on, wise beyond your years, and if you ever tell your mother what happened here, we'll never see one another again."

"I know," I said, handing him twenty cents in change.

"Goodness, how frugal we are." My lower lip began to quiver.

"Oh, Dane," he said, drawing me to him. "I was teasing, I can always get more from the bursar."

"I know *that*," I blubbered.

"What then?"

"I want you to love me."

Uncle T. engulfed me with his arms, his male smell overwhelming me. If it hadn't been for the sheer attention, I would have pulled away. I now sensed that my uncle wore cologne to mask the dark odor that made men something I could not yet grasp. I wiped away tears with the back of my hand.

"Dane," he said, his voice choking, "I will love you long after my *friends* are gone, and the older I get, the faster they seem to disappear."

"You'll become an elderly?" I thought of how *invisible* those two gentlemen seemed, shuffling among us as if ghosts.

"Yes," he said. "Yes, one day, I'll become one of the *those*, and when that time comes, I hope I have enough work to keep me busy from morning till night."

"Why?" I asked, wiping my face again.

Uncle ran his fingers through my hair and kissed me on the cheek. "I'm suddenly very hungry. Let's dress for dinner. A table alone. Just the two of us."

"Oh, goody," I said, clapping my hands, "but don't you feel sick?"

"On this beautiful evening!" He grinned and did a double-take out the porthole, where you could hear the constant slosh of waves. "Suddenly, I'm ravaged—er, uh, famished."

I remember giggling, though I had no idea what my uncle's silliness meant. While dressing, Uncle T. Rex glanced at a stiff white card and groaned, recalling it was the night of the captain's dinner. No open seating. We would pull out our formal wear and appear at the captain's table once more. I pictured it—men in tuxedos and women dressed in crinkly pastel dresses, all of whom would migrate down the main staircase and into the dining room alight with amber and gold. I thought I might die from the sheer glamour of it all. I would feel throughout the meal that we were being filmed for a newsreel in Technicolor. Sitting at the edge of my seat, with my elbows raised, I would dine with my knife and fork held like Mrs. Boatwright and Uncle T., continental style. I would sip water from my glass, ever so lightly touching my lips with the linen napkin. As I observed these rituals, Uncle T. would smile at me as if I were the only boy in the world worth his attentions. I watched him poke ruby studs into my stiff shirt and fix my bow tie. He then invited me to sit very still on the sofa while he bathed.

An hour later eight of us who had gawked at one another for days once again graced the table in the center of the oval hall. A Mr. and Mrs. Tom Marion from *Manhattan* sat across from us; Mrs. Marion was beautiful with her raven hair turned up in a flip. Randall Smythe and his sister Irma sat to my right. Captain Strombley, a white-bearded man, and Mrs. Boatwright, arrayed in a gossamer gown of silver, sat to Uncle's left. Mrs. Boatwright's face looked like baker's dough that had been given a toss of flour—smooth but unnaturally white, and she'd painted her lips with a color she called Red Red Rose. I sat next to Irma, who looked so much like Randall it was uncanny.

The evening's conversation began with literature. Mrs. Marion had recently finished reading *From Here to Eternity*.

"Isn't it fascinating?" she asked. "I assume I'm the last person in the world to have read it," she said, "since it's been out for a decade."

Mr. Marion frowned. "I liked the movie better. No one can top Sinatra for realism." He seemed to get lost in his Martini, where he focused his eyes.

Randall sipped his champagne and said, "*The Naked and the Dead* is a far better war novel. Now there's realism for you!"

Mrs. Boatwright said, "I'm afraid I haven't read much since my days at Smith, a travesty, my father always said, but with four children, a fifth, if you count Howard, when was I to read?"

I noticed that each person's comment had fallen on dead ears. All I could hear were the clinks of glasses and flatware, the rumble of lowered voices. After several more titles were dropped and there were no takers, I spoke up.

"We've seen *An Affair to Remember* three times," I said. Uncle T. cleared his throat and smiled.

"Deborah Kerr is a favorite of mine," he said, sipping his champagne. I wanted a taste, but he gently pushed my hand away, having told me *no* several nights in a row. "And Mr. Grant, of course, I do love him so." Everyone laughed.

"I always go to sleep," I said. "Mush, you know." Laughter again, as if it were a song's refrain, floated across the table. The captain, with his silver hair and barrel chest, roared, and I smiled at my little joke.

"I wonder that you sleep at all," said Irma, sipping champagne from her flute, tossing her head. The blond bun at the base of her neck bounced with fury, and Mrs. Boatwright stopped eating her soup.

"What does she mean?" I whispered to my uncle.

"Ix-nay on the itch-bay," he said under his breath, smiling. "I've had a real bout with seasickness," he said to the table at large.

"Is *that* what you call it?" Irma said. She glared at Randall. He glared back, and I felt as if some balance had been upset. Folding my arms and leaning back in my chair, I had no greater desire than to become invisible. A waiter removed our soup bowls, pouring water, bringing another magnum of champagne, a Coca-Cola for me.

Randall wore, in the fashion of a boa, the burgundy scarf, fingering its edges, occasionally sniffing it, as he ogled my uncle. Once, when he did that, he caught me staring and turned to stick out his tongue.

I was sure everyone had seen him, including Irma, who finished her champagne in one loud gulp. I averted my own eyes to the carpet, busy with naval symbols, and stared for a long time at a gold-roped anchor. At last I looked up at Randall. I can't tell you where I found the gumption.

"Are you and your sister having a fight?" I asked.

"What sister, you mean *her*?" Randall laughed into that high register again, nearly squealing like a pig. "This is Irma, my *wife*," he said.

I laughed as if it weren't true, but Irma frowned. Uncle T. excused himself to the restroom. Soon Randall left, and then Tom Marion.

"My, the men's powder room must be gigantic," Mrs. Marion said, lighting a long white cigarette. Everyone tittered except Irma. The muscles surrounding her mouth were drawn tight, a quality that set her apart from Randall. If they were married, I quickly imagined that they would be together in old age, like Mr. and Mrs. Claus, with identical rosy cheeks.

I slipped out of my chair and flew across the room, dodging waiters with silver trays, charging up to the promenade deck, where I guessed the men had gone. Spying on them through a crack in the double door, I strained to hear their voices. When I saw their black patent shoes, the three of them shoving one another like schoolboys, I slipped onto the deck and crouched under a stairway. The stink of the sea almost overwhelmed me.

"How dare you make such a claim," my uncle said, grabbing Randall by the lapel.

"How dare I!" Randall spat, grabbing Uncle's hands and holding them to his chest.

"Come now, you two," Tom Marion said, reaching out to break them apart. For a moment the rose tattoo passed unnoticed, then my hand fell across my mouth. I'd been exposed to it every day at table, and yet it was so much a part of the landscape it had become invisible.

"Why, you're both married," Uncle T. spat. "How could either of you stake a claim on me?"

"Because you promised," Randall whined. The harsh light of dusk revealed severe lines along his mouth, skin that crinkled like crepe paper around his eyes. Only through careful pampering had both he and Irma managed to maintain the look of rich, spoiled college students. "I can't bear Irma any longer, I need my Rexie." Uncle T. waved him away like a gnat.

"Marlene will give me my freedom whenever I ask," Tom Marion said.

"The few times a year you make it to Dallas?" my uncle sneered. "How enticing."

"You know what I mean. Forever, if that's what you want."

"Forever!" Uncle T. exploded. "Even the pyramids won't last that long. Both of you. Leave."

He folded his arms and faced the sea, while the other two men drifted in opposite directions along the deck. After staring at Uncle's form for many minutes, I came out from under the stairs and stood at his side. I expected him to tousle my hair, but he looked down at me sadly, as if he were sorry I had appeared. He pulled out his silver case and lit a cigarette.

"Why don't you go and finish your meal, Dane. We'll see a movie later, something fun and light. Go on."

I scuffled back to the dining room. There was no one left at our table but the captain and Mrs. Boatwright, who made me slide around so I wouldn't have to dine alone. As she placed her hand on my wrist, I heard her whisper to the captain, "That man should be shot." I ate everything put in front of me, even vegetables that looked like seaweed and a slab of meat oozing with blood. And for the next hour, the two adults forced this same food down their gullets, but not once did they ever stop talking.

When we reached Italy, I forgot about the trip over. I can't remember much about Rome either, except a few languid days, where spiders of sweat crawled down my back until Uncle made me change my shirt. We must have climbed and photographed everything that the ancient world had saved for us, but I can remember little of it now. When our trip was nearing an end, I asked Uncle about our return on the *Constitution*.

"That old tub!" he said. "We're taking Pan Am to London this afternoon and from there a 707 to New York. We'll be in Dallas by tomorrow night."

"Really!" I said.

Suddenly I was hungry for afternoons in the neighborhood pool, expeditions with my friends into the wilds that bordered Love Field, bus trips to the library, where I could check out four books at a time and spend hours reading them in air-conditioned bliss. I couldn't wait to play, once again, the tinny spinet at my piano teacher's apartment.

At the same time, I realized I might never again experience the listless inertia of an afternoon spent with the two old men or Mrs. Boatwright's kind attention or cavorting with Olympic swimmers or joking with my uncle, when he was free, of course. If he had suddenly changed his mind about flying, I would have been delighted, for there was something about the sea that would forever make me wonder, when I sailed, if I might not at all wind up where I had begun.

My Long-Playing Records

For as long as I can remember I've collected vinyl, and, as an aficionado of the stereo album, I believe there exists in it a warmth that digital sound lacks. In a well-preserved LP, I can hear sounds as if I'm facing the stage on which a symphony is playing, say, Dvořák. My ears place the brass up there on the left, above my mother's portrait. Violins fall on both sides of the living room Craig and I inhabit, violas and cellos in the center, next to the coffee table, halfway back. Percussion resonates off the hearth. If I play the same recording mastered on a compact disc, there is no hiss, no scratching. There exists, instead, a rather homogeneous sound that brings to mind the monaural LP—a sound that, when introduced, was eons ahead of its predecessor, the seventy-eight. My parents had hundreds of those. One of them I called the Laughing Record, because a number of saxes simulated giggling so convincingly that it sent our whole family to the floor in hysterics. But when I began to cry, my mother would put it away.

The first man I ever loved was, like me, a married seminarian. And so after our wives left for work each day, we entered a parallel world where I believed we were invisible. But one Saturday morning my wife dispelled such a notion when she stepped into the hall and asked, "Evan Wiseman, what're these hairs in the sheets?" After enduring carpools all week to teach elementary PE, she was now doing a wash in the basement of our married student dorm. Dallas traffic roaring up the stairs failed to drown out her words.

Sticking her head into my carrel—a closet with a file cabinet, both of which I kept locked when I was gone—she stood waiting while I scribbled my Greek translation. I let the moment pass, having believed since childhood that if you ignored a particular moment—like crying over a laughing record—the next moment would occur and the last one would be forgotten. "What're these?" my wife, a petite blonde, said. She held up several chestnut-colored pubes, pinched between her fingers like the tail of a dead mouse.

I shrugged and gathered my things. "I've got study group," I said, locking my carrel and fleeing down the stairs.

"These can't be yours," she hollered after me. "Your hair is dark."

I began to see a counselor to treat this bit of cognitive dissonance I was experiencing—striving to be a man of God, married to a lovely woman, yet writhing in the shadows with my own kind. My in-laws had funded an elaborate wedding and a honeymoon cruise in the Caribbean, thus making my betrayal manifold.

I didn't mention to my wife the free sessions where, once a week, I crossed the Trinity River on a bus, and a pastoral counselor who officed at Methodist Hospital Rogerianed his way through precisely an hour with me. *I hear you saying that you're conflicted.* This all happened in 1970 when Rogerianism was dying out, for its patronizing way of making the counselee feel like a child or worse, a moron. *If I understand correctly, you're happier with men, but you believe you're betraying your wife, doesn't you, sweetums. Why doesn't you tell Daddy all about it?* My counselor, a suave, thin-haired pastor in his forties, didn't use those exact words, but as I bounced home on the bus, they haunted me as if he had.

Sometimes on my way back to campus, I'd stop and have a beer at YurNuts, a notorious bar on Mockingbird Lane where men like me gathered. For an hour I would dance with complete strangers, our zippered cocks nudging one another like radar systems that were rather beside the point. Until then I'd taken my desires no farther; just being close to my kindred was enough. After one such time, I got off the bus in front of our dorm on Hillcrest, and one of my fellow seminarians jumped out of his Ford Galaxie and came running up to me. He and

his wife had lent us that car not long before so we could drive north for
a funeral, though I'd hardly have called ourselves friends. They'd left
the Jehovah's Witnesses to become Methodists, and they were scathing
fundamentalists—a snap judgment I made easily back then.

"I know where you've been," he said, puffing like he'd run a mile.
In that age when men were going with long tresses, he kept his salty
red hair in a crew. The freckles on his face danced as he spoke, as if he
were eleven years old. I shrugged and detoured my way around him.

"I know what you're doing, I saw you come out of that place," he
said, blocking my path. "My brother-in-law strung my sister along for
years, thinking he could have it both ways. You can't, you know."

I tried to step around the beanpole, ignoring one moment so I
could move comfortably to the next, but he put both hands on my
shoulders and glared at me. My immediate desire was to knee him in
the balls, an impulse that seemed wholly justified.

"If you don't stop this, you're going to hurt Julie, like Eddie hurt
my sister."

I withdrew from his grasp and headed toward the dorm with my
arms extended like a sleepwalker. "I'm seeing a hypnotherapist," I
said. Then I inserted a hop in my step like Popeye.

"Very funny!" he yelled after me, standing by the curb as if he were
going to catch the next bus. "You won't be laughing when she finds
out."

At my college the assistant librarian was only a few years older than I,
and he'd sort of adopted me, paying me to care for his car and apartment while he spent summers in Europe. In his absence I would tool
around in his Gran Sport 400 and entertain friends in his basement
apartment. I later discovered people thought we were lovers, though
nothing could have been farther from the truth. Near the end of my
senior year, he sent me to his office and said I could take any of the
LPs I wanted. He was converting the listening area to stereo and giving
away the monaurals. Opening every sleeve and holding each record
up to the light to search for obvious flaws, I spent hours perusing the
albums before walking away with a stack a foot high. In particular I

prized a six-record collection of the NBC orchestra led by Toscanini. When I played back Shostakovich's Leningrad Symphony in my dorm room, I could hear someone cough and fluttering programs in the background. At a dramatic point, one of the trumpeters failed by a hair to form the major third that would have completed the triad, but I didn't care. It was a historic performance from 1942 and would sound the same way every time I played it.

Wade, perpetrator of the chestnut pubes, and I became acquainted under rather tragic circumstances. A beloved couple, who'd been our dorm's residential assistants the year before we matriculated, had been motoring through a driving rain to their first church when their Barracuda was broadsided by a station wagon that hydroplaned across the median, somewhere in Idaho. The wreckage was strewn with baby clothes, and when the local sheriff called the dorm at our university, the address on both driver's licenses, he cleverly asked where Twila's baby was.

The new RA's wife began to scream: "She's not due yet, what do you mean, 'Where's Twila's baby?'"

A week later the seminary held a huge memorial service in Perkins Chapel for Twila and George and their unborn child. Even if I hadn't been acquainted with them, I felt obligated to go, and after the service was over, Wade and I spotted one other on the sidewalk outside. Our eyes locked, and when our bodies were nearly even, we threw ourselves into each other's arms, sobbing. Something about the service—the contemplative music, the anthem "My Eternal King," the eulogies, sun streaming through the white plantation shutters—had made me appreciate the temporality of life. Or perhaps Wade had only read the hunger in my eyes. Realizing we were in the midst of a crowd, I pulled away and tried to memorize his face: a nose that was pointed but bent to the left, fine but wiry eyebrows, long sandy lashes that made boats of his blue eyes, so pale they were like a gray day—all of these features framed with dull red hair swaying from side to side as he spoke.

"Could I borrow your Greek text? I seem to have misplaced mine," Wade said.

The ruse sounded legitimate enough. In the beginning we only talked, and we always ended the conversation with a hug—very fraternal. After a couple of weeks, we were seated on the sofa sleeper in my apartment, Wade's pheromones dancing with mine, begging me—*it's now or never*—and I reached across to grasp the flesh above his knee. To feel a muscular, hairy leg was akin to the first time I'd felt up a girl—something about asserting oneself as an individual and paradoxically becoming one with another. I half expected him to slug me, but when he took my hand and kissed it, I crawled into his lap. "God, you're beautiful," he said. He cuddled me in his arms and kissed me more tenderly than I'd ever kissed or been kissed by my wife. After that incident we would while away entire mornings with a slow crescendo of movements that edged slowly toward an end. And as soon as one crescendo had been fulfilled with a couple of shouts, we would begin again. It seemed to flow from an endless fountain—this fleshly, guishy love—and I couldn't let go.

On one occasion we talked about the relationships we had with our wives: how my wife had never reached orgasm and how hard I'd tried to please her; all the books I'd read, all the experiments to bring her off, including a foul-tasting cunnilingus when she'd finally pushed me away and proclaimed, "I'd sooner let a dog."

"At least she let you try," Wade said, half-smiling. "Sally only likes it on her back . . . one, two, three, oh, baby . . . and it's over."

"What would it be like to love . . . " I asked him one October day, when the weather was still warm. ". . . all the time, not just like this?" We were lying down, I had my leg thrown over his, and we were caressing one another's privates.

"God, do you think we could, Mortimer?" he asked, rising to gouge the thin mattress of the sofa sleeper with his knees. His chestnut pubes were afire with morning light, and his face had a wild look, like someone trapped at the edge of a cliff.

"It wouldn't be easy," I said, burying my face in his crotch, inhaling a scent that was both sweet and pungent. He pulled away, tossing his red hair as if it, too, were on fire, and fled the apartment. I sat dazed, feeling as if I'd awakened from a dream. *Had he even put on his clothes?* I wondered.

Still, the larger question hung in the air for weeks, as we continued our careless deception. Once a neighbor knocked at my door, alarmed because he'd heard our shouts. Another time, a maintenance man wanted to change the AC filter, and Wade hid in the bathroom behind the shower curtain. I stood outside the door with a towel wrapped around me, with Wade's saliva coating my lips, his fungal pubic taste on my tongue—as I watched the man replace the filthy filter and leave.

I figured that Wade and I would wear it out, this insatiable appetite we had for one another, and then we'd go back to the lives that were expected of seminarians, whose future was to preach the Gospel and live by example the word of God. But we fell into a pattern that then became hard to break. We spent hours talking the way other seminarians spoke with their spouses. Theology and where we might like to serve once we were out of seminary: I wanted a university ministry where I could help youth struggling with their fragile identities; he desired a downtown church in a big city where he would tackle poverty. It was an easy, brotherly relationship with Wade, peppered with long lunches, walks along Turtle Creek in one of the richest communities in the country. We attended matinees of *I Am Curious (Yellow)*, *Satyricon*, and *Oh, Calcutta!* at the Fine Arts, picking them apart over beers—hot and bothered from the nudity. And yet, the fact that we couldn't present the face of our relationship to the world made it superficial and temporal.

"I . . . only thought I loved Julie," I told Wade one day close to Thanksgiving.

We'd just returned from chapel, having assisted with the Eucharist, bending over to hold shallow silver plates, while two professors in white vestments placed wafers in the mouths of pilgrims. For the postlude the organist had played Karg-Elert's "Now Thank We All Our God," and its strains still marched through my head like ghosts in long white cloaks. I'd felt pure, like a child experiencing complete acceptance, a kind of love I differentiated from the guishy variety. For my fellow seminarians, for Julie and her family, for the poor and poor in spirit I felt this emotional purity, the reason I'd wanted to become a pastor in the first place.

My conversion had been quick and sure. Though I had shunned religion after high school, Julie finally convinced me I should hear the new young minister at the church associated with our college. Humoring her, I accompanied her one Sunday. He was a dynamic speaker, all right, weaving events from his own imperfect life with scriptural text in such a way that the message could not be mistaken. There had once existed a man who roamed the earth and so aptly loved others, especially those of us hardest to accept, that it transformed millions of lives. We all should love one another like that each day, and the young pastor laid out the steps we could take: volunteering for day care, giving succor to the homeless, even visiting those incarcerated in our own county jail. He threw down a gauntlet that was hard to reject, and I'd fallen in love—not only with Veryl, a handsome athlete—but with the idea of saving the world, one soul at a time. And when he saved mine, by listening to my lurid desires and not casting me upon the fires of eternal damnation, I was hooked. I was convinced I could do the same for others.

"Do you have to call her by name?" Wade said, holding me tight against him.

"I only thought I loved *my wife*," I said.

"Yeah, I heard you," he sighed, pulling away. I quickly thought of a catfish I'd caught once while fishing with Veryl and his family and how proud of it I was, and how it wiggled free and jumped from my arms into the lake, making me wonder if I'd ever captured it in the first place.

"I want to be with you," I whispered. "I *know* I love you."

"Yeah, me too," he said. "But we don't have to say it, do we?"

"Come, class doesn't meet for hours," I said, resting my hands on his hips, the most vulnerable part of a man's body.

"Let it go." And he pushed me away. "We have to let it go."

When he left I shivered and lay quite still on the unmade bed, listening to water course through pipes in the walls, to the squeal of truck brakes, the twitter of sparrows on the window ledge. Somewhere in there I could hear my own breath whistling through my nose like that of an asthmatic. This wasn't turning out the way I'd thought it would, the seminary experience that Veryl had convinced me would be so great. I popped out of bed, lighting a Benson-Hedges I'd hidden in a gap in the window sill, holding the crystalline menthol in my lungs, allowing the smoke to swirl in my mouth before exhaling. Staring past the parking lot to Veryl and my pledge to love Christ, I finished the cigarette and climbed back into the self I'd abandoned for Wade. Flushing the filter down the toilet, I vacuumed up chestnut pubes and changed the sheets before converting the bed to a sofa, spraying the air and blinds with Lysol to mask the smoke, as well as odors more vague.

My in-laws had booked a huge suite for the family at the Fairmont; the holiday weekend would be filled with drinking and revelry. I also had a paper due on Monday; when Julie and I returned to the apartment Sunday evening, my mind would be too occupied to consider Wade and me, a concept that now seemed as ludicrous as a Martian and me. I showered Wade's oils and odors from my body and called to cancel the appointment with my Rogerian doctor, whose *help* suddenly seemed superfluous.

In January I enrolled in a month-long course called Women in Church and Society, intently following the lectures of a female theologian from New Jersey as she spoke of changes needed regarding women's roles in the church *and* the world. The university brought in Gloria Steinem to address the student body. Fascinated, I not only thought I *got it*, but I realized that freedom for women meant freedom for me, freedom from the millions of sexist poses I'd been inclined to accept without question. I began to take more responsibility around the apartment, washing dishes so that Julie didn't have to face them when she came home in the afternoons. Using her wedding cookbooks, I taught myself to cook. I kept the apartment clean and did our laundry on Fridays. Julie seemed relieved but puzzled, as if I'd usurped an important role of hers, like childbirth—one she'd already eschewed. In spite of her resistance, I felt reborn, and I called Veryl to share my news. He laughed. And no matter how hard I attempted to explain to him how good this change was, he met my words with silence. I shivered and hung up.

Descending to the dorm basement with a huge basket of sheets and towels, I ran into Wade perched on a sorting table with another seminarian. Hot moist air trapped in the room made me sick as my basket fell to the floor. I nodded and Wade said, "Yo, Wiseman." The other guy, a handsome burly man with a beard and long auburn hair, continued to talk. "The Old Testament is complete bullshit, parallel myths written at the same time as other cultures," he said. "Do you realize how liberating that is, that the Bible is not designed by God. It's a fucking work of literature. As inspired or fallible as any other literature." I vaguely knew him as one of the draft dodgers who'd achieved 4-D status under false pretenses. By the time he finished seminary, he would be too old for the draft and maybe the war would be over and he could go about his merry way—or so the renegade thought. The arrogance of such an idea infuriated me.

I put a load of sheets in one washer and towels in another. "Got any quarters?" I asked, but they looked down and kept talking. I ran to the center stairwell and leaned against the steps long enough to stanch the tears, to gain control. Several minutes later, after digging the right coins out of my jeans, I returned to the laundry as Wade and the bearded guy were leaving. I stood in the doorway and watched them saunter arm in arm down the hall. As I started the machines, a shudder went through my body, making the roots of my hair scream, my skin feel as if it were afire. I ran up to the apartment. Standing over the toilet, I was determined not to blubber. I had nothing to compare it to, this brand of jealousy. It had no validity, no legitimacy.

"God, how could I be so stupid?" I said, sucking back the snot. I tore off my clothes and ran a hot shower. When I could no longer refrain, I peed and cried and screamed, allowing water to cascade over me, washing away all those sad liquids. I shampooed and scrubbed my body with a loofah Julie had bought the Saturday before, making my skin angry and pink. I toweled off and wiped down the steamy mirror.

Since before college graduation, I'd let my hair grow to my shoulders, but now the look seemed passé. While my hair was still wet, I walked to Hillcrest Center and had a stylist cut it Beatle length. After he'd blown it dry, I looked in the mirror and told him to take it down to the nubbin. "Are you sure, honey?" he said. "You look good enough to eat." Opening a drawer, the slender man with a blond beard pulled out clippers and plugged them in—looking at me as if I'd asked for the electric chair.

Julie didn't care for my new coiffure, but after that, when I frequented YurNuts, I got a whole new crowd to dance with me, mostly vets from Nam who reeked of BO and tobacco. I didn't care. I danced with them all and went home with a few on occasion, when I knew Julie was staying for PTA. I learned certain maneuvers I wished I'd experienced with Wade, who, by the way, thought my hair was hilarious. And strangely, Julie and I talked more now.

"I like your new domesticity," she said one evening, glancing at my apron. "It saves me a lot of time, but maybe . . . you're the only one being liberated."

"What?" I said, as she grabbed a spatula from me. Between us sat an unfrosted cake.

"You're enjoying yourself too much," she said, licking sugar off her fingers.

"I have more time," I said, retrieving the spatula and dipping it into the lemon glaze I'd mixed up. "Hey, some day, when I have a congregation and you're at home, our roles will be switched. You'll have time to do all this shit, not to mention taking care of our kids."

"I see," she said, returning to a stack of 203 volleyball quizzes. She was sailing through them like a buzz saw. "*If* we have kids."

"How do you know you have the right answers?" I asked. "Don't you use a key?"

She looked up. "ABBACDDECC."

"Oh, I see see."

She laughed, dropping the stack of quizzes to the floor. I sat on the carpet and we began to nuzzle one another. Soon we lay sprawled across the rug. We hadn't had made love in weeks, not since Wade had dumped me. I wasn't horny—I'd just that afternoon nailed a sailor's hairy ass in a garage apartment nearby—but I was hungry for *something*. Inside her I desperately wanted to trigger her pleasure, but as usual, I couldn't hold on forever and finished.

"Makes me sad," I whispered in her ear before falling on my back.

"What?"

"You never come, do you?"

"Doesn't matter," she said, standing and heading for the shower. "It's fine, really."

It had been part of my January course: make sure your woman is sated. Not in so many words, of course, but a real man considered his wife's many needs. "Don't you want to be satisfied?" I called after her.

"I don't know what that means," she hollered above the noise of the shower.

I jumped up and blocked her way to the tub. "Wade and I were lovers for a while," I whispered.

"Surprise, surprise," she said, shielding herself behind the plastic curtain.

"I stop at a bar and pick up men at least twice a week," I said. It didn't make me feel any better to say it.

"Righto." She was like Bette Davis in *Now, Voyager*, hiding an immense ache beneath her exterior. Throwing aside the shower curtain and joining Julie from behind, I wrapped my arms around her and found the little spot I'd already explored with my tongue. I began to caress her there, while cupping her breasts with my other hand. She groaned for me to stop. "Come on, beautiful cunt," I whispered. "You beautiful stubborn cunt." At that she began to writhe against me, making me hard again. "Oh, yeah, you deserve a little fun," I said in baby talk. I continued to caress her ever so softly, while nipping her ear-lobes with my teeth, and some time later—the pulsating water seemed tepid—her body stiffened. She screeched for me to stop. Putting one hand over mine and holding her breasts with the other, her breathing labored, she spoke. "I had no idea—my God—no idea." We stood holding one another for ten minutes, until the water turned frigid and we began to shiver. That night we slept in each other's arms, something we hadn't done since our honeymoon.

You can adopt a pose whereby you spend day after day doing the same thing and feel that this must be right; this must be my life. On one

of those days, after having studied all afternoon, I sat in a corner at
YurNuts, nursing a Bud. Having been seated for a few minutes, and
my olfactory senses having assimilated the stink of spilt liquor and
crushed cigarettes, I found great comfort in the place. My fellow-
ship went directly toward tuition, the apartment, books. It was Julie's
income that bought me beers, sex with strangers, and porn, and if it
hadn't been for their many pleasures, I would have gone home. When
I noticed someone standing at my table, I looked up.

"May I?" Wade said.

"Slumming, are we?"

"Not unless you think so," he said, sitting across from me. He
ordered a Bud from the waiter, a skinny black boy in tight jeans and
a white T-shirt, and I squandered more income on a second brew for
myself. "Sally's gone back to Pennsylvania," he said.

"While the bitch is away . . . "

"She took our car and all her stuff."

"Julie had her first orgasm the other day, and I think we're in love,"
I said.

He reached over and grabbed my hand. I snatched it away. "Christ,"
he said, taking a huge gulp of beer. "What's with you?"

"How's it going with whatshisname . . . O Bearded One?"

"Matthew? I, uh, tried to molest him, and he . . . he didn't take to
it. See?" Wade showed me the discoloration under his eye; it looked
like dried egg yolk. "Actually, I've blown him once or twice, but it's
different . . . ."

"So you haven't got any for a while and came down here to rustle
up some action, eh?" I pointed to the dance floor, where bodies swayed
to something slow and country.

"I followed you here, you dope. I've been walking around the
block, trying to get up the guts to come inside. Dance with me?"

"Little ole me?" I drawled. "Well, I do declare, Mr. Beauregard."

"Stop it, man. You scared the shit out of me."

"Pretty shocking stuff, two men loving one another as if it were
the most natural thing in the world," I said. I'd been poring over gay
liberation pamphlets I kept locked away in my file cabinet with some

male-on-male porn I'd bought downtown at a shop on Commerce (where I spotted one of our balding professors in dark glasses). Studying such material had placed me in a separate reality, one that was secreted, like mercury lining the inside of a mirror. Without it I could scarcely see who I was.

"Don't you want to dance?" he said, curling his lip.

"I want to smash your face in," I said, standing. We joined the others, our pelvises jammed together in harmonious symmetry. I didn't keep up with country music, so I didn't know who it was singing about ashtrays overflowing with cigarettes, beer guzzled like OJ, cars leaving tracks on your face, but at that moment I loved her. "This could be our song."

"Don't get precious. Not even with Sally could I be sentimental." Wade leaned over to whisper in my ear. "I dig you, I really do, but I don't want to say I wuv you every day forever and ever."

"How Open Marriage of you . . . "

He grunted, cradling me in his musky arms, and I hummed along with the ballad singer, a woman with a soft whiskey tenor. It was a voice I could never grow tired of, a warmth I could never reject, no matter how many times I heard the song, no matter how many times the red label made thirty-three-and-a-third revolutions per minute, the turntable clicking to a stop when the song was over.

We left shortly after, for the fourth floor of our dorm and staged a quickie in Wade's bare apartment. It was a replica of mine and Julie's, on the opposite side of the building, where the light was stunted. After we finished, Wade hopped in the shower. I joined him, but when he ignored my affections, I stepped out and dried off with the only towel in his place, a graying piece of cloth with UNIVERSITY OF ARKANSAS ATHLETICS stenciled in red. "See ya," I said.

One evening, as our lives loped along, Julie announced that she wanted to invite people over for dinner. "Let's ask Wade and Sally."

I looked up. "Sally's moved back east."

She shrugged, continuing to knead dough. She'd been shoving me away from the stove more and more. I was down to cooking Friday nights, when she allowed me to sear some salmon on the grill located between the dorms. "The kids are restless for school to be out, and it's only March," she said, placing in the oven a cookie sheet filled with small pieces of sausage rolled in dough. Already we had the AC roaring full blast. "Why didn't you tell me Sally and Wade had split?"

I shrugged, and Julie took the attic key off its hook by the door. After a while she returned with a box that held four place settings of our gilt-edged Doulton, our Towle stainless, four wine goblets and four water. Her mother had talked her into registering the patterns, which clearly didn't suit us. Unable to picture Wade and Julie at the same table, I started to dissuade her. I then sat and watched her wash and towel dry the items. She carefully placed them on our little table, which at present seated only two. When it came time to entertain, I would pull it around the corner and undo the leaf, and the surface would double in size. Julie would spread an expensive linen cloth that her mother had given her, set the table, and wait for our guest.

"Tell Wade to bring someone," Julie said, kissing me on the cheek.

"He won't accept," I said.

"Ask him."

I was dozing as *Father Knows Best* characters chattered on Channel 39, when a knock came at the door. I stood to turn the sound down, and it made me dizzy. When I opened up, Wade sailed in, presenting me with an album he'd found in a used record shop.

"What's the occasion?" I said. I removed the record from its sleeve and held it to the light. It was in what the experts called Mint Condition. How, as a youth, I'd wished, like a genie, to slither into the side of a record like this one. How my flatness would have slid against the grain of the padded turntable, how the arm would have risen from its cradle, fallen slowly, its stylus springing along the grooves of my black vinyl—sending vibrations through a needle, up the arm, through the amp, along black wires, where music from speakers would have wafted across the room like smoke in a jazz bar.

"Chet Baker, no one like him," Wade said. "He's a trumpeter, but I think his vocals are sexier. His phrasing, his intonation are perfect.

If he's a bit flat in places, it's on purpose, he knows what he's doing. I almost cream my pants."

I put the record back in its sleeve and invited him to Julie's dinner. He shrugged. "Bring someone," I said, and he nodded, slipping out the door. When I returned to the TV, the overly sentimental theme song of *Father* was playing. Within seconds Julie found me sobbing. She looked down, placing her hand over what once was my fontanel.

"My mother never let us watch that show," she said, turning the set off. "Said it was too unrealistic. 'No one's family could possibly be that happy.'"

I wiped my eyes and looked up at her—a former cheerleader, a pixie of good German stock—realizing we'd not hooked up since our scene in the shower. I'd promised myself to quit frequenting the bar, to stop picking up men, but since that day I'd discovered how weak I really was. She slid her fingers through my crew cut and then changed her clothes. "You want to cook? I'm all out of ideas."

On a day in mid-April, rainy as all get-out, Julie and I waited. We waited and waited some more. Her four small hens, marinated in red wine, garlic, and rosemary, shrank to the size of little squabs as she baked them. Every half hour until shutting the oven off Julie basted them with a warm liquid that turned a darker color of blood as it cooled. With the stereo playing, we both read until nine, when there was a knock at the door. Wade was not alone.

"Sorry we're late," he said, rushing past us into the tiny living area. "You remember Matthew. These are Julie and Wiseman." He could never bring himself to say my first name.

"Evan," I said, putting my hand out to shake Matthew's. Imagining his huge hand wrapped around my penis aroused me, so immediately I tried to think of nothing, a mental trick I'd employed since puberty. Sometimes it worked.

The bearded man strode behind Wade, and they sat together on the sofa, inches above the folded mattress where Wade and I had issued our many shouts. The records had quit playing. "Hey, I guess we need some music," I said, moving toward the stereo, as if the lack of sound might have accounted for the sudden void in the room.

"Well," Julie said, "why don't we go ahead and eat." She indicated that Wade and Matthew should sit across from one another. Lifting the plastic lid, I raised the metal arm that leveled the records and grabbed the five LPs. I turned them over, resting them atop the spindle, leveling them again, sliding the lever that would drop the first one to the turntable. I'd let them play while we waited, and now Chet Baker's album was first. I'd intended for it to be last, and if our guests had arrived on time, the music would have played out that way, ending with Baker's sentimental but edgy vocals as we all became sloshed in our wine. At this point we were stone cold sober, and those selections seemed too emotionally raw. I didn't want Wade to cream his pants, not like that, and I didn't want to cry. The needle dropped and a faint scratching signaled the beginning.

"Still love that album," Wade said, glancing up at me. "Mine is worn as hell, Sally didn't exactly take care of it."

"Yeah," I said. "I like it more every day. Thanks."

"Wade gave you that?" Julie asked, her eyes cast down, passing rice pilaf the consistency of gum. I nodded, handing Wade her oven-baked carrots marinated in olive oil and basil. Everything on the relish plate was dry: the green olives; black ones staring at us like eyeballs; even the *relish*. Hard surfaces of china, crystal, and flatware gleamed, and everyone began to eat as if it were all a great feast.

"What kept you?" I asked, my mouth full of meat strung across rubbery bones.

"Matthew lives out in the sticks. Streets were flooded, and we had to find another way back to campus," Wade said, with his mouth full.

After several minutes of watching three other jaws in motion, I spoke up. "Where'd you go to school, Matthew?"

"Yale," he said, tossing his hair, "but I'm from Ada . . . Oklahoma."

A beat passed before I began singing to the tune of "Gary, Indiana": "Ada, Oklahoma, Ada, Oklahoma . . . ." To the song's end my voice soared like little Ron Howard's from the *Music Man* album.

"Oh, Evan, *please*," Julie said, and Wade snickered, clanking his fork against our fine bone china.

"'But Ada, Oklahoma . . . my sweet home!'"

Julie's face was crimson. Wade sat back and howled, while Matthew shook his head as if I were a waif singing for coins.

"Oh," I said, pointing to Julie. "She's from Kansas City. We come pretty close to Ada to get there. How'd you wind up at Yale?"

"Connections."

"No, really," I said.

"Don't get me wrong, my SATs were respectable and I had good grades, but it was my Grampa Morrison, class of '18, that cinched it."

"Must have been wonderful to attend such a venerable institution," I gushed, downing the last of my wine.

"That's what you would think," he said, lifting a pile of meat, rice, and carrots with his knife and fork and dumping it all in his mouth. "Everyone's a valedictorian, a scholarship hound, or some kind of great musician." He chewed twice and swallowed. "But you get sick of how precious everyone is. I preferred to hang around with bums like me, who worked just hard enough to avoid a one-way trip to the Orient." He winked and smiled at Wade as if he were the only man left on the planet.

I suddenly moved to the sofa. It was more of a mental thing, whereby I flitted away and watched them from across the room. Matthew Michael Morrison and Wade Warren Williams exchanged smiles that the latter and I had not, reflecting a secure and secret union that related little to how many times they'd been to bed.

After cutting her meat into cubes, Julie placed her knife across the top of her gilt-edged plate and ate with her fork. "What was your major?" she said, lifting her eyes toward Matthew. She'd been a student recruiter for our college, *tres charmant* when the situation required it. In fact, wasn't that how she'd snared me, sauntering into the Blue Moon, a coffee house on College Avenue, and convincing me she couldn't possibly write her history paper without my help?

"Majored in philosophy, but let me say how beautiful everything looks," he said, returning her look. "Wedding gifts?"

"Yeah," I interjected. "Julie's mother made sure we got the tea pot, the coffee pot, and a huge meat platter that serves twenty. Our parishioners will love it."

"At least you're set up. I had three different girlfriends at New Haven," he said, again with his mouth full. "Not one of them worked out."

"What happened?" Julie said, touching his wrist.

"Well . . . Nancy," he said, ripping the last morsel of meat from his hen with his hands, "she wanted ten children, assuming we were gonna get married. I told her in no uncertain terms, the world has too many children. Even if a couple can afford ten, the rest of the world cannot. There are only so many resources left in the earth." Julie nodded. "But it doesn't matter now," he said, gazing at Wade.

Another record dropped. It was Rachmaninoff, the first piano concerto. I had originally timed this one to play while we were deeper into our cocktails, better able to withstand its stormy rampage. I stood, approaching the expensive amp my father-in-law had given us, and decreased the volume.

"I think couples should try and have only two," I said, looking down on everyone. "Preferably a boy and a girl, to replace us as we leave earth some day. But Julie doesn't want children." She glared at me and then into her plate like a shamed dog.

"Really?" Matthew said, glancing over his shoulder at me.

Julie smiled and shrugged, but I wouldn't let it go. "Too much trouble. Her own privileged childhood wasn't so hot, so if she can spare our genetics of such unhappiness, then we will have done the world a favor."

"You should start a movement," Wade said, leaning back in his chair, satisfied with his pronouncement, the meal, with Matthew, and with his wine, which he continued to swill at an alarming rate. "Planned Parenthood is such a joke," he added, tossing his red hair.

I watched him empty the bottle into his glass and felt as if the evening ought to explode, that the true nature of Wade's and my relationship ought to be made clear to Matthew before I crushed his skull, that Matthew and Wade ought to confess they were only buddies, though I knew it wasn't true, that Julie ought to go ape-wild over my betrayal, that she ought to scream from the rooftops that our marriage was in great peril, particularly if one of the men at our table didn't lay off her husband. Taking my seat, I expected the evening to fracture like a record of saxophones mimicking laughter, like the one I finally threw against the wall at age ten, when I'd heard enough. But the evening seemed to shimmer, complemented by apple pie and the Association's Greatest Hits, offering up one of Julie's favorites. I watched her tap a fork against her plate, as her eyes hooked mine. We'd danced to "Cherish" at our first freshman smoker, and afterward we'd stood outside her residence hall, exchanging baby kisses until the housemother shooed me down the hill to my own dorm. "I'll see you tomorrow," I'd hollered, and we'd never spent a day apart since.

As the fifth record dropped, a raucous Zeppelin album, which would have been first, the boys decided to leave. It was twenty past ten.

"Good night, Wiseman," Wade said at the door, hollering at someone down the hall. "I'll come by and we'll tackle that Greek, you have a better grasp of verbs."

"Thanks, you guys," Matthew said, hugging us. "You're both top drawer."

When the door was closed, Julie began to laugh, bending over with her face in her hands. It was the same full-bodied guffaw, with a touch of bass in it, that I'd fallen for the first night we'd gone out and I'd uttered *Good evening* as if I were Cary Grant. *You're kidding*, she'd said, taking my hand, inspiring the erection that had convinced me I was normal. I turned the stereo off, and a soft quiet enveloped the room.

"What a couple of pretentious asses," Julie said, sidling up to me.

Her mood was contagious. "Aren't they?" I said, holding her close.

"Oh, God, Evan," she said, as we stepped back from one another.

She took my hands, which were oily from the meal. "If you want a man, there's nothing I can do, you must be wired for it." She seemed like an actress who believed her lines, moisture gathering in her eyes, her skin glowing. "But surely you can do better than those two. Surely." And she kissed me on my cheek, a kind of benediction, really, whereby she set me free. After finals Julie returned to KC, and I fled to New York, where I immediately broke my relationship with Christ and his merry band of men.

My collection of LPs has grown throughout the years, and in Manhattan I've found a man who understands the warmth of analog sound. Every time Craig is away on a trip, he brings me soundtracks, which I now collect with a vengeance. I probably have three hundred—ten for each year we've been together.

"Ah, Florence Henderson, her voice was like silk back then," I say, slicing a knife through the original wrapper, removing *The Girl Who Came to Supper* from its sleeve. "Where'd you find it?" I ask, holding it up to the light.

"Estate sale near Greenwich," Craig says, running a hand through soft white hair. "An old couple who lived for fifty-six years in the same house, and yet the album was never opened. Can you imagine?"

I place the record on the turntable, the third one I've owned since 1970. The songs are unfamiliar, but I savor Ms. Henderson's voice, recorded for all times, sounding as if she's twenty-nine and in the prime of her life.

Basketball Is Not a Drug

Tikosyn is a pale apricot capsule you take at ten a.m. In twelve hours you'll take another twenty-five milligrams. This drug regulates the rhythm of your heart, since your organ, which is fifty-eight, can't seem to regulate itself. The first six capsules you ingest in a shiny new cardiology unit, because the FDA requires monitoring. Some unfortunate soul might experience violent palpitations from this drug, the very symptom it is formulated to prevent. The kidneys of another poor soul might fail. But you endure the seventy-two hours as if you're in a hotel with nurses, one of whom every twelve hours drains your blood, testing it to see if the drug is advancing the state of your death. After three days, when such does not seem to be the case, you are discharged.

Leaving the hospital, you still experience the spells where your heart becomes a squirrel digging at your ribs, but now, instead of lasting up to forty-eight hours, the spells are over in ten minutes, especially since you've begun to meditate. Upon the first irregular thump, you drop to the floor in a lotus and count breaths. You concentrate on your breathing, saying hush to the digging squirrel. If a wayward thought enters your head, as you know it will, you chant—in your head—*fie on thee,* and the thought may or may not go away. It works as a fine adjunct to Tikosyn, particularly if you don't forget to take it. You try setting an alarm, because if you miss the dose by an hour, you have to wait eleven hours for the next one. And if you wait eleven hours, Mr. Squirrel will come a-digging. You, Larry Klein, *must* remember to take

Tikosyn, along with the many others, to keep your life on its glacial rock-gathering grind.

CONDITIONS INDICATING THE USE OF TIKOSYN. At first you think you are to blame. The spells occur when you're upset. They occur when you're not upset. The spells occur when you're anxious over your father's health. They occur whether you're anxious over your father's health or not. They occur while you visit foreign countries. They occur in the bathroom, as you evacuate something one might mistake for a missile. They occur while sitting perfectly still. Before Tikosyn, they might occur thrice weekly; they might not occur for months, thus lulling you into believing your body has healed itself. As time passes, you realize anxiety only feeds the condition. It does not cause it. You realize you cannot pinpoint a cause, other than the fact that you are older than God. You finally accept that this condition is not your fault, and you become thankful for the days you have left on earth. You wonder why you are not this thankful in your thirties, as one halcyon day after another unfurls before you like a red carpet, bidding you with a crooked finger to follow the shadowy path leading to your forties. But, of course, to your fifties you follow this fickle finger of fate (thank *Laugh-In*, c. 1968).

INTERACTIONS. If a doctor prescribes something, or if you need an OTC remedy for a cold, you must ring out alarums. You thus keep in your wallet a note printed in eight-point Helvetica which lists all your meds plus the following: Tikosyn CANNOT be combined with CIMETIDINE, KETOCONAZOLE, HYDROCHLOROTHIAZIDE (HCTZ), MEGESTROL, PROCHLORPERAZINE, TRIMETHOPRIM, VERAPAMIL, or QT-PROLONGING AGENTS (such as LITHIUM, PHENOTHIAZINES, TRICYCLIC antidepressants, certain QUINOLONE antibiotics, SOTALOL, BEPRIDIL). If you fail to present this note to each concerned party, some innocent whose malpractice policy has lapsed might prescribe a substance that could advance your death.

BENEFITS OF TIKOSYN. Your heart beats in a healthy sinus rhythm, thus circulating blood more efficiently throughout your body. No near fainting if you stand up too fast. No longer, as you head for the bath-room in the middle of the night, does your body become a runaway train requiring that you brace yourself to fall against anything you can find, a wall, a door, so that you won't crash to the floor. You may now travel without experiencing something akin to agoraphobia, a fear that you may never return home. As a liberated male who helps around the house, you can now scrub the toilet without dizzying yourself as you rise to your feet. You can do tubs of laundry that have stacked up over the many weeks you've felt like shit. You can drive without fear that you might be overcome in traffic and create a catastrophic accident. Your energy is restored to the point that you might work with some verve, as you did in your forties, before this unspeakable condition comman-deered your life. Your hands are no longer cold.

SIDE EFFECTS OF TIKOSYN. You read the label. "With Tikosyn nausea or headaches may occur. You might wish to seek immediate medical atten-tion if any of these rare but very serious side effects occur: confusion, dizziness, fainting, a fast/slow/irregular heartbeat. Mineral imbal-ances can increase the chance of developing certain side effects: mus-cle cramps/weakness, severe/prolonged diarrhea, increased thirst/sweating, vomiting. You might experience serious allergic reactions such as: rash, itching, swelling, severe dizziness, trouble breathing. If you notice other effects not listed here, you might wish to contact your doctor or pharmacist."

You're learning that every drug has side effects. You've heard it said as many as seven for each benefit. It's referred to as Bradshaw's Law, after the eminent physician and researchist N. Theodore Bradshaw, who determines such a truth in 1970 and records it in an issue of JAMA. You xerox the article and, no doubt, have full confidence in its veracity.

CO-PAY. Twenty-five dollars a month, or forty-two cents a pill. Pricey, but you pay. Baby, you pay.

PERSONAL SEAT LICENSES. Each winter basketball is a sport that helps you transcend the season, from the moment that West Texas leaves trickle down in November until early buds peek out around St. Patrick's Day.

Where else, attending both the men's and women's, for a total of thirty-five games, might you enter a starkly lit, cheer-full arena designed for 15,550 souls and witness five athletes who play their wits out against five others? Where else might you gaze upon two of the grandest coaches of the game—one man, one woman—who work their wizardry on players that are, in some cases, a little above average? Where else might you go and hear a band pip and toot the same peppy songs they pip and toot every year? No, they're not the same thirty tunes played when you were a student—several directors have come and gone—but the ensemble sounds the same, heavy on pip and toot. You don't care. The same thirty tunes—including the school fight song—make you feel as if you belong, as much as when you are twenty-one and you and your wife wear cheerleader sweaters. And when you clap in rhythm and raise your fingers in the coded gesture of a pointed pistol, you do belong. Like nowhere else on earth, you do belong.

As the players warm up, you ogle the cheerleaders, the pom-pom girls. If you were to meander among them, you would become invisible, wondering why the young and delectable ignore you so. Your wife, Mona, catches you and nudges you; you nudge back. It's a joke, always has been, because on a dare you both try out and make the squad your first week on campus in '66. The girls today wear less than what might have been proper for a pole dancer back then, but you don't care, no one does, not even your Christians, who gather along with your pagans (not that there's much difference) to watch the home teams play their hearts out for thirty-five home games.

You and Mona sneak in a Dasani in your coat pockets, because paying three dollars for twenty ounces of water is highway holdup. If the game is scheduled at an odd time, you might buy hot dogs or huge pretzels and kid yourself that the money's going for a good cause, but most of the time you don't. Your wife, after all, keeps track of finances, and when she shakes her head no, you go without a hot dog she says might kill you anyway. Were it not for such thrift, you might not be able to afford your chairs.

After all, this seat you occupy leases for three thousand dollars—that is to say, the right to buy season tickets for the same seat for ten years costs you three thousand dollars—same for Mona (your daughter stays with a sitter, a much cheaper proposition). The personal seat license, this right to sit, is sort of like reserving a pew at church. Since this venue is also used for concerts given by wayward girl bands who impugn the President of the United States (secretly you think they're right), you can expect others will sit in your chair. Okay, when someone spills Pepsi on your three-thousand-dollar chair, upholstered harlot red, you become huffy and call the athletic office, demanding that it be cleaned. The next game the caramel stain has darkened, so the game after that you bring a can of upholstery spray and tackle the situation yourself, sitting in the upper level while the spot dries. The next game, an outline of the stain remains. You get over it. The sofas in your den are stained from jars of toppled salsa consumed during Super Bowls of yore. You get over these, too.

And sometimes if you miss a game—because you are puking your guts out with flu or have an out-of-town conference—your seat neighbors ask *Larry, where were you?* Like good Christians might ask if you miss Easter Sunday or even Christmas, *Where were you, Larry?* Only those who attend every game have the right to ask *Where were you?* You don't have to answer, but you do. You were at a conference. You were puking your guts out. You were blinded in one eye and wear a pirate patch to prove it. Your father died. You endure these indignities to watch a game you love more than God, and you tell this to no one, not even your wife.

COUMADIN. One tablet is flat, pink, and oval. You take one and a half, seven point five milligrams a day, and realize you will do so for the rest of your unnatural life. You accept the fact your heart will always beat irregularly, if at irregular intervals, and that as a result, you might suffer a stroke. You take the pink tablets between meals, because doing so prohibits your breakfast carbohydrates from diminishing their salutary effects. Your cardiologist declares that if your heart begins to beat regularly over a long period of time, he will take you off Coumadin. You smile. Even you realize you have a chronic condition that cannot be reversed. You and most of your older friends are on Coumadin and will be for the rest of your unnatural lives.

CONDITIONS INDICATING THE USE OF COUMADIN. Coumadin is used to prevent and treat harmful blood clots. If your heart beats irregularly (which it does, even taking Tikosyn), Coumadin will ensure that you will not suffer a stroke. Strokes can disable some or all of your body parts, rendering you inactive and senseless as a human being for the rest of your unnatural life. Oh, some people, through Sisyphean efforts, do regain some or all of their functions, but these are few. Most stroke victims will lurch along like indigestible lumps for the rest of their unnatural lives.

INTERACTIONS. You read these words from the fact sheet that comes with Coumadin: "A larger intake than usual of foods rich in vitamin K may reduce the effectiveness of this drug and make larger doses necessary." These debilitating foods include "asparagus, bacon, beef liver, cabbage, fish, cauliflower and green leafy vegetables." Boo hoo hoo, you cry and move on. Vitamin C in high doses may create Coumadin resistance, so you cut back on C tablets, except during cold and flu season. Likewise, high doses of Vitamin E may increase risk of bleeding, so you avoid this substance, too, even though you recall that when a doctor performs back surgery on you a decade earlier, Vitamin E applied to the wound makes it all but disappear. You keep this in mind should you have more surgery. Each month you take a blood test to determine your dosage, which, along with your heartbeat, must be regulated like a baby's formula.

"Coumadin should also not be taken with herbal medicines like ginger, garlic, or green tea." Therefore, if you happen to have great affection for old-fashioned ginger ale that burns your throat or the candied ginger you eat to calm your stomach after meals, forget about it. Coumadin also works in mysterious ways to *increase* the effects of acetaminophen, aspirin, or Ultram, a drug you take three times a day for chronic pain. Hmmm. You decide to ask your doctor about interactions, the very next time you see him.

BENEFITS OF COUMADIN. "This medication helps to keep blood flowing smoothly in your body by decreasing the amount of clotting proteins in the blood. Coumadin is commonly referred to as a 'blood thin-ner,' but its more correct term is 'anticoagulant.'" Preventing harmful blood clots ensures that you will not suffer a stroke or heart attack.

SIDE EFFECTS OF COUMADIN. "Nausea, vomiting, loss of appetite, stomach/ abdominal bloating or cramps may occur," although you've yet to experience any of these. "Remember that your doctor has prescribed this medication because the benefit to you is greater than the risk of side effects. This medication might cause bleeding if its effect on your blood clotting proteins is too much." This means unusually high PT (prothrombin time) and INR (international normalized ratio) results. You know this fact because every four weeks you make a pilgrimage to your cardiologist, where a nurse pricks your finger and tests your blood. She either tells you to continue the same dosage or refers the numbers to the doctor, who anon may lower or raise your dosage. "Even if your doctor stops your medication, this risk [of stroke] can persist for up to a week." In fact, should you require a procedure, say, dental work, colonoscopy, or any kind of surgery, you must cease tak-ing the drug up to seven days in advance. This move may make you vulnerable to having a stroke, but if it happens while you're under, then who will know the difference? Certainly not you.

"Tell your doctor if any of these signs of serious bleeding occur: unusual pain/swelling/discomfort/prolonged bleeding from cuts or gums, persistent nosebleeds, unusually heavy or prolonged menstrual flow, unusual or easy bruising, dark urine, black stools, severe head-ache, unusual dizziness. This drug might infrequently cause serious (possibly fatal) complications from the dislodging of solid patches of cholesterol from blood vessel walls, which can block the blood supply to parts of your body. Left untreated, this condition can lead to severe tissue damage or gangrene. Seek attention if the following occur: painful red rash, dark discoloration of any body part (purple toe syn-drome), sudden intense pain (back or muscle), foot ulcers, unusual change in the amount of urine you void, vision changes, confusion, slurred speech, weakness on one side of the body [in which case you switch hands and dial 911]. Serious allergic symptoms may include rash, itching, swelling, severe dizziness, trouble breathing. Contact your doctor immediately."

CO-PAY. Ten dollars for sixty tablets, or eleven cents per pill. A small price to pay to remain stroke-free.

EXHIBITION GAMES. These are the first games of basketball season. You do not count them in the win/loss record. These games are for practice, but in recent years the NCAA has eliminated them from the men's schedules. Your team, for example, begins the season with a tournament at home. Though you win, the first game is rough. The many new and talented players do not seem to know there exist on the floor four others, with whom they must function as a well-oiled machine. Thus saith Coach.

You keep looking at your program, trying to memorize a player's name (which is not stitched to his uniform, so as to eliminate any sense of star quality), using your binocs to memorize his face or a quirky mannerism. Some players look too much alike, whether they're white, blond, black or brown. If, for example, two men of the same stature and build both possess crew cuts, you must memorize their numbers; same for two guys with shaved heads or two guys with dreads. If two women have dark brown ponytails, you must memorize their numbers. Frizzy blondes. You can't tell by looking which crew-cut male or pony-tailed female or frizzy blonde it is. But after you get past the superficialities of appearances, you learn the most about players by watching their actions.

In particular the way players shoot a three can tip you off; some almost jackknife their bodies like Olympic divers. Others seem to levitate above the court, rising to an eerie height before releasing what is basically an intercontinental bomb. Some shots have a high arcing trajectory. This type results in one of two things: either the ball goes in slick as a whistle, or it makes a meteoric bounce off the rim, rebounding into the hands of the defense. Players who shoot a more direct, line-drive path to the basket seem to experience greater success. For one, there exists less time for the defense to react, as opposed to a high, arcing orb, during which time you could mix a highball. These shots also have a slight chance of caroming off the backboard and into the basket.

Last season your women's team loses one of its exhibition games to a squad that has seven members, one of whom limps her way down the floor every play. It is not a good season for your women; they win a total of fifteen games. They do not go to the NCAAs for the first time in sixteen years. The coach, still venerated (much more so after she resigns), ends the season with her head up, welcoming her winning and energetic successor from the Big Ten. Gone but not forgotten.

The women's game is subtly different from the men's, but each is enjoyable for its own reasons. Men have strength and athleticism going for them. Watching a player fight his way to the basket without fouling anyone or without getting the ball stolen or without getting fouled is an act that is both dancerly—like boxing—*and* athletic. But the women rely on certain finesse, more like men played fifty years ago, before the Behemoths took over the game. Women are less apt to travel, foul, or commit other errors because they don't have that pesky forward momentum working against them. And that's beautiful, you see. They can and do shoot the three as skillfully as men, maybe more so. They tend to play better as a team, because, culturally, girls stick together—going all the way back to sixth grade, when females like your older daughter make character assassination of their teacher a higher calling. Women make a better percentage of free throws, because winning close games always depends on making free throws, and women can be relentless about details. Women don't dunk the ball; in fact, it's against their rules. When the rules change some day—and you know they will, as women evolve in physical stature—their game will become more like the men's. Refs will not call walking as much, because in looking up to see what the Behemoths are doing with their elbows, they will miss the shuffle of feet. Refs will let the petty hand checks go. Unless an out-and-out brawl erupts (unlikely in this estrogen crowd), the refs will let the game proceed like the men's. Pity.

LIPITOR. You take these ten white milligrams before bedtime, say, ten o'clock along with your Tikosyn and your pain pills, since your body produces cholesterol at the fastest rate between midnight and five a.m. "Ingesting the drug blocks a liver enzyme that starts making cholesterol, thus lowering the low-density lipoproteins (LDL), the cholesterol fraction thought to increase risk of coronary heart disease. Since the amount of cholesterol is reduced in the liver, the VLDL fraction may also be decreased." It means you can eat fish and chips. A fucking Big Mac, if you want. Especially if Mona ain't lookin'.

CONDITIONS INDICATING THE USE OF LIPITOR. Back when you're forty your cholesterol totals 180. You begin to eat a strict high-fiber, low-fat diet. You are relentless about it, ordering bran by the truckload, eating only fish and poultry, growing your own organic veggies. Your body and Mona's body remain lean, but through the next decade your numbers rise (though hers do not). Your kids are svelte, too. By this time Lipitor has entered the market. When you hit your mid-fifties and your cholesterol totals 230, your primary care physician places you on this wonder drug, Lipitor. On the next test, your numbers plummet to 146, thus vindicating you, because, everything else being equal, you have proof that your sensible diet of grass, herbs, and fish works. See! you tell your doctor.

INTERACTIONS. You DO NOT take this medicine with grapefruit juice, a beverage you will miss as much as Ovaltine. Otherwise, excessive blood levels and increased risk of muscle damage may occur. You should take Lipitor with water or milk. Lipitor can *increase* the effects of Digoxin, the medication you are on before Tikosyn. If you were to take Digoxin again, Lipitor might increase the Digoxin levels, leading to toxic effects. This idea is good to keep in mind, in case your doctor should change your Master Drug Plan. You hope he won't. Digoxin makes you feel depressed and sluggish. *A depressed and sluggish slug of a slug does not accomplish much in the course of a day.* For fun you teach your daughter to say it ten times fast, until your wife puts the kibosh on that.

POSSIBLE BENEFITS OF LIPITOR. Lipitor might reduce your total LDL cholesterol (you remember this is the BAD cholesterol because the word

GOOD begins with G, which is one letter removed from H of HDL). Lipitor might decrease your triglycerides, but since you don't know how these affect you, you don't care. Lipitor is known to increase your HDL cholesterol (remember, one letter removed from G) if you have primary hypercholesterolemia or mixed dyslipidemia. Lipitor might even help prevent bone loss in type 2 diabetics, but you can't know this assertion is true, unless you yourself develop diabetes and volunteer for tests.

SIDE EFFECTS OF LIPITOR. Lipitor can spin you into a drug-induced hepatitis (without jaundice), which is rare. It can cause drug-induced myositis (muscle inflammation), also rare. It can even trigger a decrease in the coenzyme Q10, whatever the fuck that is. Not many doctors concur with you, but you happen to believe Lipitor also contributes to weight loss. You notice it in your father, who, at seventy-eight, takes Lipitor when his numbers reach 300. Immediately, because his body responds so well, his dose is reduced from ten to five milligrams; he achieves this by employing a pill splitter. You notice that by age eighty, your father has begun to lose weight, and he's still eating, according to your mother, what he's always eaten, tons. You think little about it, until you yourself have been on the drug two years, and your primary care physician believes you might be a few pounds underweight. You wonder how, because you eat tons, too. Right away, you ask, *Is it the Lipitor or the Coumadin?* You wonder, because a few of your older friends are on one or the other or both, and you observe from this, quite scientifically charting their weights in your head, that it must be one or the other. Or both.

CO-PAY. Fifty dollars for ninety pills, or fifty-six cents a pill. If you didn't achieve such excellent results, you might think the drug is a fucking rip-off.

GAME ATTENDANCE. When you first start going in 1976, attendance in the old Coliseum averages 6,000 for the men's games (forget the women, their time is yet to arrive). If they play one of their two in-state rivals, the crowd might grow to the max, eight or ten thousand (SRO). You're talking a university of 23,000 students. You're talking a city that back then is a 160,000. And this is the best attendance you can come up with? Please. Still, you kind of like it. Parking is easier if the Coliseum is not filled. You can get home faster. The Coliseum's men's rooms (both of them) are easier to negotiate. You can get a stall any time. And that is important, since your bladder, which can be quivering in agony, locks down if you are forced to urinate along a trough with ten other men. It won't happen.

At the turn of the century (this one), Spirit Temple Arena, a new basketball venue, is erected on the edge of university property, along with six city blocks of parking. The $62 million Temple is huge, rising three stories and stretching itself out to the length of a ship, built with a hint of the Spanish Renaissance architecture found around campus. Free parking is a three-block walk. You do it because it's good for you and Mona, and because the Personal Seat License parking, located across from the Temple, is higher than a cat's back and goes up thirty dollars each year—a mere trifle for the upper classes or those who aspire to join such classes, but to commoners it's a sacrifice. In windy weathers you cross the vast asphalt jungle, past the PBS station with its assorted satellite dishes, some as big as Suburbans, past Old and New Meats (a nod to Jane Smiley for nomenclature). You believe Old Meats is located in the new building, and New Meats in the old, but it's a hazy thought, something you might have read in the paper. On a given night, when a blue norther is advancing across the South Plains, you can hear the wind whistle like a train through the gridwork of the PBS tower, making you hold your parka tight around your head. Even so, you later rinse red dirt from your mouth.

When Spirit Temple Arena first opens, you are agog with joy. It holds 15,550 bodies, and the first night, against a tough Big Ten opponent, every one of the harlot-red seats is filled. That is to say, if a body is not urinating in one of the fifteen restrooms (fifteen for each gender), if a body is not in the food court buying something that will give it cholesterol overload, if a body is not picking up a hot dog at one of the dozen snack bars located along the perimeter of the arena, every body is in place for the tip-off. Every body is wearing scarlet or black, the two choices for Correct School Colors. The pep band, composed of sixty members, is playing all the old tunes, and you feel returning to your limbs a warmth that hasn't been there for eight months. Yeah, it's almost tip-off time.

Three officials are chatting up the team captains as they loiter around the oversized decal in the middle of the floor. In the 1999th year of our Lord you find your seats, the ones you've carefully selected on a given day in the fall, when all the Personal Seat Licensees flock to the Temple to select their chairs. To cram in 15,550 seats, the chairs are not configured in true stadium format. In the old Coliseum, the heads of the people in the row beneath you (there exists a subtle class distinction from one row to the next) are also beneath your line of vision. In Spirit Temple Arena, the heads of those beneath you can block your vision. But then you learn to raise your head and look at the four-screened Jumbotron suspended from the ceiling by thick iron cables. Five digital cameras record every play of the game, and the truth of each play is revealed, whether the officials abide by the truth or not. Yes, you learn to raise your vision to the blinking screen. If a crowd of people choke the aisle, blocking your view, you raise your eyes, where you can see live action. If there arises a question, you raise your eyes to view the call as it is replayed ad nauseam, until everyone in the Temple knows the truth. The officials fucked up. Or the officials got it right. Or the play cannot be determined because not one of the five cameras focused on the game was clever enough to capture the truth.

As the new millennium grinds forward a year at a time, you become less enamored with Spirit Temple Arena. A six-foot-five brute now sits right in front of you (he's actually a guest of the PSL owner beneath you, the brute's seat is behind the northern goal, you've seen the parties wave at one another like school girls), and you must view most of the game on Jumbotron. If you try to watch the action, you must move your head as this musclehead moves his. He doesn't realize how he ruins your vision at the slightest adjustment. He doesn't give a shit, a trait you find in his class of people, a row beneath yours. Of course, that's what the little lady, a grandmother who sits behind you, thinks of you, but you don't give a shit, either, so you're square with both parties.

The men's games still average six to eight thousand bodies, a number that half fills the Temple. If, when they play one of their two state rivals and "fill" the Temple with twelve or thirteen thousand, you feel good, as if the building is reaching its potential as a Temple. But again, you wonder. With a student body of 25,000, in a city of over 200,000, and you still can't fill the arena every game?

You finally accept that West Texas is not basketball country. No, now come on, it isn't. At many places in the Midwest and along the Atlantic Seaboard, denizens thrive on sitting in a starkly lit, cheer-full arena on a bitterly cold night and filling it to the brim. Think of the Phog in Lawrence. Rupp in Lexington. Cameron at Duke. Maybe it's because some of these places offer free tickets to students, who are willing to queue up for forty-eight hours in subfreezing temps. Maybe it's because some of these universities have had basketball teams for over a century now, making the sport as catholic as the Book of Common Prayer. Maybe it's because the costs to enter Spirit Temple Arena are too dear. Yes, a seat that costs three thousand up front may be *too dear*. The bitter truth is that only if your teams win and keep winning will people pay buckets of money to watch. Losers? Not so much.

AVODART. At first you take this drug every day for six months: a dull yellow, oblong capsule containing a half milligram of an androgen hormone inhibitor. This ingredient treats benign prostatic hyperplasia (BPH), which is, simply put, the swelling of the prostate, a little-known organ (until it screams out for attention) installed behind your genitals where it engulfs your urethra, choking it off when you try to urinate. Why God couldn't place this organ, say, in your wrist, for easier access, you have no idea. "This drug works by lowering the amount of the hormone responsible for prostate growth. It reduces urinary blockage and improves urine flow. Women and children should not take this drug." Yeah, since the former have no prostate, and half the latter group have one that has yet to develop. God, you'd love to meet the dopes who write this crap!

CONDITIONS INDICATING THE USE OF AVODART. Your urologist has determined through a number of means that you must take this drug. He begins by placing his longest finger up your rectum and examining in a way that seems impossible to determine anything that your walnut-sized prostate has grown to unmanageable proportions. *Ye Gods, it's as big as an apple,* he says. The doctor also refers to the result of your PSA (prostate-specific antigens)—determined by testing a vial of your blood—which is elevated above the sacred number of four. Because such a figure means you might have prostate cancer, he then subjects you to your first biopsy. You will eventually suffer through three over a period of four years. He wants to make sure.

The biopsy is an outpatient procedure, conducted on a gurneylike bed in his office, where you lie on your side, in a fetal position, with your feet shoved against the wall. Accessing the prostate through your rectal wall, your urologist removes sample cores of flesh from ten segments of each lobe. Even with a local anesthetic, you believe he's using a fondue fork. And when you bleed like a stuck pig, filling the toilet bowl as you try to stanch the flow with Northern tissue, you leave the premises with blood streaming down your leg, a substance that floods your socks and spills over to stain the waiting-room carpet. In ten days you find out you do not have cancer; this is when you begin to take Avodart daily. After six months, when your prostate has returned to normal proportions, the doctor cuts your dosage to every other day, and you thank God for small favors.

INTERACTIONS. You ask your urologist right away how this drug might interact with your other drugs: Tikosyn, Coumadin, Lipitor, and the two you've not discussed, Soma and Ultram. Oh, yes, and eighty-one milligrams of aspirin, or the occasional antibiotic you take for a scalp infection. *No problem,* he says, not bothering to research it while you're in his office. So you research it on your own, consulting the World Wide Web of Indisputable Information. "From this point forward," the website says, "before you begin taking any new medications, either prescription or OTC, you must check with your doctor or pharmacist. This medicine may be absorbed through the skin. Any woman who is pregnant or who may become pregnant should not handle crushed or broken capsules of this medicine." Ohhh, yes, *now* you see. "Any contact with this medicine by a developing male fetus might result in abnormal male sex organ development." Ohhh, wow, *now* you see, and move Avodart to the medicine chest in the utility bath, the one your wife and daughters wouldn't use if you paid them.

BENEFITS OF AVODART. You now urinate more freely. You do not rise two to four times a night, perhaps once, in the wee hours of the morning. You train yourself to go back to sleep—unless, of course, you've managed to wangle from your primary care physician a prescription for Ambien while on a trip so you can sleep in a strange bed, in which case you might conk out for seven or eight hours. It seems like so little to ask for because the benefits of sustained sleep are wonderful, sort of a temporary death from which you are resurrected day after day.

SIDE EFFECTS OF AVODART. You can and do experience a change in sexual function: impotence (even without the help of Viagra, Cialis, or Levitra—you try them all), decreased interest in sex (ever so subtle, Mona says with eyes as sad as Bambi's), a decrease in the amount of ejaculate, a quantity you once produced in great volume even in your forties (possibly the reason why, at fifty-eight, you have a ten-year-old daughter). They say these effects may go away as your body adjusts to the drug, but you think someone's lying. Breast tenderness or enlargement may also occur while you are on this drug. Thank Christ on his cross you haven't noticed anything like this. "If these effects continue or are bothersome, you might check with your doctor." But you don't because you enjoy peeing freely. You enjoy sleeping through the night. You realize you've now exchanged a more youthful form of sex for sleep, and you know you are old, older than West Texas dirt.

CO-PAY. Fifty dollars for ninety capsules, or fifty-six cents apiece. Another rip-off. You write the drug company. They never respond. They never do. They never will.

CONFERENCE PLAY. You've endured half the season now: games with Little Sisters of the Prairie and other religious colleges; state schools; schools from the North, South, East, and West. Your teams have played in tournaments and shootouts from Hawaii to Alaska to Key West. It's now New Year's Day, and your boys are facing one of the major universities in the state north of here, the one with a true panhandle. The women, as luck would have it, are playing at that selfsame university before a paltry crowd, because their women currently stink. Every year these two men's teams gouge it out until the last minute, no matter how lousy one team might be. Their coach is older than yours, but yours has more wins. The media say their coach drives drunk. Yours is portrayed as a bully, though if people try and get to know the guy, how he respects his players, they can clearly see he isn't. He isn't. Truly. You wouldn't support the games if he were.

The Spirit Temple Arena is almost full. You can see a few harlot-red seats vacant in the upper level, high up where all the banners hang. Students, mostly dudes in black-and-red face with red or black clown wigs, begin to stamp their feet and jump up and down, while the pep band plays the fight song on an endless loop. Waiting, waiting, waiting for the team to enter the arena. You know Coach is giving last-minute instructions that are akin to what those felled soldiers at Normandy must have received. And now you know why teachers make you read *Beowulf;* yes, even today, men must have dragons to slay. As soon as the band takes a breather, the sound booth plays a recording, some dude with a deep voice saying, "Put yur hands tuhgether," followed by simulated clapping, going faster until the crowd can't keep up and the sound dies out. The booth plays a CD where some dude screams, "Let's get ready to *ruuummm*bbbble." This crowd needs no encouragement.

You move to the aisle and up to the concourse to buy a bottle of Dasani because you forgot yours, and you'll have to take pills before the afternoon is over. You also buy a pretzel, because you should not take your pills on an empty stomach. When you return you have to scare some dude from your three-thousand-dollar chair, some nincompoop who sneaked past the usher, a guy who checks everyone's ticket stub (except yours, because he knows you), though evidently not, or the nincompoop wouldn't be occupying your chair. You raise your thumb (outta there, fella), and the dude, maybe eighteen, takes off toward the other aisle. You check the upholstery for stains that might have been incurred since your last game. No, there is the same dark outline the athletic office refuses to steam-clean. You get over it. Again.

You sit, and now the teams race into the arena. The PA dude announces the players on the opposing team. Then yours. With a men's game, the lights stay on. But at a women's game, the place goes dark, and there are all these spotlights with the school logo and name twirling on the floor, especially where the opposition is standing. The women's crowd spin little battery-operated lights of red that cost ten bucks (the money goes to a good cause). However, Coach doesn't stand for such nonsense; the lights stay on. The teams are announced, and before you can say James Naismith, the ball has been tipped. Their player knocks it out of bounds, and it's yours. Your point guard nails a three right off the bat, and Coach hits the roof, along with the crowd, but for different reasons. Coach likes for the team to pass the ball at least three times. But jeez, you think, the dude's wide open, and he's been hot since mid-November. Why not take a shot that takes you up three-zip? (And because it's so cool, you might keep using the word *dude*.)

Your opponent takes the possession down to the wire, and for fun, you try to analyze their defense. Is it a man-to-man? Or a junk defense (box and one, for example, where one player guards, say, your hot point guard, and the other four play *zone*, right)? Three up front and two down low? Two up front and three down low? One-three-one? Sometimes the bastards even switch defenses, trying to confuse your boys. Their defensive coach holds up a big three or a "Z" or something ridiculous. Sometimes their defensive coach stamps his foot and throws the sign down, because his players, from thirty feet away, can't see a damn thing.

Before you know it, the first official time-out arrives. The score is twelve-eleven, your team on top. You take a swig from your water, saving most of it for your pills. The pompom chicks do their little number to the theme from *Austin Powers*. They're wearing slinky black tights and glittery red tops that look more like sports bras, leaving a nifty space to display their midriffs. One of the chicks has a bit of paunch. *You think she's pregnant?* you ask Mona, who turns her head and speaks. *No, the girl likes her Big Macs and fries.* She winks. For one, your wife knows you cheat on your diet, and two, the pom-pom girls formerly wore short skirts . . . and sweater tops. You've traded views: bottoms for tops. How the world changes in a blink. You and Mona once cheered from the Coliseum floor, when she was your partner with her feet planted squarely on your shoulders, and you gazed up into her red panties as if they were a world to be conquered. Which they were, if you want to be honest.

The first half stays close and ends thirty-all. You can't wait for the second half, because this is where Coach demonstrates his superior understanding of the game and makes adjustments whereby your team can beat the opposition into submission. But first, you witness the Halftime Shootout. Two of the men's pep members roll a big slim TV onto the floor. Two male students compete at opposite ends of the court, and two female students, seeing how many free throws they can make in ten tries. Then each winner earns the chance to shoot a half-court shot that might win the big slim TV.

Over the years you've watched the TV models change. You've watched the sponsor change. Everything about this shtick has changed except for the fact that no one ever hits the half-court shot. Today is no different. The female, a rather tall one with a fiery red ponytail, nearly makes it, bouncing the ball off the back of the glass. The crowd goes "Unh!" so loud you think she's lost the war (and you know that sound). The guy lines himself up about six paces behind the time line. He eyes the basket, studies it, as many have done in the past. He takes one, two, three quick steps and heaves the orange ball, releasing it before he sails over the line. It makes a giant arc toward the basket. You remember what happens to half the balls shot with a high arcing trajectory, and your mouth snaps shut when the kid actually nails it. Maybe ten thousand people cheer; the rest are still out on the concourse feeding their faces or flushing 150 urinals as if the guy has won the game. On the Jumbotron, you watch the shot as it's shown over and over. The kid and his roommates run to the TV and caress it like a stuffed toy. Local stations interview the winner, and he says he doesn't know where he's going to put the big slim TV. He and his roommates live in the dorm. "Maybe Mom'll keep it for me until I graduate."

Yessirree. You feel good about the second half not only because your team is leading by ten at the first time-out but because something great has happened here. A poor college kid, who might not make that shot again in fifty tries, wins an expensive plasma TV, one that may not even work when and if he graduates. Yessirree.

SOMA. You take 350 milligrams three times a day: one white tablet at noon, one at five, and one at ten, along with your Tikosyn, your Lipitor. This drug and your Ultram have sustained you the longest. "This medication is used to treat pain and discomfort from muscle injuries such as strains, sprains, and spasms [for you, it's the spasms]. It often accompanies rest, physical therapy, and other treatments (e.g. anti-inflammatory medication or Ultram). Soma is a centrally acting muscle relaxant. It works on the nerves to relieve muscle pain. It may also relieve pain by calming your nervous system." Its effects are so soothing that, after several years, you become inured to them. You drive. You swim. You do Pilates. You do almost everything on Soma that you didn't do on Soma. You like the name that one of the futuristic authors used for a drug that induced more than relaxation. A Brave New Drug, one of the oldest tranquilizers, one that happens to relax your muscles so you can manage one hour to the next. One day to the next. One month. Years. A decade.

CONDITIONS INDICATING THE USE OF SOMA. Long ago, at forty-six, you lift a case of paper where you package and sell insurance, because one of the petite secretaries asks you to. It's not half as heavy as your mower or what you lift at the gym, but it's enough. You don't notice anything right away, but over the weeks you realize your doctor, who's told you to stop lifting weights, is right, when he shows you an X-ray that proves how slim the spaces between your vertebrae are. "Degenerative discs," he says. Each day, upon your rising, the electrical sensation of a buzz begins in your hip, as if someone is sticking you with pins.

But even before the Soma you take Ibuprofen, as much as 3,200 milligrams a day. You rise at seven, and the buzz begins in your lumbar region and continues through the day; as gravity applies pressure to your spine, the buzz continues down your left leg, into your toes. At times your foot feels like it must be in a cartoon where a duck hammers a rabbit on the foot and the toe visibly turns red and throbs like a squeezed balloon. Ibuprofen barely touches this buzz, but you watch the clock for the next dosage, because it's all you have. You can no longer sit at the computer, a requirement of your job. In fact, all your duties seem to aggravate your condition. Sit. Stand. Lift. You realize anybody with a buzz like this in his legs can't work. You buy a special computer chair that dials up the buzz sooner than usual. You switch to one of those new laptops. Another mistake. If you sit with it in your lap, you are forced to look down. If you put it on a desktop, your hands and arms are raised in an unnaturally awkward angle. You tire of it all, your boss grants you medical leave, and you go home to lie in the position that would provide you the most comfort if it weren't for the spasms that shoot through your lower back like fireworks.

You are referred to an anesthesiologist who also does pain management (a true oxymoron). You remember in your thirties scoffing at the notion of chronic pain. *Who could hurt all the time? You take something for it, grab a shower, rub salve into the affected area, and move on.* But your views change. The buzz that runs from your spine down your leg and into your toes worsens each day. You might take the whole bottle of Ibuprofen to see what happens. You don't care. Mona says you look ashen and runs her fingers through your hair, what's left of it. You *feel* like ashes, detritus of your former self. Your children avoid you like the plague.

The pain management doctor shoots stuff directly into your back—epidural steroid shots—to alleviate the buzz in your lumbar region that runs down your leg and into your toes. He gives you three over the course of several weeks. No good, you tell him. He prescribes physical therapy. Three times a week you go to the hospital where the therapist works. The tall strong woman who reminds you of actor Eileen Brennan begins by having you strip to your underwear. She places hot packs over your entire body, and you lie there for ten minutes. She returns and begins to massage your body. Your lumbar region. *Ohhh,*

God, that's heaven, can I take you home with me? She works lotion down into your legs, your toes. With strong, rangy arms she pulls the lotion along each leg, pulling, stretching your leg, breaking down the fascia in your muscles, trying to separate that space between discs. After an hour you feel decent. You go back to work for several weeks, while continuing therapy. But the buzz reasserts itself and you grab a beer, a substance that no longer gives you the relief it once did.

You continue with 3,200 milligrams a day of Ibuprofen (called therapeutic doses). You feel as if you're walking on a magic carpet—glide, glide, gliding along the floor. You remain ashen. You can no longer tolerate the entirety of your work day, whether you sit, stand, or lie on your sofa. Your boss begins to look at you differently. Slacking off? No, you want to say, it's this buzz you've got going in your back. Your colleagues stare at you the way they do the old agents who gather their briefcases at four-thirty and loiter in the lunchroom. You're not ready to be one of those men, but you may have no choice.

Your buzz has a definite curve. You go to bed at night, using the guest room, because your buzz—on a scale of one to ten—hovers above a nine. You now use traction to pull your feet, your legs, your spine downward. The apparatus consists of a girdle you secure around your hips. Then you hook weights to both sides, and, as you try to sleep, the weights pull your vertebrae apart (theoretically), thus reducing the pressure and some of the agony. But it has no permanent effect; as soon as you stand, the buzz returns. You at long last fall asleep, and since you are not free to roll over, you pass in and out of slumber like a train chugging in and out of tunnels. The buzz presently lowers itself to a hum, maybe a three. If you have to use the bathroom, you must unhook the apparatus and hook it up to your hips once you lie down. If you're lucky, you fall asleep once again. For two nights Mona sleeps in the space next to you, but on the third she returns to the master bedroom. Your wakefulness keeps her awake. You're still married. You love each other, but for the first time in decades, you're not sleeping together, and it feels like divorce, though you've never been through one. Not yet.

INTERACTIONS. Inconsequential. BENEFITS OF SOMA: Far outweigh risks of possible dangers, so stay with Soma forever, or until your doctor gives you a plan for gradual withdrawal. But you know it won't be easy, so you don't think about it.

SIDE EFFECTS OF SOMA. "Dizziness, drowsiness, headache, unusually fast heartbeat [hmmm], low blood pressure, or face flushing may occur. If any of these effects persist or worsen, notify your doctor or pharmacist promptly." *Remember that your doctor has prescribed this medication because the benefit to you is greater than the risk of side effects.* You keep it in mind, every time a nurse asks for a list of your medications.

CO-PAY. Ten dollars for ninety, eleven cents a pill. Cheap. You might take two.

ULTRAM. Introduced in 1996, the year of your surgery, Ultram is used to relieve pain. Plain and simple. "Ultram increases the availability of serotonin and norepinephrine in certain brain centers and also works at opioid centers, thereby relieving pain." For nearly ten years you take fifty milligrams at noon, another fifty at five p.m., and another fifty at ten (the magic hour for Tikosyn and Lipitor), each taken in concert with Soma. Because you've worked up a tolerance, you talk your doctor into prescribing another fifty milligrams (the Big Drug Book says you can *tolerate* up to 400 milligrams daily). Doc looks at you as if you're a drug addict, and you act like one, glaring back without blinking, until he relents with a scribble of his pen. Instead of taking a fourth one in a day, you halve it and combine it with your noon and five o'clock dosages. You do this because you can, and because it feels good, especially in the first half hour, when you sit staring at a syndicated *Seinfeld* for the umpteenth time, waiting for the blessed seventy-five milligrams to kick in.

You hoard pills. On rare days when you don't use them all because you're in bed with the flu or it's February in a non–leap year and your pharmacist doesn't count the three days that a month might normally yield, you harvest twelve. You wheedle a few samples from your doctor friends, each unbeknownst to the other. Online you finagle exorbitantly priced pills from a Canadian firm (whose "doctor" authorizes your prescription), to give you a cushion for when you're out of town. From your cache, from your stash, you sometimes take two, when you know you're going to be jetting across the sky on your keister for four hours or if you've lifted something you shouldn't and you're buzzing a ten. You buy Ultram and Soma by the month, on the first date your prescription is renewable, not because, oops, you've run out of pills. By renewing a day early you can hoard four more.

You dream of a day when you might go to a pain farm and get off this shit, like overweight people go to a fat farm. You dream of feeling like you did before you lifted that case of paper, but unless the medical establishment comes up with something new and different, you realize your dream is a fool's errand. You will die someday with Ultram and Soma lacing your blood, clotting your liver, creating kidney stones. Even so, you steadfastly adhere to your Ultram dosages because the alternative is morphine. You're not exactly sure what Ultram has done to you over this decade, but you do know you cannot function without it. And function you must.

CONDITIONS INDICATING THE USE OF ULTRAM. In 1996, after seven months of Mona saying you look ashen, you seek advice from an orthopedic surgeon. Actually, you consult two, because your insurance policy requires it. You like the first guy better, a shrimp with glasses, because his procedure seems more solid. What he proposes to do is remove your flat-as-a-tire disc, the lowest one in your spine, and replace it with bone slivers from your own body, and, on a cold day in December he does precisely this. Through the great tender mercies of an anesthesiologist, he makes three slits in your body. From the slit in your hip, he harvests said bone slivers to shove between the discs. Because he does it all around, the procedure is called a 360 fusion. Yes, the bone slivers, given time, bond together, thus creating a new sort of disc for you. Sort of, because it is, by comparison to the original disc, rather inflexible. Because he must do this all around, he cuts a slit along your spine, and a colleague of his slits open your front, laying your intestines out on the table so the former may work. You find it hard to believe this shrimp can wrestle with the spine of a grown man, but after four hours he's done. Oh, before he quits he drills four titanium screws between your sacrum and the lowest vertebra, functioning much like a cast—except that you know these screws are never coming out. He later that night tells you he did ten more spines after yours. It's Christmas, after all.

You spend twelve weeks at home: you read thirty-eight books, conduct video festivals of your favorite actors, like Robert Mitchum and Shirley MacLaine, and you begin to sell policies over the phone. During this time you work your way down from several opiates like Darvon, even the antidepressant Elavil, to Ultram. Your surgeon suggests that you will reach a point in the future where you may take a couple of Tylenol should you have some discomfort. Clearly, all these years later, the fucker is quite mistaken. Perhaps this is why you sign a waiver in 1996 pledging not to take legal action if your pain isn't alleviated. With scalpel in hand he says, "All I promise is to do the very best job I can." At the time it seems like a fair proposition.

After surgery, through days, months, and years of seeking nonsurgical therapy (massage, Pilates, swimming), you can honestly say that the pain has been reduced by sixty percent, if you can quantify such a concept. Pain. But you seize it as an abstraction and tell your friends. Yes, the surgery does not take away all your pain, but it reduces it by sixty percent. "Not many people can say that," you declare.

INTERACTIONS. "Ultram may increase the effects of Coumadin, requiring dose adjustments; more frequent INR tests are prudent." These are the monthly pilgrimages you make to your cardiologist where your finger is pricked and your dosage adjusted for another month. *Oh, my goodness, Ultram could effect a change in your Coumadin dosage* is a sentence that never leaves the mouth of any health care worker you know.

BENEFITS OF ULTRAM. Effective treatment of pain. You can make it through a staff meeting without screaming. You can visit with a client (standing for three minutes feels like ten thousand needles being thrust into your back), until you ask the client if sitting down wouldn't be nicer. Please. Thank you. You're welcome. You make it through day after day, a functional addict who earns a living, drives a car, makes love to his wife (with modifications). Yes, you make it through the day and pray for one more.

SIDE EFFECTS OF ULTRAM. "This medication may cause dizziness [it doesn't], weakness [nope], incoordination [maybe], nausea or vomiting [never], stomach upset, constipation, headache, drowsiness [in that first lovely half hour], anxiety [no more than you already have], irritability [no more than when some Christian or occasionally a pagan cuts you off on the Marsha Sharp Freeway], dry mouth, or increased sweating. If any of these effects persist or worsen, inform you doctor. *Remember that your doctor has prescribed this medication because the benefit to you is greater than the risk of side effects.* Many people using this medication [like you] do not have serious side effects. Notify your doctor if you develop any of these serious effects while taking this medication: chest pain, rapid heart rate [now there's a thought], skin rash or itching, mental confusion, disorientation, seizures, tingling of the hands or feet, trouble breathing. In the unlikely event that you have a serious allergic reaction to this drug, seek immediate medical attention. Symptoms of a serious allergic reaction include rash, itching, swelling, severe dizziness, breathing trouble. If you notice other effects not listed above [like major loss of libido, you want to say, or inability to ejaculate after prolonged stimulation] contact your doctor or pharmacist."

CO-PAY. Ten dollars for a hundred twenty pills, or eight cents a pill. Also cheap, the Walmart (now leading the way with a four-dollar co-pay) of drugs.

YOU ARE NOT ADDICTED. You reach the season when you would like to sell your Personal Seat Licenses. The men are playing like junior high boys and the women like little girls. You haven't paid three thousand dollars to watch this kind of nonsense, but since everyone feels this way, you have no buyers for your chairs. You and Mona continue to frequent Spirit Temple Arena. You're well into the conference season. It's even snowed once or twice. Each time you drive across town, in a climate where it might not snow for four years, the streets are crowded with four graduating classes of drivers who've never negotiated slick roads before, only watched the film or worked the simulators. Students from the Metroplex accuse local drivers of going too slow. The locals wave guns at these kids from the Metroplex, who drive as if fifty-five is prudent on surface streets even on a dry pavement. *Slowing down might be a good thing*, you want to say to the kids from the Metroplex. A hundred accidents this day, and you wonder if you should hazard black ice to see the home team play the Phog boys from Lawrence. Yeah, why not? Your men have beaten this team only once in history, so why not? Yeah.

You and Mona show early, before the streets refreeze, for one thing, and to get a decent parking spot in the free lot, for another, for there is that three-block walk. Even this many years removed from surgery, bouncing across the asphalt jars your spine, increases the buzz down your leg, but you take Mona's hand and bounce as smoothly as you can, past the public broadcasting station, past the dusty smells of Old and New Meats.

Once you take the elevator up into the Temple, you meet friends in the STA cafeteria and shell out twelve bucks apiece for a brisket buffet and as many cookies as you can carry away. When you finish, you find your seats. You look up and believe you see electricity arcing from one spotlight to another. The pep band seems to be playing with particular clarity tonight, the brass sounding as one big instrument. You watch your boys warming up, and each one seems to be making every shot he takes, whether it's a layup, a jump shot, or a three. Might you begin to hope? Might your boys beat the second-ranked team in the country? You notice a new cologne, and it smells like victory.

The Phog opponents trot onto the floor, snaking their fifteen players in a shiny blue streak around the entire perimeter of the court before beginning a warm-up. Your fans boo. It's arrogant to flaunt their team in front of your home crowd like that, as if they're privileged, as if they're entitled. But if any team is entitled, it's this one. Over a century of tradition oozes from the pores of these players like sap from a maple tree. They can't help it. It comes with their territory.

You look back at your boys. They're still hitting lights out. Strange because most warm-ups, balls are bouncing off the backboard into the pep band. The same player may miss three free throws in a row. That new cologne is tightening the air, and more and more bodies fill the harlot red seats. Maybe this will be the night, the kind of night that makes you glad you've remained a fan through the many down seasons, like the one with nine wins, through the years of NCAA sanctions.

You stand and face a giant flag at the north end, or the electronic one unfurling itself on the Jumbotron. The same gentleman who, as an opera teacher from the music school, has sung the national anthem at each men's game for the last thirty years, belts out another one, emphasizing one syllable in *our flag was still there,* sending spinets of thrills up and down your spine, thrills that make you glad to be an American, watching this game, in this behemoth temple that is filled to the rafters with fans painted in red and black. If you listen, the air crackles like you are tuned in to an old radio, and finally the band begins to play the set of songs that will lead into the last three minutes before the game. Man, it can't get any better than this. Eeeyow.

MISCELLANEOUS DRUGS FOR MISCELLANEOUS AILMENTS. Your cardiologist prescribes eighty-one milligrams of aspirin. He says it thins your blood in a different way than Coumadin. You shrug and obey, combining it with your noon pills. Your scalp itches, and when you aim your balding pate at the mirror you see you have a head full of pimples. You look like your grandfather, and your dermatologist prescribes Cephalexin in 500 milligram capsules of emerald green for what is a gerontological condition. You take one a day for the first thirty. Then you taper off to every other day, then every second day. "This medication is a cephalosporin-type antibiotic used to treat a wide variety of bacterial infections (e.g. skin, bone and genitourinary tract infections). It works by stopping the growth of bacterial infections. It will not work for viral infections (e.g., common cold, flu)." You ask about interactions. There are none, so saith your dermatologist, so too, your pharmacist.

In addition your dermatologist prescribes a shampoo, Loprox. It contains a drug that inhibits the growth of fungus. Hmmm. Isn't your problem bacterial? Perhaps it's both. When your scalp dries, you apply

Olux, a foam "which reduces the swelling, itching and redness that can occur in psoriasis, dermatitis, and other rashes." Hmmm. You wait for the side effects: burning, stinging, itching, irritation, dryness or redness when first applied to the scalp. But there are none.

You might tolerate the scalp condition if it were not for a major gathering last summer. It's bad enough you have to show up bald for your fortieth high school reunion at Holiday Inn South. You don't want your head to look like a strawberry patch, too. After a month of miracle drugs, it is clear again. It's not the scalp of a young man, but it's presentable. As Mona administers your regular crew cut, you don't feel as conscious of all that bare skin. In fact, you feel confident. Except for one thing.

You've promised Mona an overnight, but you know that sleeping in a hotel bed may compromise your back, so you ask your doctor for a sleep aid. You've seen the ads on TV, men and women with their heads atop pastel pillows, animated butterflies floating over the sleepers' heads (sorry, those are Lunesta moths). Doc prescribes thirty Ambien, which is good, because your drug co-pay is twenty-five dollars—eighty-three cents a pill. "Ambien is used to treat sleep problems. It may help you fall asleep faster, stay asleep longer, and reduce the number of times you awaken during the night. Ambien belongs to a class of drugs called sedative/hypnotics. It acts on your brain to produce a calming effect. This medication is limited to short-term treatment periods of one to two weeks or less." Your doctor hesitates to renew when you run out. "What happens over time, Larry," he says, "is that the drug loses its effectiveness. See if you can't exercise a bit more." You argue but he stands firm. In addition to the buzz you will endure for the rest of your unnatural life, you now train for insomnia.

But, of course, he's right. You have one lousy restless night, during which you re-read *In Cold Blood,* but by the next night you're so sleep-deprived you fall right off and back into your normal pattern. You are lucky; you have compadres in this world who can't sleep with the aid of five pills, some parts of their bodies buzzing like saws twenty-four/seven. All these years later, when you are horizontal your buzz does lessen. And after you've read for an hour or so you can go to sleep.

Usually, except when you travel to your fortieth reunion and wonder who's invited all these old geezers.

Your eyes search for youth in madras plaid shirts, search for girls with flip hairdos, search for black-and-white saddle oxfords and everybody sporting full heads of radiant hair, but all you see are people you wouldn't speak to if you were seated next to them on a plane. Would you? Well, of course you would. All evening at the picnic, you smile and nod and shake hands that are the same age as yours. You pull out pictures of your children; you take the guys over to check out your Land Cruiser. Of course, some of your old buddies have better vehicles than yours, but they act nice about it, admiring your car, too. Way too déjà vu, reminding you of the time you and the Woo brothers drag Avenue Q all night in their pale yellow GTO, a '65.

After all the good-byes are over, all the digi-pics taken, you board the elevator to the second floor of the hotel and look at the face beaming back at you in the bathroom mirror, but in a second the Stephen King horror of your death passes over your face like the eerie pallor cast over the earth by an eclipse. The evening of superficial jocularity roars in your ears, and you'd rather die, you'd rather *die* than stand before a hotel mirror and stare at this specter reflected back at you.

You limp to your bed. Mona takes your hand, groans, and slides it between her legs, her little signal, but you feel no stimulation. "In a minute," you say and run to the bathroom for a round orange one, film-coated with BAYER imprinted on one side and 20 on the other. Yes, twenty milligrams of Levitra will bring you that pleasure you once inspired by the mere touch of your wife's bush, the tenderness of love found there. You swallow the pill and wink at that ghost in the mirror before heading back to your love.

CO-PAY TOTAL FOR THE TAX YEAR. Over $800. You cringe, but you know your older friends, some without insurance, pay five times that much, and you are thankful. Yes, thankful for small favors.

WITH SIX MINUTES TO GO. You're on your feet. You sit. You stand. You sit. Funny, here at Spirit Temple Arena your back does not hurt. It's as if basketball is a concoction, not a drug exactly, but a vapor that seems to relieve your buzzing ganglia. Students do not sit down once as the score remains close throughout the entire game. The Phog stallions, gigantic and well-muscled, are a bit off tonight. You think back to the warm-up where your boys don't miss a shot. It's not the harbinger you've hoped for. Your boys have missed a few key shots—like every time they might have taken the lead. Yeah, they could be ahead. Instead they trail by four, which, in itself, is a miracle. The Phog coach asks for a time-out to reconnoiter. Your opponent is minutes away from losing the second of twenty games on the year; their players just don't know it yet. Yeah, you feel prescient about it. A lot on the line for your boys, too, since they've beat this team only one time in school history. The Phogs trot over to their bench for a three-minute time-out. From your seat you can see the tiny monitor the TV announcers use. It's playing a Dodge commercial that pays for the broadcast, and you wait for the floor to fill the screen once again. The timekeeper raises one finger. The band plays on.

You take Mona's hand like you used to at the Coliseum. You take her hand the minute you're elected cheerleader at eighteen. You take her hand when you marry four years later. You take her hand during hospital trips that yield three children, two now grown and living on opposite coasts. Your hands meet often until you hurt your back. Then you work your way back to holding hands weekly, yes a slower but more ardent love-making. You achieve a normal life. What say you, honey? *You're hurting my hand.* Sorry, you say, loosening your grip, but you don't let go. Not yet.

The band plays the fight song until the timekeeper's second finger goes up, and ESPN returns. The red-and-black beasts in the crowd point their fingers like guns, now splashing their painted faces all over the Jumbotron and millions of TVs from coast-to-coast. Sweaty torsos return to the floor, and a whistle begins play.

Your boys hammer away—with a stingy and dogged defense—until the last thirty seconds of the game. One of yours lobs a slick one to the center for an alley-oop. Down by two, and your boys make an important stop at the other end. Your point guard Smith will dribble the ball down the floor through a sea of soaked jerseys, amid three Phogs with four fouls each. Smith will take the ball automatically. It could so easily fall from his hands, slip away to the defender, who is treeing him like a bird dog. But Smith holds tight as his teammates head down the floor. He keeps the ball in a slow-motion dribble that might be called palming. Plunk. Plunk. Plunk. Smith plunks the ball to the top of the key.

Twenty seconds left. He makes a crisp bounce pass to Boyd, the center. All five players rotate, making skilled cuts as they've been taught, and the Phog defense rotates too. Now Boyd is at the top of the key. Seven seconds left. Raised on a farm, Boyd is heavily recruited, but his frosh average remains at three points a game. Zero for eight tonight, Boyd dribbles around himself in sort of a circle, as the defender tangos close, right outside the three-point line. When the defender falls back, almost as if Boyd has pushed him, Boyd levitates above floor, and you know what's coming.

Noooooooooooo, you scream. *You're supposed to pass off to Smith for a quick drive to the basket!* But Boyd, *who's zero for eight*, lofts the three, it arcs high, the type that will either go in or bounce off into the hands of the Phog defender, who now drools with joy over Boyd's error, and, as 15,550 souls watch, the ball does what it should do if you want to win. Slick as a whistle. You can no longer hear; you believe streamers may unfurl from the rafters. Confetti may snow down upon the heads of 15,550 fans.

Boyd's teammates run to him, but Coach is waving his arms like fucking Jerry Lewis, screaming orders in a manner that will keep him hoarse for days. Four point one seconds remain, and your boys line up for a defensive stand. The star Phog shooter is perfectly capable of hoisting one from mid-court, but as the ball is inbounded to him and he releases it way too low, the buzzer sounds, the orange neon rim of the backboard lights up, and the crowd comes undone. You feel the Spirit Temple Arena rise from footings that sink three fathoms into the caliche. Mona squeezes your hand, and the guys in soaked blue jerseys lope from the arena like bulls with spears dangling from their sides.

"Let's go," she says. "The parking lot will be mobbed."

"No," you say. "They're giving Coach the mic."

"You're the boss, Larry," she says, squeezing your fingers.

"Damned straight," you say, squeezing back.

Later, you hold Mona's gloved hand and stare up at a sky dotted with stars. The air smells clear, as if all the dirt in West Texas has been vacuumed up and rocketed to Mars, another red planet.

The writer is indebted to the pharmaceutical information distributed by Albertson's Pharmacy Answers™, Sav-On Pharmacy Answers®, and CVS Caremark, and to a book by James J. Rybacki and James W. Long, *The Essential Guide to Prescriptions Drugs 2001*. Without these sources the writer would otherwise know nothing about the medications in this story. And yes, it is but a story.

ENGINEER

When I appear at Bellwood Gardens, ten green acres and three large buildings connected with tidy asphalt trails, I'm reminded of my first visit here—not obviously, of course—but in the same way I'm reminded of being a male by entering a room lined with urinals. My brother Uriah was here in El Centro directing traffic; he'd driven my father down from New York to Texas in a large Penske truck. Over phone lines that reached 1,800 miles, he had also engaged local movers who carted in my father's belongings and placed them wherever my father pointed. Uri, a consultant for HeiTech Software, flew off to an appointment the next morning, leaving me with the rest. We'd never discussed the fact that, as the anointed, Uri should have been caring for my father, that, as Blessed Prince who lived fifty miles from my father in Larchmont, he had abdicated his responsibilities by delivering our father to my doorstep. Dear Dad now lives four miles away, a convenient ten-minute drive I make every Tuesday.

At Bellwood my father dwells in a renovated dormitory with six wings sprouting diagonally from a single round structure, and has occupied a one-bedroom apartment for almost four years. He became, by plunking down a hefty sum, a LifeTime resident. At any time he needs additional care, he can be transferred to nursing for the same monthly cost. He can even retain his apartment until a committee determines he must live in nursing for the rest of his life. Even should he run out of money, which is unlikely or Bellwood would not have approved him in the first place, the facility will care for him until the very end. Even should he live to be a hundred. Even should his progeny flee our fair city of 200,000.

My father is seated under a Japanese lantern tree whose pods are turning orange; in a few weeks, they'll brown and float to the red soil that, because of the drought, will fail to devour them. He's presently carving one of his soldiers, a doughboy crouching and rifle aimed. With a little recorder at his side, he's also taping the Bellwood carillon installed in a nondescript tower, which nearby is bonging out strains of "Some Enchanted Evening."

When he moved here from New York I would spend Wednesdays with him, but a year later I began to see Dr. Ruby and changed Dad's Day to Tuesdays. I must mean something to my father, for every time he sees me his face becomes enlivened, the way it did when my mother entered a room. He slips the figure and knife into his jacket and takes my arm, and we head toward the dining hall inside. Entering an overlit room of people who show no signs of recognizing Jacobus Verdonk and his son, we sit at a table for four. Unlike a restaurant, here he can find an entree with no cheese, something with beef, the one form of protein he will eat, and perhaps a dessert with no chocolate.

"You once ate whatever Mother placed in front of you," I say, and he returns a blank stare. For years he's looked the same, about sixty-two, but now it's not appearance so much as affect. He's always a million miles away, as if staring out to sea on a gray day.

"Did you drink your Ensure this morning?"

"I can only get down one can."

"Doctor said two."

"Gives me the trots." He opens his menu and squints through bulbous bifocals.

"You don't have to like the stuff," I say. "It's a prescription."

He frowns and begins to whistle "Some Enchanted Evening," emitting a lifeless trickle that sounds like a flute heard in New Age music.

"You weigh a hundred and twenty pounds." My father was once a stocky man of five-ten who flattened his abs for an annual military physical by completing hundreds of sit-ups. He maintained jets for the

Air Force, having eschewed his lineage as a butcher. "If you don't eat, you'll wind up in nursing with a feeding tube stuck in your belly," I say.

Sliding the menu in front of his face, he says, "I think I'll have a hamburger."

He always orders a burger, but fifteen minutes later, when the server shows up, I have to remind him. Carmelita, a short Filipino with white streaks in her hair, scribbles on her pad and leaves. "What takes her so long?" he asks. "I think she's got a grudge against me."

"She's not that organized," I say, and he smiles.

My father and I often talk more during these meals than at any other time. While waiting for our food, I tell him of a dream Dr. Ruby has encouraged me to share—although my father knows nothing of my psychologist, a giant of a man with a shock of blond hair and broad shoulders who once counseled inmates with lives more troubled than mine. At least I didn't murder Uriah Verdonk, a brother five years my junior, though at times it might have been the kindest thing to do.

"Uri and I are running down the hall." As absolute equals. "In my dream we're kids again, and I feel this great sense of joy." I don't mention the equal part—only the delight of being with the brother my father never spanked. A frown clouds his face.

"You know, Vinnie," he says. "I've always regretted that thing with your back. I was trying to catch you, to hold you in my arms—you were so quick—and I slapped your back instead." His voice drops; his face crumbles. "It's always haunted me."

I try to recall what that slap felt like, imagine the red mark it must have raised. "I don't remember," I say, picturing instead my father hoisting me up with one hand and smacking my posterior with the other, five times, after I'd shoved little Uri down. "It's all right," I say, jumping when Carmelita thunks our plates on the table.

Over the weeks, on various Tuesdays, I will be emboldened to ask my father a few questions. "Why didn't you come to my recitals?" *You know me and that longhair crap.* "Why didn't you go to church with us?" *I promised your mother she could raise you boys as Protestants, if I could smoke and drink.* "Why didn't you love me as much as Uri?"

"Opportunities never came easy to you like they did for Uri or your cousins, it wasn't fair." Sometimes he will get way off track. "Once I ran into Pop's butcher shop in Larchmont. People like Maxwell Perkins bought his chops from my father, you know, although I never met the man. It was only the missus we dealt with. I crashed into a cleaver hanging off the counter and sliced my head open. I was damned lucky I didn't die." My father's doctor won't say whether Jacobus has the Big A or not, but I have to wonder.

As he and I eat, we no longer speak. I think it's the way of his Dutch peasant ancestry. When you eat, you eat, you don't talk. The food will get cold; it might even disappear. In the summer months of my suburban childhood, he grilled burgers every Saturday; it was a rite, like taking communion. But during those warm fuzzy periods, I felt that I could never get a piece of him, that I was never manly enough to enter his domain. While Uri cartwheeled and pinwheeled (his invention) around the yard like Bugs Bunny, I tried to discuss serious things with my father, but all he could say was, "Great one, Uri, do it again." Oh, when I hit my twenties, my father liked me, approved of me; after all, I had achieved gainful employment by then. We were in a deli, and I told him how I'd loved halvah as a kid. He bought me a pound of it, and I thanked him. But when I left my parents' house the next day, it lay in the trash can of their guest room.

Now as I swallow every morsel of my meal, I can't help notice. My father eats the patty and shoves his fries around, ignoring the green beans—while I fortify my body for an afternoon of slow motion, during which I shall be required to think for two people as we complete his shopping. "Don't you already have six boxes of Ritz?" I will remind him, edging the basket toward the next aisle. When Carmelita removes our plates, mine is wiped clean; my father has pushed his food into a mound. I shall end my afternoon with a dip in the pool, swimming laps until I'm forced to crawl up the ladder. That's why I've been shoveling in all these proteins and carbs—because after two or three more hours, my father will have worn me down farther than the most willful child.

The next morning, after an early freeze coats everything with a white crust, I scuffle into the den. Kale calls me to the picture window to point out a hundred waxwings gathered in the back, gobbling berries from our trees, drinking from the feeders before they splash out all the water. He opens a cardboard box and says, "I heard an immature fly into the patio door."

"Oh, no," I say, putting my arm around him. Not much of a birder myself, I can be driven to sympathy.

Enclosed by five patio door casings, our porch is forty feet long, creating a gigantic mirror. Most of the time we move the screens and set plastic chairs near the glass to break up the space. But still, our beaked friends manage to enter this parallel world of sky and clouds. Our doors have knocked out hawks, redbirds, even some sparrows. Only the smaller birds survive.

"You taking it to the center?" I ask, referring to the wildlife rehab place south of town where Kale has begun to volunteer since leaving the university.

"Yeah, but I want to warm him up, let him get his bearings," he says. The little bird's heart is sucking a spot on his chest—in and out, in and out—and he's losing a bit more of his stunned look by the minute. The heaving chest reminds me that when I first met Kale he was a dancer, instructing those not much younger than he, nearly birdlike himself as he flew across the stage. When I taught, he often bathed and massaged my feet at night, absorbing daily war stories as he kneaded my flesh and bones like dough. Now a graying professor emeritus, Kale is no longer thin and lithe, and I recall those massages as if he were someone I no longer know.

We keep returning to the box, lifting the lid to see if the little guy's all right—his faded brown breast, the red dot on his wings, the yellow tip at the end. And each time his breathing is a bit more even, like a baby's.

Later I slip down to my office in the basement to work on my book. It's a secret. If Kale enters unannounced, he finds me e-mailing ads to unwilling clients all over the world, ads for sexual enhancement drugs, real estate, wigs. If I worked at it, I could make thousands a month, but

I prefer to labor over something that may never pay off. After a morning of hacking through a scene where a boy throws his brother from a fiery building, I leave my laptop and seek out the waxwing huddled in his box.

Hearing it flutter around, Kale takes the box to the patio. Our little baby hears his brethren outside and skitters against the cardboard. I retired from teaching the same year Mother died, the same year Uri dumped his responsibilities at my doorstep, and I've been stuck on the same chapter ever since. It's crazy, thinking I might write a book about a Blessed Prince and his evil brother, but I must prevail. It's the real reason I retired, and it's the reason I can see my father only on Tuesdays.

"I don't think we need rehab this time," Kale says. "You pick him up."

"I can't," I say, looking away.

"Loosely, as if your hands were a little cage."

I'm afraid that when I open the box he'll fly out and we'll have a permanent resident who shits all over our patio. But I crack open the flaps, scoop my arms down, and take him into my hands, his wings fluttering against my palms like little dusters.

Kale opens the patio door. "Release him," he says.

I step into the cold, bright day and toss him into the air—he deserves a boost, considering what he's been through—and he flits to the evergreens along the back fence, gathering his wits on a limb that bounces in the wind. I can't tell you how proud I feel. By being alert, Kale has saved his life, and I, with a toss of my hands, have given it back to him.

For Christmas—a holiday that my father has always manipulated to punish us, having buried his own father between Christmas and his twentieth birthday, boarding a train for boot camp twelve hours later—Kale and I sneak over to New Mexico for a few rarified days at eight thousand feet. Every time I contact my father I pretend I'm calling from the house. Even with a roaring fire, our cabin is drafty and cold, and when we fail to get a dinner reservation at the lodge atop the mountain, we eat carry-out from Allsups on Christmas day. "It's good to get away," I tell Kale, and he smiles with lips that turn an anemic shade of blue.

The week after we get back, my father opens his kitchen cabinet, where he has stored some shiny bags—one green, one red, and one white. A carillon tape of "Auld Lang Syne" is drowning him out.

"What?" I say, turning the recorder down.

"Just now remembered. White one's for Uri, this one's for you, and the green one's for Kale," he says.

These are in addition to the sizable checks he writes for the three of us. My father hasn't given gift-gifts in years, making the bags quite a surprise.

I open mine. Inside I find a coffee mug with a scene of the Jefferson Monument. "Oh, thank you," I say and give him a hug, like one I might have bestowed upon a pupil. I have a million mugs, mostly from kids: *3 Reasons to be a Teacher: June, July, & August. Hang in there, Retirement's A Comin'. World's Best Teacher.*

"There's something queer about those cups," my father says, "but I can't remember what it is." He scratches his bald head and sits in an orange recliner, next to its mate, the one my mother used when she was alive. For four years I've urged him to buy new ones, but he always stops me with a raised hand. He did that a lot when I was young.

"You know, that thing loses five minutes a week," he says, glancing up at the hutch. He points to a pendulum clock given to him by his father, who sailed with it from Rotterdam in 1911—having deserted his own father, whose butcher shop had borne the Dutch royal seal for four generations. Standing a foot tall and mounted on a round base, the clock is supported with four columns and crowned by a gilded acorn, the dark varnish now crazed. A cylindrical body suspends itself horizontally from the top, and the face is a stained cream with dainty black hands that pass over Roman numerals intertwined with a pink garland. To wind the timepiece, you open a glass door, insert a key, and wind it a dozen times, and for a week the clock continues to swing its medallion pendulum. With Super Glue and an odd spring, my father has kept the wooden heart of Verdonk history ticking all his life. He sometimes offers the timepiece to me, the eldest son, but when he does, I look away, reminded of the Cadillacs he's bequeathed to Uri, the cabin at Lake George. I hug him again and vacate the premises before I grab his damn clock and run.

The next day my father calls while I'm boiling water for tea.

"Have you used your mugs yet?" he asks.

"They're still in the car."

"Damn, I can't remember . . . ." And he hangs up.

I go and retrieve the mugs, though the plan is to drop them at Goodwill. I wash mine out, boil some water, and pour it over an Earl Grey tea bag while I step into the utility room to separate laundry. When I return to the counter, I'm stunned to see the transformation of my mug. With the warmth provided, trees along the Potomac have turned white with cherry blossoms. I call my father.

"I knew there was something about those mugs!" he says.

"Where'd you get them?" I ask, filling Kale's with hot water too. Four blackbirds turn bright with color: there's a cardinal, a jay, a finch, and a waxwing.

"I can't remember," he says.

"Doesn't matter," I say. "They're beautiful."

Later, he calls and hurries his words, like someone whose time on a pay phone is almost gone. "Gift shop downstairs."

As the weeks pass, my father becomes more obsessed with his carving. Before he moved to Texas from Larchmont, it was a minor hobby, but now he works as if he has a deadline. He used to get that way—the symptoms were vomiting and diarrhea—when his unit went on alert and his entire career seemed to hinge on a fleet of jet fighters passing inspection. Retiring in New York, he built a shop equipped with a lathe, two or three power saws, and myriad tools. He also had a sloped lawn to care for and the winter walks to keep clear. When Mother died, he had but six months to cook, clean, and do laundry before he realized he couldn't handle it all, before Uri conspired to move him down here. At Bellwood my father has no yard and no snow, and employees are paid to clean his apartment and wash his clothes. He lives like Cole Porter without cigarettes.

To aid in his artistic enterprise, my father studies pictures of World War I soldiers. He then photocopies a picture, sizing it until it's six inches high, cutting out the soldier and tracing it over carbon paper against a block of bass wood. He then marks the surface with colored pencils. From this point he begins to carve out primitive but recogniz-able figures. He works from four to six hours, and when he tires of standing at his bench, he slouches in his recliner. At the end of the day he vacuums up sawdust and chips with his Electrolux, leaving it in the corner. His apartment is aflood with things he's left out: books, half-filled coffee mugs, tins of cookies, clothing. It resembles the house I grew up in. It even smells the same, musty and sealed up.

One Tuesday, after we've returned from shopping, my father holds up a page in a book. "This is my new project," he says. "'Engineer,' it's called."

The picture is by Harvey Dunn, an artist of the period, a charcoal drawing of a gear-laden doughboy who must be hauling sixty pounds of equipment. Leaning forward, as if facing into a stiff wind, this young man is shouldering a huge backpack with what appears to be another stacked on top of it. He carries his rifle with one hand.

"His duster sure is filled to the gills," I say.

"No," my father says. "This crease separates his coat from the bag, it's full of messages." He covers his mouth. "The guy's so damned determined."

"Don't forget to eat," I say, shaking my finger. "I know you skip meals." He has sinking spells, too, where he doesn't faint but becomes dizzy and short of breath. I've reported these symptoms to his doctor, but I can't seem to get any answers. "What did you have for breakfast?" I ask, eyeing the empty sink.

"These men were my heroes," he says, thumbing through the book.

Following Pearl Harbor, my father served for two and a half years in the South Pacific, working in the motor pool to ensure that P-38s returned from their sorties. I recently stole an afternoon to read his war journals, brown-paged Moleskines with secrets scrawled in pencil. It seems he never lost a plane due to mechanical failure, and oftener than he'd like to remember he ran into the jungle to evade the bullets of Zeros screaming past him like crazed hawks. Even in his twenties, his tone is that of an Eagle Scout, a mere boy going for the top merit badge. And every day is the same. He gets up, he works on planes, he runs from the enemy.

By stark comparison my draft board awarded me a 4-F in 1966. I told everyone except my parents, that it was my spine (I could still *picture* that red smack). What I didn't say was that I had a great aversion to flying home from Nam in a box like my buddy Flip, or returning insane with no limbs, and so I spoke the truth. "I'm an avowed homosexual," I told the recruiter, parroting a phrase I'd heard from a play. The handsome sergeant smiled and said, "The Army thanks you for your candor and wishes you the best." No hearing. No psychologist. He stamped in big red letters across my name, Vincent Pier Verdonk: REJECTED. I know I ought to love a father who didn't disown me because of my cowardice, but the obligation seems too great.

One day in the spring, Kale asks if I'd like to go to Arizona. He wants to observe a species of hummingbird that frequents the border this time of the year. Though he's spent a lifetime teaching others to move their bodies and choreographing at least two shows a year, he also sets up sugar-water feeders each spring. As a spotter for a research lab, he makes weekly reports of any bird viewed in our yard. When a saw-whet owl—quite removed from its territory—once perched itself in our cherry laurel, the street became lined with nonbelievers who'd picked up Kale's sighting online.

"The Magnificent may be there in the mountains," he whispers, as if to woo me. "Its body is this brilliant apple green, it has a crown of purple. And it's huge, for a hummer."

"My father has an appointment," I say. "He's lost more weight. And his kidney readings aren't so hot." I continue to work my Sudoku, still in the hunt for a quick solve. I dive into each puzzle the way I once jammed a Marlboro into my mouth or downed shots of Haig & Haig.

Kale pulls me out of my chair and embraces me, saying, "Come on, you need to get away from here. You don't have to bird-watch. You can read, you can take the car into Tucson. If not for yourself, for me?" I can feel his ribs crushing mine, and his halitosis takes my breath away.

We check the calendar, and there exists a window of opportunity, if I want to seize it. Maybe I'll have a breakthrough on that chapter. Maybe Kale will walk in and catch me. Maybe he'll read my work and have a word of encouragement. Before the afternoon is over, I call my father and the Bellwood administrator and let them know I'm going to be gone. I reschedule his appointment. I call Uri and tell him he'll have to cover for me if anything should happen. He grunts—as he always has if he doesn't want to be held responsible. Blessed Prince once neglected to feed our spaniel because he was in a baseball tournament for three days. *I thought it was Vinnie's turn,* he kept saying. *I'm sure it was Vinnie's turn.* This is the same lad who wrote JFK in 1961 and asked for a photo. *Could you also send one of Richard Nixon? Please.*

Not long after, Kale and I head southwest, beginning an eleven-hour drive on Interstates relatively free of traffic. Kale points out bird life to me, chuckling at the turkey buzzards, marveling at hawks soaring in and out among the thermals, roosting on electric poles like sentries.

"When did you become interested in birds?" I say. This is something I might have asked when we first met thirty years ago.

"I'm not sure," he says. "I remember making this little suet feeder at church when I was twelve. I hung it in our back yard, and the birds came in droves."

"Kind of how you snagged me," I say.

"Yeah, I put it out there," he says, "and you went for it."

We met on July fourth of our nation's bicentennial, watching a huge fireworks display on Fire Island. A neighbor introduced me to Kale, and, following a week of frenzied monogamy, I moved to El Centro, Texas where it was not difficult to live out a more tranquil kind: a life with faculty parties, ten-year options on university football and basketball seats, dining outdoors with various friends when weather allowed. After our first year, while visiting my parents in Larchmont, Mother whispered to me, "Now, he's nice, you bring him back."

Our Highlander follows the long straight I-10 as if programmed, across New Mexico, flat mile after mile, until we reach our cutoff at Tucson, which heads south. We stop in a town that leads to the mountains and stock up on food. Our car climbs the slopes, and, as we reach Los Canarios Cabins, the air becomes cooler. The log structures look like WPA specials with green metal chairs placed on each porch; between them sits a little table equipped with an ashtray. Peeling away from the ashtray glass is a decal of a canary whose neck is wrapped with a red ribbon.

Inside we drop our luggage on the Chenille spread, hanging things in a small closet, stowing our food. Since we're stiff from driving, we take a walk around the site, where someone has poured crude concrete trails. Kale gazes into the dusty trees, pointing out one bird or another. I wish I were more interested. Bird life really is quite miraculous.

"Oh, wow," Kale whispers, staring up into a bleached-out tree trunk, at one time struck by lightning. "A western tanager," he says. I can see its bright plumage from here, but when Kale hands me the glasses, the lenses are filled with yellow and orange. It's like having that canary ashtray shoved in your face. Such a beautiful bird ought to hide, ought to run for its life. In this instant Uri rings my cell, which barely connects at our elevation, and says my father won't pick up the phone.

"Have you called the people at Bellwood?" I ask, my heart pounding. He grunts. "Look, Uri, you handle it. Your phone works as good as mine."

Ten minutes later Blessed Prince calls back. "He was downstairs playing Bingo in the dining room. How great is that?"

On the Tuesday after we get back, I call my father to tell him I'm on my way, so he won't be sitting in his shorts and tank top as I show up at his place. He doesn't answer. I race the four miles across town and park next to his car. Entering his apartment, I realize he's still gone. I quicken my step and take the elevator down to the lobby. "We've got twenty minutes to make his appointment," I tell the woman at the desk. Today I've planned a showdown with his doctor. I want to know what's wrong with my father, why he continues to disappear before my very eyes.

"Let me ask around," she says, phoning the barber, the gift shop, the exercise room, even the swimming pool, which he never uses. "We don't seem to know," she says, her eyes landing everywhere but my face. "I'm sending someone out to search the grounds. Why don't you wait upstairs."

"I'll do that," I say. In my father's apartment, I call the doctor. The receptionist gives me a rough time, but I convince her to work us in as soon as we can get to the man's office. I switch on the AC and sift through mail, which I've directed my father to place in a basket on his dining table, ever since he lost his bill from Bellwood Gardens. I get out the Pledge and dust where the housekeeper refuses to, along little ridges of his dining room table, scraping off crud which must be residue of my mother's cooking. I dust the rungs of his chairs. I dust his precious clock. I move his belongings and dust the top of the table. Then I throw a box of catalogues down the trash chute in the hall. I wash a sink full of dishes, and when I've done that I get out the CLR and dissolve calcium deposits from his counter and dish rack. Sailing to his bedroom, I dust his dresser and chest of drawers, clean his mirror. I groan when I see a laundry bag with a month's worth of towels. I tackle the bathroom, squirting gel under the rim of his toilet, scrubbing away dots of crap, dribbles of urine that have turned brown. Whenever my father catches me cleaning like this, he says, "You're more Dutch than I am." I'm about to head out on my own search, when I hear a knock. I rush to open the door.

There stands before me a man with his arms folded, shrunken from the days when I begged him not to spank me. *Daddy, I'll never hit Uri again. I promise.*

"Has that part come in?" he says, out of breath, grabbing my arm. His face is blank, yet confused and pale.

"Where were you?" I ask, guiding him toward the recliner, where he lowers himself with the groan of an old man.

"Needed a part."

"Part?"

"For that fighter," he says, pointing out the window. "At the end of the flight line. What're ya, blind?"

He stares at the blank TV, and I stare at him, trying to memorize his features. He begins to murmur, "How many fucks . . . would a woodchuck fuck . . . if a woodchuck could fuck wood? Yeah . . . how many fucks would a woodchuck fuck if a woodchuck could fuck wood?"

"Not that," I say, remembering the ditty he taught me when I was thirteen—swearing me to secrecy, as if we'd formed a club that didn't include Mother or Uri.

He says it faster and faster, like I used to, showing off in front of my friends. *Howmanyfuckscouldawoodchuckfuckifawoodchuckcouldfuckwood? Howmanyfuckscouldawoodchuckfuckifawoodchuckcouldfuckwood? Howmany fuckscouldawoodchuckfuckifawoodchuckcouldfuckwood?* I'm stunned, for the words themselves seem to twirl him around. Until he passes out. Kneeling by his chair, I call an ambulance and then phone Uri, who castigates me for having left town instead of taking my father to the doctor. *What are you, a complete moron?* I have no answer for him.

I sit on the hospital bed and bang my feet against the rail. A nurse in green scrubs enters and leaves, enters and leaves. When she's finished, I watch the black bulb at the end of the blood pressure hose swing like a pendulum—a good twenty minutes before it comes to a halt. My father breathes through an oxygen mask he keeps bumping off with hands floating up like wingless geese. Various nurses replace the mask, and he bumps it off. We all replace it several times, but finally a male nurse with coarse black hair on his arms restrains my father's wrists.

Kale has gone down to the lobby to wait for Uri, who's flying in at noon. My father's eyes are closed and have been ever since I called the ambulance. What's wrong with this eighty-seven-year-old man I'm not sure. Over the phone his doctor has told me that my father's body is wearing out. *This is how some old folks die.* I now overhear phrases like *renal failure, congestive heart, possible stroke,* but no one tells me anything. My father's mouth hangs open, sucking air like a fish in the shallows. His chest heaves up and down, and even through the sheet I can count his ribs. When the nurse bathes him, I can see his hairless, splotchy limbs, which call to mind the words I spoke to Dr. Ruby one afternoon. *I wish my father would go away and leave me alone.*

Dr. Ruby had raised his eyebrows and said, "Oh, he'll go away, all right."

I feel a hand on my shoulder and grab it, taking it to my cheek. Up this close, Uri is not near as bold. He treats me to lunch in the cafeteria, springing across the surface of several topics, including new software for pharmacists, *which automatically keeps the customer from taking something that is contraindicated. How great is that?* Every year he looks more like my father than I do, and I can't decide whether I love or hate him for it.

"When it comes time, I want all his carvings," Uri says.

"All?" I ask, bending my stainless steel spoon into a spiral.

He squints over a coffee cup, his eyebrows knitted. "You can have the last one."

"Engineer? It's not even finished."

"That's the one."

A few days after, when Blessed Prince has left town for a software convention in Los Angeles, my father opens his eyes. "Is the commander around?" he whispers.

"You're in El Centro . . . with me . . . Vinnie. Remember?"

He nods but his face is blank. Later, when he tries to speak, I can scarcely hear what he's saying. ". . . want to go home," he croaks.

"Soon."

In fact, he does not return to Bellwood for eleven days. The hospitalist, an Indian woman, says, "I'm required to give you his options, one of which is dialysis. But," she whispers, "*I wouldn't recommend it . . . he would never survive the procedure. And I wouldn't do it to my own mother.*"

For a minute I'm not sure what she's saying. "Thank you. If he were in his right mind, he'd never want to be kept alive like that. I have it in writing." In my valise is stashed the document I've carried for four years. I've had to wave it in the face of every doctor except Dr. Singh.

She nods, and my father is ambulanced back to Bellwood, where he's now housed in the nursing building, Bellwood Care. A hospice unit is called in, a service of Medicare, I discover, if the doctor has determined the patient has less than six months to live. Which she has.

"My father claims God watched over him in World War II," I tell the hospice representative, a petite redhead, who might think I'm a

little nuts. "He's not afraid of dying, only how he's going to get there."
I realize there are things I would not know had he not moved here,
had he not told me on one of the Tuesdays I deigned to lunch with
him. *Vinnie, we all die sooner or later,* he told me before I went to Arizona.

"He won't suffer," she says, taking my hand. "At no time will we
allow him to suffer."

I call Uri in New York, and after a notable silence, he says he'll be
right out.

"I've got tons of air miles from work," he adds.

What do you think about, I want to scream, *as you rack up your miles?
Is your mind full of nothing but Pentium circuits, do you save a brain cell or
two for your father?*

The next day the hospice chaplain, a guy named Roark, calls me.
In a deep, husky voice that sounds young, he discusses some practical
issues, including a service, which he offers to conduct, since our family
doesn't do church. He tells me *Mr. Verdonk* has been quite receptive
to his visits, his prayers. He tells me not to be concerned if we see my
father reaching upward.

"He was doing that in the hospital," I say, as if wingless geese might
be a clue, a symptom the doctors have missed.

"He was reaching for the angels," Roark says. "Bidding them to
take him away."

"I'd like to believe that," I whisper, so even Roark can't hear me.
But later, when I tell Kale, we break into at least twenty seconds of
laughter. Even later, when I share the message with Uri at my father's
bedside, Uri rests his head on my shoulder. He hasn't been this near to
me since I was seven and dandled him on a bony knee. Soon he pulls
away, saying he has to leave for Denver.

Minutes after I drop Uri at the airport, Roark calls my cell and
says my father has passed. "Don't feel bad," he says. "According to the
research, most males prefer to die alone." *Did you survey these males
before or after they died?* I wish to ask. I pull into a cvs lot and rest my
head against the wheel. This is the minute I've been waiting for, for all
this misery to be over, but I feel rotten. When I call Uri, all I get is his
voice mail.

My Long-Playing Records

At the memorial service held in Bellwood Chapel, Chaplain Roark officiates. Standing before our friends, primarily Episcopalians, this robust man, who looks more like a football player, goes into greater detail about the angel thing, saying that our service is for us, the living. I stare down at black shoes I rarely wear, watching light dance off blunt toes. "Jacobus Felix Verdonk is no longer concerned with us or with this world. He is now traversing long passages of sky and clouds to live in a place that is not beyond the grasp of any of us, should we want to reach for it." I look up, and Roark seems to be staring at me. Uri clears his throat, as he always has when trying not to cry. Kale takes my hand. I realize our hands are the same ones that first touched in 1976, in the glow of fireworks, on an island where love may last a day or two, and I squeeze hard.

After Uri has taken the ashes and left town, I awake to something feathery, spritelike, brushing my leg. It makes me jump, as if a bag of cement has been lifted from my body. I believe my father has stopped off on his way to Roark's Pie in the Sky to assure me he's fine. I rise, close the hall door, and sit in the den. On the mantel rest two objects that weren't there yesterday: my father's unfinished sculpture and the Dutch clock I jerked from Uri's arms this morning. I hear its rhythm tick with words in my head: *how many fucks could a woodchuck fuck if a woodchuck could fuck wood?* The pendulum swings as it has for a century, casting aside five minutes a week. I imagine depositing those accumulated ticks somewhere safe, wondering how many hours, how many days I might save, for what grand purpose I might now use them.

SNARKED

When I hear a snark's been killed, I figure the cops'll nail a fag within hours, but it doesn't come down that way. The paper says that Tommy Goen died from a single gun shot to his head, near point-blank range, in his own back yard. And there are no clues, no smoking guns, no shells. All the snarks think a fag did it, and all of us fags think it's a snark. But everyone knows guns are owned by snarks, not fags.

And everyone knows that all of us in theater, whether we like chicks or not, we're all fags, not to mention all the academics. Here are the real differences. Fags do drama; snarks make drama. Fags make their grades; snarks float and flunk. Fags like girls; snarks fuck them blind. Fags will go to college; snarks will sleep. But it goes further. Fags are white; snarks are not. Fags drive first-generation Explorers their dads give them. Snarks drive vintage Chevys that hop up and down with a touch of a lever under the dash, or they strut around in saggy jeans. Fags have money; snarks jingle coins in their pockets. Fags rent the robe for graduation; snarks spike the dropout rate. Fags eat lunch out; snarks commandeer the cafeteria. Fags take a chick to homecoming and buy her a huge mum with long streamers. After the game snarks sit in their cars and wait for us fags so they can steal mums and our girls. And don't forget about sports. The football team is half fag, half snark; they call a truce to play on Friday nights. They try to win one game a year, homecoming, against a 4A team from out of town. And of course, I've only been talking about the guys. All the girls are either fags or snarks, too. El Centro High has no independents. You're either a fag or a snark or you're dead, quite obviously.

Tommy Goen wasn't always a fag. That's what got him killed. Well, I don't know that for sure, but I do know he was sick of all the fighting and had started a movement to get the two sides talking, publishing little articles of understanding in *Horizon*, our newspaper. Then poof, he was gone. Unlike the rest of us fags, who transfer in from the better parts of town, Tommy lived in a house across the alley from the school. He once invited me over to rehearse a scene. Lying on his bed and staring out his window, I could see the huge smokestack rising out of the auditorium. The mother he left behind is Mexican, his father Anglo. White name, tan skin, but if he hadn't told anyone, no one would've known. He could have passed as a fag, I mean, if he'd wanted to. But he wasn't like that. He felt that if he did what God wanted, he would be safe. He told me that once between dance rehearsals when each of us was downing a bottle of PowerAde.

"God told me, 'Tommy, you have the power. You should win them to my side.'"

"And you responded?" I said, having acquired my parents' tolerant but snotty view that God may exist but only in your mind.

Tommy shrugged.

"It's so hard, man," I said. "We're the fags. We stand for everything that is decent. Snarks are dropout druggies."

"No, we're . . . they're not. Not all of them."

"See! You're a fag at heart," I said. "You *can* cross over."

"That's the point I'm making," he argued. "There's nothing to cross over. Underneath the crap, we're all the same."

I have to respect his passion, if not his opinion.

One night after a *Grease* rehearsal I go out to my car, and these snarks, about five of them, jump me. Start patting me down for my keys, which are plainly in my hand. When I jingle them in some guy's snarky face, he grabs them. Snarks tie me up with some skank's pantyhose and leave me in the middle of the El Centro High parking lot. Then they drive my car around town, in and out of bars all night long, crashing clubs with phony IDs, I'm told. Meantime, I schlub my way home and sneak in through my bedroom window.

The next day, when my parents see my Explorer isn't in the drive, it's too late. The cops have already found it south of town amid red-dirt furrows of cotton bolls. Nothing left but a charred skeleton. Nada. My parents are pissed off, not because of the car so much, but because I didn't stand up for myself, didn't call the law. My father says, "The police might have been able to find those thugs in traffic and stop them. Now they'll see you as an easy mark." Parents always use the word "police," as if it's a term of endearment, as if they're our friends. Where was the nice policeman when the snarks turned my car to charcoal?

The fag girls feel sorry for me; the snark girls laugh behind their hands. Other fags offer me rides until I find an old Corolla my dad buys for me. The snarks . . . *snark* . . . make that obnoxious laugh as I walk to my new wheels. It's said they patented the sound when a principal caught onto their yellow bandannas around the neck, trying to get around our no-can-do dress code. We can't wear earrings either, so snarks invented this laugh that makes like a loud snore attached to the syllable "ark." It's such a great sound that even the fags imitate it when no one's listening. If you want to make fun of one of your fag friends, you snark him, like this. *Snaaaaaaark!*

That's when I get into real trouble. I'm snarking my friend, Ben, in the hall one day, when a snark overhears me. He tells me to meet him in the parking lot after school, where all the snarks park. All day I debate it. Should I, or should I get a bunch of my fag friends and rumble? Uh-huh. Right before the bell rings at four-thirty, I head for the lot east of the building and loiter for the longest time. The traffic ebbs away, and there are a handful of cars left. I walk up to the one with five guys, a '63 Impala painted midnight blue. The inside of their car is swarming with smoke.

"You snark pretty good, bro," the guy in the driver's seat says, holding smoke in his lungs. I know who he is by face. "You must be one of us, bro, if you can snark like that. Ain't that so, amigos?" His friends agree with some mumbling sounds. "Why don' you snark for us right now and join up? Join the right side. The good side. Let's hear you, bro."

Now this is what I've heard from the fags ever since I started El Centro High. Fags are the right side, the good side. It's hilarious to hear the same words coming from their mouths, that snarks think they're the holy anointed ones.

"What do you want?" I ask.

"Learn my name first. Roy Boy," he says, extending his hand for a snark shake. Good thing I know how to curve my fingers at the tips and snatch my hand back and place it behind my ear before it gets burned. "And these are my *bruthahs.*" He gives me all their snark names, which I immediately forget. "And what about you, bro, what's yo name?" Not one of them is black.

"Jeremy."

"What kind of fag name is that? You look more like a Jerm. Yeah, we'll call you Jerm. Get in, Jerm." Roy Boy looks like he's eaten a million tortillas in his life, but he hops out of the Chevy, and I hump the middle.

The scrawny guy on the right gives me a gold-toothy smile and tries to hand me a joint; his mustache looks like it's been drawn in with pencil. We drive around for a while, hopping the car up and down when stopped at a light. I've always thought that looks pretty stupid, and nothing about the experience changes my mind. Roy Boy plays some Mexican polka shit, but since he appears to have nothing but an AM radio, he doesn't have much choice. Then someone pulls out a cassette, and Roy pushes it in where the dial gives way to an opening. The angriest *chicka chicka boom boom* rap comes blasting out of huge speakers hidden somewhere in the back. Sometimes in the night, I can hear this stuff pound through my bedroom walls and crawl up my skin as one of their cars roams around town. The bros finally end up at Kmart. I can't say which one because the cops might come back and study the security tapes.

"We be tired of this shit," Roy Boy says, punching the stop button. The car is filled with a deafening something, not silence exactly. It seems we're in the middle of a huge bubble filled with this sweet-smelling fog. "Go inside and get us Sean's newest D."

"I don't have any money," I say, coughing.

"Give me your wallet," Roy Boy says, fingering my cash.

"What do you know!" I say.

"Yeah, this ought to be plenty." He takes what I have and rolls it into his shirt pocket. "They all be sittin' on a display by the cash register. We all wanna D. You got a credit card?" he asks, sifting through my ID shit. "No Visa?" he says, sticking the wallet in his pocket. "You can have it back after we're through. Junior here's goin' in with you. You won't even know he's there." He means the skinny guy with the gold smile and pencil mustache, who now passes his itty-bitty roach to someone in back.

"Oh, I get it," I say. "But where am I suppose to stash 'em?"

"You talk funny," says Junior.

One of the bros in back throws me his skanky parka; you can't tell what color it is. Both pockets have been expanded to slide things down into the lining. At a light Roy shows me how deep they are. "Thanks," I say, without considering it might sound mean.

After I step out of the car and put on the parka, I start thinking how I could break into a run, but Junior's right behind me. Even if he's whanged out of his mind, I have no doubt he could chase me for blocks. Besides, the guys in the car wouldn't be far behind. I've long trusted my instincts to get me out of a jam (I love forties flicks), but this seems too hard. This one is designed to make me lose. Even if I do get out with all their CDs, what then? They'll find some other test for me to fail.

I walk through the big sliding doors and grab a cart. I look behind me, but Junior has vanished. Then I wheel the cart around and see him perusing this wall of bagged candy. Next thing I know, he's located a black overcoat he likes. In his Dockers he looks like one of the managers going to lunch. I make my way to the music section. Yep, right there by the register, which is unmanned at the moment, stands the cardboard display with Sean's latest. I can't see Junior anywhere. Maybe now I can figure out how I'm going to do this, if I'm going to do this. *Yo*, I think. *You have to do this. You have to, or you'll be one dead fag.* Then it hits me! A fag for a snark. A snark for a fag, and back and forth it'll go until we're all dead.

I inch my way over to the stand, thinking how I might slip the jewel cases into my pockets. I mean, every one of them is set in a plastic frame that'll trigger an alarm if I walk out. I pick one up and begin to finger it. Maybe with the brute strength held within in my fingers, I can get the frame off the CD and pocket it. Someone crashes into the stand, knocking it over, and me with it. I get up.

"Oh, man, I'm sorry. God, I'm so clumsy." It's Junior, sounding so un-snarky I think I might sign him up for an audition.

The sales clerk comes running from an aisle or two away. While she's futzing with all the CDs on the floor, I feel Junior brushing up against me, but he won't let go. "Go to the back," he whispers. "Run out the door when no one's looking. And put this on." He hands me a red ski mask. Uh-huh.

It seems stupid, but I get up and start to move. He bends over and helps the clerk put CDs back on the stand, getting all flirty with her. And she's eating it up, like a good little snark girl should. I've seen her in the halls at school; she works for the office, delivering messages to teachers and students.

I sprint to the back, putting my hands in the parka's pockets. God, near the hem of my coat, I can feel the plastic cases bouncing off my ankles. In the restroom, I pee forever. Emerging, I linger in the hallway, where employees seem to swarm like bees. I get a drink from the fountain and loiter, get a drink and loiter some more. The hall clears out, so I run to the back wall and shove the emergency door open. It begins to scream, this claxon. *Blaam, blaam, blaam!* And it keeps going as I run down the alley. I sprint as if someone might start shooting at me, all this plastic clanking around in the lining of my coat. There at the end of the block, there's Roy's Impala. I jump in, and he careens around the corner. The old heap can move pretty fast if you push it.

"Just now came outside," a voice in back says. "They couldn't ID us for nothin'."

Pretty soon Roy Boy's on the Interstate heading toward the center of town.

"What about Junior?" I ask, breathless.

"Don't worry about him, he'll be home in time for dinner."

All the bros laugh. At me. It would seem.

"Hey, Jerm, where's my D?" asks Roy Boy.

I reach into my pockets and distribute CDs. The bros express sounds of gratitude and crack open the frames around the jewel cases, screeching the cellophane. In a few minutes, each one tosses his D out the window and a few miles later, all the plastic crap.

"What the fuck?" I say.

"Only fags listen to that shit," Roy Boy says. "Let's bag some tamales at Josie's!" He takes the cash from his pocket, my cash, and tosses it my way.

It feels strange going to school the next day. If I were running for office this very morning—before the fags figure out I've been inducted into the snarks—I could win by a landslide. It's usually very close, a fag winning by a small margin, although snarks have been known to get everyone in their ranks to attend school on election day and sometimes win a tight one, too. Anyway, it's the day of Tommy Goen's memorial. The hall is filled with teachers wearing black like nuns, fags in black, snarks in black. There's a certain dignity, everyone's quieter than usual, and it seems very strange. The principal comes on the horn and announces the revised schedule and says the memorial will be at ten in the auditorium. We'll get out in time for an early lunch.

I go to a short first period, where my English teacher, Mr. Nunez, teaches us a poem called "Daddy." It's complex, with all these symbols that no one but him can see, like they're a secret code written in lemon juice. Someone says, "Why doesn't Syl rhyme things, and everyone would know what she's talkin' about?" We write a class poem about Tommy in small groups; each group has to write a stanza. But all the rhymes I come up with for *death* are *beth, reth, keth, seth, teth, neth* . . . and no one likes my ideas anyway. A redhead named Cass contributes the first two lines.

Tommy Goen is goin' down the line.
He's an actor, his dancin's ever so fine.

Of course, the poem makes no sense when we read all six stanzas together, but it doesn't matter, the day's already fucked. Who cares about some pathetic poem that makes even me cry before it's over. I slink down the hall and up the stairs to second period. Yikes, Roy Boy's coming right at me.

"Yo," he says, stopping me before I can get to my next class.

"Yo, Roy," I say. "Poor Tommy." He raises his hand for a snark shake and I do the same. We look ridiculous, pulling our hands away at the last second.

Roy doesn't say anything. And he doesn't look so tough now. He's shorter than me. I could take him if I was into that kind of shit, but I don't even like to wrestle. Maybe real fags like it, you know, all that slippery contact, but not me. I can still remember the tag team shit I did in eighth grade, all that underarm BO. "Me and the bros be sittin' front and center, see you there." And he's gone.

Shit. I can't sit with snarks. Not at Tommy's memorial. Well, I'll get lost in the balcony; I'll say some teacher made us sit up there because the lower level was full. Second period goes by like a flash; I can't even remember. It's my algebra class—I think maybe we do homework. Teachers like to keep their classes on the same page, and if a morning class is cut short, then they have to kill time in the afternoon to keep us all together, so they kill time in the morning, too. They tell us this like it's a big secret.

At ten to ten, the principal comes on and begins directing us to the auditorium, one grade at a time. It might work in junior high, but no one can get two thousand snarks and fags to sit where they don't want to. And it's wild, as I watch from the balcony, these swarms of kids dressed in black, sitting down and then getting back up. It's hilarious. No one can tell a fag from a snark. I laugh until I feel a tap on my shoulder. It's Junior.

"Hey," I say, trying to sound breezy.

"Roy Boy wants you down with us," he says, pointing.

"How'd you make out yesterday?" I ask.

He cocks his head. "Shut up, Doofus."

"That's the smartest thing I've ever heard a snark say."

"Roy wants you with us. Now."

I follow him along the balcony steps and into the hallway. We snail our way down the back stairs, pushing against traffic, pushing our way in and out of the groups of bustling bodies, to the front, where the king of the snarks sits dead center on the front row. There's an empty seat on both sides of him. He pats the one on his left, and I sit down. Some guy—I think it's a snark, I'm sure it is, because he looks snarky—begins playing the old Hammond organ in the pit. It's the same kind of organ that jazz groups use in dives on Saturday nights, but he has it sounding like cathedral music, all this volume coming out of the large grilles on each side of the stage. Making me sad, very sad, yet joyful, too. I can't explain it. Before an assembly, kids are talking a mile a minute. The principal sometimes pounds his shoe like a Soviet dictator (we saw a video in history) to get us quiet, but today, there's this swish of bodies moving from one place to another, trying to find a seat that isn't next to someone they hate.

"Ladies and gentlemen," the principal says (he's a fag, too). "Please locate a seat so we can begin." He pauses. "Again, I have to ask you to please find a seat at once."

The crowd heaves a sigh, politely telling him to shut up. He stands there until all you can hear is the rustle of clothing, the soft roar of air conditioning rolling over our heads like a breeze. He cues the organist and a soloist. This redhead, a fag chick from theater, begins to sing "One Hand, One Heart." I don't recognize it at first. Then, oh yeah. *West Side Story*. It seems totally wrong. I mean, isn't it a love song? But as I listen to the lyrics, I think it could be like Mr. Nunez's poem, a symbolic elegy, begging us all, fags and snarks, to join together. One hand, one heart. Something inside me gets all gnarly and rebellious. No fag's going to tell me, I mean, no snark's going to tell me . . . then it's over and this minister comes to the podium.

"Tommy wanted you to talk today," Roy whispers in my ear. "He told me before he died. 'Get Jeremy Cobb to say something at my service.'"

I do a Daffy Duck double-take, my eyes rattling in my head.

"Tommy offed himself," he says. "I saw him do it."

"But the police, the papers," I whisper back. "He was shot point-blank."

Roy points an imaginary pistol, held as far from himself as he can, about a foot and a half, and pulls the "trigger" with both thumbs, steady as a rock. I jump.

"What happened to the gun?" I whisper.

"Gone by the time me and Junior got there," he says, checking his fingernails.

"Why would he do it, Roy?"

"Dunno," he whispers.

"Come on!" I shout.

At least ten fags go "Shhhhhh," and the minister, Rev. Bill, stops speaking. I bow my head, staring at the ugly brown linoleum floor that the school board needs to replace but probably won't because the district is too poor, the state legislature too stingy.

"He wanted you to say something at the service today," Roy whispers.

I look at him, covering my mouth, wondering what I could possibly say.

"You were the only fag he ever liked. If anyone can bring the school together, it's you, he said."

"Jesus Christ," I mutter behind my hand.

"I'm just telling you what he said."

"You two young men on the front row," says Rev. Bill, a tall, silver-headed man. "You seem to have a lot to say. Why don't you come up here and share it with us."

I search his voice for anger or sarcasm, one of the adult tones, but he seems sincere, bidding us with his finger to come to the podium. Even the organist plays a little traveling music, something with a great beat. It's way cool but wrong, like we're running up there to accept an award or something. I stand and so does Roy, and we walk to the side steps and make our way up to the minister.

He asks us our names and we speak into the microphone, magnifying our voices into these monstrous echoes. "Now which one of you is a fag?" he asks. His face is red from having to use that word. Cold silence. "All right, then, which one of you is a snark?" He faces the audience. "Why don't all you fags out there stand up?" There's an immediate buzz that swells across the crowd. "No one? Well, how about you snarks? Come on, stand up!" Again, a roll of hushed whispers. "Well, now, I've been told that this school is overrun with the two of you, fags and snarks, but now, in the light of day, no one will stand to avow his association." Rev. Bill's sweating, and it sours his cologne, whatever it is, something cheap, like a poor parishioner might give at Christmas, the most he can get for his money. I reach for the microphone with my right hand, and Rev. Bill releases it. I'm silent for a few seconds, gathering my mood. Then I stand with one foot crossed over the other, like Tommy used to.

"You may not know who I am," I say, "but my name's Tommy Goen."

A large hiccup shoots across the auditorium, as if Tommy's risen from the grave. I know . . . the symbolism is cheap . . . but I feel something very deeply and begin to speak, almost as if the words are being pulled from my mouth.

"Yes, I was a snark, until I died, I was a snark." Then everyone sees where I'm going and settles down. "Every day I went to school with the fear that a fag was going to kill me, not with a gun—but with words or with silence or by not speaking, by not acknowledging my existence as a human being." I toss the microphone to my left hand and say, "My name is Jeremy. And if y'all can't tell," I say in a lower voice, "I'm a fag. I dress like a fag, you know Abercrombie Fitch, Tommy H on a bad day. I drove an Explorer until some snark burned it to a crisp." It draws a laugh. "It isn't funny," I snap. "What's next? Are we gonna burn each other's houses down?" I pause, handing the mic back to "Tommy." "Yeah, fellow snarks, no one killed me. I shot myself, like this." I hold the microphone out and snap it with my thumb to get a bang out of the crowd. Then I toss the mic back to my left. "And how do I know Tommy killed himself? you ask. Because someone very close to him, a snark, told me, a few minutes ago." Roy steps forward. With his head down, he scuffles across the stage and stands next to Officer Vestra, the school cop, and holds out his arm to be taken away. Officer

Vestra motions for him to wait. "I have no reason to doubt what Roy Boy told me. Now the question is why, why would Tommy, who had so much going for himself—I danced in the line with him on *Grease*—take himself out like that? He was headed somewhere. And I don't mean Broadway, he wasn't that good. But he was headed somewhere." I bend down and rest my forehead on the lectern a moment; when I look up everyone sits still. "Tommy cared. He wanted . . . it was his biggest wish to join us all, fags and snarks into one." Charged air seems to boil across the room, like a low rumbling of thunder. Then a groan, shuffling feet. "Shut up!" I shout. Waiting. Waiting. Waiting. "It's time we all shut up and listened to what's going on around us." Snarks and fags fold their arms in defiance.

"I'm sorry," I say, holding the mic over my chest a moment, gathering my thoughts. "I have no moral authority, I stole five CDs yesterday so some snarks wouldn't kill me. And look at all of us today. You can't even tell where the fags take up and the snarks leave off. There's a fag," I say, pointing. "You there, and you, and you, and you," pointing to my buddies from drama class. Each one of them stands. "And look, there's a snark, another, and another, sitting right there between two fags. Why don't y'all shake hands, and none of that gang shit either," I say. Miraculously, they do, these half dozen students shake hands like real people. "Now, I can't expect the rest of you to do this, not this very minute, it would be like a fagfest at some church where everybody hugs a neighbor." The black-clad students turn and talk to someone close by. Some hold hands. And some cross their arms. "Change takes time," I say. "Even if it shouldn't."

I hand the mic back to Rev. Bill, who leads us all in prayer—an ecumenical doozy that honors the Baptist god, the Catholic god, the Hindu, the Muslim, the Jewish gods, all of them. And it isn't patronizing like some ministers can make a prayer sound, but sincere, calling for the dialogue to continue, saying the obvious, something about Tommy Goen's death not being in vain. Der. After the Amen, I grab the mic away and holler, "And tomorrow, everyone wear red!" Uniting under one color has worked for a day, why not a second, a third? A whoop goes up, and for a moment I'm fooled. But I know that tomorrow we'll all be dressed in our old garb, and that we'll all be fags and snarks again, jockeying for position in a world that demands it of us. I step down from the stage and go to lunch with my fag friends.

While at Arby's, some guys lean out their car window and snark us, disgorging that stupid laugh that now sounds as crude as a fart. But we've never seen them before in our lives, and we finish our subs with curly fries as if it's a normal day. Back at school we go to the next period, where a cop interrupts our history class to talk to us about how stupid gang life is and how we ought to love and respect our parents, who've worked hard to get us where we are today in Cow Pie, Texas, USA, Earth, the universe, a speck in the eye of God. I've heard this somewhere before, but somehow the cop makes it sound brand new.

KILLING LORENZO

Lately my dreams are crowded with people I don't know, people who stand inside a horseshoe falls, water cascading past them, little mists of spray kissing my face. Many of these visions end with a headlong dive, and often, before I reach the pool at the foot of the falls, I awake in a sweaty stupor. In another dream a man begins to bathe inside the falls. I move closer, stepping into the curtain of water, but when he turns to me and I reach out to him, a deep growl escapes his mouth and I wake face to face with Brice. Hitting his shoulder, which dislodges one more *snork*, I head for the bathroom to pee. It takes a while to get things moving, but finally I finish. When I return, Brice is snarling like a dragon, so I grab my pillow and head toward our guest room at the other end of the house. A man my age shouldn't have to put up with such racket.

When I turned fifty-seven, about a month ago, I lost my job as a paralegal. In the absence of the attorney for whom I worked, I failed to secure certain information from his client—on line fifteen, page three of an Advanced Directive for Physicians. As a result, the family of a ninety-year-old man could not pull the plug on his life. Mr. Priddy, a kind man really, gave me two weeks' severance pay but told me to leave the premises. Brice had wanted me to quit for some time, so my error was, in a way, fortunate.

I've now decided to take up a musical instrument I abandoned twenty-five years ago, when I met Brice and it seemed enough to be someone's lover. Having made arrangements to pay an hourly fee so that I might rehearse on a distinguished Holtkampf installed in a church near the university, I show up on a Monday, when there isn't much of a crowd. The music director acts as if I'm a feral cat, as if I might hiss and scratch if she gets too close. I shall call that bolder part of myself Lorenzo, after an uncle who once told a priest to keep his filthy hands to himself.

The director—she looks like Olive Oyl—smiles, and without allowing her hand to touch our paw, gives us the key to the organ. I scuffle down the hall and open the door to the sanctuary. The oak pews and beige cushions that line them bring to mind an uneasiness I've had about the Church for a long time, since I nearly went to seminary, in fact. *Get over it, Glenn. You're here to rehearse, not enlist.* The voice that has penetrated my consciousness, I realize, belongs to Lorenzo. *I'm not a talking cat,* he says, jumping up on the altar. *I'm a cat who talks. You dig?*

I climb the chancel steps and sit on the bench. I reach to the side and crank the handle until my legs dangle at the right height above the pedal board. I kick off my street shoes and don my Capezios, shiny but marred with long scratches made by the heel or toe of its mate. My feet still fit the patent leather, thin-soled shoes with a one-inch heel I bought at eighteen—perfect for playing the pedals. I insert the console key and turn it. The large bellows comes to life, supplying air to the two thousand gilded pipes that rise before me. Two small fans plugged into the console begin to oscillate, one of them blowing against my face like an evening breeze. The custodian, a squat man I shall call Quasimodo, has turned on the spots high overhead, and a small fluorescent in the music stand illuminates my score.

The humpback asks in a halting voice, "Can you see all right?"

"Yes," I say. "Thanks."

I'll bet he works for food, Lorenzo says.

Though I've not utilized the technique of an organist for so long, I sit with the same feeling of awe I had at twelve when this enormous noise resounded in my ears. I shiver with a bit of wonder. All those years I could have been performing. Will my fingers find the notes that my brain tells them to? *Perhaps you expect too much,* Lorenzo says, flipping through the big Bible as if he were looking for a Pizza Hut in the Yellow Pages. *And be thankful, my son, that Miss Oyl didn't make you get down on your knees and pray to God for guidance or some shit like that.*

My urologist, a handsome Asian at the med school, has decided to conduct a little biopsy. His Nurse Barkley, plump and prissy as Truman Capote, tells me to lie on my side and slide down both pairs of pants. He snaps latex up over his chubby fingers.

"I'm going to inject you with an antibiotic," he says. "One-two-three, stick."

"Ouch," I say, and he leaves.

Then my urologist enters and says, "Draw your knees up a bit more and wedge your feet against the wall. Soon I'll be sending a probe up your bottom to take a sonogram. When I've sighted the prostate on my screen," he says, "I'll inject anesthetic where I want to take core samples. As I enter through the rectal wall, you'll hear a series of ten clicks. Ready? One-two-three, stick."

"Ouch, damn," I say.

Your bottom? Lorenzo says. *What're you, five?*

"Sorry, Glenn," the doctor says. And in several places he injects a local into my prostate. He and Barkley leave for twenty-five minutes; I watch the clock. When they return, the doctor shoots sonogram gel up my ass. It's cool and comforting, like getting a glob of Astroglide as Brice makes ready to fuck me.

"The prostate is normally the size of a walnut, but yours is a bit bigger than a plum. You do realize it's divided into lobes, don't you?" my urologist asks. "Five clicks for each one." *Do it*, Lorenzo says, *before I scratch your eyes out.*

Brice has gone mad with the November menu from Frida Kahlo's book, cooking for two days. Friends are now lying around with Brice and me in our post-dinner stupor, the aromas from several recipes lingering in the air.

"The red mole is a work of art," someone says.

A bottle of Gran Marnier sits nearly empty on the coffee table, along with a slew of crystal glasses. We've gassed about everyone's work, everyone's family, everyone's dog or cat (Lorenzo stalks out of the room), the new car, new clothes, new furnishings, and all of our latest trips to Vegas, Canada, and Majorca.

When there's a lull, Brice says, "I know! Let's play Two Lies and a Truth."

"You can't change the rules," I say. "It's like Scrabble."

"Going for the lie is so boring," Brice says. "Besides, for every situation there's only one truth, so don't you see, it's more realistic this way."

"I've always loved your flexibility," I say.

"You can go first, Glennie," he says.

"Thanks," I say, ruminating while everyone thinks of his own one truth. I kick around several ideas: Teachers I Have Loathed, Cars I Have Wrecked, Items I Have Shoplifted, Those Whom I've Fist-Fucked. Then I snap my fingers.

"My round is entitled Axe Murderers I Have Known."

"Oh, now we have to name them?" Brice says.

"Oh, sure," someone says. "It'll be fun."

"Okay," I say, "here goes. I went to seminary . . . "

"*You* went to seminary?" someone giggles. "Now that's a lie."

". . . with a guy who was indicted for killing his wife. I never believed he did it. I visited him in prison. And . . . a woman I went to college with was murdered by her minister's wife, because this woman was having an affair with her husband, the minister."

"Jesus Christ," someone else mutters, laughing, as if it were a joke.

"Finally . . . Harriet Wiggins offed her second husband, an Allstate agent, right before our twenty-fifth high school reunion." Someone makes me repeat them again.

"They all seem so real," says the second-grade teacher.

"Yes, too much verisimilitude for me," says the English prof, lighting his pipe.

"What's the third one's name?" Brice asks, and I repeat it. "It's her," he says, looking at the ceiling. "It's the very one you called by name. It has to be her."

"No fair," someone complains. "You already knew."

"Wanna bet?" Brice says, slugging back another little glass of liqueur.

My development as a musician is arrested in the yellowed pages of pieces I learned in graduate school. Fingerings are sketched in like items on a grocery list.

"How did I ever play without proper fingerings?" I say aloud.

Don' worry about it, Lorenzo says, curling up beside me.

I pull out what is, for me, a new piece by Théodore Dubois—his "Toccata" that I heard on a CD. I finish writing tiny numbers above every note of the piece, a job I started several weeks ago.

"Why wasn't I this disciplined at twenty-one or even thirty-two, when I quit playing?"

I said stop, Lorenzo says, *or I might hafta give you a smack.* He snaps his tail like a whip.

Quasimodo clatters up the chancel steps, and my pencil falls down between two blond pedals. I see eight or ten other nubs, like coins in a well, gone forever. Lorenzo raises his head, as if a fly is zooming him.

"Sorry," the humpback grunts. "I've gotta set up this place for later."

I nod and smile, but Lorenzo hisses, banging his tail against the altar wall. *Tell the moron to fuck off.* I continue to pull out lots of stops for Dubois's toccata—from *toccare,* Italian for touch—a flashy, virtuosic piece of some difficulty. So joyful and fulsome when I heard it on the CD that I ordered the score right away. Now I begin to play a trifle less than half tempo. In the margin I've listed a series of metronomic settings, about ten beats apart, and over the weeks I've checked them off as I conquer each tempo. Quasi continues to bang chairs and run the vac. After two more pages I excuse myself to the bathroom off the sanctuary and plop down to deliver my load. The minister has used this very toilet before he climbs the pulpit steps to orate his *bons mots* from God. I stare at little colonies of mold growing in the grout along the floor, finish up, and leave.

Wedging a Bible in the side door, I step out into the West Texas breeze that blows a whirl of leaves across my face. I hadn't even thought about a cigarette until the custodian banged his way into my afternoon. Now I may smoke the whole pack. I used to do that whenever Brice and I had a fight; smoking would rev me up and calm me at the same time. University students pass by in clumps of two or three, all of them talking on cells. They have it so easy. Back when I was their age, I spoke on the pay phone down the hall, and only if someone bothered to answer the fucker. It could ring fifty times before you either went insane or ran down the hall. *Yeah*, Lorenzo says, *that was in the middle of the last century, when people still sent telegrams and girls wore A-line dresses, egad.*

"Ready, Glenn?" my urologist asks. "I'm going to do the first one."

He reminds me of Tony Leung, a striking actor in *Happy Together,* a Wong Kar-wai film about two gay guys who move from Hong Kong to Argentina. A *click* resounds, like the dull thud of a toy gun. It isn't so bad. But he bores a bit deeper into my swollen prostate, and I begin to count. *Click two.* Deeper. *Click three.* I do believe he's switched to a staple gun. *Click four,* and "Ow, ow, ow," I say.

"Don't move," he says. "The further away I get from the local, the more discomfort you'll experience."

"No shit," I mumble, crumpled up on his gurney. *Click five.*

"That does it for one half," he says. "Now I want five more from the other lobe."

I breathe in and out for each one, as if I were doing Yoga. *Click, breathe. Click, breathe. Click, breathe. Click, breathe.*

"Here comes the last one," the doctor says, "but who's counting?" He laughs.

"Ouch," I say, as if it were a refrain from an old poem.

"Harriet Wiggins was my girlfriend at El Centro High," I tell everyone. "She won Miss Teenage Texas in 1966 by wowing the judges with one of the flashier Beethoven sonatas. She married when we graduated high school, but hubby left her before she was twenty."

"Yeah, but what were you doing with her?" Cord asks. I glare at our florist friend, who's blown more guys in his delivery van than I can remember cruising. In his late thirties, he's still quite stunning.

"So you didn't actually go to seminary?" someone asks.

"No," I say with exasperation. "Then, after college Harriet married this schlub, the Allstate agent, who was ten years older. One day she walked into his office and found him *in flagrante delicto* with the very woman whose job it was to detain people like Harriet. Out of her purse Harriet pulled a nine-millimeter her father had given her for self-defense and shot the agent in the back of the head, while his secretary stared up past him, waiting for hers. *But I couldn't do it*, Harriet said. *It wasn't her fault he was an asshole.*"

"You spoke with her?" Cord asks, reclining on our chaise.

"I was in town for the reunion, and I felt sorry for her. I went to see her in jail."

Everyone laughs, and I head for our bathroom, staring at myself in the mirror, then closing my eyes. Standing over the pedestal sink, I conjure up an image of my college roommate, a hairy guy named Torgelson who's remained forever young, if never my lover (we did embrace once). I stroke myself hard and am soon rewarded. Then I clean up and return to the living room, where we continue to sport with the truth.

Through the side door of the sanctuary I watch Lorenzo hop from one pew to the next, until he winds up on the altar sculpture of the Last Supper with his paws around two of the disciples closest to the end, as if he were going to bring them a chalice filled with wine. I keep an eye on Quasi, too. When the humpback finishes his work, I step into the mustiness of the room, which reminds me of my late mother's Christmas closet. Old wax. Mold. Dust. I climb into the organ loft. During my smoke break my music has been moved, and I turn the pages of the toccata back to the beginning.

Once again I pull out the stops Dubois intended for me to use. I touch the Great manual and begin playing faster than I should. Dr. Stamps used to say, "If you play it too fast, too soon, you'll wreck it." I start over, setting the metronome to guide me, but it's like when your car wants to move faster than the speed limit. I keep playing ahead of the *click click click* of the metronome, watching Lorenzo eye its pendulum, watching his tail bounce against the beat.

At last I stop the thing and let 'er rip. The tempo comes as if I've always played it this fast, and when I reach the coda, I kick the sforzando knob with my right toe. The last eight measures fall into an allargando, a dramatic slowing until the final G major chord resounds throughout the sanctuary. I sustain it for eight counts before releasing the keys as if the keyboard is on fire. My heart is pounding, my lungs heaving. I never expected to play this well again, and I wish there were a crowd of hundreds to applaud me. As a door to the hallway squeaks, I look out into the darkened sanctuary. At the back doors I can see the street where cars buzz by the university, but in the shadows there's not a soul to be seen. Not even Lorenzo, who seems to have disappeared.

"In the days to come," says my urologist, "you may see blood in your urine, your stools, especially your ejaculate. Here's a towel. If you want to clean up, the bathroom's through that door." He and Nurse Barkley leave me damaged on the table.

There seems to be a ton of gel slathered across my *bottom*. I wipe and wipe and still, I can't seem to get it all off. I sit up and stumble to the bathroom and lower my sticky self onto the toilet, trying to ignore what feels like a hot poker stuck up my ass. For ten minutes I wipe, filling one wad of toilet paper after another. I look down and almost gag. The bowl is full of blood. I reach back to flush, bursting into insane laughter that quickly turns to tears. Stanching them with a Kleenex, I fold another one and stick it between my cheeks. I pull my pants up and stagger to the door, out to my car. Again I laugh, because I'm never going through this again. Not as long as I fucking live.

Cord tells Two Lies and a Truth entitled Sex on the Veranda. "Okay, first . . . my mother dragged me into her bed when I was fourteen and enticed me with the promise of a car to fuck her three times in a row."

There exists complete silence, not even the whir of the AC.

"My father came home drunk when I was fourteen and made me blow him in the bathroom," Cord says, staring into the dark patio doors.

"That's the one!" someone shrieks.

"You can't guess until he gives all three!" I say. "Sheesh." I pour more Gran Marnier for myself and anyone who wants some.

"My high school choir teacher, Mr. Holdridge, fucked me in his office one afternoon, after he offered to pay me for filing music."

That dirty dog, Lorenzo says, entering the room again.

I've gotten all the truths right so far, and because of that, everyone looks at me to guess first.

"I'm not sure," I demur. "Someone else go." *Don't you hate moochers?* Lorenzo says, slapping Cord's face with his tail.

Three people say *Cord's mother*. Four others select *the choir teacher*.

I tap my front teeth, deliberating a bit. "First of all," I say, glancing at our cherubic friend who's provided the centerpiece for our table. "Cord's mother hasn't had sex since he was conceived." Everyone laughs. "Also, I happen to know that Cord's choir teacher was a woman, who did get fired for fraternizing with the enemy, but it wasn't Cord, I can guarantee you that. That only leaves dear old dad." I look up at Cord, and he's grinning, but the moment has a certain sadness to it.

"Damn, Glenn, you're good," Cord proclaims. "You oughta work for the FBI." A few idiots giggle, we all take a potty break, and I uncap another bottle of Gran Marnier.

When everyone returns, somewhat subdued, Brice opens with what he calls the Celebrity Round.

"You always take things too far," I say, and he smirks at me, this mustachioed mouth that I've loved for twenty-five years. Prior to teaching film at our university, Brice used to work as an aide to an assistant producer in LA.

"In 1977," he says, "I slept with Brad Davis, before he filmed *Midnight Express*." Everyone groans, as if they know it's a lie. I know it's not, but he doesn't realize that, so I groan, too. "In 1983," he says, "Goldie Hawn lit my cigarette on the set of *Swing Shift*."

"Oh, I loved that movie," someone says. "Ed Harris was so hot." Now everyone sits up straight because the first two declarations sound like such whoppers.

"Remember," Brice says, "life holds only one truth."

"Oh, shut up," I say, and he sticks out his tongue.

"In 1972," he says, "I sat in on the Burt Reynolds photo shoot at *Cosmo*. Let's say it's a good thing he has big hands."

Now the room goes berserk, guys throwing pillows at Brice as if he were a hero . . . or a liar.

I wake with a full bladder, and by the time I've stumbled in and turned on the bathroom light, I've forgotten my dream. *Does it matter?* Lorenzo says, checking his weight on the scale. *Hm, almost six kilos.* Well, yes. I've had comforting dreams, where Mother came to me and we talked about how I was getting along without her. When I woke I was so surprised to realize she was dead. After taking five minutes to pee, I check the bowl for blood, and as before, there is none. I close the door, standing over the white pedestal sink, and, thinking of Torgelson and his hairy chest, conjuring up the cock I never knew, I go to work. Soon a bright sticky stream of magenta hits the back of the sink. I stifle a scream with a hand over my mouth. *Nice trajectory,* Lorenzo says.

One afternoon, after I've been rehearsing every Monday for a couple of months, Miss Olive Oyl enters the sanctuary, standing inside my peripheral view. When I finish the Dubois, she walks toward the console buried in the floor and leans over me. The hem of her dress, a long Laura Ashley of lavender, hangs mere inches from me. Lorenzo holds it up and rolls his eyes. *Take it back to Goodwill,* he says.

"That's wonderful," she says, smoothing her dress over skinny hips. "What is it?"

I tell her about Dubois. "He hasn't as much depth as Franck, but I love this piece, so joyful, so exuberant."

"Yes, yes, it is," she says, tapping her chin. "Would you play a hymn for me?"

"I played hymns before I could walk," I say. *Good one,* Lorenzo cracks.

"Our organist, Paul, is going to be gone for two weeks," she says, "and our regular sub will be out of town, too. I'm in a bind. Do you think you could manage it?"

I realize I've been waiting for her to ask. And I've been showing off, haven't I? Lorenzo scampers to the back of the loft and hides among the bourdons—sixteen-foot pedal pipes that rattle the rafters. *Don't make me sick,* he says.

"Anyone can hear that you're quite accomplished," she says. "Your playing is so passionate, so fresh."

Meow, meow, ark, ark, ark, says Lorenzo.

I tell her I'll have to think about it, that I want to give myself a year before playing in public.

"Once," she says, sitting in a choir pew with her heels together, "when I was right out of college, I was asked to sing at Annual Conference. In front of all those people, I choked," she says. "I couldn't remember a word, my voice failed me. Except for demonstrating for my sopranos, I've never sung a note since."

I stare ahead at the Dubois score as if the notes are tea leaves, twirling with the turn of a spoon, telling me what to do, if only I could read them.

"I can find a student from the university," she says, standing, "but I think it a shame to waste your talent."

Man, that chick wants to kill me, Lorenzo says, coughing up a furball that flies out of his mouth like a bat out of hell.

I know something's way wrong when Nurse Barkley dumps me where I've never been before. The other examining rooms are far more cheerful, with life-sized charts of female anatomy on one wall, male on another, huge cutaway pictures of the prostate in various states of overgrowth. However, this room is gun-metal gray, with a gun-metal table centered under a blaring metal lamp. *This is where we give you the bad news,* I imagine Nurse Barkley saying. *Your little walnut is riddled with cancer. When the doctor rips it out next week, we'll find nothing but dead meat. Wah-ah-ah-ah-ah-ah,* he laughs like Vincent Price.

The door opens, and my urologist sits next to me at a counter, sliding a lab report between us. He's wearing a trace of Jaguar Performance, and I lean toward him, allowing his vigor and youth and utter masculinity to reel me in. If I were younger, I might hit on him, but if I were, say, in my thirties, I would have no cause to be here. And the doctor would be but ten years old. *Don't be so literal,* Lorenzo says, crawling up my back, reaching around to pat me on the cheek. *He's a hunk-o'-meat.*

"Of the ten samples I took," he says, "eight are fine. But two of them are what we call 'atypical.' There isn't enough tissue to determine whether you have cancer or not. I need to go in again."

"You'll have to knock me out," I say. *You and me both,* Lorenzo says.

"We're not set up to sedate you, but I can get you a couple of Valium and some Vicodin to take before you come in." He says he'll send Nurse Barkley in with my prescriptions. After I've had time to daydream about having no prostate and consequently, no erectile functions at all, Barkley enters and sashays across the room, where he puts an arm around me. I feel like a lump of cold Jell-O.

I do so like the color she's using, Lorenzo lisps, batting Barkley's hair, *but that eighties backsweep is the worst.*

"I still haven't agreed to do this," I say. "I don't have to sign the paperwork, you know. Men in their nineties die *with* prostate cancer, not *of* it."

"That's what we love," croons Nurse Barkley. "A nice positive attitude. After you get these filled," he says, handing me the prescriptions, "take two of each a half hour before your biopsy. Make sure someone drives you to and from the office. DeeDee up front will give you an appointment." He squeezes my shoulder. I sign the paper and run down the narrow hall to the front desk, where I can hear some twat laughing in a high-pitched voice. *And then we all ate his bird drop soup.*

"Would you rather die of embarrassment?" Barkley hollers after me.

When our little game of Two Lies and a Truth is finished, the time is quite late, so everyone sleeps over. The guys are amazed that I knew about Brad Davis, and Brice twists my arm until I confess to reading his journal. Which itself is a lie, because I heard Brice groan the truth one night—*I could fuck you blind, Brad Davis.* And it makes me wonder which is worse, invading his journal or his dreams?

In my sleep I dream that Sally Treviño looks as radiant as she did in high school. For the annual water show, I accompanied her on the spinet shoved against the natatorium wall as she sang "Try to Remember," while splashing nymphs made circular patterns in the water. The chlorine burned my nose, and light danced off her freckled face, as if someone were holding a candle to her chin. She was irresistibly Latin, continental in manner, with a dark pageboy framing her face and swaying with each gesture she made. "Are you a Republican?" I ask her. "Would I be wearing this if I were?" She smiles her brilliant smile and points to her donkey lapel pin. When I wake, I feel as if I'm seventeen, happy to have stopped dreaming of strangers.

After I inform Miss Oyl I couldn't possibly play for church yet, my rehearsals lose their focus. I sit and toy with a number of works I mastered when I was young, skipping the difficult passages and playing the bombastic parts, where I can kick the sforzando knob with my toe and rattle the rafters. About halfway through my allotted time, Olive interrupts and asks me if I'd be willing to quit early.

"I've found a university student to play Sunday," she says, "and he has two hours between finals. I'll apply your rehearsal fee to next time. You don't mind, do you?"

"Not at all," I say, canceling the registration and collecting my books from the bench, where Lorenzo sits licking his paw, casting me a look. *Well, we were here first,* he says. I remove my scratched Capezios, imagining them in a junk shop someday, after I'm dead and gone.

"My," she says, "those have seen some traffic, haven't they?"

Not as much as your face, Lorenzo says. I laugh and slide them into my big bag, putting on my loafers. In a minute a young man with flame-orange hair enters and shakes my hand. His name is Horace. Horace is gangly but handsome and wears glasses with slit-narrow lenses. A diamond stud is tacked onto each ear. He stares me straight in the face, as if he were cruising me. Jesus. As the director helps him find his way around the console, I sneak to the back and sit down. After a while she leaves Horace alone, and he plays "Onward Christian Soldiers" as a complex but recognizable improvisation—a skill I never quite mastered. As I get up to leave, the music stops. Horace stands and looks out at me.

"I must have complete silence," he says.

Stupid shit, Lorenzo mutters. *Wait until the crip with the Hoover shows up.*

I give Horace a wave and step outside to light a cigarette. When I'm almost finished, he joins me, holding a cigarette of his own.

"You're good," he says, blowing smoke straight up. "I heard you playing the Dubois the other day."

So you're the one who messed with our music, Lorenzo says, leaping at the chain dangling from Horace's side pocket.

"But I'm better," Horace says, grinning so that all his teeth show.

"No argument there," I say, checking out his crotch, which doesn't reveal much. With baggy pants sagging on their hips, the young no longer display their wares as we once did—as if there were no purpose in doing so. I follow a pebble with my toe to the gutter and kick it across the parking lot, where it clangs against someone's hubcap.

Chicken, Lorenzo shrieks like a parrot. *Me loves pretty pretty chicken.*

I swallow my two Valium and two Vicodin, and Brice drives me to the next biopsy. While we wait, I recall my dream from this morning. I'm sitting in my high school history class, looking up at Mr. Timms, the teacher. Everyone's wearing glued-on Fidel Castro beards. Staring at me, Mr. Timms asks me if I have a brain in my head.

"What the hell did he say?" I ask a kid next to me, by chance spitting in his face.

"How should I know?" the kid says, rubbing his eye.

And then I woke up and Brice drove me to the doctor.

"I'm going to take five samples from each of the two questionable areas," my urologist says. I go through the whole shebang again: the local anesthetic, the Astroglide up the ass, the skewers, the clicks. Drugs have made me more compliant, more relaxed, but I can still feel him poking at my giant walnut, as if I'm a frog being dissected by a bored tenth grader. When he dismisses me to the bathroom and I wipe, there is but one dollop of blood on my wad of toilet paper.

On the way to the house, Brice buys me a Heath Bar Blizzard, my treat for being such a good boy. At home, when I've finished spooning it down my gullet, I stagger to the bathroom and stand at the sink, but Brice walks in and suggests that I hold off.

"I'd like, Glennie," he says, wrapping his arms around me, "the pleasure of pleasuring you, myself. Later, when you feel like it." He kisses me on the neck, and I shiver as he escorts me to our room. I agree and fall into bed, where I experience a black, dreamless sleep that leaves me groggy until Brice crawls in and calls me to dinner at six. "I've made red mole for you," he sings into my ear. Lorenzo licks his balls, grinning like the very devil.

On Sunday morning I shower and dress, and in another hour, I've slipped into the back row of the sanctuary. With great skill and feeling, Horace is playing the closing section of Franck's *Pièce Héroïque*. I never performed it that well, and for all those years, I convinced myself that I had. This congregation of university people turn to one another and murmur. *Who's this child? He's fabulous.*

The pastor's sermon is transparent and uninspired. He uses everyday metaphors—like washing dishes, driving a car, whacking the kids with a newspaper—to make his three points about how we fail to love one another as Christ intended. *A C minus minus,* Lorenzo quips. Horace plays a complex fugue by Bach for the postlude, and at the most crucial passage, he leaves out half the notes. *The wunderkind ain't so hot,* Lorenzo shouts to me as he counts the money left at the altar. After the postlude and nearly everyone has filed out of the sanctuary, I walk up to where Horace is slumped on the bench, his glasses folded beside him. Both hands are buried in his face, and he's sobbing.

"It wasn't that bad," I say. *Let's not lie to the boy,* Lorenzo says.

"Oh, God," he sniffles. "I was sure I was ready to play it."

"Hang in there," I say. "A case of nerves will rob you blind."

For some reason, I drop down to the bench and hand him his glasses. I want to run my fingers through his stiff red hair, wipe the tears from his face. I want to shelter him from the pain he's going to feel in a lifetime, but then I begin to laugh.

"I'm not that pathetic," he says, beginning to gather his music.

"I was thinking of my first afternoon recital at the university. I began to play a Bach prelude from memory, and halfway through I lost my way and started over several times. After struggling longer than it would've taken to play the whole piece, I slapped on a I-V-I cadence and ended with an A major chord. Then I ran back to my dorm room and bawled for an hour."

"Is that supposed to make me feel better?" he says, rising from the bench.

"How about some lunch?" I ask.

He turns and says, "Okay, but you're not gonna suck my cock."

Nurse Barkley tries to stop me at my car, a new Solara, but even at my age, I'm too quick for his fat ass. He pounds on my window and yells, "It's not the end of the world, we can treat it." Spraying gravel, I careen over to Nineteenth Street and pull into the center lane. In my mirror, a guy in a silver 4Runner starts to overtake me, so I dart in front of him. The SUV's graying driver zooms me, falls back, then zooms me closer. It incites a rush of adrenaline, and I pull into the far right lane, where he follows and revs his engine while we wait for the light. *It's a dot of cancer,* my urologist said minutes ago. *We can inject an isotope the size of a grain of rice.* Rounding the corner, the guy dogs me. *It has a ninety-nine percent success rate.*

"Move it, you asshole," I yell at an RV over to my left. I slip in front of him, and now, on the seven-lane boulevard, the 4Runner's at my far right. I slow to let a Buick run interference. But the 4Runner maneuvers himself in front of the Buick, shoots in front of me, and jams on his brakes. I dodge into a left-turn outlet, screeching my tires across three lanes of traffic, to escape the 4Runner. *Honest, it's a very effective treatment. A ninety percent success rate.* In the middle of this residential avenue, where bare ornamental mulberries will form a canopy in May, I pull over and rest my head on the steering wheel. I hear a car pull up, and someone taps on my window. I open it.

"Yes, officer?" I say.

You should be grateful for eighty-nine percent. That's better than lung cancer, better than leukemia. Eighty-nine percent is the best you can expect.

A young man with a dark, smooth face asks for my license, and I begin to flush. "Some crazy stuff goin' on back there. We call it driving without due regard."

"I . . . I've got cancer."

Lorenzo hops out the window and wraps himself around the officer's neck, licking his mustache as if it were laden with salt. At first the guy looks at me as if I'm lying, but he gets in his car and grabs the radio mic. When he returns, he says, "I'm going to let it go, sir, you have no priors. But I urge you to be more careful." He closes his citation pad and walks back to his car, where he seems to stare at me through his dark glasses. I realize how much the officer reminds me of Torgelson, the kind of roommate that shall remain forever young. Lorenzo jumps back in through the window. *He's cute, but Brice is a better kisser.*

I wake on my side, with Brice's arm around me, his hand rubbing my stomach.

"Mmmm," I groan.

It's eighty-thirty and I should get up. My first meeting with the oncologist is at ten. But I feel protected in Brice's arms, with my ass shoved into his crotch. His caresses make me feel young, as if it's a Sunday morning in 1979, as if the *El Centro Journal* is lying on the porch and the sun's boring a hole in the door. In seconds our nightclothes are on the floor, and we're tearing at one another as if our aging spines might withstand the rigors of intercourse, which they cannot. We switch to manual labor. I roll over and grab the Astroglide. As Brice starts on me, I watch Lorenzo hop up on the headboard. He licks his paws, holding his face up to a beam of sunlight that seeps through the blind, turning his head to watch me writhe and groan at my moment. When the rusty red salvo flies over my head and past the headboard, Lorenzo falls off and disappears.

"Hey, Tiger," Brice says, climbing on me, kissing me as if I might die tomorrow. "Where've you been hiding?"

After I do Brice, we fall asleep again, and I dream of standing on a hotel balcony, where I release two remote-control American Jetliners, chrome with stripes of red and blue. One does a loop-the-loop and continues on until I assume it runs out of fuel. The other lands, colliding with a spider its own size. In my dream I stand in awe of this spectacle, unsure of the scale. Is the spider that big, or is the plane that small?

THE AGE I AM NOW

Several days before Halloween, my boss announces that I'll soon be leaving Texas to translate some tapes for the Dutch government.

"I've never been out of the country before," I tell him.

He overnights me a new passport from DC, I climb the Houston International jetway to a plane bound for Amsterdam, and twelve hours later I step off a clackety-clack that stops in Den Haag. The air bites my face, and the sky is so dark my camera won't register its light.

The Dutch office gives me a day to become acclimated, so instead of unpacking I spend most of it in Arnem at the Kröller-Müller. Amid all the Picassos and Van Goghs, I'm drawn to Verster's "Stone-cutters" and rest on a dark padded bench to study it, alongside an old woman dressed in black with a leopard-print scarf around her neck. Her dark, florid perfume seems to emanate from inside the frame, where two men and a woman sit on shallow blocks, legs extended with wooden shoes pointed to the sky. Like tikes playing in a sandbox, these three chip chip chip away, shaving the red stones into bricks. The painting gives me the peculiar feeling that someone is lying. Bricks are baked, not sculpted. I finish the afternoon in the museum tea shop, where children squeal in tongues I don't understand. Their squinty, joyful faces fatigue me, a man of fifty-four, and I soon leave. The woman, dressed in black, boards a different train than I, but her scent lingers.

On Tuesday I finish translating early and take a series of trains from Den Haag to Amsterdam, a city that sits dankly in the middle of a reclaimed swamp. A mild but pungent odor of pig shit weaves its way through the air almost everywhere, then seems to yield to the aromas of rich fried food. Yet the streets meander without so much as a gum wrapper. I begin in the section called the Jordaan, where mostly Jews have lived for some time. I've planned to see the home of Anne Frank, but the line trails around the block. The thought of standing and waiting exhausts me. Instead, I take a photo. I can show friends, though I probably won't, that I saw the home of Anne Frank.

I begin to walk east, street after street, taking in the market square, snapping ten shots of a cathedral built in the 1500s, sailing by dark rows of mossy buildings constructed along canals in the 1600s. Covered with satellite dishes, gray concrete apartments rise like huge graves before me, indicating that I've somehow strayed from my map. I stop at a pub to get directions but order smoked salmon served on hard rolls with a sharp mustard. The nutty, nostril-burning aroma of cigarettes rises like mist. Most men roll their own; a few women smoke long ones with gold filter tips.

I sip some grappa, which warms my chest, my belly. It gives me a feeling of well-being, and I take a deep quaff, finishing with a gulp. Before I can ask the waiter to clarify my location, I hear a clink against the closeness of the atmosphere, like a hammer smashing a car. I look out the window and witness the smoke of two more shots. Across the street a large blond man lies prostrate. Others immediately surround him, and his bicycle is cast aside like a broken toy. A dark-bearded man slides a gun into his pants, and, even though the blond man begs for his life, the assassin slashes the air with a knife. I blink as the dark man thrusts his weapon downward. A mélange of blurred hands and arms engulf him, and at least three people flip open cell phones. As sirens begin to toodle—they don't scream like those in America—I throw down too many euros, step outside, and push my way through the crowd, where people shriek and shout like ducks and chickens set afire. My head still floating from the grappa, I take refuge between two pairs of shoulders that both reek of tobacco.

The assassin has created an unspeakable smile in the man's throat, and, through blood spatters, I can see the entreaty in his bulging eyes, as if to say, "Please, I don't have what you want." I'm nauseated and push my way out of the crowd. I stare up into the yellowing trees, one of those times a guy looks, merely to gain ease, to see something a million miles away—perhaps a day in my childhood when I played in the front yard, enclosed safely behind a chain-link fence.

"Do any of you realize who this man *is*?" comes a voice at my feet, a Brit by the sound of it. I look down. The squat man in a tattered coat humps over the ground, near the slain's feet, as if in prayer. "Do you have . . . any . . . idea?" the man moans, seized with spasms of weeping. My heel leaves dark half-moons of blood on the pavement. I know, because I'm looking behind me as I leave the scene, watching angry men swarm like ants around the bearded one, carrying him off to a doorway. Sirens near the area, and several squad cars invade the crowd.

As I walk away, the group of police fans out across the area. A young officer pulls me back to one of the cars, a Citroën, as if my arm has been grown for precisely this purpose. I stare at the hand of this man who speaks to me in Dutch.

"Sorry, you speak too fast," I say, watching the police drag the murderer out of the grasp of the angry crowd. Very cinema vérité vérité.

"Please step into the car. You saw this. I have questions." The Dutch speak English on demand, and quite graciously, I might add.

"But . . . I was across the street eating." I point to the pub.

"Please," he says. As he closes the rear door on me, the throng's noise dims to a hum. He enters his side, and I hear it all again in a blip. He slams his door and takes a minute to get his pen out, his notebook. He turns to his side, so that he can glance back at me. His breathing is fast, but he speaks slowly.

"Why are you here in the Netherlands, business or pleasure?"

"Business, mostly," I tell him.

"What do you do?"

"I'm a translator."

"May I see your passport?" he asks, scribbling a ballpoint hard against the page in his notebook.

"It'll take a minute," I say, reaching into my pants.

"What are you doing?" he asks sharply, pulling his gun.

"Whoa, I keep it here," I say, pulling out a zippered bag looped to my belt. I remove the crimped blue booklet warmed by my body. A fifty-euro bill flutters to the floor and I grab it, holding up my passport. The officer puts his gun down, and I exhale, sliding the document under the grate between us. He glances at me, then my picture, and back again. He writes in his notebook, sliding the passport back to me.

Now the officer turns, his blue eyes scanning mine but briefly, his dirty blond hair askew. "You seem rather unmoved by this. Can you describe what happened here?"

"I was across the street." I point again, which seems ludicrous. I tell him how I jumped when I heard the clink, how I rose from my leather seat, floating across the avenue, breaking through the crowd. I describe the dark assassin. "He didn't even try to get away." I speak of the pool of blood at the base of the man's skull. I quote the moaning Brit. "Who *is* that guy . . . the one that got shot?" I ask.

Across the way several policemen hold the suspect by the arms, with two more at his legs. Others cordon him off from the crowd.

"You're positive it was he who did it?" the officer asks. "The Muslim?"

"I don't know about *that*, but yes, that man your men are holding. I saw the gun in his hand . . . the knife." I slash my throat with a forefinger, to make sure he knows.

"What were you doing in the area?" he asks.

"Actually, I got lost, and I was hungry."

He continues to write, then looks out the window for a minute as if he might suddenly put it all together. "You've been most helpful," he says. "Have you a telephone where you may be reached?"

I give him my office number. He asks for nothing else, and, as I've learned from dealing with my own government, I say no more. He releases me. I stand on colt legs for a minute and lean against the car. Seized by the smell of cooking oil, I take a deep breath to stanch the heaves. An ambulance backs its way into the crowd, which has dispersed somewhat, but I sense that something more is brewing, bubbling to the outer fringes of the city, the country. It might even boil over, making the world one big stew. I take a last look, as if the scene might reverse itself like a film, as if the big blond man might stand, soak up all his blood, and ride his bike backward into the morning.

With my grappa buzz quite blunted, I hightail it westward, discovering my error in map reading. A bit more steady, I find my station and head back to Den Haag. On the train, voices of the Dutch, usually reserved, cry out, so that by the time we've reached my stop, I can barely hear the announcement. I ask a man what's wrong, and in choppy English he shouts that a film director has been murdered by a Moroccan.

"Jesus Christ," I mutter.

Suddenly, all the Dutch media, focused on whether Bush can beat Kerry, switch to our story. At the hotel I locate a TV channel with English on a crawl at the bottom of the screen. The director's film, portraying passages from the Koran tattooed across the torsos of nude females, rolls above it. The still shot of a dark woman, his partner in cinema, imposes itself on the screen, along with the English graphic, "Muslim Women Slaves to Their Men." Faces of the Dutch in the streets reflect the same divisive feelings we've experienced at home. The word "tolerance" rolls across the bottom, and it jangles like a tin can in my ears. I ring for room service.

When my boss in Washington scheduled this trip, I protested that it would be during the election. He told me to vote early; I had one day left. Standing on line in Texas with my voter registration card in hand, I feared that something terrible might happen while I was out of the country—a coup worse than the supreme court junta of 2000—and I would not be allowed back in. I call the DC office.

"You've gotta get me outta this place," I say.

My boss tells me to forget about it. "It's not as if you're in the Middle East," he says. "Come back when you're through with the job."

Letting the phone drop, I take a big gulp—perhaps it's only hunger—and sit on the bed. When a young man knocks and delivers my supper tray, I remove the silver lid and view a dark luscious stew made with vegetables I imagine have been wrought of a fecund land a few kilos outside of town. I sit on the edge of the bed, pulling the cart toward me, fortifying myself for a siege that is all but invisible. Dutch TV can't seem to give up this historic loss; the streets are choked with rioting. When I finish eating, I push the cart away and drop to my bed, watching the screen until I fall asleep fully clothed, waiting for what's to come.

Finishing work the next day, I learn the truth about my own country. Our election has once again been determined by a single state, a state where voting machines leaving no paper trail are manufactured by a company that has funded the winning candidate throughout the election. And yet, not a cry is heard, not a moan. The loser concedes.

Daily I make my way to the government building in Den Haag and translate tapes and discs until my head feels as if it's going to pop. The recorded voices belong to Korean and British operatives that happen to fall within Dutch jurisdiction. But suddenly there are no more tapes. This day, the day before I leave Holland, I begin to converse with a local translator, a woman ten years my junior, who's been helping me with passages of Dutch that show up in my work. We've negotiated a subtle flirtation, and the way she smells of vanilla, as if she's bathed in candle wax, intoxicates me. I ask if I can take her to tea. Her apartment is close, she says, so we go there instead. Lotte Mooren is thin, nearly my height, with long brown hair piled on her head. She possesses simple features like a porcelain doll, but with a softness to her face, like my mother's when she was young. After we reach her apartment, Lotte changes behind a screen into a simple black sweater, cords, and clogs, and she shows me photos of her trip to Romania.

Seated at a small dinette with five chairs, all lacquered Chinese red, I expect to see touristy shots of arched bridges reflected in stagnant canals or gothic cathedral spires. But, in fact, this woman has spent several weeks of her vacation "helping to rebuild lives for Romanians who have so little. But," she muses softly, "they seem grateful for what they do have." Her tone casts a kind of judgment over the abundance that the Dutch, perhaps the West as a whole, have otherwise amassed in fifty years.

Her pictures depict houses that are squat, shedlike structures, where people with poor teeth and few possessions make lives. But the photos please the eye, capturing, with some empathy, turquoise walls, an orange print thrown over an opening bulging with wind. A single bare bulb dangles from the ceiling of the turquoise room. Around the bulb's base the owner has painted a series of black loops to make a kind of decal.

"I can't believe you gave up your vacation for this," I say. "I wouldn't do it, and neither would any of my friends."

She shrugs and puts on a CD of Enya, which surprises me. I thought she might like folk better. "I'll make the tea."

Lotte's place, built right after the war, is also quite spare—a second-story studio with a small galley kitchen, the water heater built in over the sink. At the Chinese red table, Lotte serves herb tea and plates of cookies. All along we've spoken in rather intermediate English, occasionally teasing one another. As we converse, we nibble the maple sugar cookies. Date cookies. Hard, sweet mocha cookies. They're all store-bought, but I realize an Oreo or Fig Newton never tasted this good. I tell her of my trip to the museum, the Verster painting, the Van Goghs.

"My God, can you believe he was shot? Theo, I mean," she says, leaping ahead, and we speak of the director descended from a Dutch painter's family. I tell her I was there, saw him fall where he lay in his own blood. She touches my arm, and I take her hand. We forget about the museum and speak of all the dolts who've allowed *this* to happen—on both sides of the Atlantic. But it's a truncated conversation. We assign blame in short, bleak, sentences—as if pronouncing death over a corpse—and drop hands.

When the late afternoon darkens, I say it's time for me to leave. Next to the red table, we stand for a long minute, staring at one another, unable to speak. With deep, dark eyes, Lotte draws me to her bed, only steps away, a hard futon covered with striped sheets that seem to bring alive the dormancy between my legs. We share hasty but cathartic sex, the hip-thrusting, sacrum-cracking kind that leads me to think I might still be alive. A quick sigh indicates she is sated, too, and we lie for a short time, until her weight becomes too much for me to support. Her flat has no shower, so we share a warm wet towel and then a dry one. The silence that follows spurs me to leave.

As I don my coat and head toward the door, Lotte hands me a small brown bag of tulip bulbs. She kisses me on the left cheek, on the right, and again on the left.

"Very silly," I say.

"It's our way," she says softly. I shiver and linger a bit. Finally, when the moment grows too long, we exchange e-mail addresses, and I go down to hail a cab.

From my hotel I call Lotte. No answer, so I message her a thank you for the lovely afternoon. "I'll send you some JPEGs when those tulips bloom. I've never had any luck with flowers, but maybe this year will be different." When I hang up, I realize I don't care if I see Lotte again and begin to pack.

I make several sashays up the aisle to the restroom, but the ten-and-a-half-hour flight from Amsterdam gives me leg cramps. Once we deplane in Houston, Americans veer to the left, internationals to the right. Inside a huge room, we migrate slowly through a zigzag maze. Because my muscles are quivering, I stretch my legs, shaking them like a dog that's napped too long. When it's my turn, a handsome ebony man waves me up to the counter.

"They may want to take a look at these tulip bulbs downstairs," he says, looking at my list of declarations.

He stamps my passport, and I move to the right, taking the escalator downstairs, where I locate my red bag. At the next checkpoint, the guy says I'm okay and throws my suitcase on the belt. Surprised that I don't have to locate the tulips stashed in a pair of shoes, I stumble toward the third checkpoint and stand in line, yawning. An Asian couple in front of me have filled two airport carts. The man doesn't seem to understand the official, a young white female.

I blink out of my stupor. *Do you have a laptop,* I say in Korean, miming the act of typing, *or a video camera with tape?*

The man turns and looks at me as if I've descended from the moon. *No, no,* he says. *I have no money for such things. Thank you, good father, for helping me to see.* He bows and smiles, and the two Koreans begin to pile items back into the baskets.

I nod and place all my metal in the briefcase, my wallet and coat in a greasy gray tray. The official tosses my shoes on the belt, and I nab them on the other side. After tying my laces, I grab all my things. The Korean couple act as if they would like to speak to me, but I run up the corridor and order a flame-broiled burger and fries, gulping them as I take a tram to the other terminal. I feel like I used to when I told people I'd quit smoking and nabbed a cigarette on the sly—a little dizzy from ingesting a foreign substance.

On a monitor I spot my flight home, to an odd city to which Buddy Holly and Mac Davis and most of my high school friends never wanted to return, home of the highest teen pregnancy rate in the country, if not the greatest number of churches—a place so dry my tulips, if they choose to come up, will wilt like wax in the warmth of a dusty March.

On my first Sunday in town, two Asian women enter the sauna at the club where I swim laps. Both possess slightly rounded hips and small breasts. I watch them count out six towels apiece as they stand outside the door. Both of them back into the room in black one-piece suits, the younger one locating herself on the upper bleacher, near me, and the older one on the lower. I say hello, but they silently go about their work, layering the towels to make pallets. No room exists for anyone but the three of us.

"Do you teach at university?" the older one asks me, once she's settled.

"No," I say. "Sorry."

"My, uh husband, he teach mattamatics." I nod and close my eyes.

At first the women are talking about food, how hard it is to find good kim chee in town. *No good noodles. Must order everything from Seoul.* They continue to speak to each other, and, even though I can't rewind what they're saying, like a tape, I do comprehend most of it.

If he wasn't so old, the young woman says, looking at me, *I might make eyes.*

Oh, daughter, says the other one, *you must not flirt with a white man old enough to be your father.*

I should say something, right? It's just plain mean to let my eyes flit back and forth between them as if I haven't a clue.

He has that ugly mole on his cheek, the daughter says. *And the hair around his ankles is gone. Maybe he can't get it up anymore.*

They both laugh, putting their hands to their mouths, reminding me of Margaret Cho and her shtick. I grin. They laugh even harder.

He's so stupid. Doesn't even know what we're talking about. How big do you think he is? the daughter asks, scratching her calves.

I don't know . . . he doesn't seem to mind showing us what he has.

The accusation is preposterous because I'm wearing a jockstrap under my trunks. I close my eyes and roll my head against the hot redwood wall behind me.

Do you think he's married? the mother asks. I open my eyes to see the daughter opening hers. *He doesn't look so happy,* she says. *Maybe he has indigestion.*

After ten minutes or so, a rather acrid odor—perhaps the excretion of kim chee through their pores—crowds the sauna like a fourth party.

What's that smell? the mother asks, wrinkling her little nose.

Ahhh, let me see, says the daughter. *Dead red meat, collected for years in his bowels. A thousand cows have given their lives for that smell.*

"Well, ladies," I say in English. "It's been real, but I have a date with a filet mignon." I step down. Their faces remain placid, so I say the same thing in Korean.

"I feel so foolish," the mother says, sitting up from her pallet. "Please, sit down."

"How do you come to speak so well?" asks the daughter.

"Government," I say, returning to my spot. They nod. "Years and years of translating messages intercepted throughout the world. At first I lived in Washington, but when I became the eldest member of my department, my boss allowed me to move back to Texas to care for my father. Both of my parents are gone now."

"Forgive us for speaking so unkindly," the mother says, bowing her head.

Think nothing of it, I say in Korean, retrieving a phrase that does not come to me naturally. *I'd call it self-defense. On the whole Americans are ruder to you than you've been to me.*

The mother giggles. *One Sunday a man wanted to sit where you are, and when I made room for him, he said, Arigato, Baby.*

"Yes," I say. "Americans don't know what do with a second language. Hell, they have enough trouble with the first one."

We all laugh and I switch back to Korean. *I want you to know,* I say, slinging perspiration from my chest, *there are Americans who don't like rap. Americans who don't talk on cell phones while driving, while sitting in a restaurant, a theater, or a doctor's office. Some of us don't own SUVs with little chrome fish tacked on the back, which you can see only after the driver's cut you off—or sped by you in a school zone. Some of us don't go to church because the hypocrisy stinks worse than thousand-year-old beef.*

The women cover their smiles with dainty hands.

Seventy percent of us did not support the war in you-know-where. There are Americans who don't salute the flag but would never burn one because it would pollute the air.

They both nod vigorously, and I feel my heart rate climbing.

Some of us have never watched Survivor *or* Apprentice *or any other* reality *show. Hah, if the networks showed a nuclear power plant leaking radiation, or if they could infrared from outer space the billions of cubic feet of carbon dioxide in our atmosphere or listen in on the president's plots to give even more money to the rich, now that would be real, my friends.*

My voice is shrill. I'm sweating more profusely than ever, my heart beginning to skip beats. I should quit, but this heady feeling has fueled my fire.

There are Americans who didn't vote because what's the point? Since the winner in Texas took all the electoral votes, why bother? My vote for Kerry didn't count in this, the president's state, so red it could be on fire.

The women seem frightened of my fist raised in protest, but I can't stop.

Some of us don't pirate music off the Internet because it's unfair to the artist; it's immoral not to pay for art. Some of us have never seen the Lord of the Rings trilogy or the Harry Potter movies or The Terminator. *Some of us know how to form a single line at Ticketmaster. Some of us don't throw litter out of our cars. Some of us don't speed through red lights or even the yellow ones. There's an America the world knows nothing about.*

I stagger out through the door to the pool's edge. I roll over on the drenched indoor-outdoor carpet. Both women follow me, and, on bended knees, dribble pool water over me. The drops feel like wet rose petals falling on my skin. My breathing evens out, my skin cools. The daughter takes my pulse and smiles. I thank her.

Good father, you must be more careful, she says. I rise to my knees, then my feet. They smile and nod, rising to stand by me in case I should fall.

"Ladies," I say. "It's been a pleasure. Till next time?"

I turn and head for the showers, where utter silence weighs on my shoulders like a cloak. Drying off and dressing, I take the elevator down to my car and drive to a home that's paid for. On the way I see three people run red lights. I love Amerika.

All night long the wind blows, a fanfare to the cold air that now stiffens my legs. The temps must be in the twenties. On my way to buy a paper and some breakfast, I shiver while waiting at a traffic light. I look over from my Avalon to this little white car, a generic Neon clone. The passenger, a woman, opens her door. She lays on the pavement, as if placing flowers on a grave, a Styrofoam bowl of cornflakes and milk, without spilling a drop. Then she closes the door and cracks the window. Sporting a pink coat with a fuzzy rabbit collar, the woman also wears a long pink stocking cap over her foam-rubber curlers. She has the pinched face of someone in her late forties, someone who has risen early all her life to ride, sometimes in the cold, to a job that probably pays less than $28,000 a year. With her lips pursed like a chimpanzee's, she flicks her disposable lighter. A three-inch flame shoots up, and she ignites a long white cigarette with the self-importance of a dedicated smoker, who's done it a quarter million times or more.

I open my door and yell, "You can't do that!"

The light is red, so I unbuckle my belt and jump out. I reach down for the bowl, a 7-Eleven promotion, and knock on the window.

"You can't leave this here."

The passenger stares straight ahead, and I pound on her window. "You can't leave this bowl of cereal!"

The light changes, but by now the driver has jumped out and runs around to where I am. Her face is like her companion's. Long, severe lines draw her cheeks down, but she's at least twenty years younger. Dressed like the other woman, except that her ensemble is all white, she wears no curlers in her pixie blond hair. She flicks her wrist and knocks the bowl against my chest, splashing milk and cornflakes all over my black leather jacket, a Bachrach sale item. Without a word, she runs back and climbs in the driver's door.

"Hey . . . what's wrong with you?" I scream, the milk stinging my chest. Cars behind us begin to sound little toots of irritation. Holding the bowl up, I shout, "I've been attacked . . . ." My body seized with shivering, I feel an earache coming on and stare down at little bits of cereal splattered across my coat like vomit. When I look up, I notice two things: a flashing red light, maybe two blocks away, and the driver, the bitch, definitely has a gun trained on me.

"Whoa," I say, raising my hands—holding the empty bowl over my head.

When I try to move toward my car, the passenger rolls down her window. The driver leans over her, still pointing the gun at me. "Get your hands up, you perv."

"The streets are a conveyance for cars, not a receptacle for your trash," I say.

"You can start mindin' your own business any minute now."

"I just got back from a country where you could eat off the streets."

"Why don't you go back there?" she yells.

The red flashing draws closer, illuminating the black trunks of old elms. The siren emits a single whoop, and an officer pulls next to me as soon as the light changes. I watch as Miss Pixie slides her gun into the same warm spot where a guy can put his passport, the same spot where an assassin concealed his weapon.

I'm reminded of a friend whose loss of power during an ice storm tripped her alarm. When the policeman appeared at the door, her big parrot screeched, "She's got a gun." I say the same thing, quietly, but the officer, a woman, pays me no mind.

She has poured her broad hips into standard khaki pants and rises a few inches above me. "All right," she says, flashing us a look. "Let's get this show off the street. I'm gonna pull onto Indiana. You both follow me around the corner into the parking lot."

When the little car's driver fails to make the turn but speeds off to the west, the officer waves me away. Something about the gesture warms my heart, the way she slams her cruiser into gear and shoots down the street with her lights and siren on, chasing Thelma and Louise toward that inevitable cliff.

In bed this night, I study "The Stone-cutters" in the museum catalog. Two men and a woman sit once again with legs extended, wooden shoes pointed to the sky, sculpting red stones into bricks. *Is it to build ourselves a house? To square our lives with the world? To save a few guilders, enough to buy some bread and a bit of meat?* they seem to say. Flipping through the catalog, I wonder what one thinks while painting. Do the little dots a pointillist makes so patiently, the solids, the cubes Picasso employs . . . do they stem from conscious thought or intuitive motion? I realize I'll never know.

I was born in 1950, my grandparents in the 1890s, their kinfolk having related to them passed-on tales of the Civil War. That world is now as yellow as the Stone-cutters' world, and it occurs to me that some day the time in which I live will be much the same for those who will have reached the age I am now. In an instant I jump up and flip on the floods outside my bedroom patio. Without a robe on, I slide the door open, and, in the stark, stabbing cold, I grab my hand shovel and dig six holes in the crusty soil. I quickly bury Lotte's bulbs five inches beneath the surface. I mark the holes with flat vertical sticks that, in the light, shine like tiny grave markers. I mumble a little something over them and jump into bed, where, under the thick covers, I can barely breathe.

Bathed in Pink

I'm a much shorter woman today. In my prime I was five-seven, but now, I'd hate to see an X-ray of my skeleton. I see the doctor every two weeks. She gives me a big shot of methotrexate to kill the pain in my riddled bones, but she can't stop the shrinking, the honeycombing that has made me shrivel to five-one . . . I guess . . . because no one really measures me any more.

I have two sons, one who calls me every day, Marty. Right about noon, as he goes to lunch. Rather annoying, really, as I've usually begun to eat. He lives on the other side of the city and drives one of those big brown trucks for UPS. He may drop by once a month for a chicken dinner, but he does call. Every day. The other son, Lawrence, calls when he wants something. He'll ring as he's leaving town and ask, *Can you stay with the kid?* As if I had nothing better to do. Is it something his father and I did to make him behave like this? (My Barry passed on twenty years ago.)

How's Helen? I'll ask.

Fine, he'll say. *Can you stay with the kid? We'd really like to go to Majorca on the sly. We have to be at the airport in thirty minutes if we're going to make the charter.* I can hear in the background the same music he listened to in high school. Kiss, I think. Lawrence is a broker, and he has more money than he knows what to do with. You'd think he'd have acquired better taste in music by now.

Is Helen still trying to gain weight? I'll ask.

If I babysit, I won't even get to see Lawrence and Helen. They will have taken a limo to the airport, typically, by the time I drive to their house. I look forward to the day when he calls and I'm not available . . . whenever that happens. I seldom go anywhere. I couldn't sit in a jet for eight or ten hours unless you shot me up with morphine. I remember visiting Spain once, and I saw all these short, hobbling women with canes. I mean, their hips looked as if they were attached at their ribcages. *I'll never be like this*, I remember thinking. But here I am, I can see the pity in my sons' faces when I do visit them, say, on Thanksgiving, at an obscenely sumptuous meal that Helen spends three days preparing.

Helen spins, while she watches Fox News, on a bicycle that goes nowhere. Feature it, she gets her exercise and political indoctrination all at once. If I didn't know better, I'd say Helen is anorexic. I sometimes watch her consume a piece of Melba toast. Oh God . . . with a quarter teaspoon of sugarless jelly, and she takes five minutes to eat it, soaking up crumbs with a damp fingertip, until her placemat is spotless. At lunch she might consume a half sandwich of tuna on rye with no mayo, no mustard. Then at dinner she'll dive into a salad of greens, small tomatoes and onions, while the rest of us gorge ourselves on whatever bit of heaven she's spent the whole day preparing. Last time it was a huge roast, with baby red spuds, carrots, and fresh bay leaf. Simple but delicious. Helen doesn't keep salt or pepper at her table.

My phone rings. "Yes, Larry," I say. "I can be there in twenty minutes. I keep a bag packed for just these moments."

"Oh, great," he says. "Be sure and check under your pillow in the guest room. A little surprise for you."

"I will," I say. "That last bracelet was a beaut. I wear it to bridge club and everyone oohs and aahs."

"Okay, well, see you in a few minutes." And he hangs up on me.

Oh, well, I'll get to enjoy the kid, anyway. But they're so different these days. Lawrence and Helen waited too long. He was nearly fifty and she thirty-five. Little Lottie's smart as a quip, I love to tell my friends.

When I drive to Lawrence's house and relieve the sitter, a teenager, Lar and Helen are already gone. Lottie draws me along the hallway to *her* computer, in *her* room that looks better than something I once stayed in at the Plaza (a digression Barry never knew about). Anyway, the little urchin is online, and up pops on the screen this huge . . . male organ, which doesn't so much bother *me*. But what about the child!

"My, my, my," I say.

"Grandma, do you want me to make the big penis go away?" she says.

With a hand over my mouth, I nod and she clicks her mousie (with whiskers and a tail painted on it) and changes the screen to little ducks dressed in pink.

"This is my story," Lottie says. "This is the mama," she says. "This is the daddee. This is the girl duckee. And this is baby brother duckee asleep in the cradle. I can make the cradle rock, you wanna see?" She turns to look at me, this angel with her father's dark eyes, her mother's full lips. I begin to hum "Rock-a-bye Baby," and she asks, "What's that song you're singing in your throat like that?"

Oh, dear, I think. I have so much to teach you about songs, about how bones shrink, and how sons do or do not call. "Would you like something to drink?" I ask, and little Lottie nods her head.

"I'll put computee to sleep," she says.

When we switch the light off, the room glows like a sunset I once saw in Spain.

"Your grandfather and I walked the streets of Madrid," I say. "As we reached our hotel, I looked over my shoulder . . . and the street, every brick along the street was just like your room . . . bathed in pink."

About the Author

Raised in Wichita, Kansas, Richard Jespers has been writing fiction for over thirty years. He graduated from Southwestern College with a bachelor of music and then earned an MA in English from Texas Tech University. He went on to teach elementary and secondary English in the Lubbock, Texas, public schools. A Pushcart nominee for his short story "My Long-Playing Records," which originally appeared in *Boulevard*, he has also been recognized by the Tennessee Writers Alliance as well as the Ledge fiction competition. His works have appeared in *Storyglossia, Mochila Review, Oyez Review, Eclectica Magazine, Gihon River Review, Beloit Fiction Journal, Blackbird*, and *Cooweescoowee*.

He currently lives in Lubbock, Texas, with his long-time companion, Ken Dixon. He draws writing inspiration from Tennessee Williams, who once stated: "Any work that has any honesty and a sufficient degree of craftsmanship or power eventually finds an outlet."

Made in the USA
San Bernardino, CA
15 April 2016